SPIDER-
MAN

SPIDER-MAN

Peter David

Based on the screenplay by
David Koepp

Based on the Marvel comic book created by
Stan Lee

BALLANTINE BOOKS • NEW YORK

A Ballantine Book
Published by The Ballantine Publishing Group
Copyright © 2002 Columbia Pictures Industries, Inc.
All Rights Reserved.

www.ballantinebooks.com

ISBN 0-345-45005-1

Manufactured in the United States of America

First Edition: March 2002

10   9   8   7   6   5   4   3   2   1

SPIDER-MAN

PROLOGUE

"Let's wake the dead, baby!"

The souped-up black Corvette roared down the main road of the cemetery, gravel blasting out from under its tires, spraying every which way. A few squirrels, foraging for food, frantically scrambled for the nearest trees as the car, its double headlights flaring, cut hard to the right. Its rear fishtailed around and the wheels spun on dirt and grass for a moment before once again finding purchase on the narrow pathway.

The road was intended for slow, stately processions: a hearse, followed by limos or regular cars bearing grieving and stricken friends and family. It wasn't designed for hot rods and fast turns, but the driver and passengers of the midnight 'Vette couldn't have cared less. They were too busy laughing at the top of their lungs, blaring the horn and gunning the engine so enthusiastically that it seemed as if they would fulfill their stated purpose and cause the deceased to rise up in protest.

Their names were Tyler, Keith, and Daniel, and they were flying high. They'd just come from a ball game over at the stadium in Flushing. It had been an extra-innings nail-biter that the home team had managed to pull out of the fire at the last moment, and the boys were pretty liquored up, so they were feeling good about baseball in general and themselves in particular.

The 'Vette had a small ding in the rear bumper but otherwise was in perfect working order. Tyler, at the wheel, had decided he wanted to open her up, and one of the best places to do that was the main drag outside the local cemetery, since it wasn't especially well traveled at night. As they had driven past, however, they'd noticed that only a single padlock, hanging on a heavy chain, was keeping the large wrought iron gates closed. A quick clipping with a pair of cutters that Tyler kept stashed in the trunk, and moments later they had the moonlit cemetery all to themselves.

The guys looked fairly alike. They all had their heads shaved down to a razor cut, and they had similarly large and sloped brows that indicated considerably advanced cranial capacity . . . if one happened to be a Cro-Magnon. Keith was wearing sunglasses, ignoring the fact that it was pitch-black out.

They were, however, easily distinguishable, one from the other, through their facial markings. Keith's face was smeared with solid blue makeup, while Tyler was wearing orange. These coincided with the official colors of their favorite baseball team, and they had festooned their faces as a mark of solidarity. Daniel had simply shaved all his hair off, down to the roots.

Tyler screeched toward an intersection, hesitated only a moment, then cut hard left. The roar of the engine filled the cemetery, barely drowning out the joyful howling of the guys in the car. Hard left again, and then right, tearing all over the place like the ghost of a driver killed in a high-speed crash.

Shooting off the road, the 'Vette hurtled across a row of graves. Daniel suddenly encountered a slight decline of nerves, and from the minimal backseat into which he was crunched, he pounded on Tyler's shoulder.

"Knock it off, man, this ain't funny!"

"They're dead, man, whatta they care?" Tyler shot back.

"Yeah, man, let the man drive!" said Keith, who was riding shotgun but had twisted around to face Daniel.

Suddenly the 'Vette slammed to a halt. It didn't happen with a screech of tires or an abrupt shuddering of medal. It just stopped, as if it had hit a brick wall, except somehow the front wasn't caved in.

"Tyler, you can't drive worth spit!" howled Keith.

"I didn't do it!" Tyler shouted in protest.

"You're drivin', man!"

"I didn't do it!" he repeated. "Something's holding us! Look!" He slammed his foot onto the gas pedal and the engine roared. The car drifted from one side to the other, the tires chewing up dirt, but otherwise it didn't move.

The full moon, which had been illuminating the graveyard, now drifted behind a bank of clouds, and the night air seemed even more chill.

"I'm getting out to see what's goin' on." Tyler unlocked the door and pushed against it. Then he pushed again. "The door won't open."

Keith tried to shove open the door on his side and had no more luck. "Okay, man, this is screwed up. . . ."

Suddenly Daniel pointed with trembling finger. "Wh . . . what's that? *What the hell is that?!*"

Something—some sort of strange, grayish strands were covering the side windows and the windshield. They were blind. Blind and trapped.

"There's something out there!" shouted Daniel.

"Oh, really? Y'think?!" Keith, the oldest, tried to sound sarcastic, but it only came out scared.

Daniel's mind was racing. "It's . . . it's a monster! Some kind of alien bug creature! It's wrapping us in a cocoon, to eat us later!"

Tyler twisted around to stare at his friend. "What're you, *stupid?!*" But the truth was that he'd been thinking the exact same thing; he'd just been too panicked and felt like too much of a jerk to say anything.

That was when the car started to shake violently. The guys screamed, cried out, shouted for someone—anyone—to help them as the car rocked from one side to the other.

Tyler let out a scream that they could have heard on the other side of the Whitestone Bridge, even as he shoved the car back into drive. And then, with a rending of metal, they were free, the rear bumper having been torn clean off.

The main gate still hung open, and they barreled through it at top speed, honking the horn like mad, which was fortunate since it was the only thing that kept them from smearing themselves along the side of an oncoming truck transporting—appropriately enough—beer. The truck slammed to a halt as the 'Vette darted around it. Before long the smell of burning rubber and the frightened cries of the trespassers faded from the night air.

In the cemetery, all was still.

Then a figure clad in blue and red emerged from the branches of one of the large oak trees, so dark that it seemed as if one of the shadows had separated and come to life. He moved so silently that the absence of sound would have prompted any onlooker to think that maybe he wasn't there at all.

His body was muscular but, at the same time, extremely well proportioned, and he moved with a lithe, skittering grace that seemed barely human. His gloves and boots were dark red, as was the design that spread up his chest and down his arms. His mask was the same color but was interrupted by two eyepieces that were impenetrable from the outside. Indeed, anyone looking at him would have wondered how in the world he was able to see at all.

Thin black web patterns covered all the scarlet areas of

the costume. And on his chest, just over his solar plexus, there was the design of a spider with its legs outstretched. Had he simply been standing up, walking along down a main thoroughfare in the middle of the day, arms swinging casually at his sides, he might have looked like a circus refugee. But here, in the still of the night, with only the eye-pieces visible as the moon once again darted behind the shadows, he looked more like a spider himself, in human form, spit out by dark forces which ordinary mortals could never even begin to comprehend except in their deepest nightmares.

He dropped to the ground, still noiseless, and surveyed the area which had—so short a time ago—been the scene of unbridled pandemonium. Looking at the tire tracks that scarred the earth, he shook his head and mentally scolded himself for not having arrived sooner and, therefore, having done more.

"But then . . . that's always the way, isn't it," he said softly.

As much as he might berate himself for not having arrived sooner, at least he had arrived just in time. The path of the racing 'Vette would have taken it directly across the one gravesite in the cemetery that was important to him. His intervention had prevented that, bringing the speeding car up short. And hopefully the lamebrains who'd been in the thing would never, ever, so much as think about setting foot in the place again.

Still so silent, silent as a ghost, silent as the grave, the masked man walked over to the headstone that was his destination, then crouched in front of it.

"Hey," he said softly in greeting. "Did you see them run? Pretty good show, huh?"

He reached gingerly toward the headstone and ran his fingers over the letters. "Least you've got a good view. That's what the guy at the funeral home promised; that you'd have a good view. Paid extra for it. But it was worth it." He paused there for a moment longer, as if uncertain what to say, or even why he had come by in the first place. "I'm sorry," he said finally. "I . . . I should have come by and spoken with you sooner. I know I haven't been by for a while. But I . . . I wasn't sure what to say. How to start the conversation, y'know. But . . . here, check this out. I figured this would be an icebreaker." He stood and turned in place, his arms outstretched to either side, like a runway model. "Like the outfit? I figure to make the best- and worst-dressed lists, all at the same time. And the pecs . . . not bad, huh?" and he flexed to prove his point. "I mean, okay, I'm no Arh-nuld, or even Kevin Sorbo, but I've come a long way, right? Not the way you figured I'd end up, right? I guess . . ." The jocularity began to fade. "I guess . . . neither of us ended up the way we thought we would, huh."

Then the masked man took a step back and placed one hand on his chest as if in surprise.

"Who am I, you ask?" he said in mock astonishment, as if a voice had addressed him from the grave. Then he leaned forward and continued in a surprisingly conversational tone. "You sure you wanna know? The story of my life is not for the faint of heart. If somebody said it was a happy little tale . . . if somebody told you I was just your average, ordinary guy, not a care in the world . . ."

Then his voice choked for a moment, and he forced himself onward, ". . . then somebody lied."

Struggling to pull himself together again, to recapture the carefree air of *joie de vivre* that typified his costumed persona, he flipped over so that he was doing a handstand with his left hand only. "Mine," he called out, like a ringmaster encouraging all onlookers to listen in, as if he were addressing all the other graves within hearing, "is a tale of pain and sorrow, longing and heartache, anger and betrayal. And that just covers the high school years. But let me assure you, this . . . like any story worth telling . . . is all about a girl. . . ."

Except . . . in the beginning . . . there had been no girl. There had just been the pain and sorrow . . . and the loss . . . . . . and the spider. . . .

I.

THE ARRIVAL

It smelled weird.

That was the first thing that Peter noticed. The moment he stepped over the threshold, he noticed the smell of the house. It was . . . it was antiseptic, somehow. Not that young Peter, standing there so neatly attired in his blue shorts, white shirt, and yellow sweater vest, would have known the word "antiseptic." That was a big, important word. Most four-year-olds hadn't heard the word, couldn't use it in context, couldn't even come close to spelling it. In this regard, Peter Parker, who had celebrated his birthday the previous August at a big and splendid party where his parents had made a marvelous fuss over him, was no different. By age five, however, he would be able to correctly define and spell it . . . along with "microbiology," "cellular," and "mitosis." On the other hand, he would continue to stumble over "photosynthesis" and "paleontologist" until he reached the ripe old age of six.

Peter, however, wasn't looking that far ahead. Five and six were an eternity away. All that concerned Peter at that moment was the here and now. And what was here, and what wasn't.

He was here. These strange people whom he had supposedly met once, when he was a baby—but he sure couldn't remember—were here. That weird smell was here.

His parents were not.

The living room in which he was standing didn't seem even remotely inviting. The cushions of the couch were covered in plastic. He'd tried to sit on one and hadn't liked the way it had stuck to the underside of his legs. So he'd slid off it, but it had made this really weird squeaky "ripping" sound, and he hadn't liked that either.

The man and woman who were bringing the last of his things into the house, who were speaking in hushed whispers to the woman named Miss Hemmings—the "social worker," she'd been called—those people weren't paying any attention to him. That suited him fine. Perhaps he could simply reside there like a ghost, no one noticing him. When he was hungry, he could snitch food from the kitchen, presuming they had one, and otherwise be left alone.

He wanted that more than anything . . . particularly to be left alone by the man, who reminded him a little of his father. Except it wasn't him, and that made him feel all the more uneasy.

The door closed, shutting out the outside world. The smell of the plastic cushions threatened to suffocate him. He would have screamed if he could have worked up the energy to do so, but he felt wrung out, like a sponge.

The carpet was weird, too. It felt slightly moist under his feet, as if it had been just washed. Just to add to the assault, there was a lemony smell coming from all the wood furniture. He stared down at his reflection on the coffee table. There were flowers arranged neatly on a small lacy thing in the middle of it. He leaned forward to smell the flowers. The flowers, he realized belatedly, were fake. They were the only things in the whole living room that *didn't* smell.

"Well, Peter," said the man, coming into the room. He clapped his hands once and rubbed them briskly together. The magician at Peter's birthday party had done something similar, right before he'd produced coins from out of nowhere. He'd pretended he'd pulled them from thin air, but Peter had spotted the sleight-of-hand. In a loud voice he'd explained every single one of the magician's tricks, to the irritation of the conjurer and the endless amusement of his parents. His mother's laugh still rang in his ears. He hadn't yet been able to grasp the notion that he would never hear that laughter again.

"Well, Peter," the man said again, "would you like to sit down?"

"No, sir," Peter said politely, addressing the older man as "sir," just as his parents had always taught him.

"Land sakes, child," the woman said. "You can't just plan to stand there forever. Why won't you sit?"

He saw no reason to lie. "I don't like the plastic."

"The plastic protects the cushions," she said reasonably. "You understand that, don't you, Peter?"

"No, ma'am."

"Oh." She seemed vaguely disappointed. He felt as if he'd let her down in some way.

"Peter . . ." And the man got down on one knee. Closer up, the resemblance between this man and Peter's father was more striking. He had that same square jaw, that same laughter in his eyes. His hair was a different color, more red in it, and his eyebrows were bushier. Peter's nostrils flared. The man smelled funny, too.

"Why are you sniffing me, Peter? Are you part cocker spaniel?"

"You have a funny smell, sir."

"That would be my aftershave."

"It was his Christmas present," the woman said proudly. She sat down on the couch, her hands neatly folded in her lap. The couch made that same weird plastic-creaking sound when she sat on it. "Do you like it?"

"Smells like poop, ma'am," Peter said.

Her mouth immediately stretched to a thin line, while the man guffawed heartily. "He has his father's tact," the man said . . . and then immediately looked contrite. "I'm sorry, Peter. I spoke without thinking."

Peter's eyebrows knit. "You *have* to think to speak, don't you, sir?"

"Less often than you've been led to believe. And please, Peter, call me Uncle Ben. Have you ever heard of your Uncle Ben?" Encouraged by the boy's prompt nod, he said, "What have you heard?"

"That you make . . ." He frowned, trying to recall the word. ". . . perverted rice."

Now it was the woman's turn to laugh, as Uncle Ben's cheeks reddened slightly. "Different Uncle Ben, Peter. And I think you mean 'converted' rice."

"Oh." He was studying the woman now, comparing her automatically to the only woman who'd had a major place in his life. Her face was narrower, her eyes a bit more sunken. Her hair, which was brown with gray streaks, was tied back in a severe bun. She had a long neck and her hands tended to flutter toward it, as if she was trying to cool down waves of heat. "Okay," he added, to fill the silence.

"I'm your Aunt May," she told him. She said this with a great deal of gravity, as if she were revealing one of the great secrets of the universe.

"Okay," he said again.

The man clapped his hands together again. Peter waited for a dove to appear or a coin to drop out of the air. None was forthcoming. "Would you like to see your room, Peter?"

Finally something he understood. He nodded eagerly. "Do you wanna see where I drew some cowboys on the wall?" he asked.

Ben and May exchanged puzzled glances. "What do you mean, Peter?" Ben asked.

"Where I drew some cowboys. When I was little. Mommy yelled at me, and tried to wash them off, but you can still see them, 'cause I used markers."

"Ohhh," Ben said, and it sounded a little like a moan when he said it. "Peter, I mean your new room. Here."

"Can't I go back to my old room?"

"Peter, dear," said May, and she took his hand in hers. Her hand felt cold, but smooth, as if she'd put some sort of lotion on it. He noticed a few brown spots on the back of her hand and wondered what it would be like to connect them. "Your old room is back in Wisconsin. I thought the social worker explained it. . . . You'll be staying here, in New York. With us."

"Can't we stay at my house?"

"But Peter, this is where we live. And this is where you're going to live now," Ben told him, trying desperately to sound upbeat about it. "We'll make a good home here for you."

Obviously this Uncle Ben and Aunt May weren't getting it. "I have a home," Peter explained, politely but firmly.

"Peter . . ."

"You know what you need?" Aunt May suddenly said briskly. She didn't clap and rub her hands. Instead she patted them on her knees. "Some nice, freshly baked cookies. Why don't you go upstairs and get your things unpacked, and I'll whip up some cookies. Do you like chocolate chip?" When Peter nodded eagerly, she flicked a finger across the end of his nose in a playful manner. "I thought you might." She rose as she asked, "Is there anything else you'd like?"

"Yes, please."

"And what would that be?" She leaned over, hands resting on her knees. "What would you like?"

"My mommy and daddy."

She winced at that, and Ben, trying to sound kindly but firm, said, "Peter . . . you have to understand, you're going to live with us now."

"I don't want to," Peter told him firmly. He wasn't rude, wasn't whining or crying. He couldn't have been more polite if he'd been ordering a meal in a restaurant. "I want my mommy and daddy. Please," he put in almost as an afterthought.

"They're not here, Peter . . ." Ben began.

"Can I talk to them at least? Can you call them?"

"Peter," and Ben took him firmly by the shoulders. "Your parents . . . they're with God now."

"When are they coming back?"

Ben's lower lip was quivering. Peter had never seen a grown-up cry, and the feeling made his stomach queasy. He didn't think it was something that grown-ups did. Ben coughed loudly, took a deep breath, and said, "They're not coming back, Peter."

"I want to talk to them."

"You can't. They . . . they went away. . . ."

"I want to talk to them. Make them come back."

"Peter . . ."

"Make them come back!" And the sound and agony that ripped from Peter's throat terrified the child himself, because he couldn't believe that it was his own voice sounding like that. His eyes went wide, pupils tiny and swimming in a sea of white, and without another word he turned and bolted up the nearby steps.

Looking a lot older than he had a few minutes earlier, Ben turned to May and sighed dryly, "Well, *that* went well."

Peter sat on the floor in the middle of the room, his knees drawn up to just under his chin. He could have been a statue; he was that immobile. The room itself wasn't terrible, but it didn't feel especially warm. In Peter's room—his real room—all the furniture kind of looked like it went together. Here it seemed as if some random stuff had been stuck together in one place. At least none of it was covered in plastic.

Uncle Ben had brought up the last of his suitcases some time ago. Peter hadn't spoken to him. The truth was, he was embarrassed about his outburst and was quite certain that Uncle Ben was angry with him. So he had felt it wisest not to say anything and hope that, eventually, Uncle Ben would forget that he had shouted in such an inappropriate manner. That's what his mother would have said. "In-ap-pro-pri-ate, young man," with her finger waggling one quick downward stroke on every syllable.

Uncle Ben didn't try to strike up a conversation with him; he didn't seem to know what to say. For his part, Peter was busy focusing all his attention on the spider that was up in the corner of his room. It was quite big, hanging in the middle of an intricately designed web that stretched from the edge of the ceiling down to the upper portion of the wall. He had never seen anything so morbidly curious. On the one hand, it was incredibly ugly; on the other, it possessed such an elegant beauty that he couldn't look away. So Uncle Ben would come and go from the room, grunting slightly and wondering out loud why Peter was packing anvils in his suit-cases—which puzzled Peter, who couldn't remember bringing any—while Peter sat there and watched the spider. The sun moved across the sky, the shadows lengthened, Uncle Ben stopped coming in and out, and Peter and the spider stared at each other until time ceased to have any meaning.

The smell of fresh-baked cookies wafted upstairs, seeping in through the doorway and wrapping the tempting fingers of their aroma around him. For a moment he was sorely tempted to abandon his vigil, which had boiled down to waiting for the spider to move. He resisted, however, although he did shift his posture so that he was sitting cross-legged.

Finally he heard footsteps again. He recognized them as belonging to Uncle Ben, but he didn't bother to turn around. Then he heard his uncle chuckling softly, and that distracted him. He swiveled his head and regarded his uncle, who was standing in the doorway, leaning against the frame, his arms folded. He was holding a small, wirebound book tucked under his right arm. "What's funny?" asked Peter.

"You just remind me so much of Ricky, that's all," said Uncle Ben. "Same serious face. I'll show you pictures of him at your age, if you want."

"Who's Ricky?"

"Ricky. Richard. Your dad."

Peter blinked in confusion. "How come you know my dad?"

Uncle Ben's jaw dropped. "How come I . . . ? *Peter!*" he said in astonishment. And then he sat down on the floor with Peter, just like his mom and dad used to. "Peter, your dad . . . he was my little brother! Didn't you understand that?"

Peter shook his head. "I thought you were my uncle."

"I am! An uncle or an aunt is what you call someone who is a brother or sister of a parent . . . in this case, your father."

Peter frowned, digesting that bit of information. "So . . . so Aunt May is my dad's sister?"

Ben made that odd sound that was a combination of laughter and a cough. "Peter, Aunt May is my wife!"

"You married your sister?" Peter was by now hopelessly confused.

"No, Peter." Rubbing the bridge of his nose between beefy fingers, Ben said, "We call her your aunt because she's married to me, which is the other way someone can be an aunt or uncle. By marriage. Understand?"

"I guess so," said Peter, who thought he did but wasn't 100 percent sure. Then he took a deep breath and let it out unsteadily. "My mom and dad aren't coming back, are they?"

"No, Peter," Ben told him, as gently as he could. "They were killed in an airplane crash. It was an accident."

"No," Peter said flatly. "It wasn't."

"It wasn't?" said Ben curiously.

Peter shoved his hand into one of the bags and extracted a stack of comic books. "They were secret heroes. Like . . . spies. And they were helping their country, and a bad guy, like the Red Skull, killed them." He held up an old issue of a comic, spine-rolled and tattered.

Ben flattened it carefully and looked at the cover. "*Captain America*. You like these old comic book heroes?" Peter bobbed his head. "And you think your mom and dad were like that? Why?"

"Because they were special. Too special to get killed in a stupid airplane accident."

"I see," said Ben, very seriously. "That's an interesting possibility you've got there, Peter. I'll have to think about that one."

Peter nodded and, satisfied that the conversation was over, went back to what he was doing . . . namely, watching the corner of the room.

"I see you have a roommate," Ben commented after a time. "Heck of a spider. They're good luck, you know."

"They are?" That surprised Peter. His mother had always hated them and called on his father to squish them whenever one happened to wander unwarily into the house.

"Oh yes. They eat harmful bugs, like mosquitoes. They protect people. That's what they are, Peter. Protectors. They're helpful. And in this world, folks need all the help they can get. Right?"

"Right," Peter agreed.

"Who knows? Maybe my brother—your dad—sent him to watch over you."

"Maybe," said Peter. He was looking back at Ben, staring at him as if seeing him for the first time. "I thought only kids had brothers," he said.

"No, grown-ups have them, too. I, uhm . . . I brought you something." He took out the notebook that he'd tucked under his arm and handed it to Peter. "Here you go."

Peter turned it over and over, then opened it. "There's nothing in it," he said curiously.

"I know that. It's for you to write in. You see . . ." He shifted on the floor, perhaps to make himself comfortable, or perhaps because he felt uncertain of exactly what to say next. "You said you wanted to talk to your folks. Well . . . they're in heaven now, Peter. But they can see you. They can see whatever you're doing, and they're watching you all the time."

"They are?" Peter asked, looking around, brushing a hank of tousled hair from his face.

"Oh, yes. And if you write to them, in this book . . . they can see it. So it's just like talking to them."

Peter stared at the pages, running his hands over the paper respectfully. "But . . . what will I write to them? Say to them?"

"Whatever you want. Tell him about how things are going with you. About your life, about school . . . whatever you want."

"Can I tell them I wish they were here?"

"As much as you want." Ben smiled, resting a hand on Peter's shoulder.

Peter considered it a moment more. "If I'm talking to them," he said at last, "how will I know when they're talking back? Will I hear them?"

"You won't hear them with these," he said, tapping his ears, and then he reached down and tapped Peter's chest gently. "You'll hear them with this."

"My heart? Who listens with their heart instead of their ears?"

"The wisest men in the world, Peter. The wisest men in the world. And I think you can be one of them."

"Oh." He riffled through the pages once more. They made a most satisfying noise as he slid them across his thumb. Then he frowned. "Uncle Ben, I don't know how to write."

"Ah." Apparently Ben hadn't remembered that. "Well . . .

tell you what," he said after pondering the problem. "At first you can tell me what you want to say, and I'll write it for you. As you get older, you can write it yourself. How's that?"

Peter's head bobbed up and down. The entire idea sounded rather exciting to him. The notion that his parents could be watching right over his shoulder, without being seen, was an exciting one. It made them almost like invisible heroes or something. More importantly, it eased—ever so slightly—the aching melancholy that had threatened to overwhelm him.

Uncle Ben pulled out a ballpoint, balanced the notebook carefully on his knees, and waited expectantly for Peter to start talking. He had a very serious demeanor, like an executive secretary about to take dictation from the president of the United States.

"Mom and Dad," Peter said finally, "I love you and I miss you. Maybe I'll see you soon. Uncle Ben is nice," and he glanced surreptitiously at his uncle to see his reaction. The only hint of it was the edges of his mouth twitching upward. Peter took that as a good sign. "Aunt May is nice, too. I think she made cookies. They smell good."

"They are good," Ben assured him under his breath.

"Uncle Ben says they're good. I think maybe I'll have one, if that's okay. But I won't sit on the couch or chair or anything to eat them, because I don't like how they feel."

"Know what? Neither do I," said Ben, even as he continued to write. He spoke very distantly, as if thinking aloud. "I think I'll have a chat with your aunt about removing them. No reason we can't make the house more little-boy friendly."

"That'd be good," Peter said.

Ben hesitated, waited. "Anything else you want to say?" he inquired.

"No. That's all for now," said Peter after thinking about it a little.

They went downstairs and had cookies and milk while

Aunt May insisted that she would attend to putting away all Peter's clothes, just to help him feel more at home. Uncle Ben kept telling Peter how pleased he was to see Peter's mood improve, and how they were going to be great friends and a great family, just you wait and see. Peter's spirits improved with each bite of a cookie and each sip of milk. It was the warmth of the freshly baked cookie versus the chill of the refrigerated milk, and the warmth won out, giving him a pleasant feeling in the pit of his stomach.

Then he went upstairs, and the first thing he noticed was that the spider was gone. "Oh, that awful thing," said Aunt May. "Don't worry, Peter. I vacuumed it right up. That nasty spider is dead."

For the next hour it was very difficult to hear the shouts of "Thanks a *lot,* May!" and "How was *I* supposed to know?" over Peter's pained howls. It took a full day of coaxing and an entire tray of brownies to get Peter to even talk to his Aunt May, and even then there was occasional snuffling or hurt looks. As time passed, the relationship between Peter and his aunt and uncle smoothed out and became a consistent and loving one.

His relationships with the rest of the world, on the other hand, were a bit more problematic. . . .

II

THE
DEPARTURE

Why did I listen to her?!?!

Peter Parker adored Mary Jane Watson. There was no question in his mind about that. She was, indeed, hard not to adore. With that luscious red hair . . . with that exquisite mouth that could start as a pout that could crush your heart, then transform into a smile that could send it soaring into the stratosphere . . . with those stunning green eyes that could evoke a spring day in the dead of winter . . . with that laughter as light as a meringue . . . from head to toe, the girl was as close to absolute perfection as any high school senior girl could be.

She had just one teensy, tiny little problem.

The girl had no sense of time.

At all.

Not only that, but she could never remember times that were told to her. Times of meetings, of appointments, of tests . . . there and gone. Her mind was filled with the simple joys of living each day to the fullest, and didn't do well with being bound by such inconveniences as deadlines. Timeliness was for lesser mortals.

So what in the hell had possessed Peter to believe her for so much as a microsecond when she'd said that the bus for the field trip left the school at precisely 8:30 that Friday morning?

Probably because he'd seen her the previous day, late in the afternoon. This wasn't all that unusual an occurrence, considering that she lived in the house opposite his, their backyards adjoining. Nevertheless, even though he'd known her for twelve years, since she had moved in at the age of six, Peter had had occasional bouts of being tongue-tied around her.

This had been one of those times. She'd been weeding in the garden in the postage-stamp-sized backyard, and noticed Peter coming out of his house to get a hammer from the toolshed for Uncle Ben. She'd waved to him; he had waved back. Then she had stood up, dusting off her hands with an air of having finished her task, and picked up a small stack of books. But rather than going into her house an off-white A-frame with red shutters she'd simply stood there, her arms wrapped around the books. He'd had a feeling she was waiting for him to say something, so he'd said the first thing that popped into his mind: "When are we supposed to be at the school again, for the science class trip?"

Without hesitation she'd replied, "Half past eight." Then she'd flashed that gorgeous smile.

"In the morning?" he asked, and immediately mentally kicked himself for such an utterly lame follow-up.

"Well, yeah, we don't do that many class trips at 8:30 at night."

"Right, right." He ran his fingers through his dark hair, and shuffled his toe on the sidewalk. *You're shuffling your toe? What are you, an* infant? *This is Mary Jane Watson . . . M. J. The woman you've loved since before you even liked girls! Say something, for the luvva God! Something intelligent!*

"Well . . . later," he said, and immediately he pivoted on his heel, ran inside, sprinted up the steps to his room, and thudded his head repeatedly against a wall that already had a bunch of peculiar marks that constantly mystified his Aunt May.

So it was that 8:30 lodged in his brain. And when he

arrived at Midtown High at 8:25, it was just in time to see the yellow Laidlaw school bus hanging a left turn out of the parking lot and heading off down Woodhaven Boulevard.

"Awww, crap!" Peter howled, and he started to sprint. He was grateful that, a year ago, he had actually managed to convince Aunt May to let him start wearing sneakers to school. Through his junior year, she had insisted that school was where you wore some of your best clothes, second only to your Sunday go-to-meeting clothes, whatever those were. Aunt May had this occasionally annoying habit of talking like she'd stepped out of a Mark Twain book. Every time she'd say something like "Land sakes!" he half-expected to be able to look out the back window and see a paddle wheeler cruising up the mighty Mississippi, instead of the tree-lined streets of Queens that typified their Forest Hills neighborhood.

So if it had been a year ago, he would have been trying to hotfoot it after a bus wearing a pair of neatly tied Oxfords, slipping like a madman on the highly polished soles. Fortunately enough he was wearing a good pair of running shoes instead, which was what he was going to need if he had any hope in hell of catching up.

The bus was inching its way up Woodhaven, which gave Peter cause for hope. But then a car, which had been in the process of parallel parking, and thus holding up traffic, finally managed to angle its way into the space, and the bus took off like a rabbit.

With a choked groan, Peter sped up.

The bus driver turned onto Queens Boulevard and started to open her up. Most mornings Queens Boulevard would be choked with traffic. Today, naturally, it looked like the Wall Street area on Easter Sunday. The school bus chugged along the outer road of Queens Boulevard, picking up speed, and Peter's lungs were slamming against his ribs.

A kid in the bus saw him. He pointed out Peter to another

kid, and within moments all eyes were on him. For one fleet-ing moment Peter Parker thought he was going to catch a break, and then the sounds of laughter and taunting floated through the air toward him. The bus, which had started to slow for a red light, lurched forward when it abruptly changed to green, and a belch of smoke erupted from the tail pipe. Peter held his breath as he ran through it; one inhala-tion and it would probably have collapsed his lungs. This sign of open disrespect from the bus itself only jacked up the amusement level among the kids, who laughed even harder at his predicament.

His bookbag was slamming against his back as he ran. He shouldn't have even brought the stupid thing. But no, no . . . he'd had to decide that he might as well bring stuff to read on the trip. Try to get ahead on some courses. Peter Parker, the big brain who just couldn't get enough of books that he had to haul them along on a class trip. Part of him wanted to pitch the stupid things down the nearest sewer, but he con-tinued to clutch them tightly.

His large rectangular glasses were bouncing around on the end of his nose. Twice they almost slid off, as his face became drenched in perspiration. With his luck, they'd fall off and he'd wind up trampling them. Wouldn't *that* cause unbridled hilarity for the troglodytes that constituted the senior class.

The bus put its left signal on. It was about to shift lanes, to move into the Queens Boulevard express lane. If it did that, he was finished; the only way he'd catch up with it under those circumstances would be with a rocket.

That was when he heard a female voice—*the* female voice—and even though the motor of the bus was roaring, and even though all the kids were hooting and hollering, she made herself audible over the hullabaloo.

"Stop the bus!!" came Mary Jane's voice. "He's been chasing us since Woodhaven Boulevard!"

This caused a collective and disappointed *awwwww* from the kids on the bus. Naturally. Mary Jane had terminated the fun before it had led to something really entertaining, like a coronary or a blood vessel exploding in his head.

The bus slowed, and for a moment Peter thought it was yet another tease, another false hope. But then it glided over to the curbside, and the doors opened to admit him. Peter nearly collapsed on the first step, clutching the handrail. The bus driver looked down at him, not with concern but with undiluted annoyance, obviously irritated that this idiot teenager had disrupted her carefully prepared schedule.

"Thanks . . ." Peter managed to gasp out.

The driver grunted, shoving forward on the bar and slamming the door shut behind him while he was still in the stairwell. She didn't even wait for him to get into the body of the bus as she pulled the bus forward, grumbling to herself in a steady stream of indecipherable muttering.

Peter staggered forward, fighting not only his own exhaustion and pounding heart but the swaying of the bus as it practically vaulted into the express lane and hurtled forward. He bumped against kids who were seated, and muttered, "Sorry . . . sorry . . ." to each one as he went.

He got a particularly nasty look from the teacher, Mr. Sullivan. Peter always got nervous when he looked at Mr. Sullivan, with his thick glasses, thinning hair, and expression of perpetual pain, because Peter couldn't help but worry that he was looking at a future version of himself. It was a disconcerting, even terrifying thought. Mr. Sullivan gestured impatiently for Peter to go find a seat, then looked down at his clipboard with such intensity that Peter felt as if he was in the midst of translating a newly found section of the Dead Sea Scrolls. Peter glanced over Sullivan's shoulder and saw a list of the students' names on it. Sullivan was putting a little black X next to Peter's name.

That can't be good, Peter thought.

Seated about three-quarters of the way down was Liz Allen. She had a mouthful of braces, glasses thicker than Peter's, and blonde hair so wiry that it could have scoured clean a pan with two inches of hardened grease on it. She had books with her. And here Peter had thought he was the only one obsessive enough to bring along stuff to read. The seat next to her was empty. Peter, his legs weak, made eye contact with her.

She promptly slammed the armload of books down into the space and fixed him with a fearsome glare that could have chilled the sun. "Don't even think about it," she growled.

Wonderful. Liz was to the high school social whirl what the fox trot was to a mosh pit. Yet even *she* was concerned enough about her standing in the Midtown High community that she didn't want to share a seat with him.

As he made his way down the aisle, he couldn't help but wonder what he'd done to deserve this. Was he really that ghastly looking? He caught a glimpse of himself in one of the windows as he passed. Granted, the window was covered with grime and dead bugs, but even with all of that, he wasn't *that* ugly. His face was round, his attitude honest and open. He was physically unimposing: Some would call him scrawny, but he preferred the term "svelte" or "lean." And in his eyes . . . well, he thought his eyes were his best feature, deep blue and filled as they were with quiet intelligence and authority. . . .

Oh, well, and isn't that just what high schoolers adore: intelligence and authority. Intelligence blows the bell curve, and authority is what teens are supposed to rebel against. And here came Peter Parker, the living personification of both. With all that taken into consideration, it was a wonder that he was still walking around at all. . . .

And then, without warning, he was on the floor.

At first he had no idea how it had happened; it had oc-curred so quickly that his mind didn't have the time to process it. All he knew was that one moment he was making his way down the aisle, and the next he was flat on the floor. Unsurprisingly it was filthy, littered with gum wrappers, candy wrappers, stray bits of food and detritus that had been lying there for who knew how long? To add to this joy, he had banged his elbows severely when he'd hit, and the pain running up and down his arms was excruciating. More painful, however, was the humiliation, and the stinging of the blood rushing into his cheeks was the sharpest pain of all.

Because Peter knew that he hadn't simply stumbled. He'd been tripped.

He twisted himself around, shoving his glasses back into place as he looked up with pure, unbridled fury at the occu-pant of the seat he'd just gone by.

Sure enough.

Flash Thompson.

Flash Thompson, the swaggering, arrogant, overarching, self-confident football hero, with a heart the size of all out-doors and compassion to match, if all outdoors happened to be the Arctic Circle. As far as Peter was concerned, Flash was living proof against Darwinism. Because Flash was ob-viously a throwback to an earlier era, and if Neanderthals were anything like Flash, then mankind could never have evolved. NeanderFlash and his caveman cohorts would have made life for any new species an endless torture of trip-ups, poundings, wedgies, and verbal taunting. "You put the 'homo' in 'Homo sapiens,' " they'd doubtless be shouting, grunting and howling. The best and brightest future incarna-tions of man would have scampered back up the trees, never to descend again.

Oh, and they'd get the best women. They'd just overwhelm them with their raw animal magnetism, sling them over their shoulders, and swagger away.

Case in point:

Mary Jane was sitting next to Flash.

She clearly hadn't seen that Flash had been responsible for sending Peter tumbling to the floor, but she was regarding him with clear suspicion. Flash, his hands upturned in a gesture of total innocence, was saying, "What?" And why shouldn't he? Even his lowbrow intelligence was enough to assure himself that Peter wouldn't rat him out, and he was right. The only thing worse than the way this morning was going would be for Peter to point accusingly and say, "He tripped me!" How utterly lame, how whining, would that sound?

No, Peter had to suck it up, which was what he did.

Without a word he staggered to his feet and fired Flash the fiercest, angriest look he could. This intimidated Thompson about as much as could be expected; he curled his lip contemptuously and turned back to Mary Jane, making a point of draping an arm around her shoulders.

There was an empty seat toward the back on the right. It was one of the two seats that nobody ever wanted to sit in: Directly over the rear wheels. It hit all the bumps and potholes, jostled constantly, and was in short the most uncomfortable seat in the house. Peter, sliding into self-pity, exiled himself there. No one gave him a second glance.

Alone amongst a crowd, Peter did what he frequently did under such circumstances. He pulled out a small journal from between two larger books and laid it neatly on his lap, balancing it with accomplished expertise. The journal looked identical to the one that Uncle Ben had bought him over a decade ago, but it had the number 29 neatly inscribed in the upper right-hand corner of the cover. It was the twenty-ninth journal that he'd started since his youth. It was fortunate that Uncle Ben had purchased a common and popular brand of notebook. It gave him a sort of continuity between the young man he'd been and—with any luck—the old man he would become. It made him feel almost like a time traveler.

Writing on the bouncing bus was no easy thing, and this wouldn't be one of his neater entries. Then again, compared to the chicken scratchings from when he was six and still trying to master cursive style, it would be a masterwork.

He dated the page and wrote:

Mom and Dad:

Well, it happened again. Flash made me look like an idiot in front of M. J., and she didn't even realize it was him. I don't understand it. I have about a hundred times his brainpower, but he gets the best of me every time. Uncle Ben says you can beat ignorant people by out-thinking them, and arrogant people by appealing to that arrogance and using it against them, but that people who are ignorant and arrogant are the toughest to deal with.

And the worst is that he sits there with M. J. That's killing me. I don't think he even really likes her . . . not really likes her. He treats her like she's a trophy or something. Like, since he's the best athlete and everything, he deserves to have the best looking girl in the whole school. Like it's divine right or entitlement or something. When it comes down to it, Flash Thompson doesn't love anyone as much as he loves himself. She's there to make him look good.

She must know that. She's got to know that. So why the heck does she put up with him? Why does she even like him? She deserves so much better than him.

Mom, Dad . . . you know I don't ask favors of you, hardly ever. But the next time you're sitting around, shooting the breeze with God . . . do you think maybe you might mention Flash to him, and ask for some divine intervention? Nothing fancy. Nothing extraordinary. An anvil, maybe. A hundred pounds. On second thought, better make it five hundred pounds. With his thick skull, he probably won't feel anything less.

Whatever it takes. In short, any strings you could pull that would provide just a little balance, a little justice, would be greatly appreciated.

Harry Osborn shifted uncomfortably in the back of the chauffeur driven Bentley, sneaking looks at his father, Norman, while fervently wishing that he was somewhere else—anywhere else—at this particular moment in time.

Norman Osborn, for his part, hadn't glanced at Harry for the last twenty blocks. Instead he'd been utterly absorbed in coordinating his day of meetings via his handheld PDA. Harry's attempts at casual conversation had been met with occasional grunts or nods, and not much more.

Osborn the Elder exuded an odd mix of power and barely controlled anger. Harry had never been able to figure out just with whom his father was mad, exactly. The world, it seemed. He was frustrated at all he wished to accomplish . . . and able to focus only on failures rather than successes. And Harry was often the target of his misplaced frustration. At least, that was what Harry chose to believe.

He had never forgotten that time, on his sixteenth birthday. His father had thrown a sizable bash, with a guest list comprised mostly of Norman's friends, with a couple of Harry's friends du jour tossed in for appearances. It was more a business opportunity for strategic meeting and greeting, but Norman had gotten himself seriously liquored up as the evening progressed. That was unusual for him. Usually he prided himself on his total control.

Late in the evening, however, Harry had found himself alone in a hallway with his dad hanging with one arm on his son and speaking in a voice filled with alcohol and contempt.

"I look at you, Harry," he'd said, "and I see myself at your age . . . except without the potential for greatness."

Harry had gone to bed shortly thereafter, and hadn't come out for two days, claiming a headache. His father, mortified over what he'd said while in his cups, finally coaxed him out of his room with a dirt bike he'd been coveting and a vacation to the mountains. It had been a glorious outing, but the circumstances behind it still rankled.

As the Bentley approached the curbside at Columbia University, Harry could see the kids offloading from the school bus onto the sidewalk. He wished for all the world that he'd been able to ride along with the other kids. Norman had put a quick end to that notion, of course. No son of his rode creaky, dirty, disgusting school buses. What if someone he knew saw Harry on it?

The limousine window was slightly rolled down, and he could hear the teacher, Mr. Sullivan, shouting in his perpetually put-upon voice. "Okay, people, no wandering! Proceed directly up to the . . . *knock it the hell off!*" he bellowed as the teen horseplay, laughter, and shouting reached terminal levels. For a microsecond he had caught their attention, and he continued in that same tone, ". . . up the steps and into the building . . . !"

But then all eyes turned toward the Bentley. Harry wanted to sink into his seat, through it, and into the trunk. Hoping to salvage the situation, he muttered, "Dad, could you drive around the corner?"

Norman glanced up from his work toward the entrance to the building. "Why? The door's right here?" he said.

Harry lowered his voice to an urgent whisper, as if the kids could somehow hear them from outside. He saw that they were congregating into one lump of curiosity, focused entirely on him. "These are public school kids," he reminded his father. "I'm not showing up to school in a Bentley."

Norman Osborn laughed bitterly. "What? You want me to trade in my car for a Jetta just because you flunked out of every private school I sent you to?"

Harry winced at that. The only thing worse than the reproach in his father's voice was the knowledge that his dad was right. Trying to mount some sort of defense, he said, "They weren't for me. I told you that. It wasn't for me."

"Of course it was!" Norman shot back. But then, seeing Harry flinch at the abruptness, he sighed and then smiled wanly. He reached across Harry to unlatch the door on his side. "Don't ever be ashamed of who you are," he said, not unkindly.

"Dad, I'm not ashamed. I'm just not what you—"

Norman frowned. "What, Harry?" he asked, trying to get to the source of his son's discomfort.

"Forget it, Dad," he sighed, sliding out of the car.

He squinted, as his eyes had to adjust from seeing the world through the smoked glass of the Bentley to being assailed by the brightness of the sun on the crisp autumn morning.

He stepped onto the curb, bobbing his head slightly in recognition of the awed and impressed expressions on the kids' faces. They were approaching the car as if it was the Holy Grail, which made Harry even more uncomfortable. He'd been speaking the truth to his father: He had never felt like he fit in at private school. Now his money and status were going to set him apart in public school, as well.

"Hi ya, Harry," said a familiar voice.

He felt a quick surge of relief as Peter Parker stepped out of the crowd. Immediately Harry noted that the knees of Peter's pants were dirty, as if he'd taken a spill. Well, he could always ask him about it later.

"Hey, Peter," he said.

Then Harry remembered: He'd borrowed some science books from Peter and had intended to return them this morning, but he'd left them in the car. He started to turn back to the Bentley to get them, but his heart sank as the other back door opened and Norman Osborn stepped out. He didn't so much emerge from the car as grow from it, as if he were an extension of the power and prestige such a vehicle afforded.

He was holding the book bag. "Won't you be needing this?" he inquired.

He handed the bag to Harry, but his gaze was riveted on Peter, sizing up this person who had addressed Harry in such a friendly and outgoing manner. Realizing that an introduction was not only required, but inevitable, Harry cleared his throat and said, "Peter, this is my father, Norman Osborn."

"Great honor to meet you," Peter said, shaking Norman's hand. He winced a bit.

Norman laughed good-naturedly. "Oh, come on, son. You call that a handshake? A man is judged by the strength of his grip. Let's see what you've got."

Peter made an obvious effort, and Harry couldn't watch. Instead he looked around at the girls who were gathering around the Bentley, oohing and aahing. He couldn't help but notice that Mary Jane Watson was one of them, looking at the car almost reverentially, as if it was the most magnificent thing she'd ever seen. He made a mental note of that. It might be that showing up in such a fancy vehicle might not have been such a bad thing after all.

Apparently Peter had made a worthy enough effort, because Norman nodded approvingly and released his hand. "I've heard a lot about you. Harry tells me you're quite the science whiz."

"Well, I don't know about that . . ."

Quickly, Harry said, "He's being modest. I told you, Dad, he's won all the prizes."

With a touch of reproach, Norman said, "Anyone who can get Harry to pass chemistry shouldn't be modest."

"Harry's really smart. He didn't really need my help."

"We have to go, Dad," Harry said.

But Norman obviously found conversation with Peter too engaging to end it quickly. "I'm something of a scientist myself, you know," Norman said with genuine enthusiasm.

"I know," Peter said immediately. "I know all about

OsCorp. You guys are designing the guidance and reentry systems for the first shuttle mission to Mars. Really brilliant."

Norman blinked in surprise at Peter's obvious and total knowledge of everything that his corporation was up to. "Impressive. Your parents must be proud."

Sounding slightly apologetic, Peter said, "I live with my aunt and uncle. They're proud."

The girls were now moving away from the Bentley at the urging of Mr. Sullivan, who was trying to herd them up the steps into the building.

"What about your folks?"

Harry wanted to say something to get Peter off the hook. But Peter took a deep breath and said, "My parents died when I was little."

Norman seemed a bit taken aback by this, and when he spoke again, he sounded sympathetic. "I lost my parents as a young boy, as well."

Harry, sounding a bit more sarcastic than he would have liked, said, "Which no doubt strengthened your iron will to succeed, huh, Dad?"

From the door at the top of the steps, Mr. Sullivan—looking on the verge of apoplexy—called down, *"Hey, you two, I'm closing the door!"*

Norman released his grip on Harry's shoulder, and it was all he could do not to sag in relief. "Nice to meet you, Mr. Osborn," Peter said.

"See you again," Norman assured him before sliding back into the Bentley.

Mary Jane was standing near Flash but watching the Bentley as it pulled away. She shifted her gaze to Harry, and suddenly Harry felt a lot more . . . more powerful, really . . . than he had before. Radiating confidence in a manner that would have made his father proud, Harry said, "Hi."

She smiled back. That alone was enough to put some

additional spring in his step, and then she moved away, Flash blocking her from view.

The class was standing in a corridor with arched ceilings, lined with neatly framed portraits of various scientists, or reproductions of noted scientific documents. Sunlight filtered in through a series of skylights, and the acoustics were terrific as far as the kids were concerned . . . and a horror show as far as Mr. Sullivan and the other chaperones were concerned. As their voices reverberated up and down the hallway the frantic "shushing" from the adults only made things worse.

"He doesn't seem so bad," Peter said, standing at Harry's right shoulder.

Harry looked at him in confusion, not entirely certain who "he" was. Then he realized that Peter was talking about his father, and it was all he could do to suppress a laugh. "Not if you're a genius," he said ruefully. "I think he wants to adopt you."

Then Harry noticed that Peter was looking beyond him, and turned to see that his friend was staring at Mary Jane. Flash had drifted away—apparently a rendering of Da Vinci's famed drawing of man was one of the most hilarious things he'd ever seen, and he was laughing it up with his friends. Mary Jane, for her part, was about two feet away from Peter, studying a portrait of Isaac Newton.

As intrigued as Harry was with Mary Jane, he knew two things beyond question: First, that Peter had been interested in her far longer, and second, that any guy who tried to take her away from Flash Thompson would probably get himself killed. Still, it might be worth the risk . . . provided M. J. was actually interested in breaking it off with Thompson, the Id that Walked Like a Man. Better for his long-term health, Harry realized, if Peter were used for the litmus test of M. J.'s availability, rather than Harry himself. Not that Harry had any intention of sending his friend into danger. Certainly if push came to shove—particularly shove-through-the-wall—Harry could intercede and charm—i.e., bribe—Flash out of it.

Harry snapped his fingers in front of Peter's face to catch his attention. "Hey," he whispered, and, nodding toward Mary Jane, said, "Say something."

Peter squared his shoulders, which struck Harry as rather funny. Peter couldn't have looked more serious if he'd been preparing to enter a ring with a maddened bull, armed with only a dish towel. He approached Mary Jane, who saw him coming, turned and smiled that million-watt smile at him. No wonder, Harry mused, that her last name was Watson. She looked expectantly from Peter to Harry and then back to Peter, and Harry waited for his friend to say something.

And waited.

And waited.

The moment morphed from energy-charged to awkward. Mary Jane tilted her head slightly, expectantly, like a dog trying to pick up a high-pitched noise. Desperate to have matters progress, Harry stepped forward and said to M. J., "Hi. How ya doing?"

Mary Jane smiled in return. "Hey," she said conversationally, and waited once more for Peter to say something. It was difficult for Harry to get a read off her. It could be she was just being friendly . . . or there might be some interest. He needed Peter to keep it going in order to tell for sure.

Peter's jaw twitched once, twice more, which was good since it indicated that he was, in fact, alive. Then he walked away as quickly as he could. M. J. looked to Harry quizzically, and he made a vague noise in his throat and hurried off after Peter. The moment he drew alongside him he asked in annoyance, "Why didn't you say something?"

"I was about to," Peter said defensively. "It . . . wasn't the right moment." Looking around for some sort of exit, he ducked into the nearby men's room, leaving Harry shaking his head.

Suddenly a large shadow was cast over Harry. He turned and looked up, and up, at Flash, and for a moment wondered if there might be a problem, wondered if Flash had figured out what he was up to.

But Flash quickly disabused him of that notion. The jock was obviously only capable of figuring something out if it involved tormenting someone smaller than he. "Explain me something, Osborn," he said.

I'm not sure I know enough small words, he thought, but said gamely, "Sure, Flash. What?"

"You and Parker. I mean, he's such a loser, and you're Mister Megarich Dad and riding around in a Rolls Royce . . ."

"That was a Bentley."

"Whatever," Flash said impatiently. "The point is, why do you bother hanging around with the guy? What's the big attraction? You and Parker ain't . . . uh . . ." and he flipped one hand forward and down in a decidedly limp-wristed manner.

"Huh? *No!*" said Harry with extreme vehemence. "No, it's nothing like that. It's . . . look, you really wanna know?"

"I asked, didn't I?" Flash's disposition wasn't improving.

Harry glanced right and left to make sure no one was paying attention, and was sufficiently satisfied with Mr. Sullivan's fruitless endeavors to get everyone to pay attention. He was reasonably sure they could chat undisturbed for a few moments. "Okay, look . . . my previous schools, all the best, preppy, private schools there were . . . I got bounced out of them, okay? I couldn't cut it scholastically. In point of fact, I didn't even want to."

Flash let out a whistle. "I wondered how you wound up at our dump of a school."

"Yeah, well, if I'd been left on my own, I'd probably have

flunked out of yours, too." He leaned against the wall, shifting uncomfortably, as if his shoes were suddenly too tight. "I'd been at Midtown for about two weeks, and I had this biology report due. I didn't have a clue how to approach it. So I figured I'd do what I always do when I run into a problem: throw money at it. I track down Parker, the biggest brain in school, and offer to buy a biology paper off him. He writes it, I sign my name, pay him off, everybody's happy."

"I get it! So you're Parker's meal ticket!" Flash grinned broadly, as if pleased to learn that Peter Parker's feet were as made of clay as any other guy's.

But Harry shook his head vehemently. "No. No, not at all. Because Peter wouldn't do it. He says it's wrong. He says it won't accomplish anything. I double the offer. Two hundred bucks, I offered him. He still won't take it. I say, 'What? Don't you need the money?' He says, 'More than you know. But that would be wrong,' he says to me. Instead he says to me, 'Look . . . I'll help you do it yourself. Help you pick a topic, show you how to research it, the whole nine yards. And I'll proofread the paper for you once you've written it. Make sure all the facts are right. That way, it's really your paper and it's all aboveboard.' I ask him, 'How much will that run me?' And he says, 'Nothing.' I say, 'So why would you do this for me?' He says, 'Because you look like you need the help. And that would be right.'

"So I take him up on it, because I figure I can still talk him into it. The thing is, thanks to him, I really started getting into it. As I found out stuff in my research, I really did get excited about the idea of seeing it through, for maybe the first time in my life. So I did, and I got a B+, and it was the sweetest grade I ever got, 'cause it was mine. And Peter never took a dime from me.

"Y'see, Flash, most people are like you. They see me, they see a walking dollar sign. Not Peter. He's barely got two nickels to rub together, but I realized—thanks to hanging out with him—that some things, like integrity, are beyond price." He put a hand on Flash's upper arm, and cringed slightly as he felt the rock-solid muscle beneath the shirt-sleeve. "You hear what I'm telling you, Flash? Does that tell you something about Peter Parker?"

"Yeah," said Flash with a snort. "Parker's even dumber than I thought. Walking away from two hundred bucks! He probably would've enjoyed writing the stupid paper. And he could've had you as a customer for the rest of high school. What a jerk!"

Harry moaned, closing his eyes and shaking his head. "Noooo, Flash . . . I think you kind of missed the point . . ."

"The only point that matters is the one on top of Puny Parker's pointed head. What a maroon! What a ta-ra-ra goon-de-ay."

Harry stopped talking, realizing that nothing he was going to say would change Flash's mind about Peter. Indeed it was possible that nothing in existence would do that, short of Peter caving in Flash's face. But as Flash swaggered over to Mary Jane, draping an arm around her as if she were a side of beef, Harry realized that the odds of Peter ever laying out Flash were very, very slim indeed.

The Ascot Club, situated in a neatly adorned brownstone on Lexington Avenue, was one of those men's clubs that seemed hopelessly out-of-date. That, of course, was exactly what its uniformly male membership enjoyed about the place. All one had to do was walk in and take a deep breath. It was easy to detect, with just one whiff, the history, pipes, fine cigars, and testosterone that filled the atmosphere. There was a sense of gravitas in the air, and a serene quiet. In a number of rooms, discussion was banned entirely, allowing blissful silence to hold sway.

Norman Osborn wasn't especially in the mood to talk, but all the truly comfortable chairs in the silent areas were taken. So he had opted to settle into an overstuffed easy chair in the far corner of one of the conversational rooms and bury his face behind a newspaper in hopes of being left on his own. This hope proved to be futile, although at least it made a perverse sort of sense when he was interrupted.

"At least you're reading my newspaper, Norman. I appreciate the show of solidarity."

Osborn folded the *Daily Bugle* in half and looked with surprise at the person who had addressed him. "Jonah!" he exclaimed. "A bit early in the morning for you, isn't it?"

J. Jonah Jameson, publisher of the *Daily Bugle,* didn't need the excuse of his club to puff away on a cigar. He did so whenever and wherever he was inclined, ignoring everything from prohibitive signs to city laws. But he'd been heard to say that, at his club at least, he could smoke without having to worry about getting dirty looks.

Jameson's face had a lived-in look. He had a habit of walking with his chin thrust out, like a boxer daring people to take their best shots. Jonah Jameson also had said on any number of occasions that he led a life without apology. It had been observed by others that he didn't need to apologize; that's what he had a staff for.

In contrast to the impeccable designer suit that Osborn was sporting, Jameson was attired in one of his customary ill-fitting gray off-the-rack things that looked like he'd slept in it for two days. Since he seemed to spend every waking hour either in the office or at the club, he might very well have been sleeping in it. It was a total mystery to Osborn how anyone with as much money as Jameson had could pay so little attention to personal appearance.

Mustache bristling, Jameson dropped into a chair opposite Osborn. "Early for you as well, Norman. Me, I just walked out of a meeting with my idiot accountants."

"Ah. So you came out of an unpleasant meeting. Me, I have to head into one. So I figured some quiet time with a good newspaper . . . and a better brandy . . . ," and he held up his brandy, swirling the contents slightly in the glass, ". . . might be just what the doctor ordered, to help get through it."

"Where is it? Your factory out on the Island?"

Osborn nodded and leaned back in his chair. There was a look of amusement on his face. "Yes, Jonah, it's my factory out on Long Island, and no, I'm not going to go into details. With an old newshound like you, less is always better to say than more."

Jameson didn't laugh, since Jameson never laughed. The most he ever managed was a sort of gruff bark, which was what he produced now. "Don't overestimate yourself, Norman. The day-to-day workings of OsCorp aren't exactly the kind of banner headlines that leave readers begging for more."

"Is what readers are begging for of particular concern to you these days, Jonah?"

Jameson growled this time. Osborn was starting to wonder if the man wasn't part wolf. "Readership in general is what concerns me. That's what my meeting was about, if you really want to know—"

"No, I don't especially."

But it was too late. Jonah was off on a rant. "Blasted accountants, telling me that the newspaper lost a million last year, and will lose another million this year, and very likely another million next year. You know what I told them?"

"That at this rate, you'd have to shut the paper down in about thirty years?"

Jameson blinked in surprise. "How did you know?"

"Because I saw *Citizen Kane,* Jonah. You lifted the line from a sixty-year-old movie."

"I did?" Jonah frowned, and then his eyes went wide. "Son of a gun, I did. Damned good movie, too, if you ask me."

"I didn't ask you, but yes, it was."

Truth to tell, Osborn enjoyed these rare verbal fencing matches that he indulged in with Jameson. But J.J.J. didn't seem in the mood to appreciate it all that much this particular day. "Know what's killing our circulation, Norman? Would you like me to tell you?"

"Could I stop you?" said Osborn hopefully, attempting to get back to his newspaper.

"Our readership is dying out, that's what," Jonah said, as if Osborn hadn't spoken. Osborn sighed and put the paper flat in his lap. Jonah continued, "Older readers, who grew up reading newspapers and fully realize and appreciate the depth of news coverage that only a paper can provide, are dying out. And these new kids . . . they get stuff off television or the Web . . . when they express any interest in learning about the world around them, that is. They aren't going to plunk down fifty cents to read intelligent, in-depth reporting when they can get facile news in small, easy-to-digest, bite-sized bytes."

"Now that's a doomsday attitude to have, Jonah."

"It's realistic." Jonah sounded uncharacteristically self-pitying, even morbid, as he said, "I wonder . . . when the dinosaurs were sinking into pits, their days of glory at an end . . . I wonder if they made the same kind of howls of frustration that old-time, ink-under-the-fingernails newsmen make as our medium goes straight down the tubes."

"You're being much too hard on yourself, Jonah. And you're forgetting something."

"Oh, yeah?" Jonah shifted the cigar from one side of his mouth to the other without using his hands. He just rolled it over from left to right, smooth as pudding. "And what might that be?"

"All you need is one big story. Just one. Something to fire the attention of New Yorkers. If it's a big enough story, people will seek out information on it anywhere they can get it."

"You may be right," said Jonah. "The question is, what sort of story would be big enough?"

"I don't know, Jonah. I'm just a dumb scientist, not a media genius, like you. It's the oldest commandment of showbiz: Give the people what they want."

"What the people want are short, punchy stories with no depth. Black and white, good guys and bad guys, heroes and villains."

"So what's the problem with that?" asked Osborn.

J. Jonah Jameson laughed contemptuously, settling back into his chair with the air of someone who was very much in his element, both physically and philosophically. "And here I thought, Norman, that you were a man after my own heart. Don't you know? There are no heroes. Not anymore. If you want greatness, and great men, crack a history book and look at the founding fathers. There were great men. Men of conviction. Men willing to put themselves on the line. They put their names to the Declaration of Independence, knowing that they were signing their death warrants. But they did it because they believed in something. That's gone now. You know what killed heroism, Norman?"

"No, but I suspect you're going to tell me," Osborn said dryly.

"This whole Internet thing. With people having no respect for copyrights because they're busy stealing entire printed works off downloads, or going around ranting and raving at each other, striking from hiding behind names like 'Fuzzydice' or 'The Destroyer' or 'Bob1123' or similar nonsense." Jonah was waving his cigar around, ashes flying all over. One of the attendants, long used to Jameson when he went off on a rant, was busily sweeping the ash into a dustbin. "How much impact do you think the Declaration would have had, Norman, if it had been filled with signatures like 'Deathscream' or 'Hoppybunny27'?"

"Not very much," Osborn allowed. "But to be fair, Jonah . . . why should anyone want to be a hero, in this day and age fostered by your own media. Whenever someone does something heroic, the newspapers grab ahold of him and dig and dig until they find some sort of dirt, and then splash it all over the front pages. Why should anyone want to make themselves such a target?"

"If you're a hero, you don't think about what might happen if you take a risk. You just do what needs to be done," Jonah retorted. "I've tried to live my life as scrupulously as possible, Norman. You can't go around bringing down corruption if your own hands aren't clean. People want to investigate me, let 'em. I have nothing to hide. But do people follow my example? They do not. No heroes anymore, as I said. Don't blame the messenger for the message."

Osborn kept telling himself that he shouldn't be baiting Jonah this way, but he was apprehensive enough about the meeting he had to get to, and the old windbag was starting to grate on him. "So what is the message you're getting out there that you shouldn't be blamed for? That nobody's good enough to withstand public scrutiny, no matter how well-meaning their actions may seem."

"Exactly," Jonah said with an emphatic wave of his cigar, sending more ashes tumbling. A couple danced on the lapels of Osborn's jacket, and he brushed them away. Jonah didn't seem to notice. "That's exactly it."

"Funny," said Osborn, scratching his chin thoughtfully as he rose from his chair. "I seem to remember a man who lived about two thousand years ago who had a touch of the heroic about him. A lot of people looked up to him. A lot of people didn't. So tell me, Jonah . . . if a man of that caliber of heroism showed up today, would you be listening and learning from him? Or would you be first in line to crucify him?"

A number of men had been listening to the exchange, and

there was a collective guffaw when Osborn said that. Jameson fired looks around, and the laughter was quickly silenced as they went back to their own newspapers.

"That's not funny, Norman," Jameson said quietly.

"No. It's not." He patted Jameson on the shoulder. "Jonah, I hope—for your sake—you get your hero, and you get your story, and you get your circulation numbers back up. God knows we still need newspapers and heroes . . . and you need someone to tear down."

"Or build up," he added quickly.

"That's up to you, isn't it?"

And as he walked out of the men's club, Jonah called after him, "Mark my words, Osborn: The closest we come to heroes these days is some schmuck with bad timing who falls into it by accident!"

"Jonah," Osborn called over his shoulder, "I think you may just have defined 'hero' for the ages."

III.

THE
ACCIDENT

It was the smallest of the small. It tended to stay away from the others, daunted by the disparity in size. While the others moved in leisurely groups, clumps of mandibles and black furred abdomens, the smallest—the runt—kept to itself. Food was plentiful, and the larger ones got most of it, simply because they were bigger and didn't hesitate to hog it. The smallest of the small got the leftovers. As a result, in addition to its diminutive stature, it had a lean and hungry look about it.

So while all the others would sit around, fat and contented, the smallest of the small explored every nook and cranny of their home, endlessly and meticulously studying every centimeter. It did not do so out of any sort of plan or long-term strategy. It did so because it had nothing else to do to pass the time.

As a consequence, it was the only one that discovered the break in the seal.

It found the break purely by accident, as it moved around the edges of the grillwork that covered one of the air vents. It wasn't a break that a normal creature its size would have been able to exploit . . . but this was not a normal creature.

The creature pulled experimentally on the edge of the seal, and its strength was sufficient to bend it ever so slightly, in the place where one of the screws hadn't been driven in as tightly as it should. The others, fat and content as they were, did not notice what the smallest was up to.

*They did detect the slight vibration of the small metal grill-
work overhead moving, but the vibration abruptly ceased
and their attention immediately wandered. They gave no
further thought to it, to its source, or to the smallest of the
small . . . which was no longer there.*

As he entered the Columbia Genetic Research Institute,
Peter Parker didn't know where to look first. The laboratory
was cavernous, lined with instrumentation the nature of
which he could only guess. He saw some stuff that looked
vaguely familiar . . . even a bit similar to things that Peter
had worked with. But the equipment he'd used was on a
much smaller scale than what he was looking at now.

The domed ceiling was so tall it was hard to believe that
the building contained it, and the equipment itself was
shined to within an inch of its chrome life. Peter's camera
was hanging around his neck, the nice sturdy Konica his
aunt and uncle had gotten him for Christmas. "Too bad
we're not Jewish. I could have gotten you a Konica for
Chanukah!" Ben had said cheerfully, prompting a moan
from Peter and an annoyed thump on his chest from May.

The tour guide, a thin, black-haired Asian woman, was
guiding them past a large exhibit on spiders. "There are
more than 32,000 known species of spider in the world," she
intoned, managing to sound both important and deathly
bored at the same time. The thirty-three students on the trip
responded to Mr. Sullivan's get-over-here gestures by
crowding into a circle around their guide, who didn't even
appear to notice that anyone was paying attention. "They are
in the order Aranae, which is divided into three suborders:
Mesothelea, Orthognatha, and Labidognatha. All spiders are
carnivorous, ravenous eaters who feed on massive quantities
of protein, in liquid form, usually the juices of their prey."

Peter, however, was getting severely distracted from such
riveting topics as spider juices. Instead he was keeping an

eye on Mary Jane, who was joking around with some friends of hers. He was still stinging over the way he had fumbled the ball, yet again. He had fallen into a depressing routine: trying to talk to her, perhaps getting out a few words of no consequence, before folding faster than a tent without a center pole. It was a pretty crummy way to go through life, particularly when it concerned a girl as important to Peter as M. J. was.

But that could change. *He* could change. All he needed to do was make that resolution, and decide that he was going to start doing things differently. Yes, yes, that was it. That was all he had to do. And it was going to start with Mary Jane.

"Arachnids from each of the three groups possess varying strengths which help them in their constant search for food," the tour guide informed them.

Yes, that was it: M. J. was a sort of food to him. Soul food. Food that could provide him emotional nourishment, if he could only get himself to try her. Well, he was going to do it, that's all. *Just do it*, like they said in that stupid commercial.

He took a deep breath to steady his pounding heart, then took two steps toward her. That was as far as he got before Flash Thompson, with a timing bordering on the supernatural, swept in while Peter was still a good two yards away, stepped in behind her, partly obscuring her from view. He put his arm around her, nuzzled her neck. Peter gulped deeply, his Adam's apple bobbing up and down. Well, that was certainly all he needed to see.

The guide was going on about the jumping spider, family Salticidae, genus Salticus. On and on, and Peter turned away from Mary Jane, from Flash, from that which was so upsetting to him that he couldn't even articulate it. For a fraction of an instant, he thought he saw Mary Jane looking in his direction and then pulling away from Flash, looking embarrassed over his overt and clumsy attempts at affection. But no. He was certain that it was a product of his fevered imagination, a wish fulfillment that M. J. would realize that a guy like Flash wasn't right for her, no matter what her father might say.

Her father . . .

Peter had been watching that time. . . .

He'd been daydreaming, staring out his window, when he'd seen Flash Thompson pull up to her house. Flash had walked up to the door, knocked, and M. J.'s father had opened the door. Seeing the two of them together, Peter was struck by the similarities, in terms of build and deportment. They'd laughed together, there on the stoop, and although Peter couldn't hear what was being said, he had no doubt that it was bursting with enough machismo to grow hair on anything that didn't normally sport hair.

When Flash had left with M. J. on his arm, he'd received a pat on the back from her dad, and even a few bucks that M. J.'s dad dug out of his jacket pocket. It was perfectly obvious: M. J.'s dad felt he had a lot in common with Flash, and had willingly "given" his daughter over to him.

And Mary Jane had gone along with it.

That struck him as unutterably sad, although he wasn't entirely certain why.

Peter was abruptly jolted from his thoughts by Mr. Sullivan's loud, pinched voice. He was bellowing at the other kids, who had been looking anywhere and everywhere except at the tour guide, and talking about anything and everything except spiders. Sullivan was standing so close to Peter when he shouted that Peter thought he was going to suffer permanent hearing loss.

"Excuse me! Is anyone paying attention to the genus Salticus?"

That brought everything screeching to a halt. Even the

guide looked shaken. Mr. Sullivan nodded slightly in her direction and said, "I apologize. Go on."

The tour guide started speaking again, but it was rather tentatively, and she wasn't taking her eyes off Mr. Sullivan, as if concerned that there would be another outburst "The . . . genus Salticus . . . can leap up to forty times its body length, thanks to a proportionate muscular strength vastly greater than that of a human being." She was about to continue speaking when she noticed that Peter was trying to catch her eye. She raised her eyebrows in response, clearly inviting a question.

Peter held up his camera and gestured to it. "Okay to take a few pictures? For the school paper?"

The tour guide nodded, and Peter—to his chagrin—noticed that the guide looked more irked than anything. Obviously she hated being interrupted. But Peter didn't have much time to dwell on any faux pas he might have committed, since he was immediately distracted by nearby snickering and mutterings of "geek." These days it seemed like any words out of his mouth, no matter how innocuous, managed to attract snide commentary and disdain from either Flash or one of his cronies. It shouldn't be getting to him; he knew that intellectually. All of Flash's friends put together had the collective IQ of a dust bunny, and their opinions should have carried just as much weight. But it bothered him nevertheless . . . and worse, it bothered him that it bothered him.

He tried to put it out of his mind, concentrating instead on the nice shot that was set up at that moment, of the tour guide standing just in front of one of the spider displays. It was well framed, and would make a good accompanying piece of art for the article. But with remarkable timing, just as Peter pressed the shutter release, someone banged into his arm, jostling the camera and giving Peter a superb photograph of Harry Osborn's elbow.

Peter fired a glance over his shoulder and saw one of

Flash's pals—a guy who'd picked up the nickname "Hoops," due to the number of small rings he had adorning his various piercings—backing away and snickering.

The tour guide, unaware of the struggle touched off by the mere act of Peter's trying to take her picture, droned on as if anyone cared. "The funnel-web spider—family Hexathelidae, genus Atrax—one of the deadliest spiders in the world, spins an intricate, funnel-shaped web whose strands have a tensile strength proportionately equal to the type of high-tension wire used in bridge building."

Hoping to salvage the moment, Peter started to aim his camera, and once again his elbow was shoved. Hoops wasn't even bothering to be coy about it this time. He shoved Peter's arm deliberately, challengingly.

Even though he knew that Hoops could probably break him in half, Peter whirled to face him. Seeing the anger twisting Peter's features, and probably welcoming an opportunity to tap dance on Peter's face, Hoops took a step forward in a threatening manner. But then a voice, low and commanding, said, "Leave him alone."

Hoops and Peter turned to see the speaker, Harry Osborn. As opposed to both Peter and Hoops, who were wearing their respective outrages openly on their faces, Harry's mien was one of utter calm. Obviously he wasn't going to give Hoops the satisfaction of seeing him angry, as if Hoops wasn't worthy of the privilege.

Nevertheless, Hoops said defiantly, "Or what?"

Flash, without batting an eye, replied, "Or his father will fire your father."

Hoops blanched at that, and several kids standing around, who had overheard the exchange, laughed loudly. Harry didn't seem perturbed by the attention, although Peter flushed a bit.

But Mr. Sullivan had clearly had it. In a loud, clear voice

he called out, "The next person who talks is going to fail this course. I kid you not."

Peter didn't think that should be much of a threat to Hoops, Flash, or any of their ilk; he was reasonably sure the only time they ever saw a D, C, B, or A coming their way was if they were standing on a subway platform. Nevertheless, Hoops backed off, although he did spare a fairly nasty glare for Harry.

Harry, for his part, didn't seem to notice or care.

Continuing along the display the tour guide said, "The crab spider—family Thomisidae, genus Misumena—spins a web to catch its prey, but hunts instead, using a set of reflexes with nerve conduction velocities so fast, some researchers believe it almost borders on precognition . . . an early awareness of danger . . . a," and she dropped her voice and waggled her fingers to make it sound mysterious, ". . . spider sense."

They reached the center of the rotunda floor, where researchers were working at computers surrounding an electron microscope. Large video screens around the room displayed giant images of what was obviously the microscope's area of scrutiny: spider DNA. Peter found the entire thing incredibly fascinating and could tell from a quick glance at his classmates that he was the only one. Was there something wrong with him, or with the rest of them?

"Over five painstaking years, Columbia's genetic research facility has fully mapped the genetic codes of each of these spiders." The guide walked with measured strides around the rotunda, speaking with such pride that one would have thought she personally was in charge of designing a map to track every strand of every chromosome. "Armed with these DNA blueprints," she continued, "we have now begun what was once thought impossible: interspecies genetic transmutation."

Flash had drifted just within Peter's earshot, and just outside of Mary Jane's, and he said very softly, "I thought they managed that when you were born, Parker." He guffawed to himself and stepped back just before M. J. noticed that he'd said anything. Once again Peter felt a sharp stinging in his face as the blood rushed to it. He didn't know which was worse: Flash making jokes at his expense, or the knowledge that Mary Jane was Flash's and Peter was left with nothing.

"In this recombination lab," the guide said, gesturing with one hand to take in the entirety of the amazing complex, "we use synthesized transfer RNA to encode an entirely new genome combining genetic information from all three spiders into these fifteen genetically designed superspiders, the first mankind has ever produced."

Just ahead of them was a glass tank. The aforementioned mutated spiders were crawling along the walls. Peter noted with wry amusement that something had finally presented itself which fully captured the students' attention. They were staring with fascination at the disgusting creatures creeping along the glass.

They seemed to be congregating in one area. Peter decided that if he could manage to get a shot with all fifteen of them in it at once, that would be extraordinarily cool. Mary Jane had already positioned herself near "spider central." If he could get her in the shot, so much the better. Harry was also drawing near, but Peter held back a bit in order to get the wider angle and make sure that the fifteen were in the shot.

"Dis*gust*ing," said Mary Jane, but she didn't sound especially repulsed. Indeed she seemed almost enthused, as if they were beautiful in their sheer nauseating appearance.

Harry, however, misread her tone of voice. "Hateful little things," he said, thinking he was agreeing with her.

"I *love* it," said M. J.

Quickly realizing his error, Harry amended, "Really? Me, too."

It was all Peter could do not to laugh. Certainly the last thing he wanted to do was start enjoying himself at his friend's expense. He didn't exactly have an abundance of friends, and he sure didn't want to alienate the very few he had.

"Just imagine," said the tour guide, "if one day we can isolate the strengths, powers, and immunities in human beings, and transfer that DNA code among ourselves. All known disease could be wiped out. Of course we're nowhere near ready to start experimenting with humans, so for the moment we're concentrating on these fifteen spiders. Any questions?"

"Fourteen," M. J. said abruptly. All eyes went to her, and Mr. Sullivan laughed nervously in a "why is she doing this?" manner.

"I beg your pardon?" called the tour guide.

Undaunted by the challenging looks from the others, and the clear chagrin from the teacher, M. J. said, "There's only fourteen spiders."

"No," the guide said firmly, "there's fifteen." And then, a little less firmly, she asked, "Aren't there?"

The smallest of the small didn't have the strongest of memories when it came to events. The things that it did, it did as a result of instinct, hardwired into it by century upon century of evolution.

So the smallest, having departed the case that had been its home, had no recollection of ever having resided there. The only home it now knew was the web that it had delicately spun for itself, up among the recesses of the ceiling.

Nor did it have a clear recollection that, once upon a time, it had been given food by a mysterious benefactor that was the closest to the concept of God that the creature could come to. All it knew now was that food was no longer forthcoming, and that it had to forage for itself. The craving in its belly was growing by the hour, and it hadn't been able to spin its web fast enough to gather sustenance for itself.

The gossamer web it had spun was indeed quite a beauty, and the smallest of the small was now waiting in the middle of it. Waiting for the unwary, waiting for its prey, waiting for something it could trap and cocoon and drain dry. Unfortunately nothing seemed to be cooperating. No flies or insects of any kind were presenting themselves as an entrée, and the smallest was beginning to go mad with hunger.

And something else was disrupting the poor creature—thunderous vibrations from the—from the whatever they were—a far distance below, which were no doubt serving to drive any potential meals away from the web.

The creature did not know, could not experience such emotions as anger. But as it became more and more famished, its frustration level built and built. . . .

The picture, and the opportunity, could not have presented itself more perfectly.

There was Mary Jane, looking into the glass case, checking out her makeup. It was hard for Peter to believe that she saw any need to take such measures. She was perfect; how could she conceivably improve upon herself? But he didn't question it too closely, because he was busy seizing the chance that had been tossed his way.

A few quick steps and he was by her side. He said, "Can I take your picture? I need one with a student in it."

Mary Jane turned to look at him, and Peter felt as if he was being pulled completely out of the depressing, frustrating world inhabited by Peter "Big Brain Loser" Parker and into the sphere where dwelt the magnificence that was Mary

Jane. It was a happy, glorious place, and he was pleased just to be the most transient of tourists there.

In response, she immediately struck a pose, hiding a small smile behind the practiced pout of a model. She flipped her hair back, eyed the camera as she would a lover, and said in a playfully sulky voice, "Don't make me ugly!"

"Impossible," Peter scoffed, gazing at her through the viewfinder. He could have remained that way all day, but he felt he had to be thoroughly professional. "Right there . . . good!" He snapped a picture, and the autowind shot forward. "And one more—!"

Except she had vanished from his viewfinder. She had moved out of frame, drifting toward a group of her friends. "Thanks," Peter called after her. He'd gotten her to smile at him, even if only for a photo. This was turning into a memorable day.

The spider had lost its mind.

It wasn't as if it had a large mind to begin with, but hunger had overridden its desire for caution. Eat eat eat was the imperative hammering through it, and it decided to go on a hunt, rather than wait for something unwary to come to it.

There was a target just below it. Its spinnerets lowered it gracefully down, closer to its prey. Had the spider been thinking properly, it would have gotten nowhere near this . . . this monster. This gigantic thing. But the spider was only concerned about making a last ditch effort to fill its belly, and when it lunged at its prey, it had no clue that it was the last conscious effort it would ever make. . . .

"Ow!" Peter yelped.

He had just been turning to look at a huge display of electron microscopes when a sharp pain had gotten him in the right hand. Instinctively he'd snapped his wrist, and he caught out of the corner of his eye some sort of . . . of bug. An insect. A mosquito, perhaps?

Peter held up the back of his hand and saw two tiny red marks flaring up on it. There was a moment of morbid amusement as he wondered if he'd been assaulted by the world's tiniest vampire, and then he saw a brief movement on the floor. He looked down, his eyes narrowing, as he watched what appeared to be a spider flip over onto its back, its legs curling up like something out of a commercial for Raid.

A spider . . .

Peter Parker felt a surge of momentary panic as he looked back in the direction of the spider tank. There had seemed to be some confusion as to whether there were fourteen or fifteen spiders. Could one of them have escaped? And . . . and could this be it? If he'd been bitten by some sort of genetically mutated spider . . . it could make him sick as anything.

Thoughts of blood poisoning tumbled through his head, and he moaned softly. *Great. Just great.* Everyone else goes on a nice, ordinary class trip, and good old Peter Parker gets bitten by a toxic spider.

But even as the possibility occurred to him, he was inclined to dismiss it. How in the world could a spider have escaped from there, anyway? It's not as if one of its relatives could smuggle in a teeny tiny hacksaw. The spiders weren't about to start punching their way through the thick glass. No . . . despite Peter's tendency to ascribe a worst-case scenario to everything in the world, even he had to admit that the chances were that this was a normal, garden-variety spider. Heck, it didn't even look as big as the others had been. The others had been huge, relatively speaking. This one just looked like . . . well, like a dead arachnid.

It was kind of puny, really.

And the kids—Flash, in particular—did tend to refer to him as Puny Parker. So if he had to be bitten by a spider, it was probably appropriate that it was this one.

Peter stood there, rubbing his hand, as the array of electron microscope display screens flashed around him, images of DNA strands dancing over him. He didn't consider it to be particularly ironic in any way.

That would change.

IV.

THE
MEETING

Norman Osborn could remember clearly the day that the proud OsCorp Industries factory in Commack, Long Island, had first opened. He had stopped going home in those final days, as they rushed to make certain everything was ready for the opening day. He ate, slept, and breathed that building, checking every rivet, every switchplate, every window seal.

The first time he saw the neon letters of the huge OsCorp logo flicker to life, he felt a swelling of pride. The first time he beheld a black, noxious cloud belching out of the towering smokestacks, he knew that everything for which he'd been striving all these years had finally been attained.

So here he was, years later, and if driving a wrecking machine through the place—leveling it, reducing it to nothing but a pile of rubble—had been an option, he would have grabbed it in a heartbeat.

Explosives would serve just as well.

"General Slocum and the others have already started the inspection," said his somewhat high-strung assistant, Simkins. "Mr. Balkan and Mr. Fargas are with them."

Above the elevator door, the square that read RESEARCH AND DEVELOPMENT lit up. R&D was situated a fifth of a mile underground, which was a compromise as far as Osborn was concerned. For his full comfort level to be reached, he'd much rather have had it situated somewhere near the earth's core. Industrial theft was his number-one concern, and he was prepared to do whatever it took to avoid having enemies swoop in and steal that which he had labored so long to achieve.

There was a soft ping as the elevator doors slid open. Osborn stepped out onto a dizzyingly high catwalk, and his hard green eyes, while appearing to be focused straight ahead, took in everything around him, with peripheral vision that would have rivaled the capabilities of security cameras. Simkins gulped audibly, fighting off a momentary flash of vertigo before gripping the rail and moving behind her boss. She had to pick up speed, because Osborn wasn't slowing down.

"Why wasn't I told about this?" Osborn growled.

"I . . . don't think they wanted you to know, sir," admitted Simkins.

Osborn moved quickly down a narrow flight of steps, taking two at a time. He hoped Simkins could keep up but was too focused on his destination to be concerned if she didn't. He practically vaulted down to the polished floor, ignoring the greeting of "Morning, Mr. Osborn" he got from every employee he passed. As if there was anything good about this morning. As if any of them were remotely happy to see him. Every single one of them was a security risk, no matter how many nondisclosure forms they signed.

On the other hand, there was nothing to be done when the enemy strolled right into your lair. Or, for that matter, rolled right in.

That certainly described Mr. Fargas, sitting imperiously in his wheelchair, his eyebrows thick, his head bald, making him evocative of the professor character from that mutant movie. Mr. Balkan, as always standing beside Fargas, was tall and distinguished looking, but no less irascible.

There were other people in suits standing nearby. Dammit, how many people was the Pentagon going to dispatch whenever they wanted to look in on OsCorp's activities? It seemed there were more and more each time, and each one—as far as Osborn was concerned—represented a potential security leak.

There was General Slocum, in the middle of the lab, doing a slow, measured tread around the project that they had all come to see and, very likely, criticize. Slocum was square-jawed, steely-eyed, beetle-browed, and pea-brained. As for the project itself . . .

It was breathtaking.

For all the anger he was feeling toward this intrusion, Osborn was still able to take pleasure in his achievements, when his vision was combined with the talents of his people.

He remembered the time he had gone to the beach, at Harry's pleading. Harry had just gotten a boogie board for his thirteenth birthday and was thanking his father profusely for his thoughtfulness. It seemed silly to Osborn, but the boy really *did* seem to be trying lately in school, and it seemed the least Osborn could do.

Well, off they'd gone to the beach. At first Osborn had felt self-conscious splashing about in the surf, but he was making the effort for Harry. It wasn't easy; it was contrary to Osborn's business-first nature and his own upbringing. But no one seemed to be paying attention to him, and he started to relax a bit.

But then he started watching Harry and other kids with the boards, skimming the tops of waves, controlling the things with remarkable dexterity.

And as they did so, Osborn took a mental snapshot of their actions, and found himself transporting the concept in his mind. Instead of skimming waves, they were hurtling over battlefields, deftly maneuvering around enemy troops. In his imaginings, they were wearing armor—tight-fitting, lightweight suits, designed for protection but more than that: They had a cybernetic link to the board. Yes, that was it— they could take it to the next level. It wouldn't be all that much of a jump, really. Rather than depending upon the reflexes of the rider, the board would respond to their very thoughts.

When Harry had emerged from the water, his father had been grinning and nodding and clapping his hands with delight. Harry couldn't have been more thrilled at his father's support. Osborn, for his part, was looking right through his son, seeing a vast army of armored boogie board-riding soldiers.

It had taken four years, a government contract, and two breakthroughs in cybernetics to bring them to the point where they were now. There, in the lab at OsCorp, was the the result, mounted atop a servo pole. Since this board was designed for air, rather than water, adjustments had been made to make it aerodynamically stable. Fins had been added, and footholds for a more sure grip, and naturally there was the jet tubing down the middle that would propel the thing.

Next to the device, a technician was outfitted in the armored suit, moving his legs and arms while the board obediently responded to every change in his posture.

By rights it should have been eliciting ooooh's and aaaahhhh's from the onlookers. Instead they just stood there and scowled. They were bereft of imagination, nor did they possess the slightest vision, and yet they were coming here and standing in judgment of Osborn's work.

He was entering the lab just in time to hear Dr. Mendel Stromm, his head of R&D, embark on a detailed explanation of everything that made the glider work. There may not have been a more personally annoying individual on the planet than Stromm, with his affectations and slightly mincing manner. But when it came to quantum leaps in cybernetic breakthroughs, the only scientist who had better chops than Stromm was probably Dr. Henry Pym, and Pym simply wasn't for sale.

"Individual Personnel Transports are moving along splendidly," Stromm was saying, clearly about to go into detail on the program's progress.

"I've seen your glider," General Slocum said, pausing momentarily over the word "glider" with such faint disdain that Osborn wanted to throttle him. "That's not why I'm here."

Osborn forced pleasantries. "General Slocum," he said convivially. "Good to see you again. Mr. Balkan, Mr. Fargas," he continued, acknowledging each of them in turn. They didn't respond. Just glowered.

"Always a pleasure to have our board of directors pay us a visit."

Slocum didn't seem impressed by Osborn's greetings. "I want a progress report on Human Performance Enhancers."

Doctor Stromm paused a moment, glancing at Osborn, who simply nodded. Gesturing toward a glass-walled isolation chamber on the other side of the lab, Stromm started toward it, speaking as he went. "We tried vapor inhalation with rodent subjects. They showed an eight hundred percent increase in strength."

Fargas rolled his chair forward. "Eight hundred percent. That's excellent."

That gave Osborn a momentary surprise; he didn't think Fargas was capable of praising anyone or anything. Slocum, however, was naturally looking for the downside. "Any side effects?" he asked.

"In one trial," Stromm began to reply, "yes, the—"

Osborn quickly interrupted. "It was an aberration. All the tests since then have been successful."

But Slocum continued to pointedly ignore Osborn as he addressed Stromm. "In the test that went wrong, what happened? What were the side effects?"

Stromm didn't hesitate. It was clear that he was extremely concerned about the situation, and was welcoming the opportunity to make that concern known. "Violence. Aggression. And eventually, insanity."

A silence fell over the group for a moment, and then Slocum said, "What's your recommendation?"

Before Stromm could say anything else that could possibly sink OsCorp lower than the R&D level, Osborn stepped in, physically interposing himself between Stromm and Slocum. Meeting the general's gaze, he assured him, "With the exception of Dr. Stromm, our entire staff has certified the product ready for human testing."

And then the human submarine known as Dr. Stromm fired his torpedo, striking the good ship OsCorp across the bow. "We need to take the whole line back to formula."

Feeling betrayed, Osborn whirled to face Stromm. *"Back to formula?"*

"Mr. Osborn," Slocum said stiffly, "this department has missed seven consecutive delivery dates. After five-and-a-half years of R&D, the United States government has a right to expect the supersoldier you were contracted to deliver."

This was madness! The formula was safe! Stromm was just being paranoid!

Trying to sound reasonable and assured, Osborn said, "These are quantum leaps in science, gentlemen. We are unlocking the secrets of human evolution. I never said it would be cheap or fast, only groundbreaking."

Slocum drew himself up so that he towered over Osborn, and fixed a cold stare upon him. "I'll be frank with you. I never supported your program. We have my predecessor to thank for that." There was another word that he spoke with dripping contempt: predecessor.

Osborn sensed that the other shoe was going to drop, and it was Balkan who dropped it. "The General has given the go-ahead to Quest Aerospace to build a prototype of their exoskeleton design. They test in two weeks."

My God . . . they're that far along? Osborn fought to

keep any look of panic off his face, even as General Slocum, twisting the knife, said, "If your so-called performance enhancers haven't had a successful human trial by that time, I will pull your funding and give it to them."

"Norman," Fargas said, very slowly and very dangerously, "we are *not* going to lose this contract."

All eyes were now on Osborn, obviously waiting for him to say or do something. At that point, all he could manage was a nod and a forced smile. Then he glanced back over his shoulder at the armor and the glider, and instead of a foreign battlefield with enemy soldiers strewn around, he was picturing sailing it over a ground littered with the bodies of Slocum, Stromm, and the entire board of directors.

It gave him some momentary comfort.

V

THE SIDE
EFFECTS

May Parker thought she was going to have a heart attack.

She had just walked into the living room to discover her brilliant husband standing precariously on a chair, stretching his arm as far as he could to try to change a light bulb in the overhead fixture. Ben was grunting, his full concentration on the job at hand. Pale sunlight was filtering through the just-vacuumed venetian blinds, causing him to squint as the chair tilted ever so slightly on the carpeted floor.

For a moment all May could think about was that he would fall forward, crack his head open, and blood would permanently stain her couch, making her wistful for the plastic coverings that they'd removed years ago to keep Peter happy. Then she decided she really had to reorder her priorities and instead prevent Ben from getting himself killed.

"Why aren't you using a ladder? You'll fall and break your neck," she admonished him. Indicating the bulb, she continued, "Wait for Peter to do that."

Ben ignored her as he was wont to do. Instead, with a final triumphant twist, he got the bulb in and it illuminated. "God said let there be light," he intoned. "Voila. Seventy-five soft glowing watts of it."

He started to step down off the chair, clutching the burned out bulb with one hand, and Aunt May stood just behind him to break his fall should it come to that. Not that she'd do him all that much good; if he landed on her he'd likely kill her. But she felt as if she had to do something.

"Good boy," she said sarcastically. "God'll be thrilled. Just don't fall on your ass."

The moment his foot was on solid ground, she headed into the kitchen to continue preparing dinner. As she went about doing so, Ben called after her, "I'm already on my ass. When the plant senior electrician is laid off after thirty-five years, what else would you call it? Of course I'm on my ass!"

She'd heard him rant about it so much that she was able to mouth it along with him. Standing at the stove, she checked on water that was about to boil. Ben walked in behind her, tossing the burned out bulb into the garbage can. Figuring her husband might as well make himself useful, May said, "Hand me the bowl. The green one."

Ben picked up the requested kitchen implement and then went to the newspaper that was spread out on the table. He flipped to the classified section and shook his head dispiritedly. "Corporations firin' people left and right so they can have a few billion more. What do they know about standing on a stool, screwin' in a light bulb?"

Standing around in pitch-blackness was beginning to sound preferable to listening to Ben carry on. "Ben, you'll get another job somewhere."

"Well, let's see," Ben said with mock joviality, running his finger along the job notices. "Computer analyst, computer designer, computer engineer, computer . . ." His point made, he let out a melancholy sigh. "I'm sixty-eight years old. I have to provide for my family."

She hated to see him this way. So dispirited, so frustrated. Ben was of a generation that set a great deal of store by the ability of a husband to keep a roof over his loved ones' heads. The loss of his job had been an unmanning experience for him. Granted he wasn't a young man anymore, but Ben had a natural ebullience that belied his advanced years. That was missing now, consumed by doubt and self-pity.

Turning the flame down under the pot, she stepped in behind him, embraced him, and kissed him on the cheek. "I love you," she assured him. "And Peter loves you. You're the most responsible man I've ever known. You've been down and out before, but somehow we survive." Not wishing to dwell too long on maudlin concerns, she stood up and said, "Where is Peter, anyway? He's late."

At that moment the front door opened and then slammed. Ben quickly turned the newspaper to the comic strips and called heartily, "Here he is!"

"Just in time for dinner," May said. The roast she was making in the oven was already giving off pleasing cooked smells that were filling the kitchen. She dropped some potatoes to be boiled into the water on the stovetop.

"How was the field trip?"

May's back was to Peter, but when he didn't respond promptly, she turned and glanced at him. She was taken aback by his wan look. It seemed as if he could barely stand up.

"Don't feel well . . . I wanna go to sleep," he moaned softly.

She immediately wanted to start making a fuss over him but knew how that made him feel, and every time she did it he'd complain she was overreacting. So, keeping a lid on her natural impulses, she instead said with just a touch of disappointment, "You won't have a bite?"

For some reason he gave her the oddest look when she said that. Then he shrugged and, heading for the stairs, said in what sounded like a bleakly amused tone, "No thanks . . . had a bite . . ."

"Did you get some good pictures, Peter?" asked Ben.

But Peter was already at the stairs, trudging as if he had lead weights attached to his ankles. "Gotta crash . . . everything's fine." And with that, he vanished. Moments later they heard the slamming of his bedroom door.

Ben, his own concerns forgotten, turned with a mystified air toward May. "What's that all about?" he asked.

May was already moving toward the base of the stairs, but trying to sound nonchalant, she said, "He's a teenager."

"He's depressed," said Ben.

"He's a teenager," she told him again, as if that was all the explanation that could possibly be needed. And perhaps it was.

Ben paused, considering her explanation, but then said firmly, "I better go up."

May was even more firm. "Stay put," she ordered. "He'll let us know if he needs help."

"Help," Peter whispered.

He had spoken so softly that his voice didn't carry beyond the confines of his bedroom. It wasn't that he was being macho or trying to tough it out. At that point, he really didn't have the strength to get up any volume.

Peter had dropped to his knees in his bedroom, clutching his abdomen in pain. "Help," he gasped again. Writhing in agony, he looked at the spot where the spider had bitten him. It was completely red and swollen.

He'd been an idiot, a total idiot. Trying to save Aunt May and Uncle Ben a few bucks on a doctor, when he'd obviously been poisoned by that . . . that stupid, stupid spider. Well, enough was already way too much. He was going to stand up, throw open the door, call down to Aunt May and Uncle Ben that he was sick and they should haul him immediately to the ER while alerting the toxicology and animal venom unit—presuming there were such things—that they were going to have a major case on their hands.

At least, that was what his mind was telling his body he was about to do. His body, however, wasn't the least bit interested in cooperating. Instead, just when he thought it couldn't hurt any more, it got worse. His legs curled up into

a fetal position, and sweat was pouring off his body like a
sumo wrestler working a Stairmaster. The carpet beneath his
head was soaked with perspiration, and he was shaking un-
controllably, extreme heat and lethal chills taking turns
pounding through his system. His teeth were chattering, and
if he'd been able to make it to a mirror, he would have seen
that his eyes were sunken, his face the color of vanilla pudding.

He made one final effort to stand, but it would have been
impossible to tell by looking at him, because he didn't budge
from the floor. Instead he curled up even tighter, his arms
clutching around his legs, drawing his knees up to just under
his chin. His eyes rolled up into the top of his head, and the
final jolt of pain was too overwhelming for him to handle.
With a final, low moan, he passed out dead away. Under his
lids, his eyes continued to flutter.

Tortured dreams cascaded through his mind, and *he was
climbing a strand of DNA, and suddenly the strand was
twisting around and back on him, and it broke down into
strands of thin, gossamer consistency that were like flutter-
ing threads from a spider's web. He struggled to break free
of them, and then he saw a spider descending toward him,
except Flash's face was reflected in one of its eyes, and Mary
Jane's dad in another, and M. J. was standing to the side
with her friends, posing for pictures and laughing, and as
Peter screamed, his voice made no sound, no sound at
all . . . and there was a screeching in his head, like something was trying to warn him of incredible danger.*

*And the spider was coming closer and closer, and it
seemed to be talking to him; he thought he could hear its
voice in his head . . . but most of what it was saying was in-
comprehensible. Just two words echoed in his head . . .* **great
power** *. . .* **great power** *. . . all the things he'd wanted to do,
everything he'd ever wanted . . . popularity, and Mary Jane,
and wiping that smug look off Flash's face, all of it, his for*

the taking, except he didn't want it, he just wanted to wake up, wake up. . . .

"Wake up! Peter, you'll be late for school!"

Peter snapped awake, blinking against the sunlight that was pouring in through the window. For one delirious moment, he thought that the sun had come out at night, and then his mind settled down as he realized that, no, the night had passed. And to his very great surprise, he had not woken up dead.

Not only that, but the venom had obviously worked its way through his system. He'd probably . . . sweated it out somehow.

"Peter," came Aunt May's voice a second time, and he heard her tentative footsteps on the stairs.

Peter's head snapped around as he saw that he'd more or less trashed his room in the throes of his pain and delirium. Plus he was still wearing the clothes from the night before. If Aunt May saw him like this, she'd probably panic and become convinced that he was desperately ill, just at the point where he was feeling 100 percent better.

"I'm up! I'm up! I'm getting dressed!"

The steps paused, and then she said, sounding a bit relieved, "All right. Better move along."

"Right, right. Moving."

He stretched his legs tentatively. For a moment he felt some tightness around the calves and, even more strange, a tingling around his toes. But those quickly disappeared and movement became unimpaired. He took several deep, experimental breaths, and even took his own pulse. Everything seemed fine.

And yet, it was a little odd. He felt as if he was a new inhabitant in his own body, learning his way around it like a newborn.

He glanced over at the clock and saw that Aunt May had

been right: Time was wasting. Then he looked down and saw that his glasses had fallen off, and felt mild surprise. With his glasses on, his vision was 20/20, but without them, things were a blur. Yet he'd been able to make out the digital readout on the clock with no problem. He picked up his glasses out of reflex and put them on his face as he stood . . .

. . . and he knocked into a chair.

He staggered back, utterly confused, as the chair tumbled around. Quickly he removed his glasses and looked down. Sure enough, there was the chair, big as life, perfectly clear to his vision. But when he tentatively replaced his glasses on his face, the chair blurred out as if he was looking through the bottoms of a pair of soda bottles. On, off, on, off, he tested the glasses repeatedly. There was no question about it: Not only could he now see better with the glasses off, he could see *perfectly* with the glasses off.

"Weird," he muttered.

He had completely soaked through the T-shirt he was wearing. Not even the standard teen tactic of sniffing the armpits was going to salvage this one. He pulled the shirt off over his head and, stripped to the waist, headed over to his dresser, passing the full-length mirror on the wall.

Then he stepped back in front of the mirror, still bare-chested, and gaped.

It wasn't his body. It was his head, all right, staring back at him from the mirror, but somehow, for some reason, it was sitting perched atop someone else's torso. It wasn't the frame of a bodybuilder, not hugely overmuscled. But he was definitely ripped. There was serious muscle definition, as if he'd been working out steadily for weeks on end. His stomach was hard and washboard flat, his gut in the muscle cutout commonly referred to as a six-pack. His pectorals weren't Schwarzenegger level, but they were impressive nevertheless.

He raised his arm, watched it move up and down in the

mirror, matching the gesture. He turned his head slowly left and right, never removing his gaze from his reflection. For a moment he thought he might still be dreaming. He dug a fingernail into his finger and felt the pinch. Then, just out of curiosity, he tried flexing his pecs as he'd seen muscle men do.

They jumped like a couple of cheerleaders.

Peter let out a shriek and jumped back, still never taking his eyes off the reflection of someone who could never, ever, under any circumstance, be addressed as Puny Parker.

Then there was an insistent knocking at the bedroom door. Peter had been so distracted by the mirror that he hadn't heard Aunt May coming up the stairs. She'd probably been alerted by such little clues as Peter's annoying girllike scream. "Peter? Are you all right?"

"Fine!" he called back, his voice an octave too high, and he forced himself to lower it. "I'm fine! Just fine!"

"Any better this morning?" she asked tentatively. "Any change?"

He flipped his glasses into the garbage can, even as he called back unevenly, feeling shell-shocked. "Change? Yes . . . yes, big change."

He grabbed some clothes at random from a drawer and, as he did so, happened to glance out the window and across the way. He couldn't believe it; his vision was even better than 20/20, maybe 20/10. And what Peter was seeing now was Mary Jane, standing in her bedroom window, doing a last minute check of her hair. He watched, mesmerized. Finally she tucked her hairbrush into her purse and darted out of view.

Suddenly all the setbacks of the previous day, all the condescension that he'd had to endure, came roaring back to him. Something in him cried out for justice, for the ability to put everyone on notice that things were going to be different from now on. There was a minor buzz of warning in the back of his mind that he should still be panicked. He had, after all, undergone some bizarre metamorphosis. His life had changed overnight.

Then again, it had only changed for the better, so what could there really be to be nervous about? Maybe the smart thing to do was just accept this, go with it, and milk it for all it was worth.

Peter pulled on a sock, and then discovered there was a huge hole in the heel . . . so large that it would be visible over the top of his shoe. "Wonderful," he muttered, and yanked the sock off again.

It ripped.

He stared down at it in confusion. For some bizarre reason, the toe end of the sock had torn clean off and was sticking to the end of his foot. "What is up with that?" he muttered as he pulled the material off his toes and yanked on a new pair of socks. He finished dressing, shoved the edges of his clean T-shirt into the tops of his jeans, and sprinted out the door and down the stairs. He vaulted the banister, landing behind Uncle Ben with the poise and confidence of an Olympic gymnast who just nailed a complicated dismount. He was desperate to run out the door after Mary Jane, but Aunt May was just emerging from the kitchen with a plate of pancakes and strips of newly made bacon. Peter wanted to stay and savor it. In many ways, it was as if he was truly alive for the first time in his life. Still, he didn't want to let Mary Jane get away. So he compromised, grabbing food off the table and shoveling it down with the efficiency of a black hole. Uncle Ben, sitting at the table, was taken aback, and made a point of keeping his fingers away from Peter lest they be consumed as well.

"Hi. Gotta go," said Peter between mouthfuls.

Ben looked on, hypnotized by the rapid motion of food to mouth. "We thought you were sick."

"I was. I got better." Except this time he wasn't waiting for his mouth to be clear of food, so it came out more like, "Iduz, Igobedder."

"Sit down, dear," Aunt May suggested as an entire plate of eggs disappeared into Peter's mouth.

"Can't. See you later." Peter slung his books over his shoulder, leaving behind a table of dishes that he'd had an impact on—not unlike the impact a tornado has on a trailer park.

"Don't forget, we're painting the kitchen today! Home right after school, right?" called Ben.

His voice disappearing into the distance, Peter called, "Sure thing, Uncle Ben, don't start without meeeeee. . . ."

And then he was gone.

May and Ben stared at each other. "What was *that* about?" asked May.

Ben stared down at his own empty plate. "He ate my bacon."

Peter had just emerged from his house when he spotted Mary Jane coming out of hers. She was walking as quickly as she could, and her father was leaning against the door frame. He was speaking with the kind of slur that indicated he'd been drinking. *At this time of the morning?* Peter wondered, astounded.

"I don't care what your mother said! It's not okay with me!" M. J.'s father called after her. "You're trash! You'll always be trash! Just like her!"

Peter stopped in his tracks, paralyzed, all of his energy forgotten. How could anyone, much less her own father, say something like that to M. J.? M. J., the most perfect, the most wonderful of females? How could someone who should be loving and adoring her and thanking God for blessing him with her—okay, maybe that was a bit over the top, but still . . . —be speaking to her in that manner?

"I have to go to school," M. J. said quickly, turning on her heel.

"Who's stopping ya?" her father said with a sneer.

From over his shoulder, M. J.'s mother stepped up and said angrily, "Leave her alone!"

M. J. didn't wait around to see how the confrontation between her parents was going to work out. Instead she bolted down the sidewalk. Her movement snapped Peter's own paralysis, and he hurried after her.

Everything he'd been planning to say to her had gone out the window, because in his imagination, she'd been the smiling, bright, chipper M. J. that he knew so well from school. An M. J. who was emotionally overwrought, who had to deal with parents—or at least a father—who didn't appreciate her for who and what she was, was outside of Peter's ability to handle. With all the energy bursting in his sinews, he was sure he could overtake her in a heartbeat, but his own uncertainty slowed him. "Talk to her, talk to her," Peter kept saying to himself as he drew closer to her at a steady but cautious pace. But she was wiping away tears, and Peter's usually nimble mind wasn't able to come up with anything to say, given her emotional stress. . . .

There was a loud honking from behind them, and a car packed with her girlfriends pulled up alongside. If Peter thought the transformation he'd undergone from the night before was remarkable, that was nothing compared to the lightning-fast transformation of M. J.'s face. Immediately all the despondency and frustration vanished, to be replaced by a broad smile and a party-girl demeanor. The car slowed enough for M. J. to hop in and, like Cinderella off to the ball, she was gone. With the girls laughing merrily, the car zipped away, angling around the school bus. . . .

School bus?!? Aw, crap!

Peter bolted down the street. Once upon a time, such a hurried, determined sprint would quickly have left him breathless, but not this time. His breathing was slow, steady, and sure, as was his heartbeat. It was as if he wasn't even straining himself, as if the rapid clip at which he was moving was only a fraction of just how quickly he could truly move.

Even so, it wasn't quite fast enough as, with a belch of smoke, the bus moved off from the curb. Peter was starting to wonder if the driver was actually waiting until he spotted Peter coming and then gunned the engine and roared away.

Peter got to the side of the bus just as it angled away from the curb. There was a GO WILDCATS banner on the side. Running into the street after the bus, he slammed his hand against the banner, with the intention of pounding repeatedly on the bus in order to get it to stop.

The bus pulled away.

The banner stayed behind.

To be specific, the banner was sticking to his fingers, in much the same way the sock had clung to his toe but much more forcefully. He tried to pull the banner clear of one hand, but found it adhering to the other one. Why the hell was the banner so blasted sticky? It was as if it were made out of flypaper.

Except his eyes told him there was nothing unusual about the material that the banner was made from. It just was clinging to his fingers. . . .

No . . .

No . . . that wasn't it at all. His fingers . . . *were clinging to the banner.*

And suddenly something pounded through his head, something with such force that it almost split his skull in two. It was a warning, a sensation, a fight-or-flight response, all clamoring for attention simultaneously, and as he tried to sort it out, a horn blasted above all of it. But the horn was outside his head, not inside, and he whirled just in time to see a truck bearing down on him. He could feel the heat coming off the radiator, could practically smell the rubber of the tires, it was that close.

With a scream, Peter leaped out of the way, all the while knowing that there was no way, *absolutely* no way, that he was going to be able to get out of the way in time, even as the brakes locked and the tires screeched.

And then it was gone, the heat, the smell—all gone, to be replaced by a dizzying sensation as if he were flying. He angled up, up, the breeze of his acceleration hitting him in the face, and below him the ground sped by as if he were a jet lifting off from a runway. That sense of glorious freedom, of not being bound by such trivialities as gravity.

And that was when he hit the wall of the building. It wasn't a particularly tall building, a three-story office structure that housed a law firm. But its bricks were just as solid as any Manhattan skyscraper, and when Peter slammed into it, forty feet above street level, it almost knocked him unconscious. In his dizzy, confused state, he did something that made absolutely no sense at all: He reached out and tried to hold on to the side of the building, so that he wouldn't fall.

What made even less sense was that it worked.

He clung there, batlike, his mind trying to process the insanity of what was happening to him.

He glanced over his shoulder and saw, twenty yards away, the truck driver standing on the street, staring at his front grillwork as if unable to comprehend why there wasn't a teenager smeared all over it. The fellow hesitated a moment, then got down on his hands and knees to inspect the underside. For a moment, Peter thought he was actually dead, and that he would see his body lying there like in those movies with ghosts and angels and such. But then the trucker shrugged, shook his head as if doubting his senses, climbed into the cab, and drove off. He left behind him a street that was decidedly devoid of corpses.

At that moment a woman in the office building slid open a window, with the intention of watering some flowers in a window box. Upon seeing Peter, she let out an astounded yelp, enough to startle Peter loose of the wall. The ground yawned up at him, and in his desperation he grabbed out for a drainpipe to avert the fall and perhaps even pull himself up to the roof and safety. Instead the urgency of his grip caused him to crush the pipe beneath his steel-hard fingers, and it gave way. Peter fell, his arms waving desperately around, and then he hit the ground . . .

. . . on his feet.

It made no sense. Falling as he had been, even if he'd landed standing up, his leg bones should have been driven somewhere up into his chest from the impact. Instead he hit the ground in a crouch, as if he'd fallen only a foot or two, and when he stood it was with no effort, no ache or pain. It was as if dropping off a building and landing unhurt on the ground were the most natural things in the world.

The woman overhead had been moving her mouth without benefit of sound emerging from it, and finally she found her voice and let out a high-pitched scream. Peter ran from the alleyway as fast as his legs would carry him, which it turned out was pretty damned fast. And still his heart continued beating with that slow, steady calm. It was as if his body was already acclimated to his new situation and was patiently waiting for his mind to catch up.

VI.

THE FIRST FIGHT

Human beings are blessed with an infinite capacity to rationalize away or ignore anything their senses cannot comprehend. Peter Parker was no exception, and as a result he had managed to explain the oddities of the morning by the time lunch rolled around. The banner had been pasted to the side of the bus, and the paste had gotten on his fingers. When the truck had been bearing down on him, he'd managed to jump out of the way but had hit his head in doing so, stumbling against the side of the building. In his concussed haze, with the events surrounding the spider bite still fresh in his subconscious, he had imagined himself as a giant spider on the side of the building.

It all made perfect sense . . . certainly far more sense than that he was somehow transforming into a . . . well . . . well, that was just ridiculous.

Utterly ridiculous. Kafkaesque.

"As Peter Parker awoke one morning from uneasy dreams he found himself transformed in his bed into a gigantic spider." Yeah, like *that* was going to happen.

Nevertheless his newly acquired appetite could not be ignored. The cafeteria woman, who was accustomed to Peter being the lightest of eaters, gaped as he loaded up his tray with enough food to feed the marching band. He made his way over to a table, moving with unaccustomed grace as he easily balanced the overladen tray. No one else in the cafeteria gave him a second glance as he sat, which was nothing unusual. Peter Parker, after all, wasn't someone who generally registered on most people's radar.

Out of the corner of his eye he saw Mary Jane approaching, and for a moment he thought she was going to sit next to him. Instead she maneuvered toward her customary group of friends, who were seated at their table and waving her over.

Suddenly Mary Jane skidded on a wet patch on the floor, the souvenir of a previous lunch period when someone had spilled some milk. In trying not to lose her footing and also to hold onto her tray, M. J. accomplished neither, and she started to fall with her tray angling toward the floor.

Instantly Peter was on his feet. It was as if he were moving before the incident unfolded. With his left hand he snagged her tray, righting it so quickly that nothing spilled from it. At the same time he dropped his right shoulder so that M. J.'s flailing hand could clutch onto it. Not having yet realized what had happened, M. J. regained her footing, then looked around desperately for the tray as if hoping she could still catch it. Her eyes widened as she saw Peter holding it effortlessly.

She turned and looked at him as if seeing him in a new light. "Wow. Great reflexes!" she said.

Peter himself couldn't really believe that he had pulled it off. He'd been operating purely on instinct, and it was only now, when the moment had passed, that he fully realized what he'd done. But he also understood that nonchalance was the key at times like these. So he shrugged as if it were nothing and handed her tray back to her.

"Thanks," she said.

"No problem."

He expected her simply to walk away. But instead she was staring into his eyes . . . no. Not staring. She was gazing, and he felt as if some sort of electrical connection had been made. "Hey, you have blue eyes," she observed. "I never noticed without your glasses. You just get contacts?"

No. Actually, I've got eyesight that would make a hawk jealous, and for all the newfound strength I feel coursing through me, none of it means a thing when compared with the heady sensation of your eyes upon me. . . .

"Uh-huh," was all he managed to get out. Then his throat constricted, and while he tried to manage an oral presentation of some of the thoughts tumbling through his head, all of them crowded forward at once, and none of them managed to make it to his mouth.

"Well . . . see ya," Mary Jane said and, shrugging, she turned and walked away.

He felt totally devastated. Forgotten once more, angry at his own uncertainty and incompetence, and then—to his astonishment—Mary Jane did something she'd never done before.

She glanced over her shoulder at him and smiled. An after-the-fact acknowledgment of him.

He couldn't believe it.

Despite the fact that she then sat down at the "popular kids" table—right next to Flash, of course—he still treasured that brief look she'd sent his way. The look that promised . . . well, it hadn't promised anything, really. But it had hinted at something he hadn't even dared consider before. Namely that she found him . . . what? Interesting? Handsome?

Peter sat back down at his table and started to eat with the same aggressive bulldozer approach he'd taken at breakfast. He started to set his fork down so that he could pick up the can of soda to his right.

The fork stuck to his hand.

He stared at it as if it was someone else's hand. Then he tried to pull the fork free with his other hand, only to discover that a long, gooey strand of . . . of something . . . was stretching from his hand to the fork. At first it was like whitish gray mucous, as if he'd blown his nose out through his wrist. But then he pulled on it, and pulled, and it reminded him of that stuff he'd had when he was a kid: Silly String. Except the tensile strength was far greater, and somehow it was managing to secrete through his wrist, and *what was he doing scientifically analyzing it when the fact was that, Holy God, he had some kind of supersnot oozing out of his forearms, what the **hell was up with that?!?***

He pulled even harder on the fork, but rather than separate it from the strand, he instead managed to shoot out another strand, this time from his other hand. And suddenly all the rationalizing, all the reordering in his mind of the morning's events, went right out the window as he realized, *It's webbing! It's webbing! I've got spinnerets in my forearms, oh jeez, what if somebody notices but now it could be worse, could be worse, at least I'm not shooting webbing out my butt, which is where spiders generally secrete their webbing, and perhaps it might bear some further investigation as to precisely why the spinnerets choose to manifest themselves and **Holy God, I'm shooting freaking webs outta my freaking arms!!!***

The only thing more horrific to Peter than the webs was the notion of someone spotting them. That would be it for him, over, done, no chance of normalcy, no chance of Mary Jane, no chance of nothing. If the other kids saw him oozing white gook out his arms, he might as well just put a paper bag over his head and slink out of high school forever.

But things were just going from bad to worse, and the paper bag over his head looked to be a very probable future for him. For the strand he'd just fired shot across the aisle to the table across from him, and smacked into Liz Allen's tray. Liz was chatting with someone and hadn't noticed, thank heavens, but he only had seconds in which to act before she did spot it, and look to see where—and to whom—it connected.

Hoping to yank the web strand free of the tray, Peter pulled as hard as he could. In retrospect, he should have realized what would happen, but he wasn't thinking especially clearly. Unfortunately, the inevitable did occur. Liz's tray took off like a rocket, arcing through the air straight at Peter. He ducked under the tray as it soared over his head. He heard the tray crash behind him, heard an uproar and shouts, and turned to see what had happened.

Flash Thompson was sitting there, wearing the girl's lunch. Jell-O was trickling down his shirt, milk was in his hair, pasta was on his shoulders, and murder was in his eyes. Mary Jane, sitting next to him, wasn't helping the situation by desperately trying to cover up her laughter and failing miserably.

M. J.'s barely stifled laughter was the only noise in the cafeteria at that moment. Like an infuriated rhino trying to find a target, Flash's eyes swept the room, looking for the guilty party. And Peter realized that if there was one thing Thompson the football star was capable of doing, it was chart the trajectory of an incoming object. With rapid-fire calculations he could never have articulated, Flash figured out what direction the tray must have come from. He glanced in Liz's direction, but probably realized that she didn't have the arm strength to hurl the tray that far. So he tracked it to the closest source, and his piglike stare fell upon a sweating and loudly gulping Peter Parker.

"Parker?!" Flash said.

If he had discovered that Peter Parker was actually Britney Spears in a cunning disguise, he couldn't have reacted with greater incredulity. Instantly Flash was on his feet, and that same warning of danger was buzzing in Peter's head, except this time there was no doubt where the jeopardy was coming from. Peter jumped out of his chair, knocking it backward, and he motored out of the cafeteria, dragging the still-snagged tray behind him.

As the doors swung closed after him, the tray didn't make it through in time. It slid up and down the gap between the doors, tapping against them as if pleading to be let out. Finally, the strand broke and the tray fell to the floor with a crash.

In the hallway just outside the cafeteria, Peter paused next to a row of lockers and checked the undersides of his wrists. He didn't have a clue as to exactly what he was going to see. His shirtsleeves were rolled up, and on each of his wrists there was a single, nearly invisible slit.

Wonderful. Just wonderful. If anyone ever spotted them, they'd think he'd tried to commit suicide. Then again, considering that Flash Thompson was on his tail, they probably wouldn't blame him. Nevertheless he quickly rolled down his shirtsleeves as far as they would go in order to cover them.

And that was when the warning signals that had been sounding in his head went off again, with even greater strength and clarity than before. This was beyond a simple signal that something was wrong. It was as if he was seeing outside himself, aware of everything around him—all at one time. The very movement of air was an alert to him, and in his mind's eye, he was able to "see" a fist coming in at him, fast, from behind.

Peter whipped around, darting to one side, just in time to avoid Flash Thompson's roundhouse as it slammed into the locker just to the right of his head. Flash hit the locker door with such force that he left an indentation in the metal, then let out a yelp of irritation, shaking the stinging out of his fist, as Peter backpedaled to put some distance between him and the outraged sports star. Mary Jane was coming up behind

Flash, and Peter saw Harry coming from another direction. M. J. was calling Flash's name, but he wasn't paying the least bit of attention.

"Think you're pretty funny, don't you, freak?" Flash demanded, wiping some stray ketchup off his brow. Even under the circumstances, Peter was forced to admit that Flash had good fighting form. His fists were up and cocked, ready to unleash a flurry of punches at Peter the moment he was within range.

"It was an accident!" Mary Jane tried to tell Flash, grabbing at one of his arms. He shook her off, never taking his eyes from his target.

"I'm sorry. It really was," Peter said, and the apology was genuine. Despite all the dirt that Flash had done him, he didn't want to sink to Flash's level. . . .

Except . . .

Why not? Why the hell not? It wasn't as if Flash would ever rise to his level, and he would teach him a lesson by giving him a sound thrashing on the debating team. If Flash was ever going to learn that he should leave Peter alone, descending to Flash's level was the only way the lesson would ever be taught.

But . . . could he really do it? Defeating Flash was more than a matter of strength and agility; it was having enough confidence to *believe* that it was possible. And that was a pool Peter was going to wade into with very tentative steps.

Unaware that he was in any physical peril, Flash dismissed Peter's protests by growling, "My fist breaking your teeth . . . *that's* an accident."

Flash's cronies were closing in, but they weren't going to give Flash any help. Why should he need it, after all? It was just Puny Parker. They did, however, close a few stray class doors to make sure the teachers within weren't going to see what was about to happen.

Peter felt himself moving with strength and certainty.

Once again it was as if his body knew what to do and was just waiting for his brain to catch up. Suddenly he started to feel genuinely sorry for Flash, as it dawned on him that the bully very likely was going to get more than he bargained for. Endeavoring to give him an out—and yet half hoping Flash wouldn't take it—Peter said, "I don't want to fight you, Flash."

"I wouldn't want to fight me neither."

Well . . . can't say I didn't try, Peter thought. He balanced carefully on the balls of his feet, his center of gravity low.

Flash swung a quick right, then a left. Either of them, had they connected, would have put Puny Parker down for the count . . . had Flash been dealing with Puny Parker, of course. But Peter easily dodged them, making it look effortless, as if he knew where they were going to be coming from and had already arranged to be elsewhere.

On some level, one of Flash's cronies realized that this wasn't going according to plan. Perhaps it was the befuddled look on Flash's face when his punches failed to connect, or perhaps it was the blinding speed with which Peter was moving. Either way he decided things would go more smoothly if Parker were held immobile. So he lunged from behind with the intention of wrapping his arms around Peter's torso and keeping him still.

Peter, however, wasn't about to let that happen. Just as easily as he'd sensed Flash's attack from behind, he perceived this one, as well. He ducked under the grab, leaving Flash's pal overextended and grasping air. Peter then immediately straightened up, catching his assailant off balance, and sending him tumbling heels over head to the floor.

Flash clearly couldn't believe it. With a roar of outrage, Flash lunged at Peter, swinging an impressive combo of punches . . . right jab, left jab, right roundhouse, left haymaker. Not a single one connected. Peter wasn't even backing away. He simply twisted this way, that way, pivoted, and then leaned back as if he were a limbo dancer. With each movement, his confidence swelled all the more. It wasn't just that he wasn't getting pummeled. He was actually making Flash look like a fool. In comparison to Peter Parker, Flash Thompson was moving in slow motion.

He heard Mary Janc call out to Harry Osborn, "Harry, please help him!"

"Which one?" asked an obviously impressed Harry.

That was it. That was the final validation for Peter, and he was filled with a surge of complete certainty that he had nothing to fear from Flash Thompson, ever again. Every prank, every trick, every jibe Thompson had ever tossed at him throughout the years came back to him, like a bottled volcano which had been building up over a decade, then came unstoppered all at once. Flash lunged at Peter once more, and this time Peter didn't try to get out of the way. Instead he threw a punch that landed solidly on Flash's jaw. He'd always heard that hitting bone upon bone was painful, but he felt nothing aside from giddy and heady satisfaction.

There was a pleasing crunch as Flash sailed back, slamming against the far row of lockers with a crash that seemed to echo back through the years of torment, signaling an end to all the harassment and ushering in a new age where nobody stepped on Peter Parker's face anymore, ever again.

Flash sunk to the ground with a moan, his eyes closed. "Jesus, Parker," someone exclaimed, "you knocked him out!"

Damned straight I did, and it served him right! Peter wanted to shout. But he was still partly in shock, staring at his clenched fist as if it belonged to someone else. Other students were crowding forward, gaping at the unconscious Flash, and someone else said, "Parker did that? Yeah, right."

Flash started to sit up, his hands covering the front of his face, and he was groaning. Peter scoffed inwardly, figuring that Flash was playing for sympathy. How pathetic. After all, he hadn't hit him *that* hard. He couldn't help it if Flash Thompson had a glass jaw and a tendency for melodramatics that would have been more at place in a Spanish soap opera.

Then one of his cronies, crouching next to him, pried his hands away from his face, and there was blood everywhere. All over his face, still trickling from his nose, down his chin, onto the front of his shirt. His eyes were already swelling; within the hour he'd look like a raccoon.

Peter stepped back, horrified, looking at his hands as if an alien had invaded them. The strength in them, the power that he had just displayed, which had made him feel so giddy, so alive, now terrified him.

He turned and bolted from the school. Once upon a time, the notion of cutting in the middle of the day would have been unthinkable. Now he gave it no consideration whatsoever. Instead the only thing on his mind was putting as much distance as possible between himself and the blood-soaked thing that was Flash Thompson.

Once in the street, he stopped and looked at the place on his hand where the spider had bitten him. Whereas yesterday it had been red and inflamed, by now it had subsided considerably. Well, why not? The damage had already been done. Peter's life was totally trashed.

VII.

**THE
LEARNING
CURVE**

There was an alleyway near the school, and Peter stopped there, distracted for a moment. A glorious spiderweb, spun between a Dumpster and the alley walls captured his attention. The sun was glinting off its fresh strands.

Peter glanced right and left and saw that he was alone. Then again, somehow he had already known that. He had a feeling that if someone had been watching him, had posed some sort of danger, he would have . . . well . . . sensed it. Spider sense.

Once more he looked at the web, and then to his hand. He flexed his fists a couple of times, stretching his fingers, waggling them, and felt a sort of prickling from his fingertips. At first he thought they were becoming numb, but then he slowly brought them closer to the wall, palm upright and flat, and it was as if there were a small surge of static electricity between his digits and the surface of the wall.

He placed each hand flat against the wall, very tentatively, then pulled back ever so slightly. The palms moved freely away from the wall, but the fingers remained adhered to it.

He slid one of his hands along the wall, and it continued to stick. Then, as if jumping and trying to reach something, he pushed his other arm up and over his head, and that hand stuck, as well. He was hanging about half a foot off the ground, his entire weight supported solely by his hands.

He started to climb, his feet not actually adhering, since

they were covered by fairly thick shoe soles, but not needing the additional support or thrust. He just used them for balance, and climbed higher and higher, each passing moment bringing more and more confidence. He reminded himself not to get overconfident; he'd become that way with Flash, and a teen with a rearranged face had been the result. He didn't want it to be his turn to have parts of his anatomy rearranged.

He achieved the flat rooftop. Rather than hauling his legs up over the edge, he instead vaulted onto the roof, effortlessly swinging the lower half of his body up and over. He dropped into a crouch, then stood upright and bowed slightly as if to a nonexistent audience.

There was a series of rooftops, all approximately the same height, stretching out before him, and he studied the array with the same eagerness and sense of unconquerable confidence one usually saw in an accomplished athlete such as a surfer. And that was, in effect, what Peter Parker became: A surfer. Except instead of searching out waves, he was going to surf the rooftops.

With total abandon and a sense of fun he previously thought had been denied him, Peter started leaping from one rooftop to the next. Just for amusement, he held his arms outstretched as if he were riding a major wave.

And then he wiped out.

Not entirely, and not terminally, but damned close. He'd been barreling toward the edge of one roof, preparing to vault to the other side, when he got to one where he realized, at the last moment, that the gap was simply too wide. Or, at the very least, it was wide enough that he didn't want to chance it. So he came to an abrupt halt, teetering on the edge. The chasm yawned before him. He could turn around, head back the way he came. Or else he could simply climb down the side of the building. Either option was available . . .

. . . or perhaps . . . there was a third option.

He looked down at the slits in his wrist, pushing aside the fact that it still looked as if he had tried to end his life. Although he had to admit the irony, considering where he was and what he was doing. One wrong move, one mistake in judgment, and he'd be putting an end to himself a lot faster than he could by hacking at his wrists.

Still, there was no reason he couldn't try to make this webbing goop work for him. So he tried to force the web to spray out by sheer willpower.

Nothing.

Then he tried wiggling his wrists, but had no more success than before. He saw it as trying to crack a combination lock. It was just a matter of putting together the right assortment of numbers in the correct order.

So he opened and closed assorted fingers, combined with twists of the wrist this way and that. At one point, he tried, just for laughs, a variation on "bunny ears": His palm facing up, he extended all five fingers, and then brought his ring and middle fingers toward his palm.

Even though he'd been trying to achieve the affect, he was still extremely startled when a loud *thwip* sounded from the area of his wrist, and a single strand of webbing shot out, straight up. Thankful that he didn't snag a passing pigeon, Peter tried aiming at the building across the way, hoping that the same combination of wrist-twist and fingering would produce the same result. His wish was granted as another strand of webbing zipped out and anchored to the far side of the other building.

Peter tugged on it as hard as he could, trying to guess how much strain it would undergo if his full weight was put upon it. It seemed solid. Heck, it was more likely that the bricks would fall out of the wall than that his webbing strand would snap—now *there* was a cheerful thought. Nevertheless, he was still understandably apprehensive about what he was going to do.

He warned himself not to look down, promptly looked down, and then mentally kicked himself for having done so. Just to play it safe, he wrapped the trailing end of the strand around his hand once, twice. Then, muttering a prayer and fighting an urge to give out a Tarzan yell, he jumped off the roof.

He had prepared himself for the possibility of the web breaking free, but it held perfectly. The world whizzed past him, wind in his face, as he held onto the strand and experienced something akin to the exhilarating feeling of flight. This lasted for as long as it took the web line to have its arc terminated by the wall.

Peter slammed into it with jaw-rattling force and hung there, flattened, looking like the Coyote after an abortive pursuit of the Roadrunner. Or perhaps one of those plush toys some people kept suctioned against their car windows.

"Ouch," he muttered.

"Ouch," said Madeline Watson, Mary Jane's mother. "One punch, you say?"

M. J.'s father was seated at the kitchen table, knocking back a beer. His night shift at the train yard didn't start for some hours yet, and he was glowering with red eyes at Mary Jane, who was fixing herself a snack from the refrigerator.

"I don't believe it," he growled.

"She saw it with her own eyes, Phil," Madeline said, pouring herself a cup of coffee.

"I did. So did everybody else, although a lot of them still don't believe it," M. J. said cheerfully. She swung a right cross in the air. "One shot. *Bam.*"

"You sound awfully chipper about it," Philip Watson observed.

"Well, I wouldn't say Flash had it coming, but . . ."

"But you'd think it without saying it?" suggested her mother. This prompted a ready grin from M. J.

Philip, however, was not grinning. M. J. noticed that he was scowling even more than before. "I'm glad you both think this is funny. The fact is that anyone can get in a lucky punch. Flash was probably taking it easy on him. . . ."

M. J. had been about to bite into her sandwich, but she put it down as she shook her head. "No way, Dad. No way. Peter just . . . just took him down, that's all. It wasn't luck. Flash did everything he could and never laid a hand on him."

Her father harrumphed loudly at this, and then said, "Sounds to me like Flash needs work on his technique. Maybe I'll give him a few pointers when he stops by."

Mary Jane's jaw dropped, and she exchanged a look with her mother, who appeared just as surprised. She didn't know which comment to process first. She tried the less inflammatory one. "When is Flash 'stopping by?' "

"Oh, he called. Did I forget to tell you?"

"Ye*essss!*" She managed to turn "yes" into a two-syllable word.

"Oh. Well, he's coming over to pick you up," and he glanced up at the wall clock, an annoying present from his equally annoying sister, Anna, replete with pictures of birds that gave off birdcalls every hour. "Said he wanted to show you his birthday present. Just about any minute, he should be here."

"Thanks for telling me! And what do you mean, you'll give him a few pointers?!"

Philip looked annoyed that she would question his intentions. "What, you think I can't? In my day, I was all-county—"

"I know what you were, Dad, that's not the point!" she said in exasperation, pacing the kitchen. "You want to give

Flash some tips on how to pound Peter into the ground? He's your neighbor, for God's sake! How could you?" She dropped into the chair opposite him, her sandwich forgotten, and folded her arms resolutely. "I'm not going out with Flash tonight. I don't feel like it."

Bristling, Phil shot back, "I told him you were. Are you trying to make me look like a fool?"

"Not everything is about you, Phil," Madeline snapped.

"In this house, it sure as hell is!" He leaned forward, stabbing a finger into M. J.'s face. "You better realize this right now, Mary Jane: Flash Thompson is the luckiest break you ever fell into. I've seen that boy play football. He's going to be All-American. He's going to make a ton of money. You could do a lot worse than be married to someone like him."

And the words were out of her mouth before she could control them: "Damned right. I could be married to someone like you!"

Instantly, with a roar, Phil was on his feet, nearly knocking the table over. M. J. rolled off the chair, frantically crabwalking backward on the floor as she tried to put some distance between herself and her outraged father. Madeline quickly interposed herself between the two. "Phil, calm down! She didn't mean it!"

"The hell she didn't!" he bellowed, saving Mary Jane the trouble of saying much the same thing. "She's got a future tied up in a perfect bow, and instead she worries about a loser like Peter Parker!"

"He's not a loser!" Mary Jane cried out defiantly, pulling herself to her feet.

"And you would know about that, wouldn't you!" he shot back. He was trembling with rage. "You go out with Flash, as I promised him you would, or don't you bother coming back!"

"Fine!" she howled, fighting back tears, and charged out the back door, furiously kicking it shut behind her.

Between the constant practicing and the one or two brief bouts of unconsciousness, the time had totally slipped away from Peter. It was getting on evening when he finally dashed into the kitchen of his house, calling out for Aunt May and Uncle Ben. He immediately sensed that they weren't around, however. This required no advanced spider-given technique or nearly psychic ability. He'd always been able to tell when they were out. The house seemed . . . sadder when they weren't around, as ludicrous as that sounded.

His nose wrinkled as he smelled something odd. He turned and experimentally touched the wall, taking extreme care to do it delicately so that his finger didn't stick to it. It came away with a dab of fresh yellow paint on it. Then he noticed, in the corner of the room, some buckets, a neatly folded drop cloth splattered with paint of a color identical to what was on the wall, and the ladder.

He moaned, remembering that he was supposed to have gotten home early so that he and Uncle Ben could paint the kitchen. But when he'd fled from school, he'd become disconnected from everything else he was supposed to be doing. He'd turned totally inward, and now he'd let his uncle down. He felt like a creep, and even worse when he spotted the note on the wall that read, in Aunt May's delicate hand, "Meatloaf and vegetables in the oven. Cherry pie on the shelf. We've gone to play bridge at the Anderson's."

Great.

Not only had he broken a promise, but also, instead of leaving an angry note or even being there to chew him out, they left him a dinner . . . and pie. It was the pie that hurt the most, since cherry was his favorite.

"Aw, shoot . . ." he muttered.

Then he heard shouting from across the street. From Mary Jane's house.

Peter began to wonder if it had always been noisy over at her place, or whether—since a single spider had completely reordered his life—he had just become more attentive, more aware of the world around him.

He walked out onto the back steps, giving him a plain view of the back of M. J.'s house, over the fence that separated the two small yards. He heard words being shouted. Words like "loser" and "future" and, he was pretty sure, "Flash." *Figures,* he thought sourly, and started to turn to go back inside when Mary Jane stomped out into her backyard. Even from where he was standing, he could see that she was trembling with fury.

She looked up at him, her eyes wet.

Suddenly he felt utterly mortified, like some sort of disgusting Peeping Tom, poking in on other people's lives. The thing was, he wasn't accustomed to thinking of M. J. as "other people," but rather as an angel on earth who should, by rights, have no problems at all. He wanted to dart back into the house, but it was way too late for that. He stood there, paralyzed, and finally managed to accomplish what was, for him, a major achievement: To initiate something approaching a casual conversation with her. "Oh. Hi."

It wasn't much of a start, but at least it *was* a start.

She wet her lips, brushed away the tears that were obviously brimming in her eyes. She looked mortified, but also defiant, as if daring Peter to feel pity for her. "Were you listening to that?"

"No!" he said quickly, sounding very guilty, and when he realized how obvious the lie was, he quickly tried to amend it, words tumbling over each other. "Yeah. I . . . heard something but wasn't listening. To what?"

Mary Jane blinked at the babble, then seemed to take a bit

of amusement in his obvious discomfort. "I guess you can always hear us," she said, trying her best to sound casual.

"No. I was . . . just taking out the trash."

She paused to note the obvious lack of garbage bags in his hands and raised an amused eyebrow. Well, at least she was capable of finding humor in the situation, no matter how uncomfortable. "You always do your chores, don't you, Peter?"

"Well . . ."

When she spoke to him next, she wasn't looking at him. Perhaps she was too embarrassed. "I'm sorry we do that all the time," she said softly. "Your aunt and uncle never scream."

"Oh . . . they can scream pretty good, y'know," Peter assured her, and that much was true. Granted, they'd never screamed at *him*. Their patience with him, and for him, bordered on the infinite. But he'd heard Uncle Ben scream enough at blind umpires on televised baseball games, and Aunt May scream back at him that it's just a game, for pity's sake, grow up, and let's turn this silly thing off because there's an interesting program on the Discovery Channel about the lifecycle of the luna moth. That kind of thing. He certainly didn't want to rub M. J.'s nose, however, in the fact that he was better off without parents than she was with parents.

"So . . . where to after you graduate?" she asked, obviously ready to change topics.

A real live conversation. How about that? Peter strolled forward, suddenly feeling at ease, his hands in his pockets as he approached the fence. "I thought I'd go into the city, get a job as a photographer. Work my way through college. What about you?"

"Headed for the city, too," she said, matching his steps as she approached the fence as well. "I can't wait to get out of here. I thought I'd . . ." Then she looked down, embarrassed. "Oh, I don't know . . ."

Obviously she had some sort of career in mind. Figuring he could see her in just about any profession except for the oldest one, Peter said, "Try me."

He'd never known Mary Jane Watson to look as vulnerable as she did at that moment, as he realized that she was concerned he would laugh at her. "I want to . . . ," and she lowered her voice as if afraid her parents would hear, ". . . to act. On stage. Be an actress."

"Hey, that's great! You were really awesome in all the school plays, Mary Jane."

"Really?" She cocked her head eagerly, like a cocker spaniel needing to be petted.

"Yeah. I cried like a baby when you played Cinderella."

Mary Jane blinked in confusion, and then she barely suppressed a smile. "Peter, that was in first grade."

"Well . . . even so," Peter said, rallying. He was leaning up against the fence now, and she did as well, just to his right. He could smell the perfume wafting from her. He wanted to vault the fence in one jump. He knew he could do it, so easily, but he felt—correctly—as if he was dealing with something very delicate, and such an overt move would only shatter the mood. Trying to stay focused on the topic, Peter continued, "You know how sometimes you can know something, like what's going to be? Like . . . tell what's around you, what's coming?"

He wasn't sure if that had sounded at all coherent, but M. J. simply nodded and said, "Sometimes."

Encouraged, he continued, "And you can just see things coming that aren't exactly there, but you just believe . . ."

Again she nodded, apparently fancying the thought that Peter had been able to see a first grade performance of *Cinderella* and intuit, from that moment on, that she belonged in the theater. "What do you see coming for you?" she asked.

Lately? Fists and brick walls.

"I'm not sure . . . but it feels like something I never felt before, whatever it is." That much was true enough. However, at that moment, he couldn't have said whether he was referring to his newfound spider abilities . . . or to the fact that he was talking to Mary Jane and she was actually listening to him, and even seemed interested in him.

"And what for me?" she asked.

"You?" He laughed as if the answer was self-evident, a foregone conclusion. "You're . . . why, you're gonna . . . light up Broadway."

She smiled, and then the silence fell between them. There was so much he wanted to say, but as was usually the case at such times, he couldn't even begin to know where to start. M. J. was eyeing him, and after a moment she said, "Y'know, you're taller than you look."

"I hunch," he said.

She reached out and put her hands on his biceps.

In all the years he'd known her, it was the first time she'd ever touched him. It was as if someone had touched a live wire to him, and he stood bolt upright, a small gasp emerging from between his lips.

"Good. Don't hunch," she told him.

For all his newfound physical prowess, for all the liberating feeling he'd had when vaulting rooftops, never had he felt more energized or alive than he did at that moment. Whereas before his heartbeat had remained steady, no matter what sort of physical exertions he'd been subjecting himself to, now he could feel it pounding like a trip-hammer against his chest.

Suddenly there was a loud, irritating *aah-oooo-gahh* from the front driveway. And Peter heard an all-too-familiar voice calling, "Hey, M. J.! Come take a ride in my birthday present?"

Stay. Stay with me, he urged her with such force that he

was positive she could hear the words in her head. And indeed, for a moment she did seem torn. There seemed to be more to her indecision than just not knowing with whom she wanted to hang out. When she looked in the direction of Flash's honking, Peter detected, or thought he detected, fear. But . . . fear of what? Fear of being with Flash? Or fear of not being with him?

He had no time to inquire or figure it out, though, because suddenly Mary Jane's uncertainty was replaced by her "party girl" face . . . a face Peter was slowly starting to realize was a mask she slipped on whenever she wanted to confront the world without letting it know what was going on in her mind.

"Thanks, Pete," she said, patting him on the shoulder. "I gotta go."

She dashed around the side of her house, and thankfully Peter couldn't see her as he heard her *ooh* and *ahhh* over what was obviously Flash's new car. Then there was a grinding of gears—apparently Flash didn't have the hang of it yet—and the car peeled out of the driveway. It roared away, and he caught the briefest glimpse of Mary Jane, laughing, her hair streaming out behind her.

Peter watched the car disappear, and then he sagged against the fence like a puppet with its strings severed. He hung there for a time, feeling sorry for himself, and then he reached over and gingerly touched the bicep that she had rested her fingers on. He raised his arm, flexed it, and made a muscle. Made a considerable muscle.

And the wheels started turning.

Dear Mom and Dad:

I've been getting a heck of an education lately. Learning about how these new . . . gifts, I guess, I hate saying "powers," it sounds so pretentious . . . work. And also learning about girls. About Mary Jane, especially.

I'm starting to realize how much she's hurting. And I think that she likes me, or could like me...but she also desperately wants to be happy. And Flash's folks are loaded. He's got money. He can make her happy. I mean, jeez, he got a car for his birthday. My last birthday, I got a sweater, not to be confused with the birthday before, when I got a sweater, or the birthday before that, when I got a sweater and that weird knit stocking hat that pulls down over my face...a baklava, I think it's called.

I mean, don't get me wrong, Uncle Ben and Aunt May are great, and I remember when he blew a bundle to buy me my camera and I know it set him back. So there's no way they'll wind up getting me a car. And a photographer doesn't pull in big money either, and if I do get into a career with science, it's not like the starting salaries of research assistants are anything to write home about.

And M. J. deserves to be happy. She deserves to have a guy who can surround her with fancy stuff. She's had such a crummy home life, it's the least she deserves. I think that's one of the reasons she still hangs with Flash. That and some other reasons I don't really have to go into now.

Anyway, I think I've got a plan how to make some serious money. Uncle Ben always says things happen for a reason. Well, when I was cleaning up the kitchen, putting away the drop cloths and getting ready to toss some of the old newspapers he'd been drying the brushes on, I found an ad. I've got it right here. It says, ATTENTION AM-ATEUR WRESTLERS! THREE THOUSAND DOLLARS! FOR JUST THREE MINUTES IN THE RING! COLORFUL CHARACTERS A MUST!

Let's face it: I didn't just beat Flash. I clobbered him, and it was no effort at all. None. I wasn't even trying. Sure, I don't have any wrestling experience, but if I was able to do that to Flash when I wasn't trying, imagine what I can do to someone when I am trying.

So I've been putting a plan into motion.

They want colorful characters? I'll give them one they'll never forget.

The first thing I needed was a costume, of course. I've got to have a mask. Anybody sees my teenage face that I shave maybe once a week, and they'll be too busy laughing to take me seriously. Besides,

I've seen pictures of those Mexican masked wrestler guys, so no one should think anything about it. So I started with costume designs. I must have gone through a hundred different kinds, with wings, and antennae, and extra legs hanging off it... anything you could imagine. I finally came up with a design I liked, with web lines and a spider design on it. And I'll just use that baklava as a mask.

There's so much to do, though, and I'm doing it all alone. I also started practicing with the webbing. It's going to be of absolutely no use to me if I can't find a way to make it go where I want, when I want. Heck, it could wind up hitting me in the face, and I don't think I'm ready to depend so completely on my weird "spider sense" that I'd want to get into a fight with my eyes closed.

So I set up two empty glass bottles on a bookcase, went to the opposite side of the room, and tried to hit them with a web strand. Didn't even come close. I tried again, and again, thwip and thwump, thwip and thwump, and inside of five minutes I'd managed to cover nearly every object in my room with webbing except for the freakin' bottles. Luckily it dissolves away to nothing after a while. Aunt May must've heard it, because she came knocking on my door and asked me what was going on. I told her I was exercising and wasn't dressed. "Well, don't catch cold," she said to me. She didn't have to worry. With my aim, I couldn't catch an elephant, much less a cold. It was like trying to precisely aim water while using a broken hose.

But after a while, I got the hang of it. It went just where I aimed it. I can't tell you how thrilled I was. I started shooting right and left, like a gunslinger taking out bushwhackers. And it wasn't enough to just "shoot" stuff with the webs. I snagged stuff with pinpoint precision and pulled on it, sending it flying across the room. I was totally into it, not thinking about what I was doing. I don't know, maybe I kind of blanked out or something. All I know is that suddenly Uncle Ben was pounding on the wall, calling to me, "What are you doing in there?!" That snapped me out of it, and I looked around at my trashed room and said, "Studying! Hard!" Which sounded so incredibly lame, but I couldn't think of anything else to say.

Mom...Dad...God, I wish you could be here to see this. I mean,

I know, I know, if you had lived...if I'd been with you...then this whole accident could never have happened. And don't get me wrong: I'd trade all the wall climbing, all the feats of strength, all this incredibly exciting bizarreness that I'm experiencing right now for eighteen years of mundanity with you guys.

Like I said before: Uncle Ben claims things happen for a reason. Well, maybe my winding up here, and everything I've been through... maybe this was the reason for all of it. I'd be lying if I said I'd figured out all the ramifications and long-term ins and outs of these powers, but as far as the short-term goes, I'm on the verge of making some serious breakthroughs. And wherever you're watching from, all those times you've had to sit there in frustration while people walked all over me and called me Puny Parker...well, you don't have to worry about that anymore. Things are changing, starting today...

...as soon as I get my room cleaned up.

VIII.

THE TEST

Norman Osborn, standing just outside the glass-enclosed isolation chamber, deep in the bowels of OsCorp, checked the readings for the third time in as many minutes. Incongruously he was wearing only a pair of green trunks. A gurney lay nearby, with restraining straps hanging open and waiting for an occupant. He thought about the number of times he'd seen movies with mad scientists trying out some sort of formula on themselves, transforming themselves into human guinea pigs. And he'd always shaken his head and wondered, how could any scientist ever be that dumb? It was like the old advice about never investing with your own money; use someone else's. Same thing. Never test formulae on yourself. Always use volunteers, cat's-paws . . . whatever is available.

Yet here he was, realizing that for such a scenario to play out, one didn't need to be a scientist, or stupid. Just someone who was desperate. And as he checked the latest printouts for the fourth time, he realized that he, himself, was just that desperate.

His head snapped around and his eyes narrowed suspiciously as he realized that Doctor Stromm was looking over his shoulder, checking the results as well. Stromm looked positively ill. And to think that not long ago, Stromm had been the picture of confidence and heroic defiance as he'd advocated starting the project over from scratch. Yet now here was Osborn, ready to put his own butt on the line, and Stromm was showing a marked lack of nerve. That just went to show who was a real man, when it came down to it.

"Mr. Osborn, please," Stromm said, "I'm begging you for the last time. . . ."

"Don't be a coward," Osborn said disdainfully, drawing strength from Stromm's fear. "Risks are part of laboratory science."

Stromm's brow was soaked with sweat, and it wasn't because it was hot in the room. "Let me reschedule this with a proper medical staff and a volunteer. If you'll just give me two weeks . . ."

Osborn put down the pages he'd been checking and fixed a level gaze on Stromm. "In two weeks, this project, this company, will be dead," he said in a flat, implacable tone. "Sometimes you have to do things yourself. Now give me the barium phosphate."

Obviously Stromm was confused by the sudden change in direction. "Sir?"

"Decreases nausea when the vapor hits the bloodstream."

Stromm let out a heavy sigh, apparently realizing that nothing he could say would dissuade Osborn. This was of great relief to Osborn, who had a lot to accomplish that evening and didn't have time for misguided debates. Stromm handed him the bottle of phosphate.

Osborn stared at it for a long moment, as if he were about to drink from the Holy Grail. "Forty thousand years of human evolution, and we've barely even tapped the vastness of human potential." He drank it down and then offered a belated toast: "To the realization of man's true physical and intellectual capability." Stromm simply nodded in response and offered a weak smile.

Osborn took one, final deep breath, then lay back on the gurney. Obediently, Stromm went to it and—in quick motions—buckled one strap across his legs and another across his waist. Then he stepped to the control console, breathed a silent prayer, and hit an array of switches.

The gurney, with Osborn still strapped to it, was lifted up, up, and slid neatly into place in the glass tank. As frantic as Stromm obviously was, Osborn could not have been more calm. It was as if he neither knew nor cared where he was or what the possible consequences of his actions might be. He was convinced of the rightness of what he was doing and was perfectly content to let all other aspects of the adventure play out.

There was a petri dish in the middle of the tank, and from it a thick, noxious, white gas arose. Osborn could imagine that the gas was forming faces; demented specters with their mouths twisted into sneers. But instead of fear, all he felt was rage, even challenge, as if he were more than willing to take whatever was thrown at him, by all creatures real or imaginary.

The gas, lighter than air, crept over Osborn's body, starting with the feet and working its way upward. Despite the fact that he'd asked for this, despite the fact that he wasn't afraid, Osborn reflexively took a deep breath. The white cloud enveloped him and—for just a moment—he felt a surge of fear. But then he reminded himself of just how sniveling, just how useless the emotion of fear could be. Newly resolved, he opened his mouth and forced himself to take in a tiny bit of air.

It was no doubt his own vivid imagination that made it look as if the gas were leaping, like an entity that had developed intelligence, into his mouth. It was that selfsame imagination that caused Osborn to choke on the gas for a moment, but then he calmed himself and forced himself to breathe normally.

The gas flowed in and out of his nostrils; he could actually see it moving. He saw Stromm looking in on him, felt more relaxed than he'd ever been, and started to speak to Stromm, to tell him not to worry.

And suddenly his entire body was seized by convulsions. From his fingertips to his teeth, it was as if someone had touched a hot poker to his every nerve ending. His body shook violently, straining against the straps, and if he'd been able to see his eyes at that moment, he would have seen only white.

He heard frantic beeping, alarms, and distantly realized that it was the body monitors. He heard flatlining noises, which he couldn't understand because those would only be going off if someone were dead. And that certainly couldn't be applying to him, because he definitely wasn't dead. Hell, no, he'd never felt this alive before, every fiber of his being, every pore of his skin, wide-open and receptive to everything it could possibly experience. He felt bigger, stronger than his body, as if his skin couldn't contain the amazing sensations that were hammering through it.

That was when he heard a ringing that soared above everything else. It was the panic button, the emergency abort button. Stromm had hit it. Stromm, the lily-livered, weak-kneed insult to the human race. Stromm had displayed a complete lack of vision and conviction in hitting the panic button, and Osborn felt a surge of fury at Stromm's weakness.

The white gas was being sucked out of the tank as the giant vacuum vents in the ceiling roared to life. Osborn wanted to laugh and cry at the same time, to beg the gas to return to him. To give him the strength and stamina that he was positive he could obtain. No, not just "could." Should. The abilities that should by right be his were being sucked away via the ceiling vents.

It was more than he could bear.

He felt hands fumbling at the straps, and it was only then that he realized his eyes were clenched shut. His body wasn't responding to the instructions of his mind. It was like having an out-of-body experience while still being in your body.

Osborn decided to inform Doctor Stromm that he was perfectly fine, thanks, and to get his hands off him.

It came out as a shriek.

Osborn continued to scream, and he had no idea why he was doing it, but it felt good on some sort of primitive level, like a caveman with his foot planted on the body of a recently slain foe, informing everyone else that he was a force to be reckoned with.

The straps were gone from his chest, and Osborn could hear all the emergency monitors going off. In his haze, he didn't associate them with himself anymore. They were just noise, something he could join if he so chose. And he did, screaming louder, matching them in pitch and taking an insane delight in doing so. His heart rate leapt, his blood pressure, respiration, everything, shot off the charts.

His eyes snapped open, alight with the fire of inner madness, and he ripped the sensors off his chest. Stromm tried to hold him back and lasted for exactly as long as it took Osborn to notice him. When he did notice him, he knocked him away with one sweep of his arm.

The strength of the gesture was horrifying in its casualness, devastating in the damage it caused with such minimal effort. Stromm sailed into the glass of the booth, and through it. The glass exploded from the impact, shards flying everywhere. Stromm kept going, flying through the air as if some great invisible fisherman had tied a line to him and was reeling him in.

He sailed across the lab and smashed into a pillar on the far side, some fifty feet away. He sagged to the floor, blood pooling under his head.

Osborn watched Stromm's life ebb from him and didn't care in the slightest. He had other things to worry about.

His attention was far more drawn to the battle suit and the personnel carrier prototype. The two devices were sitting there in the darkness, filled with power waiting to be used. Osborn felt exactly the same way, like a source of considerable power—if only it could be utilized properly.

He felt as if his mind were splitting in two. On one level, he was fully aware that Stromm was dead, dead at his hand, and the aspect of Norman Osborn that realized it recoiled in shock and horror.

But there was another part of him that not only didn't care, it reveled in it. Stromm had been weak, and the new Osborn despised weakness.

The world was filled with sheep, and the wolf went among the sheep and devoured them.

The component of Norman that had no tolerance for weakness leapt to the forefront, brought there by the gas, by the chemicals that it had unleashed in his mind. A great green haze fell over him, and Osborn trembled, twisted, convulsed as if something was trying to fight its way out from the most primordial roots of his soul. And then Norman Osborn threw his head back and howled in pain, confusion, and transformation.

Gone was any trace of guilt, gone was any consideration for ramifications, gone was any hint of a man who would have felt the least bit of remorse for his actions.

He began to leap and dance and cavort around the glider and armor, like a devout worshipper giving thanks to the totem of a dark and slavering god. He waved his arms around, gibbered and howled like a cross between a baboon and a wolf, and the last conscious thoughts fled him.

The next thing he knew, he felt as if he were being lifted up, as if his god were taking him up to heaven. There was the heady sensation of flight, of the world speeding below him. And there was more than that; he felt as if he had power, ultimate power of life and death over all the puny mortals who sprawled beneath him, going about their pathetic little lives, sleeping or watching movies or making love, all unaware that a new dark god and his greatest disciple were abroad upon the land.

They would know him and fear him and worship him, and he would take their fates in his clawed hand, for they, like Stromm, were just sheep. Just sheep. And he was the shepherd, and he would guide them and herd them and sheer them and slaughter them. For what else did one do with sheep?

Harry Osborn hated his father's den.

Partly it was because some of his earliest memories involved being chased out of that haven of his father's, when all he'd wanted to do was spend a few minutes with his dad. But his dad had been so busy, always so busy.

The other part of Harry's antipathy for the den stemmed from his father's grotesque collection of masks.

He had no idea what had prompted his dad's fascination with such hideous things, but they had been there for as long as he could remember, and every year there were more of them as Norman acquired them in his business travels. Medieval jester's masks, masks from New Orleans during the Mardi Gras revels, masks allegedly worn by witch doctors in the heart of the Congo . . . all these and more adorned the walls, staring down in silent judgment and condemnation of anyone—namely Harry—who dared to set foot in the den without approval of the master of the house.

Some of the masks even had eyes painted on them, and Harry always felt as if they were watching him. Sometimes, when he was a child, he'd had dreams that they were observing him while he slept.

Truth to tell, he had similar dreams as a teen.

The problem was that the den extended off the main hallway in the opulent Osborn apartment in Tudor Hill, and there was no way Harry could avoid walking past it whenever he was on his way out. So he always made a point of hurrying by as quickly as possible. The passage was made simpler by the fact that the doors were usually closed, so there was no temptation to slow and glance in to see if some new repulsive mask had joined the others.

This day, however—one which was supposed to be dry, but nevertheless had a considerable number of clouds in the sky—Harry saw that the doors were wide-open as he walked by. Against his better judgment he slowed, hesitated, then peered around the corner of the door frame with the intention of speeding on his way once his curiosity was satisfied.

To his utter astonishment, his father was seated in the middle of the den. If it weren't for the fact that he didn't smell of alcohol, Harry would have thought Norman Osborn had been out on a serious bender the night before. He was wearing the same clothes he'd worn the previous day, and he looked disheveled and disoriented.

Long years of being told in no uncertain terms that the den was off limits prompted Harry to pause in the doorway. He almost felt like a vampire, unable to enter unless he'd been invited.

"Dad? What is it, Dad?"

Norman Osborn looked up at his son, seemingly aware of his presence but unable to focus on him. "Harry?" It was partly an acknowledgment, and partly an inquiry as to whether this was, indeed, his son standing before him.

Harry immediately shook free of the old childhood worries and quickly walked in, crouching in front of his father and making no attempt to hide his concern. "You look sick. What's happened?"

"I . . . don't know."

He'd never heard his father sound like this: vulnerable. Even scared. For once his dad actually needed him. "Where were you last night? I didn't hear you come in."

Osborn frowned, as if trying to reassemble pieces of a fractured recollection. "I was . . . last night," he said thickly, "I was . . ."

"What?"

His shoulders sagged in defeat.

"I . . . don't remember."

Before Harry could pursue the matter, he heard noises from down the hallway. He immediately recognized one of them as the houseman, Edmund. The other took him a moment to place, but then he realized it was his father's assistant from the factory, Ms. Simkins. He'd only met her one or two times; his father had taken great pains to keep his life at the factory separate from his home life. Sometimes Harry got the feeling it was because he was embarrassed about his son and wanted to minimize Harry's exposure to any business associates so he could spare himself humiliation. Now, though, clearly wasn't the time to dwell on old hurts.

"I have to see him," Simkins was saying urgently. It was obvious that she had forced her way past Edmund in her attempts to get to Norman.

"He can't be disturbed now," Edmund told her, sounding more irate by the moment.

"This can't wait!"

It was Osborn who settled the matter. "Who's there?" he called out. Harry couldn't believe how weak he sounded, how confused. He wondered if maybe his dad was getting Alzheimer's or something equally horrible.

"Mr. Osborn," said Simkins, entering the den.

She looked distraught, but Harry immediately felt protective of his father, not wanting him to be subjected to any undue stress. "My father's not well, Ms. Simkins," he started to say.

But Simkins spoke right over him. "Mr. Osborn, Dr. Stromm is dead."

The name didn't mean anything to Harry. It obviously meant something to his father, though, because Norman looked up at Simkins, stunned. "What?"

"His body was found this morning in the laboratory," Simkins took a deep breath to steady herself and then continued. "He was murdered, sir."

"Murdered!" said Harry. He might not have known who Stromm was, but a murder in the middle of his father's factory? That couldn't possibly be good.

Norman Osborn got to his feet, some of the confusion falling away as he focused on this new situation. "What are you talking about?" he demanded.

"And the flying wing prototype, sir . . ."

"What about it?"

Simkins said, all in a rush, "It's missing. It's been stolen."

There was a dead, stunned silence for a long moment.

"Take me there," Osborn said.

With a quick nod, Simkins headed out, Norman following her. Harry remained behind for a moment, then looked at the masks that were watching him and hurried out of the den. He hurried after his father, ran out the door and down the stairs just as Norman was getting into the back of the car that Simkins had driven there. His father looked up at him and said, "Where do you think you're going?"

"You . . . you weren't well," Harry said. "So I figured maybe I should come along, maybe be of help . . ."

"Simkins will help me. That's what I pay her for. I'm not the kind of man who lets a little headache bother him."

"But Dad, I . . . I thought . . ."

"You thought what?"

His every word becoming softer and softer, until by the end of the sentence his voice was barely audible, Harry said, "I thought you might . . . need . . . me. . . ."

Norman reached out, squeezed his forearm briefly, and said, "I do. But not for this." And with that, he swung shut the car door and the vehicle rolled away from the curbside, leaving Harry feeling a bit depressed . . . but also oddly elated.

IX

THE RIDE

Dear Mom and Dad:

Boy, did I have a day.

I saw M. J. walking home, and for once Flash wasn't with her. I think maybe they had a fight or something. So she goes into her house, and I keep thinking about the way that Harry was looking at me, so disappointed in me when I couldn't just, you know, talk to Mary Jane. So I decided, what the hell, what's the worst that could happen?

So I go over and start heading up their front walk, and before I can knock on it, the door opens and there's M. J.'s father. In all these years, it's the first time I've ever really seen him close up. I know they say that girls are attracted to guys that remind them of their fathers, but boy, I never realized how much that was the case with M. J. and Flash, because her dad is like what Flash'll be in about twenty years.

And he just looks at me with this contempt. I try to ask if Mary Jane can hang out, just to bum around the mall or something. But he just stares at me, like I landed from Mars, and my throat closes up.

So he says, "You're the Parker kid from across the way, aren't you." He's got a voice like a dump truck spilling out gravel. I manage a nod. And then he says, like he looked right into my head, "She's got a boyfriend. And even if she didn't, I wouldn't let her see some bookworm type."

And then he closes the door in my face.

In.

My.

Face.

And I took it. I wanted to pound on the door, I wanted to shout,

"You think you know me? You don't know anything about me! A book-worm, huh? Well, worms turn, Mr. Watson!" But instead I just took it, took being treated like I was dirt on his shoes. I stood there like a dope, and then I heard M. J.'s voice from inside saying, "Who was that?" and her father snapping back at her, "Nobody."

That's all I am. Nobody.

How the heck was I supposed to talk to her after that? "Hi, I'm the nobody who was just talking to your dad." She'd just look at me with pity, and that's the thing I can't stand, above anything else. I'd rather she looked at me with love or hatred or not at all, but pity I just couldn't stand.

So I turned and walked away.

The worm turns. But even after he does, he's still a worm.

It's not fair. It's just not fair. Instead of doing something about how I feel, I'm just sitting here, on the front steps of my house, writing to you.

I wish you guys were here. I can't talk to Aunt May or Uncle Ben about this stuff. Heck, Uncle Ben'll probably get himself so worked up that he'll stomp over there and confront M. J.'s dad, and how humiliating would that whole scene be? And Aunt May will just tell me how wonderful I am, and how some girl will appreciate me some day, and then she'll bake brownies. It's amazing I don't weigh four hundred pounds.

Then again, if you guys were here, I don't know what you'd do, either.

Better finish off this letter. Aunt May and Uncle Ben are going to start getting worried about me.

I keep thinking about the way her dad looked at me. And how it made me want to . . . I don't know. Do something.

Wouldn't it be great to be someone who could do whatever he wanted?

Well . . . I'm working on it.

It was as if Aunt May and Uncle Ben were waiting for him. As if they knew he'd come sprinting down the stairs—

which he did—heading for the door at full steam—which he was. They were seated in the living room, Aunt May darning a sock and Uncle Ben reading a newspaper, but it seemed as if those were just poses as they waited for him to appear.

With his backpack slung over his shoulder, Peter said quickly as he moved toward the door, all in a rush, "Going-downtothelibraryseeyoulater."

"Hold on! I'll drive you," Uncle Ben called to him, getting up from the chair. He did so with a slight grunt, as he always did. It was as if his body were scolding him for subjecting it to an exertion.

"It's okay, I'll take the train . . ."

But Uncle Ben was already taking his jacket off the coatrack, and Peter could tell by the jingling coming from the pocket that the keys were already in there. And when he spoke it was in a surprisingly firm, take-no-guff voice, as if he'd just caught Peter with his hands in the cookie jar. "I said I'll drive you. Get in the car!"

Taken aback by the sharp tone, Peter meekly climbed into Uncle Ben's car, a 1988 Oldsmobile Delta that his uncle had fallen in love with and refused to sell, no matter how many things he needed to repair on it. He thought he saw Uncle Ben winking at Aunt May but had no idea what that might have been about.

To his surprise, most of the ride passed in silence. He couldn't figure it out. He'd hoped Uncle Ben just wanted to spend some quality time with him, chitchat about what was going on in his life. Truth to tell, Peter hadn't much been looking forward to it. Because of course there was only one thing of true significance that had been going on in his life. He didn't want to lie to Uncle Ben, and to a great degree it was easy to avoid doing so. After all, unless Uncle Ben said, "So, Peter, did a bite from a genetically engineered mutant spider give you spider powers recently?" Peter wouldn't be put on the spot.

But he also knew that was a technicality. Peter firmly believed in concepts such as sins of omission. The very fact that he wasn't being completely forthcoming was, in and of itself, deceitful. Anything less than an honest answer to a question as straightforward as "What's been going on with you lately?" was going to be a lie. He hated the notion of lying to Uncle Ben. Uncle Ben, who had such an open, honest face . . . it was like clubbing a baby seal, lying to him.

It was dusk when the Olds rolled up to the library. Peter turned to get out, with still nary a word having passed between them. He said, "Thanks for the ride."

Ben drew a breath and said, "Hold on a minute. We need a talk."

Dammit. Peter sagged back against the car seat, faced with his worst case scenario. "Not a lecture, Uncle Ben! I gotta go . . ."

But Uncle Ben reached across Peter and placed a hand firmly on the door. Granted, Peter could have pushed the door open. He suspected he could have pushed the door clean off the car, if he'd been so inclined. But that would have been totally out of line, and secret or no, Peter simply wasn't prepared to go that far.

"Your Aunt May and I don't know who you are anymore. I wonder if *you* know who you are. Starting fights in school . . ."

So they did know! Peter had thought he'd dodged a bullet, that the school hadn't called to let them know about the scuffle with Flash. Obviously he'd thought wrong, but his aunt and uncle had kept the knowledge to themselves, probably trying to determine the best way to approach it. Or perhaps they'd just been giving him enough rope to hang himself . . .

Or, in his case, webbing.

"I didn't start that fight," Peter said defensively.

"Something new is happening to you," Ben pushed on. "You're changing."

That froze Peter in his seat. How much did Ben know? How much had he and Aunt May figured out? He thought he'd cleaned up all the webs . . . but . . . but there was no way they could have figured it out, right? No way . . . right?

"How would you know?" asked Peter, very cautious.

"Because," was Ben's knowing answer, "when I was your age, I went through exactly the same thing."

It was all Peter could do to stifle a laugh. For a moment he had a mental image of Ben Parker scurrying along a wall or vaulting rooftops. "Not exactly," he said. Then he took a deep breath to steady himself and fight down any other laughter. "I have to go."

But Uncle Ben wasn't ending it that quickly. "These are the years when a man becomes the man he's going to be for the rest of his life. Just be careful who you change into. You're feeling this great power, and with great power comes great responsibility."

And Peter started to get angry. Here Uncle Ben was lecturing him about stuff, and he had no clue, *absolutely* no clue, what was going on. Sure, sure, everyone was entitled to their opinions, but the truth was that everyone was entitled to their *informed* opinions. And Uncle Ben simply wasn't informed on the matter. Plus . . . he could have trusted Peter just a *little*. Even if Peter had been inclined to tell him what was going on, Uncle Ben didn't seem the least bit interested in hearing it. He'd already made up his mind. Didn't all these years of hard work, of good grades, of staying out of trouble, mean anything?

"What are you afraid I'll do, become a criminal?" Peter demanded in irritation. "Stop worrying about me, okay. Something is different, but I'll figure it out. Stop lecturing me!"

Ben hesitated a moment, and Peter took that hesitation as an opportunity to push the door open and get out onto the curb. "I know I'm not your father, Peter . . . ," Ben began.

And then came the words that Peter would, in later years,

wish that he could call back before Ben heard them. The words that, if Peter could go back in time and throw a gag around his mouth to prevent him from uttering them, he would have done so in a heartbeat. Instead they emerged, hostile and hurtful.

"Then stop pretending to be!"

Ben's face grew cold then. Peter had never seen him look that way. So angry, so hurt, so . . . so old. "I'll pick you up here at ten," he said frostily, and then eased the car into traffic.

Feeling contrite, Peter shouted, *"I'm sorry!"* But he wasn't sure whether Ben heard him as the Oldsmobile drove away.

His shoulders sagged. That shouldn't have happened, that fight. He should have been more honest, should have told Uncle Ben what was happening. But if he had, he knew that Ben and May would never have let him do what he was planning to do. Instead they'd probably just try and take him to doctors and specialists and clinics to expunge these abilities from him. And then it really would have all been pointless.

Well . . . he'd make it right. That was all. He'd make it right. He'd make sure that Uncle Ben and Aunt May knew he was sorry, and he'd make it up to them. Hell, if everything worked out this evening, he'd make it up to them in a big way. He'd hold up the three thousand dollars in Uncle Ben's face when Uncle Ben came to pick him up, and the expression would be worth everything. "Money problems solved, Uncle Ben," he'd tell him, and when Uncle Ben was positive that Peter was involved dealing drugs or something—because how else could one come by that much money that fast?—why, Peter would just bend a lamp post or climb up the side of a building.

It would all work out. Things always did.

X.

THE
SECOND
FIGHT

Every so often at school, someone would accidentally drop a tray in the cafeteria. At those times, shouts, catcalls and all-around bellowing from the students would serenade the unlucky clumsy individual. Up until this moment, it had been the loudest group noise Peter Parker had ever heard.

It was nothing compared to what he was experiencing now.

The arena was wall-to-wall sound, unending, feeding upon itself and just building and building, and Peter thought that he was going to start bleeding out his ears. The place was huge, packed with more drunk people than Peter had ever seen in one place in his life, and they all wanted the same thing: to see some guys get their heads kicked in.

Every so often, Uncle Ben would watch wrestling on television. It was one of the few things he did despite knowing it drove Aunt May completely nuts; indeed, that might have been one of the reasons he did it. Just to keep his hand in, to let her know he was the man of the house, darn it. And sometimes Peter would join him, which would send the *tsk tsk*ing from Aunt May to an entirely new level. But seeing it on TV, nice and safe on a couch back home, had done absolutely nothing to prepare Peter for the reality of actually *being there*.

He was standing on a line behind other amateur wrestlers, most of them wearing remarkably garish outfits. At the front of the line sat a bored-looking blonde with too much makeup and a bad perm, checking them in and taking down vital information . . .

. . . *like next of kin,* he thought bleakly. The hallway he was standing in, along the outer perimeter of the arena, was cramped and smelled like mildew. A pipe overhead dripped water steadily into a bucket that needed to be emptied, and soon. When Peter heard another massive roar, he took a step back and peered through an exit door into the arena itself.

The wrestler in the middle of the ring was known as Bone Saw McGraw. Peter had never seen him in action during any of the fights that he'd watched alongside Uncle Ben. That might have been a good thing, because if he had, he might never have screwed up the nerve to come. McGraw was at least six-feet-nine-inches tall and three hundred pounds of pure muscle. His massive chest was glistening with sweat, he had long, dark, messy hair and a dark beard, and he had a look on his face of such dementia that Peter couldn't help but wonder whether McGraw might not be overdue for a distemper shot.

At that moment, McGraw was busy polishing off an opponent who had been billing himself as Battling Jack Murdock. He had flaming red hair and some muscle of his own, and he was dressed in a costume of yellow and dark crimson. But if he'd ever had a prime, he was clearly past it, and McGraw was making short work of him. He slammed Murdock to the ground and delivered a crushing flying-elbow to his opponent's chest so hard that Peter thought he could feel it from where he was standing.

"Down the hall, to the ramp," said the check-in woman to the man immediately ahead of Peter. The man was tall and lean and dressed like Robin Hood. "And lose the hat," she added sourly. He reluctantly removed it but gave her a nasty look, which only succeeded in earning him a derisive chuckle. "Yeah, yeah, nice tights, tough guy," she said. "Next!"

Peter pulled himself away from the exit door and turned to face her. She looked him up and down once and said briskly. "There's no featherweight division here, small-fry. Next!"

Watching the three thousand dollars evaporating before his eyes, Peter said quickly, "No, no . . . I know."

She stared at him as if trying to figure out—not *whether* he was insane—but just how insane he was. "Ooookay," she said slowly. "You understand the NYWL is not responsible for any injuries you may . . ." She looked him over one more time and continued, "and probably will sustain while participating in said event, and that you are at sub one hundred and fifty pounds, indeed participating under your own free will."

"Yes," he replied.

Sighing as one would when saying farewell to a condemned man, she said, "Down the hall and up the ramp. May God be with you."

Behind Peter, a man dressed as Xena waited his turn. The blonde rolled her eyes and said, "Let's go, princess."

Aunt May, drawn by crowd shouts from the TV, walked into the living room to find Ben sitting there, staring at the screen. She gave a low moan as she realized he was watching wrestling. She hadn't even heard him come home. "How did the talk with Peter go?"

He grunted.

"That doesn't sound good." She stood in front of the TV. "Do you want to discuss it?"

"No," he said. "I want to watch large men pound on each other."

"Why?" she asked him, for what seemed the thousandth time in the course of their marriage.

"It vents frustration. One side, May, please."

With an extremely loud *tsk tsk,* she stepped aside. Then,

after a moment, she walked primly over to the couch and sat down next to him. Ben looked at her as if she'd just dropped down from Mars. "What do you think you're doing?"

"If you can take it, I can," she replied. "You're not the only frustrated one here."

Ben moaned softly, then picked up the remote and turned the volume up, hoping the noise would drive May away. Instead she simply sat there, watching, shaking her head slowly to display her obvious disbelief that anyone—much less she—would watch this voluntarily.

"Who is this person?" asked May after a moment.

Sighing, knowing that she wasn't going to disappear anytime soon, but not wanting to give in to the unspoken pressure to change channels, Ben said, "That's Bone Saw McGraw."

"Oh. I wonder if that's his given name."

"No, May, his birth name was Bone Saw Liebowitz, but he wanted to avoid possible anti-Semitism."

"My," she sniffed, "*someone* is in a mood."

Bone Saw McGraw, possibly née Liebowitz, was in the process of dispatching an unfortunate-looking fellow dressed in a clown suit. Bone Saw hurled the clown into the ropes, which sent him careening back into the middle of the ring. For the coup de grace, Bone Saw then picked the clown up bodily and tossed him into the stands.

The crowd went insane with enthusiasm as McGraw roared with rage.

"How brutal," said May.

"It's rehearsed, May. It's . . . it's like a big show," Ben assured her. "It's all fake."

It was obvious that someone in the audience concurred with Ben, because a fan standing a couple of rows back from the ring shouted, "Hey, Bone Saw! You big fake! You suck!" And he kept shouting it, over and over. The camera zoomed in on him, the TV screen filling up with his sneering face.

Abruptly the contempt in his expression disappeared, to be replaced by panic Laurence Olivier wouldn't have been able to fake on his best day. The TV camera whipped around and focused on the infuriated Bone Saw as he lurched toward the fan. People, trainers, the referee, a guy with earphones, were all trying to hold him back, and he was shaking them off as if they didn't exist.

The camera stayed with him as he caught the heckler, who was just trying to make a break for it. Bone Saw swung him around, leered with a distinct lack of sympathy into the heckler's face, and hit him just once. The heckler's nose became a geyser of blood and he let out a shriek as he collapsed to the floor.

Bone Saw then grabbed up the heckler's folding chair, waved it over his head like a trophy, and bellowed into the camera, *"Fake my ass!"* He turned and stormed back toward the ring, pausing just long enough to notice that the fallen clown was trying to crawl away. He smashed the folded chair over the clown's head before climbing back into the ring.

Slowly Aunt May turned and fixed a gaze on a speechless Uncle Ben.

"That man," she opined, "has some *serious* issues."

Hidden from view by a black scrim, which in turn hung behind a large curtain, Peter was trying not to panic.

He was starting to get a feeling for what it was like for the Roman gladiators when they were about to be marched into the center of the Coliseum. Hearing all those spectators howling for blood—their blood—would have undermined the most experienced and confident of warriors. And Peter didn't have a lot going for him in either category.

He heard the ring announcer shout, "Are you ready for more?" And, when he apparently wasn't satisfied by the audience's shouts of bloodlust, he bellowed even louder, *"I said, are you ready for more?!"*

The crowd gave him what he wanted. *"More, more, more!"* they shouted, over and over, stomping their feet rhythmically until the whole place was shaking. Peter started to wonder if the arena was going to collapse, rendering this entire harebrained stunt completely moot. He noticed a monitor mounted nearby that had the ring on the screen. Bone Saw was sitting on a stool in the corner, where he was being tended to by his bikini-clad ring maidens who were collectively known as the Bonettes. They were sponging him off, giving him water, massaging him.

He sat there with a smug expression on his face that reminded Peter of Flash Thompson, and the fear within Peter began to burn away, to be replaced by an overwhelming desire to smash that grin into the ground.

Bone Saw, apparently having had enough pampering, rose and started flexing. The crowd went nuts. Peter rolled his eyes. "Bone Saw's ready!" the wrestler announced, his voice so loud that it carried even over the barely controlled pandemonium of the spectators. Then the image on the screen changed, and the announcer reappeared.

"Will the next victim please enter the ring at this time!" he called dramatically. Then he was gone again from the TV monitor, and Peter realized it meant he was heading up the ramp toward the curtain. He was, however, momentarily distracted when he saw two girls on the screen, with breasts the size of ham hocks. They—the girls, not the breasts—were marching around the ring with a banner reading 3:00 FOR $3000.

Then the announcer finished his trek and ended up standing just outside the curtain as he continued, "If he can withstand just three minutes in the cage with Bone Saw McGraw, the sum of three thousand dollars will be paid to . . ." Then he peeked around the curtain, cupping his hand over the mike for some momentary privacy, staring at Peter with open skepticism. "The Human Spider? That's it? That's the best you got?"

Peter, already feeling uncomfortable, graduated to ridiculous. "Yeah."

Making an annoyed huffing sound, the announcer said, "Nah. You gotta jazz it up a little." Then, without hesitation, he started speaking into the mike again, continuing as if he hadn't left off. ". . . the sum of three thousand dollars will be paid to . . ."

The curtain started to open. Peter took a deep breath, steadying himself, trying to calm his pounding heart.

". . . the terrifying . . . the deadly . . . *the amazing . . . Spider-Man!*"

The black scrim, which had been revealed by the curtain, rose perfectly on cue, and Peter Parker didn't feel the least bit terrifying, nor deadly, and certainly not amazing. When the crowd's reaction combined laughter with . . . well . . . more laughter . . . what he felt was still, quite simply, ridiculous.

Uncle Ben guffawed at the sight. "Big overture, little show," he snorted.

Bone Saw's challenger apparently was nothing more than some undersized idiot dressed in blue sweatpants, a red sweatshirt with a spidery design on it, and . . .

"What's that stretchy hat thing he's wearing?" asked Ben. It looked like some sort of hooded garment, covering his neck, face, and head. Only his eyes and the bridge of his nose were visible.

"It's a balaclava," May told him promptly. "You remember. I gave Peter one for his fourteenth birthday. Looks a bit like that one, actually. Maybe his mother gave it to him."

"Well, she didn't do him any favors, that's for sure. 'My mother dressed me funny.' There's a battle cry for you. *Humph.*

Wrestlers who dress like teenagers. Pitiful. Pitiful. Gorgeous George, now *there* was a wrestler with fashion sense."

Aunt May looked at Ben with an arched eyebrow. "I'm starting to worry about you, Ben. I really am."

The challenger, meantime, didn't seem pleased with his introduction. "That's 'The Human Spider,' " he said.

"Get out there, dipstick," said the ring announcer, who apparently didn't realize the microphone was on.

The masked figure walked slowly toward the ring, looking right and left, clearly overwhelmed by what he was seeing. The Bonettes were waiting for him on the ramp, like a pack of hungry wolves. They mercilessly heckled him as he went, made as if they were feeling his muscles and yawning while doing so. They taunted him and berated him, and as they did so they egged on the crowd to join them, and the crowd did so with gusto.

The clown contestant was wheeled by, and the camera's microphone picked him up saying, "I can't feel my legs . . . I can't feel my legs . . ."

"Oh, Ben, enough is enough. Turn this off. It's grotesque."

"I know, I know, but . . . damn," and Ben shook his head, "I can't help but feel sorry for the poor guy. Maybe I'm hoping a miracle will happen."

"What, that he'll have the sense to turn and run? I wouldn't count on it," said May.

The challenger, meantime, had crawled into the ring with McGraw and was looking around in bewilderment as the chant "Cage! Cage! Cage!" arose from the crowd. Obviously he didn't know what was about to happen. It made Ben pity him all the more.

Abruptly, from overhead, a flat structure with metal bars appeared. The challenger stepped back in surprise as the cage dropped down around him and hit the padded floor of the ring with a muffled thump.

"Will the guards please lock the cage doors!" came the voice of the ring announcer, and stagehands promptly wrapped huge metal chains around the corners of the cage, locking the combatants in.

The challenger was yanking at the bars when Bone Saw, who was standing in the middle of the ring, caught his attention. "Freak show!" bellowed Bone Saw, and the crowd roared its approval. "You're going nowhere! I've got you for three minutes. Three minutes of playing with Bone Saw!"

Ben stared at the TV screen. "He's going to get his head handed to him," he said, realizing the inevitable.

"It's horrible. Just horrible," said Aunt May. "Suicidal, even. You have to wonder the kind of home life someone like that would come from, to put himself into a situation where he'll likely get himself killed. That costume, this insane stunt . . . I'm telling you, Ben, this is a cry for help."

"Help," muttered Peter beneath his balaclava as he flattened himself against the bars. "What am I doing here?"

Bone Saw didn't waste any time. Maybe he just loved giving the crowd what it wanted. Maybe he had a hot date and wanted to get out quickly. Whatever the reason, he came in fast and hard, straight at Peter.

Peter leapt upward and Bone Saw crashed into the cage wall with teeth-rattling force. He had been so confident that Peter wouldn't be able to get out of the way that he had fully committed himself to the charge. Consequently he hit the cage walls so hard that he actually bounced off and crumbled to the ground. His vision swam and he had to shake off the impact, even as he stared stupidly at the bars in a vaguely accusatory fashion.

Then he looked up. Peter, clinging to the top of the cage, waved down at him.

"What do you think you're doing?" demanded Bone Saw, staggering to his feet.

"Staying away from you for three minutes," Peter replied, sounding more cheerful than he felt.

With a roar of indignation, Bone Saw leapt up at him. His leg muscles were powerful enough to carry him within reach . . . except the lithe teen had already vaulted out of the way, somersaulting to the opposite side of the cage. He clung there for a moment, then dropped to the ground.

And then he heard something that completely astounded him.

"Yeeeeeeaaahhh! Go, Spider-Man!"

It was the heckler whose face Bone Saw had rearranged. He was back in his seat, dried blood on his face, and he was shouting encouragement and pumping the air. Other people in the crowd were joining in, as well, apparently pleased by the show that Peter was putting on.

Then his spider sense kicked in. It had been warning him since the moment he set foot in the ring, starting with the buzzing signal that began in his head as the cage was descending. But he'd had too many distractions to know where to look first. Now, however, he was beginning to focus on what was important, and he realized that not only was it necessary to defeat Bone Saw and win the money . . . it was also important to do so in a way that would be entertaining to the crowd. If he was going to do this with any degree of regularity and get the big purses—money that would make this three-thousand-dollar payday look like chump change—he'd have to give the crowd what they wanted. What Bone Saw gave them.

A show.

His spider sense had warned him that Bone Saw was coming at him again, and Peter leapt effortlessly between his outstretched arms. To him, it was as if Bone Saw were moving in slow motion. But this time he didn't settle for just getting out of the wrestler's way. Instead he landed in a one-hand handstand on Bone Saw's head. Beneath his balaclava he was grinning, his confidence growing.

"Not a bad costume," he said to his opponent as if chatting in a Laundromat while watching clothes dry. "What is that? Spandex? I used Lycra for mine, and it itched like crazy."

But Peter had gotten too cocky, too quickly. With a fast, economic move, Bone Saw grabbed one of his outstretched legs and shouted, "I got you now, insect!" And he swung Peter in a spin that sent him crashing against the side of the cage.

"Owww," Peter moaned softly.

The crowd's reaction was mixed. Some cheered the violence, but others were rooting for an upset. Clearly they liked this upstart with his dazzling gymnastic style.

Bone Saw hauled him away from the edge of the cage and let him loll back on the floor. "You know," said Peter, feeling woozy, trying to pull himself together, "technically it's 'arachnid.'"

If the students in Peter's class hadn't seemed interested in the specifics of spiders, Bone Saw seemed even less so. He barreled toward Peter, whose spider sense was now screaming at him over the imminent danger. Peter, his mind snapped clear by the intensity of the warning, looked up in time to see Bone Saw leaping at him with a flying-elbow. In a second, that elbow would be slamming down into Peter's chest, very likely breaking several of his ribs.

Fortunately for Peter, he didn't need a whole second. Instead he brought his feet up, catching Bone Saw in the chest just in time to use the brute's own speed and strength against him. At exactly the right moment, Peter uncoiled his legs like a python snapping at its prey and sent Bone Saw hurtling across the cage, slamming with full force into the iron bars. The entire cage shook from the impact, and Bone Saw sank to the mat unconscious.

Peter couldn't believe it. Neither could the crowd. For a long moment there was dead silence. And then, as if with one throat, the crowd erupted in a joyful chant.

"Spider-Man! Spider-Man! Spider-Man!"

Springing to his feet and realizing that he didn't feel the least bit winded, Peter spread his arms wide, drinking in the adulation.

"Ahhhh . . . showbiz," he said.

"Spider-Man?" Aunt May said in slow amazement, unable to believe what she'd just witnessed on the TV screen. *"Spider-Man?"*

"Apparently he does whatever a spider can," Uncle Ben said as he pointed his remote control and shut off the TV.

"What nonsense. I'll tell you, Ben, if I were his mother, I'd give him a piece of my mind. I mean, anyone who's clever enough to come up with tricks like he used should be able to put his mind to more creative things than . . . than brutality!"

Ben reached for his keys and headed for the door. "If I ever happen to run into him, I'll be sure to tell him you said so. In the meantime, I've got more than enough to worry about in trying to figure out what I'll say to Peter." The door closed behind him with a click.

And as it did, Aunt May felt a chill pass through her. She had no idea why. There was just . . . just something about the way the door had clicked shut, a sort of finality to the sound. . . .

Then she shrugged it off and went to put on a sweater.

Peter, still in his costume but holding the balaclava in his hand, stared at the single hundred-dollar bill that the promoter was handing to him.

They were up in his office, upstairs at the arena. It was seedy and the corner of the desk was propped up by a phone book. The promoter dabbed at his sweaty, balding head with a handkerchief as he said brusquely, "Now get outta here."

"A hundred bucks!" Peter said incredulously. "The ad said three thousand!"

"Check it again, webhead," said the clearly irritated promoter. "It said three grand for three minutes. You pinned him in two. For that I'll give you a hundred, and you're lucky to get it." He came around the desk and waved a fat cigar in Peter's face. "You made my best fighter look like a girl out there."

Peter felt rage building up inside him. He'd punched Flash Thompson into the middle of next week, and Flash still got Mary Jane and was the big hero. He'd flattened the terror of the ring, the great Bone Saw, and now this yutz wouldn't even give him the money owed him. What the hell did he have to do to get some respect?

Barely containing his fury, Peter practically snarled in the guy's face. "I *need* that money."

For a moment the promoter looked intimidated. But then he looked into Peter's eyes and obviously realized that despite his ire—Peter posed no threat. He wasn't going to break the guy in half, no matter how tempting it might be.

"I missed the part where this is *my* problem," he said coolly.

Peter fairly trembled with rage and then, disgusted with the promoter for his trickery and with himself for what he perceived as weakness of character, he turned and stalked away. As he walked out the door, he passed a squirrelly looking man on the way in, his hair dyed platinum blonde, his gaze darting about in agitation. For a heartbeat he met Peter's eyes, and then he looked away. *Good,* Peter thought, *at least someone has respect for me.*

Stalking down the hallway, he clutched the hundred-dollar bill in his hand, muttering under his breath. Part of him tried to find the upside. It was, after all, a hundred bucks for two minutes work. It was the most money he'd ever seen in his life. But it really wasn't about the money; it was about what he'd done to earn it, about what he'd risked—the pain, the humiliation. And in return, all he'd received was more humiliation at the hands of that weasel promoter, refusing to fork over what he'd been promised, what he'd earned, what he'd . . .

"Hey!" It was the promoter's voice, shouting from his office. *"What the hell do you—?!"*

Peter thought, just for an instant, that the promoter had been yelling at him. Maybe he'd had a change of heart and was going to try and do right by him. That was when the door of the office banged open, shattering the glass, and out darted the blonde-haired man, clutching a canvas bag.

"Help! That guy stole the gate, *he's got my money!*" came the outraged howling of the promoter.

From the far end of the corridor, a security guard—middle-aged, out of shape, huffing and puffing—ran down the hallway as best he could. The thief was charging right toward Peter, and just behind the teen, the elevator door opened, accompanied by a cheerful *ding.*

"Hey! You!" the security guard shouted to Peter. "Stop that guy!"

Peter instantly knew what he was going to do, was going to say.

And the moment he came to his conclusion, he reviewed it from all angles. He knew it was contemptible and spat in the face of all the conscientiousness he had practiced throughout his lifetime.

Yet all he could think was that all that conscientiousness, all that fair play, had come down to two things and two things only: Flash Thompson had Mary Jane, and the promoter had his money. Except now the thief had the promoter's money, and dammit, sometimes karma evened out faster than expected. All he had to do was stay out of karma's way, and the unjust would get what they deserved.

So with smug satisfaction, with more of a sense of rightness than he'd felt in ages—perhaps ever—Peter stepped back and allowed the thief to dash into the elevator.

"Thanks, pal," grunted the thief as the doors slid shut.

The security guard got there a heartbeat after the doors closed and slammed his fists against them in frustration. He whirled toward Peter and bellowed, "What the hell's the matter with you?! You just let him go!"

And sure enough, there was the promoter. Better and better: There was a large red welt growing on his forehead where the thief had clocked him. So Peter had taken the high road and the promoter had still gotten the worst of the deal. Oh, yes, payback was definitely a bitch. And then the promoter said exactly what Peter had hoped he'd say: "You coulda taken that guy apart! Now he's gonna get away with my money!"

Savoring every syllable, Peter responded, "I missed the part where this is *my* problem."

He stared at the promoter long enough to watch the guy's face turn purple with rage, then he turned his back on him and walked away, humming. It hadn't been such a bad evening after all. Granted, he was out $2,900 dollars. But it was almost worth it just to see payback occur that quickly.

Almost.

XI.

THE
SHOOTER

Peter was running late, and that alone was enough to make him nervous.

His original plan was to get back to the library early enough that he could come trotting down the stairs to meet Uncle Ben, who was supposed to give him a ride home. He didn't want Uncle Ben to see him emerging from the subway station down the street, having taken the subway over to the arena.

Unfortunately he'd wasted so much time arguing with the promoter that he was returning to the vicinity of the library later than he'd intended. Well, why not? Every other thing in his evening had gone wrong. Why not this? He just had to hope and pray that Uncle Ben didn't spot him coming up from the station or that Uncle Ben was running late himself.

Dressed in his street clothes, Peter trotted up to the corner where his uncle was supposed to meet him. He let out a sigh of relief. Uncle Ben was nowhere in sight. He looked around, trying to see if perhaps he'd parked across the street, but there was no sign of him. So he was running later. Or maybe he'd gotten there early, and some cop had told him he couldn't stand there, so he was circling the block. That also made sense, particularly since Peter spotted a police car at a far corner, its light blinking steadily. Yes, that was definitely it; the police had turned out to make sure no one blocked the front of the library. So Uncle Ben would likely be pulling up any moment, Peter would jump in quickly, and off they'd go.

The only question in Peter's mind was whether to show Uncle Ben the hundred dollars . . . no. No, his new vocation would only pass muster if Peter had some serious money in hand. Maybe he—

Then another police car raced by, its siren blaring, stopping short to join the first one. There was an ambulance siren in the distance, drawing closer.

That was when Peter started to get a gnawing, uneasy feeling in his stomach. Because there were two police cars here, and an ambulance approaching, and Uncle Ben wasn't here. The calm, logical part of his mind told him that it was pure coincidence. There couldn't possibly be any sort of connection.

Even as he thought that, though, he started walking toward the corner where the police cars were. Pedestrians, onlookers, rubberneckers were also starting to gather, and wasn't that a considerable number of people, and wouldn't Uncle Ben drive up at just about any moment and wonder what all the hubbub was about? And as Peter climbed into the car, Uncle Ben would make some sort of comment about how blasted nosy people could be, and what the hell was happening to people in this country, anyway, that they were so obsessed with other people's misfortunes. Then Peter would agree with him and, having found common ground, Peter would apologize for earlier and this time he'd know that Uncle Ben heard him, and maybe they'd go to Carvel for a sundae, and Peter would tell him everything, be totally straight and just take what came, because when it came down to it they were family, and always would be family, and they'd make everything better.

The entire rosy scenario, and a dozen variations on it, played through his mind as he headed down the block, walking first and then walk-running and then a flat-out run. He got to the outer perimeter of the crowd and it was as if people weren't even there. He just started pushing them out of the way as a pounding began to throb in his temple, and it had to be that he was just imagining another worst case scenario. *Uncle Ben, you're gonna laugh. I saw these cop cars and heard an ambulance and I was thinking that something happened to you! Just me being paranoid, right?* And Uncle Ben would look at him solemnly, although with a twinkle in his eye, and intone, *Just because you're paranoid doesn't mean they're not out to get you, Peter.* And they would laugh and laugh . . .

He shoved through to the front of the crowd, ignoring the shouts of "Hey!" and "Watch it!" and he stared, dumbfounded, at the body of some old man lying in the street. There was blood pooling on the pavement under his body, and on his chest where he'd obviously been shot, and the old man looked very small and very unimpressive, really. Peter had never actually seen a dead body before, or someone about to die—whichever this guy was—and he realized on some level that he should be repulsed or horrified. Instead he was just disconnected, as if he was in shock over seeing his Uncle Ben lying in the street like leftover rubbish, except this guy wasn't Uncle Ben. No, heck no, hell no, he didn't look a thing like Uncle Ben. Yeah, okay, there was a faint, passing resemblance, and he *was* wearing the exact same clothes that Uncle Ben had been wearing earlier, and his hair was pretty much the same color as Uncle Ben's. And there was some similarity around the eyes and nose, but this definitely was not Uncle Ben, no way, no how, because the big difference was that Uncle Ben was safe and sound and alive, whereas this poor schmuck was lying in the street, and either he was dead as a doornail or was going to be soon, and therefore could not possibly, no way, no how, be . . . be . . .
. . . be . . .

"Uncle Ben!" screamed Peter as his world collapsed around him, and he lunged toward the corpse, but the police

held him back. In truth Peter could have picked them up and juggled them, but he was too unfocused in his confusion and shock. As a result the policemen were able to restrain him, but just barely. They exchanged silent, surprised looks with one another that such an unassuming-looking teenager could give them such a tussle.

"Hang on, hang on!" shouted one of the cops, who was wearing a name tag that said, LIEBER. The cop next to him, Ditko, was almost knocked on his ass by Peter's struggles.

"My uncle! That's my uncle!"

"That's not gonna help him!" Ditko said, trying to brace himself against Peter's onslaught.

"What happened?!"

"Carjacker," Lieber told him. "He's been shot."

Peter tried to shove past to get to him. He nearly succeeded, lifting Lieber clear off his feet and slamming him back down again with such force that Lieber almost collapsed from the impact. Ditko, standing behind him, his arms wrapped around Peter's waist, nodded for other cops to help them as he shouted in Peter's ear, "Hold on, kid! You can't help the guy!"

"The guy?! He's not 'the guy!' He's my uncle!"

And then they couldn't hold him anymore, because Peter yanked his arms clear of them and ran over to Ben. He dropped down onto the street, cradling his head in his lap, and cried out, "Uncle Ben! Uncle Ben, it's me! Peter!"

He can't be dead he can't be dead, the words kept going through his mind, as if he could bring Uncle Ben back through sheer force of will. And then, slowly, Uncle Ben opened his eyes, his mouth forming a smile that seemed to be coming from very far away. He mouthed, "Peter," and that was when Peter knew beyond any doubt that Uncle Ben was going to make it.

Then Uncle Ben's head slumped back, and there was that

rattle, that awful rattle that Peter would remember every minute of every day for the rest of his life. And Ben was off to be with his brother.

Peter let out a howl like the damned, and the people in the crowd who had been babbling to one another lapsed into silence, not so much out of respect but out of shocked fascination for this naked display. The ambulance siren continued to wail in the distance, like a banshee announcing a dead soul on its way to the hereafter.

The world blurred out for a moment, threatening to go away entirely, and then Peter heard another cop call out, "They've got the shooter! He's headed south on Fifth Avenue!" And that brought his surroundings snapping sharply back into focus around him.

No . . . "they" aren't going to get the shooter . . .
I am.

In a dark alleyway, Peter pulled on his wrestling sweats and, without hesitation, leapt into the air and onto the nearest wall. He skittered up the building, higher and higher, no longer caring about the heights he was scaling, or the danger he was facing, or anything except getting his hands on the bastard who had ripped his uncle away from him.

He leapt onto a flagpole, swung around it by using it as an anchor to build up speed, and then released it, his momentum carrying him to the next building, which he ascended as rapidly as he had the first one.

Achieving the rooftop, he looked far ahead to the cluster of police lights, the cop cars screaming down Fifth Avenue in pursuit of the shooter. Peter fired a webline—a silver strand twinkling in the moonlight, adhering to a building two blocks down. It was the longest swing he had ever attempted. He didn't hesitate. He wasn't even thinking about it.

Everything now was a means to an end, and even as he

swooped down, down toward the street, and then snapped upward on the arc . . . even as he fired another web line in midswing, caught another building, and continued his journey, never slowing, moving with an ease and defiance of gravity that would have turned the most experienced of acrobats green . . . even as all that was happening, all he could think of was Uncle Ben.

Worse, all he could think about was that last conversation. Except it hadn't been a conversation. It had been . . . a fight, a temper tantrum, a horror show. The petulant words of a brat and an ingrate, and Peter was sure that was what Ben Parker had carried with him in departing this life. It was horrible and unfair and it fueled his rage all the more as his swings overtook the police pursuit.

Then he saw it.

For a moment he felt as if he was seeing a ghost. There was Uncle Ben's Oldsmobile, barreling down Fifth Avenue, the driver himself hidden by the long shadows of the night. In short order, Fifth Avenue was going to effectively dead end into Washington Square Park, and they'd probably have roadblocks set up there. The shooter obviously knew it. He cut hard at Eighth Street, misjudging the angle, his speed carrying him too far. He slammed through a row of newspaper boxes, sending the unsold papers flying. Three police cars also cut hard, continuing the pursuit.

Given time, they might or might not have caught up.

Peter wasn't about to give them any time. If there was one thing he'd learned, it was not to assume that there would always be time enough for anything.

Webbing left, right, left, right, unseen in the shadows, Peter outsped the police cars and landed with a thump on the roof of the Oldsmobile. Without hesitation, he funneled his full rage into his fist and effortlessly smashed through the roof of the car. He reached around, not knowing what he would grab, and was pleased when he felt what had to be the shooter's face cupped in his hand. All he had to do was squeeze and the man's face would become a pulped and bloody mass in his palm.

He was all set to do it, even as he cringed inwardly at the thought, but then the car began to swerve wildly, back and forth, trying to shake him off. The natural adhesion of his feet and his one free hand enabled him to stay attached to the roof, but it wasn't easy. Still, if he crushed the guy's head, that would solve the problem, wouldn't it.

The car went against the light where Eighth intersected with Broadway. Cars slammed to a halt to avoid getting smashed. The Oldsmobile whipped right onto Broadway, with its wider lanes and more maneuverability. It fishtailed briefly, then kept going.

Peter, meantime, discarded the notion of killing him outright. Instead he wanted to growl at him, *"Remember the experience of being born? Well, you're going to relive it right now,"* whereupon he would proceed to pull the shooter, headfirst, through the hole in the roof.

But he didn't have the opportunity, because suddenly his spider sense was screaming in his head. Then bullets, fired from inside the car, started punching through the roof. Peter's agility kept him one step ahead of the rounds of ammo that came blasting up at him, but he knew it wasn't going to last forever.

A truck was moving down Broadway alongside them, and Peter vaulted onto the top of the truck. He crouched, watching the Olds as it raced alongside them. . . .

Then he looked up. There was a traffic-light arm extending across the street, right at Peter's chest level. And another a block beyond that, and another . . .

Peter jumped, executing a triple somersault over the traffic light and landing back on the roof of the truck. But he wasn't about to spend the rest of the evening vaulting traffic lights. The moment his feet touched the bus, he ricocheted off and landed back on the roof of the speeding Oldsmobile. This time, though, as if defying gravity itself, he managed a much softer landing so that the driver was unaware that he had reacquired a passenger.

Light-footed, he vaulted onto the hood and swung around so that he was peering right through the windshield. He had a satisfying glimpse of the stunned, terror-stricken shooter, clearly not comprehending what he was seeing.

The car cut hard to the left, barreling down a sidestreet toward the East River. Peter saw the driver fumbling around on the seat, probably for his gun, but not for a moment did Peter know the slightest fear. Later . . . later he would tremble with an awareness of how much danger he'd been in, but at that moment, nothing—least of all his own self-preservation—could penetrate the haze of fury that had seized him.

Not giving the shooter an opportunity to start firing again, Peter slammed his fist through the windshield, releasing webbing as he did so. In a heartbeat, the entire front of the car was filled with webbing, completely blocking the driver's vision.

The car screeched wildly, the driver losing control, and the Olds smashed through the front gates of a creepy-looking building near the East River. The impact nearly knocked Peter off the hood, but the incredible adhesion of his fingers stabilized him. Then his head whipped around as he realized that the car was hurtling straight toward the front door of the building, with no intention of stopping. The gates had been held closed by a lock which easily broke upon impact, but Peter had the distinct feeling that the door was going to be a lot less yielding. If he didn't bail, and quickly, he'd be crushed.

He leapt straight up toward the building, just as the car

smashed into the door and through. The sound was absolutely ear-splitting, the collision so forceful that he felt the vibration even though he was well out of harm's way.

And the blasted car kept going.

If the vehicle had been of more modern vintage, it would doubtlessly have ended its automotive life right then and there. But many was the time he could remember Uncle Ben proudly saying, "Dammit, this *is* your father's Oldsmobile," as he would crow over the car's old-style durability as compared to . . . as he said . . . "the tinfoil they're making cars out of these days."

Well, it turned out that Uncle Ben had been right, as the car vanished into the interior of the building.

Just thinking about Uncle Ben's words, dwelling on times that would never come again, fueled Peter's rage all the more. Police cars were now approaching, searchlights sweeping the exterior of the building, but Peter wasn't waiting around. Nor was he allowing any chance that the carjacker might somehow slip away.

He made his way into the darkened building, which turned out to be a warehouse. Whereas before he'd been reluctant to trust his spider sense, now he utterly turned himself over to its guidance. It didn't take long at all. Despite the grim blackness of the interior, he zeroed in on his prey, locating him on the second floor of the dilapidated structure.

The shooter was cowering in the corner, clutching a gun, glancing around desperately and peering into the darkness. He was wearing a cap. He might very well have sensed that he wasn't alone, but he didn't have a clue as to who else was there or from where an attack might come. It never even occurred to him to look straight up.

Peter practically slithered across the ceiling, undetectable by any ears that didn't belong to a citizen of the planet Krypton. Outside, police boats were cruising the East River. Slowly the shooter arose and went to the filth-encrusted windows, trying to peer out. As the carjacker checked his options, Peter released a webbing strand and slowly lowered himself to the floor.

He landed softly, just behind the shooter, still not making a sound.

And then a stray searchlight came through another window and, for just a moment, Peter's silhouette was projected on the wall to the shooter's right.

The shooter whirled and fired in one motion, and had it been a normal man standing behind him, the killer would have claimed another victim. But Peter simply leapt away, the bullet smacking harmlessly into the wall behind him.

Exterior lights played across the interior of the dank warehouse, elongating shadows, throwing false targets. Peter still couldn't see the shooter clearly; he was just a shadow with a gun. But it didn't matter. His spider sense was all he needed to guide him as the shooter blasted away randomly, desperately, and Peter effortlessly kept one step ahead of him the entire time.

Peter heard footsteps from all around the building, hammers being cocked, rounds being chambered. The cops were moving in, but there was no way—no way—he was going to let them get to the shooter first. The carjacker fired once more where he thought Peter was, but Peter was already sailing through the air, and he connected with the shooter's arm, sending the gun clattering across the floor. The shooter turned as if to go for it, but Peter grabbed him by the shoulder and whirled him around.

"This is for the man you killed!" howled Peter from the bottom of his soul, as he drove a roundhouse that connected with the carjacker's mouth. He felt a satisfying crack of bone under it; with any luck, he'd broken the man's jaw.

The carjacker was sent hurtling through the air, his cap flying off, and he slammed into one of the unbroken windows. The impact shattered the window, allowing floodlights to pour through freely, although the security grill outside held. The carjacker teetered for a moment, almost falling, then tumbled forward onto the grimy warehouse floor. Peter leapt into the window frame, grabbed the shooter up and hauled him to his feet.

The shooter was trying to talk, his speech hampered by the damage Peter had done to his jaw, but he managed to get out, "Don't hurt me . . . give me a chance, man, give me a chance . . . !"

Peter couldn't believe what he was hearing, and he shook the man furiously like a tornado molesting a tree, a force of nature that could not be stopped. *"Did you give him a chance?"* he raged. *"The man you killed! Did you? Answer me!"*

And in that moment, a moment where Peter was so filled with frenzy that he might well have torn the man's head off, Peter saw the man's face . . .

. . . and a piece of Peter's soul broke away and went screaming down into a hell of his own making.

Dear Mom and Dad . . .

You know. You must know, because Uncle Ben's with you now, and he told you about the guy. About what happened. About how we fought. The guy . . .

My fault. All my fault.

I went after him. And the whole time I was going after him, all I was thinking about was how I was at least going to do this one thing right, this one thing, after everything I'd screwed up. Except when I cornered the guy, when I had him right in my hands, I looked straight into his face, and he looked back at me with this . . . this terror in his eyes, and part of me was thinking, "I recognize this guy . . . where do I know him from?" I figured, you know, maybe from a post office wall or something . . .

And then I knew. It was him.

He'd run past me at an arena where I'd gone to be a big shot, to start a career as a high-priced wrestler. He'd run past me with a bundle of cash that he'd taken off some guy who I figured deserved it. Because I figured, you know, this guy, this promoter, he'd stiffed me, so the way I added it up, one bad turn deserved another. I kept thinking, karma, you know? Karma. And what I didn't stop to think about for a second was that by letting the guy go when it was in my power to stop him . . . by letting him commit a criminal act and laughing up my sleeve about it . . . I was performing my own bad turn. I was turning my back on the needs of society, a society that should be protected from creeps like that.

So the karma came back at me, and why couldn't it have come right for me, huh? Why couldn't it have bitten just me on the ass? But no, no . . . it went straight past me and nailed your brother, Dad, just . . . just nailed Uncle Ben.

It was the same guy. The thief from the arena was the same guy I was gaping at, up in that warehouse.

I dropped him, just staring at him, lights from outside flashing all over. He stood up and aimed a gun straight at me, and I didn't care. No, I take that back. I cared. Because at that second all the anger I'd been feeling, that I'd been turning outward, was turning inward. I started toward him, not more than ten feet away, and all I could think in my blind rage was, "C'mon, c'mon! Shoot me! Put a bullet in my chest! In my brain! Send me to be with Uncle Ben, because that's what I deserve!" At that moment I was in so much pain that the thought of living with it was unbearable.

He aimed at me point blank, grabbing up the canvas sack with his money in it, the blood money that Uncle Ben had died for. He squeezed the trigger and for a second I flinched in anticipation. Except nothing came. His eyes went wide and he fired again and again. Click click click, nothing, just . . . nothing. I couldn't believe it. He was out of bullets.

I let out a scream, then, and I have no idea what it must've sounded like to him. But the next thing I knew, he'd backed up too far, and he tripped over a piece of rotting paneling and smashed into a window. Unlike the previous one that had kept him from falling, this one didn't.

*There wasn't time for me to get a web shot off to snag him, so I
lunged forward, trying to catch him barehanded. I missed....*

I missed because I was too slow.

Or I missed because I didn't want to be fast enough.

I'll never know.

*And then he was gone, out the window and down, down. The side of
the warehouse faced out onto the river, so there was no sidewalk there.
There was, however, a wooden dock below...fifty feet below. He hit it
with a thud that sounded like a watermelon exploding. Money from his
canvas bag fluttered all around, some of it landing on his dead body, the
rest of it landing on the water and washing away. He'd lost his money.
He'd lost his life. Uncle Ben had lost his. The scales didn't seem balanced because...the one who'd started it off...was still there.*

*A police patrol boat was roaring down the river, and its spotlight
picked up the shooter's body. Then it swung up toward the window
where I was standing. I flinched back, throwing my arm over my face,
as much from the brightness of the light as from wanting to keep my
features obscured. One of the cops on the boat shouted, "There's the
other one! I told you there were two of 'em!" They didn't give me any
chance to surrender, to come out with my hands up, no matter how
much you hear that they're supposed to. They just raised their guns
and got ready to start shooting, probably figuring that I had the advantage since I had the altitude. They didn't want to take any chances
with a "cold-blooded murderer" like me.*

*They came pouring into the building as quickly as they could. Like
it did them any good. Like they could keep up with me. By the time they
were all running around on the first floor, I was already out and gone.
None of them saw me. None of them knew me. No one knows me. No,
while they were trying to find me, I was blocks away, crouched on a
rooftop next to a stone gargoyle, and I was sobbing like a baby. Saying "Uncle Ben...oh God...I'm so sorry..."*

Like God was listening.

Like God cared.

*You're with God, Mom and Dad. Next time you see him...you ask
him if he's satisfied. Is he pleased I got the lesson?*

He gave me these powers, and I tried to cash in on them, and I became selfish and self-centered. And I have to carry that with me every time I see, in my mind's eye, the body of Uncle Ben lying there in the gutter. And every time I see, in my mind's eye, the putrid face of that shooter, the one who got away. Who I let get away.

And I had to carry that with me when I saw Aunt May's face, when I had to share with her that her husband was never coming back, that he'd been taken away from her because of a violent world... a world that I did nothing to improve, except try and get into show business.

I'm like... like Scrooge, being told by the Ghost of Christmas Present that mankind should have been my business. I spat on gifts and ignored those who loved me, all for a power trip and the hope of making some fast money, and I can never, ever tell Aunt May about it because she would hate me forever.

If anyone should have died, it was me. I'm the one who had the opportunity to do something great with this power. Instead I'm left with the only father I've ever really known, lying in the cemetery. And the only mother I've ever really known mourning his passing.

You tell God... you tell him that I get it, okay? I get it. It's what Uncle Ben said... that with great power comes great responsibility. But responsibility for who? For what? It's sure not to my pocketbook, or to a life of fame and fortune. I saw what happened when I made those things important.

I have to look inward and outward, all at the same time.

I have to do something... before I go crazy with grief.

Something.

But what?

XII.

THE
GREMLIN

General Slocum was extremely impressed by the setup at Quest Aerospace, and with every passing moment he was feeling better and better about the prospect of dumping Os-Corp.

The facility itself was about as advanced as they came. Indeed, Slocum was almost looking forward to returning to the Pentagon and telling them that Quest was working on things that made current military technology look sickly. There was no doubt in his mind that Quest—and not Os-Corp—was the outfit with which they should be doing heavy-duty business.

The night air was stiff and exhilarating as Slocum and the project coordinator, Dr. Maddux, walked along the back of a concrete bunker at the Quest testing facility, moving past a sign that proclaimed in bold letters, BUNKER 6 QUEST AERO-SPACE PROVING GROUNDS.

Maddux was a remarkably personable man, devoid of Osborn's irritating intensity and arrogance. Instead, Maddux wore his confidence like comfortable shoes. "Our exoskeleton's got real firepower, General Slocum," he was saying proudly.

"If it does what you say it can," Slocum assured him, "I'll sign the contract tomorrow." But he wasn't looking at Maddux; instead his attention was focused on the war machine standing out on the test area.

The project's name was B.A.D.G.E.R.: Ballistic All Defense Guerrilla Explorer/Recon. However, some of the guys in the development team had claimed—rather tongue-in-cheek—that it really stood for BADass GEaR. The metal exoskeleton was situated on the tarmac, crouched like an oversized cross between a praying mantis and the ferocious little animal that it was named for. It glistened in the moonlight, and Slocum felt a chill of anticipation as he and Maddux stepped into the protective bunker. "I think I'm in love," Slocum said.

Maddux peered at him over a small pair of horn-rimmed glasses perched on the end of his nose. "I'm afraid I'm married, General."

Slocum laughed heartily at this. "Sorry, Doctor. I believe the object of my affections outweighs you just a bit." He peered through the slits of the bunker, admiring the B.A.D.G.E.R. as it awaited the test procedure.

"Now under ordinary circumstances," Maddux said, making some last minute checks via his handheld computer, "the B.A.D.G.E.R. would naturally be controlled by an on-board human operator."

"Like the fellow there," said Slocum. Sure enough, a test pilot was climbing into the unit, strapping himself in, and running a series of last minute checks on the control panels.

"Exactly right, General. That is, after all, the entire purpose of an exoskeleton: to be a sort of second skin to both protect a soldier and augment his strength." When Slocum nodded, he continued, "however, there is an auto-program built into the unit, which is designed to kick in should the human operator be rendered inoperative through a fluke or by an enemy. That's what we're going to be testing this evening. The human pilot will simply be along for the ride; everything else is going to be preprogrammed."

"Let 'er rip. Let's see the soldier of the future."

Cautiously, Maddux said, "And . . . what about your commitment to OsCorp?"

At that, Slocum chortled. "Nothing would please me more than to put Norman Osborn out of business." And he absolutely meant it. He'd endured Osborn's smug, insufferable manner for years now. It was one thing to have that attitude when you were producing things that made you irreplaceable. But Osborn was talking the talk without walking the walk, and Slocum's extremely limited patience had finally run dry. "Let's just hope no gremlins spoil the test."

"Gremlins?" asked Maddux, looking blank.

Slocum smiled in recollection. "In the old days, during World War II . . . something went wrong with the planes, the pilots always claimed a gremlin had gotten into the works."

"Well, General," laughed Maddux. "I assure you, the only gremlins that exist these days are odd-looking used cars. Nothing's going to go wrong."

The only equipment in the bunker was a radio unit that would enable them to hear communiqués from the test pilot in the B.A.D.G.E.R. "Jacobs. Can you hear me? Over."

"On line, over," came back Jacobs, the test pilot.

Maddux glanced toward Slocum, who gave him an encouraging thumbs up. "Bring mission profile on line, Jacobs," ordered Maddux.

"Beginning mission profile," replied Jacobs, "and . . . mark."

The B.A.D.G.E.R. trembled slightly as a roaring filled the air. The bunker did not vibrate in response, indicating that the walls were sufficiently sturdy and they would be safe enough should any unfortunate mishap occur. Not that Slocum was expecting any. It was clear that Quest had its act together.

Then the B.A.D.G.E.R. began to lift off, spewing a cloud of exhaust, rotating ninety degrees as its onboard jets prepared to send it at an angle across the tarmac.

Maddux was all smiles, about to issue another order, and suddenly the alarmed voice of the pilot came over the speaker system. "What the hell is that?" he demanded.

For a moment, Slocum thought this might be part of the test, but then he watched as the expression on Maddux's face moved from confusion to barely controlled alarm, and he knew something was wrong.

"Jacobs," Maddux started to say, "Jacobs, come in, what is . . ."

And suddenly the pilot's voice went up an octave as he screamed, "Oh my God! What is that?!? *Nooooo!!!*"

"Maddux," Slocum said warningly, not liking the way this test was going.

"I'm . . . sure it's just a glitch—"

That was when the B.A.D.G.E.R. exploded.

It happened utterly without warning. There was no sign of anything going wrong with any of the onboard mechanics. One moment the unit was there, hovering a few feet in the air, and the next it was a fireball of burning and twisted metal, the sound so deafening that Slocum was moaning as he held his ears. Pieces of the unit flamed toward them and ricocheted off the bunker. Maddux was gaping uncomprehendingly through the slit. The smell of burning metal wafted through the air.

Then something loomed out of the sizzling and smoky ruins. Some sort of . . . of creature, it appeared to be . . . a mechanical demon spat up from a techno hell, limber and tinted green, with a metal crest on its head, glowing yellow eyes, and a wide-open mouth filled with jagged teeth. It was flying, hovering on what appeared to be a . . . a glider . . . a glider that looked familiar, it looked . . .

. . . it looked . . .

Oh . . . God . . . thought Slocum, realizing where he had seen it before. And in doing so, he knew the true identity of the beast hovering twenty feet away, inspecting its handiwork. *Oh . . . my dear God . . .*

The green-tinted creature, looking like an oversized, monstrous gremlin, glanced right and left as if searching for new enemies. Then its attention fell upon the bunker, and if its mouth hadn't already been frozen into a grin, it would have split wide with mirth.

And the general reasoned that it couldn't be, simply couldn't be *him*. Couldn't be the man with the hard expression and the self-satisfied, smug air. Couldn't be the man whom the general had been gleefully planning to put out of business.

He started to shout, *"Osborn, what do you think you're doing!?"* and it was at that moment—when the high-powered missile detached itself from its holder beneath the flying platform and hurtled toward the slit in the bunker as if it had eyes—that Slocum realized Osborn in fact knew *precisely* what he was doing.

The missile struck the bunker, and although the structure had been designed to withstand a significant amount of punishment, the damage it sustained from the missile was far more than it was able to take. The bunker erupted in flames. Maddux barely had enough time for a scream; Slocum, not even that. Within seconds the conflagration had consumed the bunker and its inhabitants.

And with a demented cackle of glee, the gremlin spun joyfully in the air and bellowed, "B.A.D.G.E.R? B.A.D.G.E.R.? *We don't need no steenkeeng B.A.D.G.E.R.!*" Then he threw his arms around himself in a joyful expression of self-adoration, and jetted away into the night sky, his laughter drifting behind him.

XIII.

THE
TRANSITIONS

Peter wanted to feel good about it.

As he looked up at the clear blue sky, his view of which was suddenly interrupted by hundreds of mortarboards spiraling into the air, he wanted to do nothing but rejoice over the fact that he was about to leave high school behind. That his life was, in effect, about to begin, with everything up until now serving as a sort of lengthy preamble. But as the overjoyed cheers of his fellow graduates rang in his ears, all he could do was dwell on the fact that Uncle Ben wasn't there to see it, and he should have been. And it was Peter's fault that he wasn't.

But he knew he had to push such grim and depressing musings far, far away from him. Aunt May was like a bloodhound. If she scented the guilt that he was carrying, she would immediately start asking him what was wrong. So he forced a stiff-upper-lip grin, determined that no one would see the heaviness in his heart, and looked around for her.

Instead he spotted Harry, who was grinning with absolutely delirious joy. Peter couldn't blame him. Harry had, with Peter's aid, studied his butt off for the regents exams, and he'd nailed them. Harry war-whooped when he saw Peter and threw his arms around him. "We made it, buddy!" Peter said, smile plastered on his face. Truth to tell, with the infectious joy that Harry was giving off, it was hard not to share in the happiness.

Harry nodded, and then gripped Peter's upper arms in

excitement. "Good news! My father owns a building downtown with an empty loft he said we could have. Why not move in with me when you get to the city?"

Peter blinked. He'd been wrestling with the notion of how he could possibly support himself in the face of Manhattan prices, and had almost resigned himself to having to stay living with Aunt May. Still, it wasn't that easy. "I'm . . . not sure I can afford the rent," he admitted.

"We'll work something out!" said Harry with assurance.

Peter crossed his fingers. "Gotta get a job, first." Then he looked around, trying to spot Aunt May in the surging mass of parents and students surrounding one another.

Then he spotted her, standing much closer than he would have thought. And he was stunned when he saw to whom she was speaking. "Harry, look!" and he pointed.

Harry looked where Peter indicated, and his jaw dropped. "What're the odds?" he wondered as they pushed their way through the crowd.

They drew within range of Aunt May, and Peter caught the tail end of what she was saying. ". . . thought you might be Harry's father. He's the spitting image of you." Then she spotted Harry, who was in front of Peter, and called, "There's Harry!"

Harry made it over to his dad, Peter right behind him, and held up his diploma in his left hand as if it were the Olympic torch. "Hey, Dad!"

"You made it," Osborn said. "It's not the first time I've been proven wrong. Congratulations."

Jeez, I wonder if this guy plays tennis the way he compliments his son, because he's got a hell of a backhand, thought Peter, feeling irritated on Harry's behalf. But for Harry, apparently, it had the impact of a feather on a rock face, because when his father held out a hand, Harry shook it firmly. "Thanks," Harry said.

Obviously looking to bring some genuine warmth to the

moment, Aunt May embraced Harry and said, "Congratulations, Harry."

Suddenly Osborn's eyes focused on Peter, spotting him over Harry's shoulder. For no reason that he could determine, Peter felt a slight chill, as if his spider sense was making a vague attempt to stir to life. But Osborn certainly wasn't saying anything threatening. In fact, he looked happier to see Peter than he was to receive his own son. "Ah, hah! The winner of the science award!"

It was certainly hard to miss. It was a plaque about the size of Peter's forearm. He almost felt embarrassed to be hauling such an ostentatious thing around. He bobbed his head in acknowledgment of the compliment as Aunt May hugged him and said, "Here's our graduate!" She draped an arm around Peter. "You two looked so handsome up there!"

Osborn stepped forward and, to Harry's obvious annoyance and Peter's discomfort, put his arm—not around Harry—but around Peter from the other direction. "I know this has been a hard time for you, but try to enjoy this day. Commencement: the end of something. The start of something new."

"Thanks, Mr. Osborn."

"And if you ever need anything, you just call. And if and when you do, I'll be there to pick up the phone and say—"

"—you gotta be kidding me!"

Mary Jane's gaze darted back and forth in mild self-consciousness. She was holding her mortarboard under her arm, shaking out her hair, and she was doing everything she could to look nonchalant in the face of Flash's obvious fury. "No, Flash, I'm not kidding you. . . ."

"But we had everything planned out! About what we were gonna do when we got out of school!"

"Flash, *you* had everything planned out. Not me." There was still no sign of her parents. She couldn't have been more relieved. Having her folks there might have made this more difficult, if not impossible. She'd planned to tell Flash that evening when they went out, but she suddenly found that she simply couldn't wait. That even one more date with him would be giving more encouragement than she felt comfortable with. She brushed her hair back again; she tended to do that a lot when she was nervous. "I have a career I want to pursue . . . acting . . ."

"*Acting?* How about this, M. J.: You start acting like my steady girlfriend, which is what you're supposed to be. . . ."

"You know what the problem is, Flash?" she said, her green eyes burning with anger. "You were too busy listening to yourself to listen to me."

"You are being totally unfair!"

"I'm sorry you feel that way, Flash. Look," she said, "I just . . . I feel like I want to explore options."

He bristled, his face getting red with fury. "And what about how I feel? Isn't that at all important?"

"Flash, it's been nothing *but* your feelings for years now. You don't give a damn about my hopes, my dreams. . . ."

"You?" He snorted. "You dream of partying, and you hope there's another party after that. What, there's more?"

Something in his Neanderthal intelligence obviously warned him that he'd made a mistake just then. But it was too late to repair it, as Mary Jane yanked the steady ring off her finger and shoved it in Flash's hand. Without a word, an infuriated Flash cocked his arm, and for a moment Mary Jane flinched, thinking he was going to belt her. Instead he swept his arm around and let fly with the ring, sending it hurtling over the crowd. Then he turned back to Mary Jane, trembling, facing her with . . . rage? Embarrassment? Frustrated love? Any, all of the above?

And he growled, "There's gonna be payback for this. You won't know when or where . . . but definite payback." Then he spun on his heel and stalked away.

Mary Jane took in a deep breath, then let it out. She thought she should feel good . . . but all she felt was empty. For the first time in ages, she was alone. Totally, completely alone. All around her were her classmates, laughing, joyful, and almost all of them with their families. And here was M. J. with nothing. She knew her parents. They were probably fighting, and when they fought, they tended to lose track of time. When they started in on each other, nothing else mattered . . . least of all their daughter.

Her chin quivered as she fought to hold back tears, and suddenly there was someone standing next to her. She thought it might be her father; she feared it was Flash. She turned and reacted with surprise.

"You okay?" asked Harry Osborn. "I couldn't help but notice . . . Flash looked kind of pissed off. Is everything okay with—?"

And Mary Jane let out a soft cry and buried her face on the arm of a very surprised, but not the least bit displeased, Harry Osborn.

Peter let out a low whistle. "So they broke up, huh?"

They were standing outside the Parker home. Norman Osborn had given Peter and his aunt a lift home, and Harry was standing at the curbside next to the Bentley. Although Harry's father had made a point of saying that they couldn't stay, he relented to May's urging and was now inside the house, looking at the long and proud collection of Peter's various science awards. Peter was so mortified by the whole thing that he was staying out on the sidewalk with Harry, waiting for the ordeal to be over. Peter had his gown draped over his hands. "You're positive?"

Harry nodded. "She told me. I would have let you know, but you were busy talking to my dad. . . ."

"Yeah, I hope that doesn't bother you, him making a fuss over me—"

Harry shrugged. "Hey . . . if he likes you, and you like me, then maybe he'll like me better." Then he laughed. "Man, I wish you could have seen Flash's face. He looked like the guy from that movie poster for *Scanners* . . . you know, the one where his head looks like it's about to blow up. That's some timing, huh? On graduation day?"

"Well," sighed Peter, "I can't say I'm entirely surprised."

"You're not?"

"Look," and Peter shifted uncomfortably, glancing around as if concerned he was going to be overheard. "Just between us . . . ?"

"Sure."

"I'm pretty sure M. J.'s father has been giving her all kinds of crap about . . . well, about everything."

"Her?" Harry obviously could scarcely believe it. "You mean some guy's got a terrific daughter like M. J. and he rags on her?"

"More than you can believe." Peter lowered his voice even more, though there was no one around. "But as near as I can tell, he really liked Flash. So I think she stayed with Flash as . . . well . . . kind of protection, y'know? To survive. And also to feel a little bit less lonely in a family where love was hard to come by."

"Wow," Harry breathed, leaning against the lamppost.

"And by dumping Flash," concluded Peter, "it was almost as if she was signing her own Declaration of Independence."

"You've really got this whole thing worked out."

"Well," Peter admitted, "I've been giving her a lot of thought."

At that, Harry raised an eyebrow and looked at him sideways. "Hunh. Really. So are you planning to . . . y'know . . . make a move? Now that Flash is out of the picture?"

"Harry, she just broke up with the guy, for crying out loud. What, I want to be the guy on the rebound?"

"What's wrong with being the rebound?" Harry said reasonably. "Rebounds get played into slam dunks, too, y'know."

"I just . . ."

"You just what . . . ?"

Peter knew that if he happened to be looking in a mirror at that moment, he would have seen the haunted, dispirited look in his eyes. Because as much as he'd been fighting it up until that point, all he could think of was who wasn't there that should have been. . . .

She deserves better than me. . . .

"Peter . . . ?" Harry prompted him.

And Peter just shrugged. "We're too different. We'd never work. It'd be a train wreck. Trust me."

Harry started to reply, but then Norman Osborn came out of the Parker house, walking briskly. Peter noticed that when Osborn walked, his arms didn't swing at his sides like other people's. They stayed straight down, taut, contained. He looked as if he was capable of jumping into a few quick movements from *Riverdance.*

"You have a lot of awards, Peter," said Osborn. "Your aunt showed me every one. Every. One."

"Ouch," Peter said sympathetically.

But Osborn gave a wan smile. "I understand. She's proud of you. It's good to have children you're proud of. Just as I'm proud of Harry."

Harry looked thunderstruck, and as he climbed into the back of the Bentley with his father, he gave Peter a cheery thumbs-up. Peter grinned and stood there, watching the car pull away. Then he turned and walked slowly into the house.

Aunt May was beaming, looking at the science award, turning it around in her hands and examining it from every angle. His diploma was on the coffee table; she already had a frame picked out for it, poised and waiting next to it on the table. She glanced over her shoulder as Peter entered and started to trudge up the stairs. "May I fix you something?" she asked.

"No. Thanks."

He was trying to keep back the sadness, but he could tell from Aunt May's expression that he was failing miserably. Peter continued up to his room, not even bothering to close the door. Sitting on the edge of his bed, he interlaced his fingers and stared off into space. He had no idea how long he'd sat like that when Aunt May finally entered.

She knocked on the door, peering around the open corner of it, looking in at her nephew. Peter didn't stir, just sat there. She apparently took that as leave to enter, for she walked across the room and placed the science plaque on a shelf next to some other trophies. The diploma was already framed, and she placed it neatly on his desk. She took a step back, considered it, then moved it slightly and nodded with satisfaction over the minuscule adjustment.

Then she turned to Peter and just stood there, as if waiting for him to say something.

Finally he filled the silence. "I missed him a lot today," he admitted.

She nodded. "I know. I miss him, too." She took his hand in hers and said, "But he was there."

Peter was in no mood to hear about how Uncle Ben would always be there with them in spirit. *He was Ben Parker, not Ben Kenobi, for crying out loud. And having him in our hearts just isn't the same thing, so let's stop pretending that it is.*

But he didn't say any of that. Instead he just nodded, and then he started to say, "I just wish I hadn't—" *Let the thief go. Caused Uncle Ben's death.* All the real, true completions for the sentence, he didn't dare say.

"Peter," sighed Aunt May, "don't start that again."

No, he didn't dare talk about the true reason for Ben's

passing. So instead he focused on the only aspect of his guilt he felt safe discussing. "I can't help thinking about the last thing I said to him . . ."

"Stop it," she said firmly.

"He tried to tell me something important, and I threw it in his face."

There were many things Aunt May tolerated, but self-pity was not among them. "You loved him and he loved you," she said, her tone strong and certain. "He never doubted the man you would grow into. How you were meant for great things. You won't disappoint him. Or me."

She waited another moment, then squeezed his hand, stood, and headed to the door. She looked as if she wanted to say something else but refrained from doing so, instead walking through and allowing the door to click shut behind her.

Peter remained there alone for a time. And then, without even being aware that he was doing it, he was up and at his dresser. He pulled one drawer out completely, removed some sweaters that he'd piled in there, and proceeded to dig all the way to the bottom of the drawer.

It was there. The makeshift costume he'd worn when pursuing the crook. The red sweatshirt with the spider outline sketched onto its chest.

"Remember," echoed Uncle Ben's voice in his head, *"with great power comes great responsibility."*

But responsibility to whom? To what?

The answer became clear to him. To the living. To the dead. To those accused but not convicted. To the people who need help.

And to those who, faced with death, deserve to live and have a second chance to make things right.

But he couldn't do it from here. Not from the house where Uncle Ben—whom he had let down—no longer resided. And Aunt May, jeez, she'd be watching his comings and goings like a hawk. He needed mobility. He needed freedom.

He needed to do the job.

Dear Mom and Dad:

I'm going to keep this short, because a lot's been going on in the last few weeks.

I've moved in with Harry. It's great.

I've got a job. It's great, too.

The costume's done, which may or may not be great, because if I get myself killed, then the apartment and the job are pretty much moot.

But I have to try. That's really the lesson of all this, isn't it? I have to try.

If this works, I'm going to be making it a better world for a lot of people. If not . . . well . . .

. . . then I guess I'll see you soon.

XIV.

THE SPIDER-MAN

She missed him.

That's what it really came down to. She missed him.

Mary Jane stood at the pay phone on Fifth Avenue, hesitating for what seemed the hundredth time. Why should it be so difficult to speak to him?

Did he even think about her? Wonder where she was? What she was up to? Or was he busy with his own life? If she tried to contact him now, after all these months, would he think she was crazy? "What are you calling me for?" he might ask with real confusion in his tone. That was high school. High school is gone. We're adults. Go off, be an adult. Don't bother me, little girl.

A couple of people went past her, talking excitedly between them, and she heard the words "spider monster" being batted about. She rolled her eyes in annoyance. How long was *that* going to go on. There'd been some sort of mass hysteria throughout the city in recent weeks. People kept claiming there was some sort of human spider scuttling around the tops of skyscrapers, hiding in alleys. How in the world did these idiot rumors get started, anyway? And before this spidery creature, there had been albino alligators in the sewers, and Elvis pumping gas at truck stops in New Jersey. How did people let themselves be so gullible, anyway?

She took a deep breath, trying not to let the uncertainty that had infested her undermine what little strength she had left. The city had undergone a real cold snap, and she drew her threadbare coat more tightly around her.

Mary Jane Watson, party girl. Well, the party had sure gone on without her, hadn't it.

A half block away, a vendor was hawking pretzels to tourists. They were insanely overpriced, but because of the cold, people were snapping them up anyway. She actually considered it for a moment, but then checked her pockets and found that she had precisely four bucks on her, and that had to last her for the day since she wasn't getting paid until tomorrow.

The truth was . . . she was homesick. The problem was, home itself held no happy memories for her. But she wanted something. Something that would make her feel better about herself, that would remind her of at least the facade of happiness she once displayed.

Screwing her resolve solidly into place, she dropped the money into the slot and dialed the phone. It rang a couple of times, and then she heard a comforting voice on the other end.

"Hello?"

She took a deep breath and, putting as much upbeat inflection in her voice as possible, she said, "Hi, Mrs. Parker . . . it's Mary Jane."

"Mary Jane?"

Feeling slightly crestfallen, she said, "Watson."

There was a pause, and then sudden recognition that made her feel as if a weight had been lifted off her heart. "Little Mary Jane! From the house behind us!"

She nodded into the phone, which of course was a silly move, but she wasn't thinking about it. "Yes, that's me. I got your number from information. I hope you don't mind. . . ."

"Sakes, child, of course not! Little Mary Jane . . . well, not so little, of course. Not anymore. You were so wonderful as Cinderella, you know. In the school play, I mean."

She suppressed a laugh. "Yes, I still get lots of comments

about it." Then, taking a deep breath, "Well, look, Mrs. Parker, I was just wondering . . . is Peter around?"

"He doesn't live here anymore, dear."

For a moment, she felt utterly defeated. With her luck, he was in Chicago or Los Angeles . . . someplace like that. "Well, uhm . . . do you have a number for him?" She looked nervously at her watch, timing the call. The money would be falling through soon, and if Mrs. Parker had to rummage around in some shelf for five minutes to turn up Peter's phone number, that would be that.

"Of course, yes. I keep it pinned right here on the bulletin board next to the phone. Do you have a pencil?"

M. J. closed her eyes, prepared to recite the number to herself repeatedly to get it down. "Go ahead."

"It's area code 212 . . ."

Her eyes snapped. "That's Manhattan. That's here."

"Yes, dear."

"Here in New York City."

"Yes, dear, unless Manhattan's been moved to Illinois and no one told me." She paused. "That was a little joke, dear. Although, you know, perhaps it's not so funny. I remember when the Brooklyn Dodgers left. I thought my father, rest his soul, was going to throw himself off the Brooklyn Bridge. . . ."

The money fell through. The call had thirty seconds left and then would be automatically cut off.

"His address, Mrs. Parker. Could you tell me where he is? I just," and she took one last shot at sounding convivial. "I just figured I'd see where Peter is hanging around these days."

The robber bolted out of the Korean deli, not caring about the alarm the grocer had set off behind the counter. There were no cop cars around; he'd been too careful. By the time any responded, he'd be long gone.

He heard a string of invectives behind him, and turned to see the grocer coming after him, waving a baseball bat. His feet pounded the pavement, and when he glanced back over his shoulder, the idiot was still right behind him. It was incredible. The guy had to be in his fifties if he was a day, and he was keeping up. What was he, on the freakin' Korean Olympic sprinting team?

Well, enough was enough. There was no reason to let this farce continue.

The robber spun, yanked his gun from the inside of his jacket, and aimed it at the grocer. The grocer didn't even seem to notice; he kept coming at him, waving his bat, shouting in Korean.

"Fine, your funeral," snarled the robber.

But before he could fire, strands of gossamer white that looked fragile but were strong as steel wafted down from above, snared the gun, and yanked it from the robber's fingers.

He gaped as the gun flew through the air and, an instant later, stuck to the wall of a nearby building, held there by what looked like some sort of . . . webbing.

Uncomprehending, he completely forgot that he was in any sort of jeopardy, but he was promptly reminded of it as the baseball bat slammed him upside the head. He went down faster than dot-com stock. Even the grocer looked a bit surprised at what had transpired, but when he looked around to see what had happened, all he saw was a quick flash of blue and red disappearing down an alleyway . . . on a wall six feet above the ground.

"Did you see that?" he asked the robber in Korean, but then realized that the guy was unconscious. He kicked him once for good measure, and then went to phone the police.

Mary Jane took a deep breath and buzzed the street-level intercom at Harry and Peter's apartment. The writing on the tag said, in neat felt tip lettering, OSBORN & PARKER. Beneath that, in the same hand, the words "Attorneys at Law" had been scribbled. She smiled at that. Nice to know someone up there was keeping his or her sense of humor. Then she tilted her head back and studied the townhouse. Very nice. If she'd been living there, her sense of humor would probably be in much better shape, as well.

The door buzzer sounded without a voice speaking to her over the intercom. She shrugged, pushed it open, and entered the immaculate front hallway. She knew from the apartment number that Peter and Harry's place was one flight up, so she trotted up the stairs, her heels clicking on the wooden steps. When she got to the right door, she knocked.

"It's open," came Harry's voice from within.

She entered the apartment, glancing around. She'd been expecting something of a disaster area, considering it was two guys living on their own. But, startlingly, the place was immaculate. Harry was lying on an elegant living room couch that had black leather cushions, reading a book. The couch looked nice. Indeed, everything in the place was nice. Somebody in the apartment had money, and she had a sneaking suspicion it wasn't Peter.

"Hey, Harry," she said.

Harry both sat up and turned so quickly that he almost fell off the couch. He was wearing a T-shirt and gym shorts, and looked baffled and confused.

"Mary Jane?!"

"Last I looked."

"What are you doing here?"

"I was in the lady's room at Grand Central, and someone had written, 'For a good time, go to . . .' and this address was listed."

He stared at her blankly, reflexively straightening his hair. "What?"

"I was kidding. Peter's aunt gave me the address."

"And how'd you get up here?"

"You buzzed me up, Einstein," she laughed.

"Oh. Right." If Harry had looked any more sheepish, M. J. could have used him to knit a sweater. "I thought it was Peter. He forgets his keys sometimes."

"Ah."

There was a pause. Then Harry, as if suddenly remembering his manners, said, "Sit down! Sit down! Can I get you something to drink?"

"Anything. What'cha reading?"

He padded barefoot into the kitchenette, which was just off the living room. "*Interview with the Vampire*. Have you read it?"

"No. Saw the movie. The little kid in it creeped me out."

He came back with a couple of glasses and handed one to her. "Cheers," he said and they clinked glasses.

She sipped from the glass. "Ginger ale?" He nodded. "Harry, you wild man. Off and living on your own and you're getting crazy with ginger ale."

"You should see us scarfing Cheez Doodles. We're practically animals."

They laughed together, and then they were silent for a moment. "Do you know when Peter will be back?"

"Not sure. Think he might be at the lab. He's got a job at a lab, you know. So . . . you came by to see Peter, then?" Harry asked.

"Both of you, actually. I just . . . happened to be in the neighborhood, really. Thought I'd say hi. Uhm . . ." She looked down into her drink, feeling a bit embarrassed. "I should say thank you. For your help at graduation, I mean."

"Oh. No problem. Whenever anyone needs a shoulder to cry on, I'm more than happy to be there."

She got up from the chair, her glass empty. "Wow, you were thirsty. Want another?" When she nodded, he said, "Help yourself."

As M. J. poured out another glass, she leaned against the countertop and smiled sadly. "You must have thought that was some kind of timing on my part. Me breaking it off with Flash on graduation day."

"I guess it was. But it was understandable."

His casual tone of voice surprised her. She turned to look at him. "It was?"

"Well, sure." He appeared to be pondering the matter, reaching for a thought, or perhaps trying to recollect something he'd considered earlier. "Let me take a guess: You didn't get on great with your father, right?"

Mary Jane was utterly taken aback. "How did you know?"

"Takes one to know one. He put you down, right? Made snide remarks, made you feel worthless. Am I getting warm?"

"You're scalding!" she said in wonderment. Harry had had his feet up on an ottoman, but M. J. came over to him and sat on it now, so he put his feet on the floor. "I'm really impressed, Harry."

"Like I said, when someone's got the same difficulties in their life as you do, you just get a knack for telling. Let me guess," and he leaned forward, fingers steepled. "As much as your dad didn't like you . . . he adored Flash."

"Yes! That's exactly right!" Her face was flushed with excitement.

Warming to his subject, Harry said, "So, in a way . . . you stayed with Flash as long as you did because he offered a kind of protection. He helped you survive by giving your father something to like about you. And it made you feel a little bit less lonely in a family where love was hard to come by. But by dumping Flash, it was like you were sending a message to your father. Almost like you were signing your own Declaration of Independence."

"Holy God," breathed Mary Jane in awe. "I swear, Harry," and she took his hand in hers. "It's like you know me better than I know myself! I mean, some of that stuff I hadn't even really thought of before . . . but I think you're right! It's like you figured it out before I did! You are something else!"

"Aww," he said modestly.

"No, really! You're like . . . like Sherlock Holmes and Dr. Joyce Brothers all rolled into one."

"I'm just here to help," said Harry.

That was when Mary Jane's stomach rumbled, rather loudly. Her face colored with embarrassment. "I'm . . . I'm sorry."

"You're hungry."

She tried to laugh it off. "Yeah. I think the people downstairs probably know I'm hungry after that. Sorry . . ."

Briskly, Harry clapped his hands and bounced up from the chair. "Tell you what," he said. "I'm not sure when the heck Peter'll be home. How about I take you out to dinner. My treat. We can catch up on what each other is up to. Just lemme throw on some clothes."

But I wanted to talk to Peter . . . to tell him how I feel . . . but Harry's being so nice, and my stomach is killing me. . . .

"You got it, Mr. Osborn," said M. J.

Harry winced as he headed into the bedroom to grab some clothes. "Do me a favor; don't call me that. I hear 'Mr. Osborn,' I look over my shoulder for my father."

The alarm at the jewelry store at Forty-seventh and Seventh was screaming into the night air when the police car pulled up. Officers DeFalco and Owsley jumped out of the car. The two cops couldn't have been more physically opposite. DeFalco, the senior officer, was heavyset, middle-aged, and Italian, while Owsley was black, in his early thirties, and something of a health nut. Their nightsticks out, they saw the shattered doors at the front of the building. There were no signs of the perpetrators; more than likely they had hightailed it out the back.

Nevertheless they were cautious when they entered the building. But because the alarm was blasting so shrilly, they didn't hear the muffled noises of grunting and protest until they were already inside the room. Owsley and DeFalco looked around, trying to locate the source. It sounded like someone had been gagged.

Then they looked up.

For a moment they thought that what they were seeing was the staff of the jewelry store, rendered helpless by the crooks. But then they realized that there was a thick bag of loot attached to the two men who were dangling from the ceiling, helplessly wrapped head to toe in . . .

"What the hell is that?" DeFalco said, prodding it with his stick. The robbers—for that was who they were—shouted in protest over the fact that the cops were in no hurry to get them down. But since the white material was covering their mouths, they couldn't really make themselves understood.

"Man . . . looks like . . . some kind of cocoon . . ."

"What," DeFalco said skeptically, his voice thick with disbelief, "you're telling me that these two jokers were nailed by a giant caterpillar?"

Owsley rubbed some trailing threads between his fingers, noting the adhesion. "Or," he said with an air of great significance, "a giant spider, man."

"Great," snorted DeFalco. "Well, it's better than last week, when you read about those soldiers getting trashed in New Mexico and said some kind of incredible hulk did it."

Mary Jane still couldn't believe it, looking around the restaurant in wonderment. "*Sardi's,* Harry? I can't believe we're eating at Sardi's!"

Harry shrugged as if it were no big deal. All around them, framed caricatures of famous actors smiled out from the wall. The place was incredibly busy, and the aromas of the glorious food all around them were so pure and inviting that M. J. literally had to fight to stop her mouth from watering.

"And we walked right in!" she continued, waving the menu around. "It's usually impossible to get a reservation here! But we just walked in and the maître d' goes, 'M'sieur Osborn! Eet ees excellent to zee you again!'" she said, imitating his French accent.

Harry laughed and surveyed the menu. "You might try the roast duck. It's really good here."

"My God, the prices . . ."

He waved dismissively. "My treat, I said. Remember?"

"I know, but . . ."

"No buts," he said firmly. "You deserve it. You deserve some happiness."

Mary Jane leaned back in her chair and smiled sadly. "It's been a long time since I thought I did. Thank you, Harry."

"You're welcome. And anything I can do in the future to treat you the way you should be treated . . . you just tell me. Because you know why? You're high class, Mary Jane. High class, all the way."

"That's . . ." She almost felt breathless, giddy. "That's so sweet of you. I don't know what to say . . ."

"How about if you say," Harry leaned forward, taking her hand in his, "that you'll go out with me tomorrow night?"

And M. J. couldn't help but think how funny it was, the way things turned out. She'd gone to the apartment to see Peter . . . happened to run into Harry . . . and now here they were, at dinner in this gorgeous restaurant, and . . . and . . . and she was happy for the first time in ages. Yes, she felt happy with Harry and, even more . . . she felt safe with him.

"You're on," she said.

Mrs. Iola was hurrying home, the fish from the Krause Fish Market safely on ice in her bag, when the assailant stepped away from a lamppost that he'd been leaning against. Her eyes went wide and she took a step back as he pulled out a gun. "Give me the purse."

Intellectually she knew the thing to do was just hand him the purse. But she was too benumbed with fear. All she could do was stand there, trembling, slowly shaking her head—not in refusal to cooperate but in disbelief that this was happening.

"Now!" he snarled, cocking the hammer of the gun.

It was that noise, that distinctive, terrifying noise, that snapped her from her paralysis, and the purse almost leapt on its own from her hands to his. He snagged it. . . .

And then he was gone.

Except he had hadn't run off. He had simply disappeared.

Mrs. Iola blinked, then reached under her glasses to rub her eyes in confusion. She'd thought for a moment that there had been some sort of quick motion in front of her, a flash of blue, a blur of red, just before the mugger had fled the scene, but . . .

And then she let out a little shriek, startled, because her purse suddenly dropped down from overhead. The mugger, however, was nowhere to be seen. Slowly, her hands shaking, she knelt down, picked up the pocketbook, and only then did she notice a note attached to it.

It read, *Courtesy, Your Friendly Neighborhood Spider-Man.*

The TV newspeople were having a field day.

Since no one knew anything about him, no experts were required. It was the purest example of the old saying that everyone was entitled to his or her opinion, and this was certainly one of those instances where everyone had an opinion. Even the most low-rent of news operations could cover the story, because all they had to do was send out a camera crew to ask people in the street what they thought, and they were more than happy to spout off for the ten o'clock news.

"This is not a man," intoned a cabbie, parked at the cab stand outside Penn Station. "My brother saw it building a nest in the Lincoln Center fountain."

"Have you ever seen his face?" inquired a construction worker at a half-finished office building on Forty-ninth Street. When the TV reporter shook her head, he said, "Neither have I. Wait until his wife figures out he's running around in tights."

"Never mind the vigilante thing," said an irritated police officer outside the precinct house on Twentieth Street between Seventh and Eighth Avenues. "You see all those webs he leaves all over the city? I'm gonna cite the guy for littering."

The front page of the Daily Bugle *carried a story that was headlined,* COSTUMED FIGURE SAVES FIRE VICTIMS, *and above that an even larger headline that screamed,* WHO IS SPIDER-MAN?

At that moment, someone else was screaming back.

"He's a criminal! That's who he is!"

J. Jonah Jameson stalked his office as if he were ready to start chewing paint off the walls. He was clutching a copy of the bulldog edition of his own newspaper, and he was twisting it between his fists. His office was cluttered and chaotic, and all over the walls were citations of public service, framed front pages of news stories that Jameson had written back in his reporter days, and photos of Jameson with an assortment of world leaders. The office should have been a place that brought him much joy, considering how jammed it was with souvenirs of his accomplishments. Instead it was the place where he tended to vent most of his aggravation. It wasn't a happy place for him.

Nor was it a particularly happy place at that moment for

Robbie Robertson, Jameson's city editor. Robertson was a middle-aged African American with a head of close-cropped graying hair, an avuncular way of speaking, and a general air of confidence and erudition. And never were his powers of calm and patience tested more than when he was having a meeting with Jameson.

"A vigilante!" Jameson continued in his rant. "A public menace! What's he doing on my front page!"

Before Robertson could reply, an advertising manager named Ted Hoffman, bespectacled and nervous-looking, walked into the office, rapping on the door for a perfunctory knock. Jameson didn't especially like advertising managers. That was because he didn't especially like advertisers. He considered them a necessary evil, nothing more . . . and maybe even a good deal less. Hoffman knew that and looked as if he'd rather get a root canal or be sunk headfirst into a vat of warm monkey vomit than have to talk business with Jameson. "Mr. Jameson, we have a page six problem. . . ."

"We have a page one problem! *Shut up!*"

Hoffman was momentarily taken aback, and Robbie seized the momentary silence—a rare enough event in Jameson's presence—to say, "He's news."

Jumping in, Hoffman said, "They're a major account, it can't wait."

"It's about to," Jameson informed him.

Hoffman started to open his mouth, but this time it was Robertson . . . obviously feeling that he was nearing the end of his patience tether . . . who ignored Hoffman and said to Jameson, "He saved six people from burning to death—"

"—in a fire he probably started!" When Jameson saw Robertson's incredulous expression, he tried to sound friendly, as if it were all a big misunderstanding. As if, once Robertson had come around to Jameson's rock solid point of view, everything would work out. "Something goes wrong, and this creepy crawler's there! What's that tell ya?"

"Jonah, he's a hero!"

Jameson circled his desk so that they were standing face-to-face and said reasonably, "Then why does he wear a mask? What's he got to hide?"

Forcing himself into the discussion, Hoffman, said, "We double sold page six. Both Conway and Macy's bought three quarters of it."

"We sold out all four printings, Jonah," said Robbie.

That stopped Jameson cold. He stared at Robertson, trying to digest mentally what he'd just heard.

"Sold . . . out?"

Robertson smiled in that way he had when he knew resistance from Jameson was about to melt away. "Every . . . copy," he said, savoring each syllable.

Immediately Jameson's discussion at the club with Norman Osborn came to mind. That discussion in which Osborn had told Jameson that if he wanted to get his circulation on the rise again, he needed to put forward a hero to the public. One they could embrace and would desperately want to read about.

But . . . this masked man? A hero?

Jonah didn't like it. It went against the grain. Anonymity . . . it was a sickening notion to an old newsman who had attached his name to stories for decades. Stories that could have gotten the crap kicked out of him. Spider-Man was definitely hiding something, and if someone had something to hide, it was never anything good.

But . . . a hero . . . newspaper circulation . . . copies jumping off the newsstand, sales going up, money flooding back into the coffers. Jonah's newsman instincts collided head on with his desire to turn his newspaper, his beloved *Daily Bugle,* back into a profit-making venture.

And then, as if receiving a burst of enlightenment from

above, Jonah reached a magnificent compromise. Who did the public adore, become fascinated with, even more than heroes?

Villains. The Dahmers, the Mansons, the Sons of Sam . . . those types captivated and engaged the attention of the buying public. Jonah Jameson could have the best of both worlds. On the one hand he could present Spider-Man as a heroic individual, at least to start, to get people back into the newspaper-buying habit. At the same time, he could point out to people that there was likely something very sinister, some dark secret, that the wallcrawler was hiding. That would give him a dangerous edge and make him even more interesting.

All of that went through Jameson's mind in a flash, and then he declared—as if he had just suddenly hit upon the notion that carving bread into slices might be a truly nifty idea—"Spider-Man, page one, tomorrow!" He scowled at the front page and added, "With a decent picture this time!"

Hoffman cleared his throat to catch Jonah's attention. Casting an annoyed glance in his direction, Jameson snapped, "Move Conway to page seven."

"There's a problem with page seven," began Hoffman.

Jameson, however, did not want to hear it. "Then move them to page eight and tell 'em we'll give 'em an extra column inch. Now get out of here!"

Bobbing his head in agreement, and looking extremely relieved to be distancing himself from the whole matter, Hoffman backed out of the door. Robbie Robertson didn't even watch him go. "Can't get a picture. I've had Eddie Brock on it. Nobody ever gets more than a glimpse of him."

Jameson was appalled at the apparent ineptitude of his staff. "What is he, shy?"

"Perhaps," Robertson said, trying to sound reasonable. "Not everyone is out for fame, Jonah."

That excuse didn't fly with Jameson at all. Thudding his

fist on his desk, he barked, "If we can get a picture of Julia Roberts in a thong, we can certainly get a picture of *this* nut!" He rolled his cigar from one side of his mouth to the other as he considered the situation. "Put an ad on the front page," he said finally. "Cash money for a picture of Spider-Man. Doesn't want to be famous? Then I'll make him . . . infamous!"

XV.

THE
MYSTERY
GIRL

It was everything Peter could do not to hack violently as he buttoned his shirt while running across the Empire State University campus. He was starting to wonder if he was going to cough up a lung. But he had to be cautious; he was wearing his Spider-Man uniform underneath his clothes, a habit he had taken to in recent days. He certainly didn't want to be running around the campus with his oxford shirt hanging open and his costume visible.

He tried to button the top button, and this time when the coughing seized hold of him, he couldn't keep it back. He knew he should consider himself lucky. He had, after all, inhaled a lot of smoke yesterday while rescuing those people. If he'd taken in too much—and it wouldn't have required a lot—he could have been dealing with a collapsed lung by now. The smart thing would have been to get himself to a hospital to be checked over as soon as he'd gotten those people clear. But he was afraid a barrage of questions would be forthcoming, to which he wouldn't have answers. In his worst case imaginings, the hospital would call the police, more questions would be posed that he couldn't answer (such as why he was near the burning building) and in no time he'd be in jail, suspected of arson.

No, better to tough it out.

As a result, his chest was aching from the miserable night's sleep he'd had. When he'd finally managed to get some shut-eye, it was close to five A.M., and then he slept through his alarm going off. His only chance of getting to school on time had been to websling over, except on his way he'd wound up helping a would-be suicide who'd climbed out on a ledge. That delayed him even further, and by the time he'd arrived on campus—muscle-weary, still-sharp pains in the chest—he felt like something that'd been scraped off someone's shoe.

He darted across the campus, getting to the science building just as Dr. Curt Connors emerged. Indeed, if not for a quick warning from his spider sense, he would have gotten slammed in the face with the door. Connors hadn't seen him coming because he'd been busy shoving the door open with his shoulder. He only had one arm, and in his existing hand he was holding a small cage with an iguana in it.

Connors looked down at Peter. The scientist wasn't espe-cially short-tempered, never flying off the handle easily. If anything, as the lantern-jawed scientist stared at Peter, he ap-peared more disappointed than anything else. He was wear-ing a long, white lab coat, and the empty sleeve was pinned up. "Dr. Connors . . ." Peter began.

"You're an hour late, Parker," Connors said, allowing the door to swing shut behind him. "Class is over. You missed another . . . session . . ." He allowed the word to trail off, be-cause he was staring at Peter's general demeanor. Peter glanced at his reflection in the glass of the door, and quickly realized why. He was disheveled, and part of his hair was still singed from the heat he'd endured in the burning build-ing. Connors looked as if he was about to ask Peter what in the world had been going on in his life, and Peter quickly started formulating responses.

But instead the professor just shook his head. "I'm sorry, Peter, you have a hell of a scientific mind, but you can't seem to get your priorities straight. You've been late six times this semester."

"Professor, please, let me explain. . . ."

Connors put the caged iguana on the ground and said with a heavy sigh, "This is a paid internship. Do you know how many freshman applied for it?" He put his hand on Peter's shoulder, shook his head, then turned and picked up the iguana cage.

Peter couldn't believe it. The look on Connors's face was clear. Urgently refusing to believe this was happening, Peter said, "Dr. Connors, I *need* this job!"

"I like you, Peter," Connors said, not unkindly, as he walked away. "Come see me when you grow up a little."

Peter stood there, numbly staring after the departing Connors. Just like that. Just like that, he was unemployed.

It just seemed so damned unfair. Here he'd been nearly running himself into the ground, just trying to help people. And he'd gotten himself fired because of it. Anger welled up in him, stinging at his eyes, and he wiped his arm across his face to make sure no tears flowed, because he'd be damned if he stood there crying on the ESU campus, even if the tears were flowing mostly because he was so blasted tired.

He tried to take an emotional step back and see it from the professor's point of view. On that basis, he supposed he could understand. Connors hadn't taken him on because he wanted a series of excuses. He wanted an enthusiastic freshman who would be there when needed. And Peter hadn't been there. You snooze, you lose. The race is to the swift. All those other clichés came to mind as Peter tried, really tried, to view the situation the way the professor probably viewed it. On that basis, he supposed he could understand why Connors had just given him the heave-ho.

On the other hand, part of him, a nasty, insidious part, couldn't help but hope that stupid iguana would mutate, bite

Connors, and turn him into a giant lizard. Then Connors would get to see life from Peter Parker's point of view.

As if *that* would ever happen . . .

Trying to take his mind off matters, Peter trekked over to the ESU library, took a couple of hours to get some studying done, and then headed home. Considering he was feeling a bit down, he decided to walk the distance that he normally would travel by subway . . . or, if he was feeling adventurous, by webs.

On the way, he picked up a newspaper from the stand. Leaning against a wall, he flipped to the want ads. There seemed to be a few possible prospects . . . none of them particularly interesting. But at least they'd put food on the table. Harry had been incredibly elastic about Peter's share of the rent. The main reason, of course, was that Peter was helping him with his studies. Harry had made a point of saying that, as far as he was concerned, Peter could live there rent free and Harry—for getting his grades salvaged—was still getting the better part of the bargain.

But Uncle Ben and Aunt May had spent long years drilling a work ethic into Peter. Consequently, if he didn't chip in for the rent, he'd feel like a freeloader no matter how many tutorial skills he was bartering.

He found one address, of an employment office that wasn't too far away, and he started heading in that direction.

But as he walked, he did so with a very different attitude than he'd once had. Once upon a time, he would have just walked along the sidewalk like anyone else: involved in his own thoughts, occasionally glancing at others if they did something interesting, but otherwise utterly self-absorbed. Or even, God forbid, yakking on a cell phone. That Peter Parker was gone, however. In his place was a young man who was constantly looking all around him, sizing people up.

There was a woman whose little boy was pulling urgently on her hand. Was there a danger he might slip loose and run into traffic? No, it was okay . . . she scooped him up so that he wouldn't wiggle away.

There was a man, glancing right and left before entering a jewelry store. Was he going to rob it? No, it was okay . . . a minute later, he reemerged, quickly slipping a small box into his pocket as a young woman, obviously his girlfriend, walked up to him and kissed him on the cheek. He must have picked up an engagement ring on the sly, and they were going somewhere where he'd propose to her.

Yet another false alarm.

Peter's head felt as if it was whirling. He was starting to think he was responsible for the safety of every single person in Manhattan. He realized that if he didn't start reordering his thoughts, if he didn't start coping with his power, it was going to overwhelm him. He'd likely end up curled into a sniveling ball, not knowing where to look first.

But he couldn't help it.

Over there . . . a guy approaching an elderly woman. She was clutching her pocketbook nervously while standing on the edge of a curb. Was he about to knock her down, grab it? No . . . no, it was okay. He spoke to her softly, extended an arm. She looked exceedingly grateful as he walked her across the busy intersection, tipped his hat, and walked away.

And over there, at some seedy-looking diner with the word MOONDANCE in neon letters overhead, except the first N was burned out, so it seemed as if it were someplace that cows went to boogie, there was a nervous-looking, red-haired young woman, emerging with a raincoat drawn tightly around her, as if concerned she was in danger from some . . .

He did a double take as she walked right past him. "Hey!" he said in astonishment.

"Buzz off," she snapped back.

"Mary Jane Watson?!"

She froze on the sidewalk. It was as if . . . as if her own name frightened her.

Peter approached her, cautiously, delicately, as if she were a deer in the headlights about to bolt. "M. J.? It's me . . . Peter . . ."

Mary Jane tried to laugh lightly, but she seemed embarrassed to see him. "What are you doing around here?"

He held up the classifieds and said, "Begging for a job. What about you?"

"I'm, uh . . ." Her mind seemed to be racing, ". . . headed for an audition."

The way she said it struck Peter as wrong somehow, but he wasn't about to call her on it. "So you're an actress now! That's great!"

She still hadn't turned to face him. "Uh-huh," she said, and in a voice that sounded as if she were choking back a sob, "It's a dream come true."

Suddenly the door of the diner burst open and a surly looking cook stepped out. He was clutching a pile of restaurant checks in his large fist, and a smell was coming off him that was reminiscent of rotting meat. Peter wasn't sure if it was his own personal aroma or an odor that was clinging to him from the food.

"Hey! Glamour girl!" he growled "Your drawer's off by six bucks! Next time I take it out of your check, y'get me?"

M. J. didn't look at him. It was as if she were pretending he wasn't there. And Peter's heart went out to her in her mortification, because the truth of the situation was so apparent that a blind man would have seen it. The cook, meantime, wasn't letting it go. "Excuse me, Miss Watson. I am speaking words to you. You get me?"

Her shoulders sagging in defeat, she choked out, "Yes, Enrique, okay? I 'get you,' Enrique."

Peter saw red at that moment, and it wasn't in the color of M. J.'s hair. Enrique, although he didn't know it, was a heart-beat away from finding his teeth situated somewhere in the back of his throat. Either that or being hauled up the side of a building, across the rooftops, and finding himself hanging naked from the top of the Washington Square arch. All it required was for him to open his big mouth and say one more rude word, just one, to Mary Jane.

Fortunately or unfortunately, depending upon how one chose to look at it, Enrique picked that moment to stop speaking. He simply turned and stomped back into the diner.

M. J. let out a long, unsteady sigh, and then turned around for the first time. She did not, however, look up. A chill wind blew across her, ruffling her hair. With a self-deprecating laugh, she quickly opened and closed the raincoat, like a flasher, just long enough for Peter to see the stained waitress uniform she was wearing underneath. "It's just temporary. Few extra dollars," she said.

He tried to put on his most Uncle Ben–like tone. The voice that assured the listener that things weren't remotely as bad as they seemed. "Well, that's nothing to be embarrassed about. I've been fired from worse jobs than that." He paused and was about to ask her out for a cup of coffee . . . or maybe a drink . . . or maybe even dinner. He had a few bucks in his pocket, he could splurge, treat her. Nothing fancy. Catch up on things.

All the old feelings came flooding back to him. He re-membered feeling as if he didn't deserve her, or couldn't do enough for her, but things changed, and—

"Don't tell Harry."

That stopped him cold. Peter stared at her in bewilder-ment. "Harry . . . ?"

Now she actually looked up at him. She looked just as confused as he did. "We've been going out," she said as if it was common knowledge. Her eyes narrowed. "Aren't you guys living together? Didn't he tell you?"

He blinked, trying to kick start his brain back into motion. "Oh, yeah!" he said, as if it had simply slipped his mind. "Right . . ."

"I think he'd hate the idea of my waiting tables," she said. "He'd think it was . . . low."

"Well, Harry never has lived on a little place I like to call Earth," Peter said with such chipperness in his voice that none of the bitterness he was feeling at that moment was evident.

M. J. laughed at that and visibly relaxed. Feeling buoyed by her reaction, Peter continued, "M. J., probably half the people starring on Broadway were waiters or even dishwashers."

She looked at him with that tilt to the head she often used. "How come you always make me feel better?" She jumped up and down slightly to keep herself warm, and then obviously feeling the need to get moving, she said, "Well . . . bye, Peter."

Mary Jane started to walk away, and part of Peter's mind shouted at him to run after her. But the man who was capable of vaulting rooftops without batting an eye, who swung heartstopping distances supported by nothing except strands of webbing and thought nothing of it, was too afraid to do anything except remain rooted to the spot. He settled for calling down the street, "Maybe I'll come down and have a cup of your Moondance coffee some day!" Then quickly he added, lest she be concerned, "And I won't tell Harry."

"No, can't tell Harry," she affirmed with a glance over her shoulder.

And then she was out of earshot as Peter said softly to himself, "No, I won't. I won't tell Harry. Harry . . . and Mary Jane. Wow." Then he turned and walked in the opposite direction.

He wanted to be angry with Harry. He wanted to feel that his supposed friend had swiped Mary Jane out from under him. But he had learned all too well the importance of taking responsibility for one's actions, and the fact was that it was his own actions—or inactions, for that matter—that had led to this. Without realizing he was doing it, he'd given Harry a clear path to Mary Jane, and his roomie obviously had taken it without hesitation.

Don't tell Harry.

He muttered, "Don't tell Peter."

Except, of course, it was too late.

Evening was just settling in after a long, fruitless, and frustrating day for Peter, who was wondering just how things could possibly get worse. When he opened the door to the Tribeca apartment he shared with Harry, he quickly found out.

Harry was seated at the dining room table, books spread out all over the place. That was nothing unusual. However, the new addition to the picture of Peter's domestic life was Norman Osborn, pacing and talking into a cell phone. Peter couldn't help but remember that those things were purported to cause brain cancer, and wondered why no one seemed to care about that anymore. Maybe he could do a study on it. Either that or just get a cell phone and use it in hopes of rotting away the brain cells that caused him such worries.

Osborn spotted Peter and nodded in acknowledgment of his presence. Peter felt honored. He headed over to Harry and dropped into a nearby chair as Harry looked up ruefully. "Stormin' Norman, making his weekly inspection," he muttered. "Spends half of it on the phone. Man, am I glad you're here," he continued, indicating the open books. "I need your help. I'm hopelessly lost." Harry had been so caught up in his father's presence and the challenge of the material in front of him that it took him a while to actually look at his roommate. But when he did, he frowned. "What's wrong with you? Somebody run over your dog?"

I don't have a dog. I don't have a girlfriend, either, thanks to you, you—

"No," Peter sighed, feeling that a portion of the truth was preferable to manufacturing something from whole cloth. "I, uh . . . I was late, and Dr. Connors fired me."

Harry leaned back, stunned. "Late again? What is it with you? Where do you go all the time?"

"Around," Peter answered vaguely.

Shaking his head, Harry said, "For a completely responsible guy, you're completely irresponsible."

There was a definitive snap from Osborn's cell phone as he closed the cover and turned toward Peter, all smiles. "Peter Parker!" he said, as if having just discovered the cure for the common cold. "Maybe you can tell me who she is!"

Peter stared at him blankly. "Who?"

"This mystery girl Harry's been dating."

Peter's spine froze. The one thing in the entire world that Peter would rather not have been discussing at that moment, and guess what was being shoved in his face. At that moment he felt like walking over to the wall and thudding his head against it, repeatedly. Then he tried to recall if there had been one day since Uncle Ben was killed—just one—that was a genuinely, sunrise to sunset, good day. Nothing was coming to mind. He wondered if he'd ever have one again.

"Dad . . ." Harry moaned, clearly chagrined that Peter was being yanked into the discussion.

Osborn was still talking to Peter, looking hopeful, even good-humored. "I think he wants me to meet this one, and believe me, it's the first time that's hap—"

"Dad!" Harry couldn't have acted more mortified if his father had hauled out naked baby pictures and passed them around at the prom.

His father looked at him questioningly, wondering why his son was raising such a fuss.

Very softly, and trying to keep any accusatory notes out

of his voice, Peter said, "Sorry . . . Harry hasn't mentioned her."

Making a very obvious attempt to change the subject, Harry said, "Hey, Pete, you're probably looking for work now. Dad, maybe you can help him find a job?"

Spider sense tingling

It was so odd. Here they were, in their own apartment, and there was no threat to him. No danger present at all. And yet somehow, for some reason, he was feeling the slightest warning of danger rattling around at the base of his skull. For reasons Peter couldn't even articulate, he suddenly felt the need to distance himself from the table. He got up and headed for the kitchen, saying, "Oh, no. I appreciate it, but I'll be fine."

"It's no problem," Osborn assured him. "I'll make some phone calls. . . ."

"No!" Peter said far more sharply than he would have liked, so forcefully that Harry actually jumped slightly. Reining himself in, he said in a more moderate tone, "I couldn't accept it. I like to earn what I get. I can find work."

There was silence in the apartment for a moment as Harry looked nervously up at his father. But Norman simply nodded and, somewhat to Peter's surprise, said, "I respect that. You want to make it on your own steam. That's great." Then, very pointedly, he said to Harry, "Interesting, isn't it? Peter is *looking* for work. As in, actively seeking, as opposed to strenuously avoiding . . ."

Harry eyed a nearby pen thoughtfully, as if considering whether he should drive it into his own eye or not. "What do you want from me?" he sighed. "I'm trying to keep my grades up."

"I want you to be able to do more than one thing at a time, son," said Norman reasonably. "The world will always pull you in different directions. If you don't learn to cope with it, well . . . that way lies madness."

Peter tried to take a philosophical attitude toward the situation as the Osborns talked. Considering the burden he was carrying in school, and the expectations of his father, should Peter really begrudge Harry what little happiness he was able to garner with Mary Jane?

Hell, yes, he thought bitterly.

He picked up a copy of the *Daily Bugle* off the kitchen table, hoping that perhaps the want ads in that newspaper would be more productive than the washouts the *Trib*'s classifieds had provided. He flipped open the front page, looking for the index, and stopped dead.

He focused on the headline, his eyes widening in disbelief.

Harry's father was saying something to him, but it wasn't registering. Instead he was staring at the crude sketch of Spider-Man's face, under the headline, WANTED: PHOTOGRAPHIC PROOF! BUGLE OFFERS REWARD!

"Parker!" Osborn repeated, commanding Peter's attention, "Do you have any other skills?"

With a small smile, Peter said, "I'm thinking of something in photography."

XVI.

THE
PHOTOGRAPHER

The 35mm camera had been carefully suspended in the cornice of the third floor of the building. Peter peered through the lens one more time to make sure it was properly targeted and working. The words AUTO SHUTTER flashed in red in the lower right corner of the viewfinder.

The view through the lens was a wide angle, giving him a nice view of the entire front of the bank. Moments later, the doors of the bank burst open and three robbers burst out, waving guns. Pedestrians fell back with terrified screams.

"Showtime," Peter muttered beneath his mask.

Battling Jack Murdock, still walking with a limp after his encounter with Bone Saw McGraw months ago, was on his way into the Citibank when he stopped dead in his tracks. He couldn't believe it. It was the kind of thing he saw only on television or in the movies.

The robbers charged out of the bank, shouting for people to keep back. Jack was no fool. This was no wrestling ring. This was real life. So he stayed right where he was, making no sudden moves, lest he draw their attention.

Police sirens sounded in the near distance and the robbers, all of whom were masked in ski caps, looked at each other nervously. Obviously they hadn't expected the cops to get so close, so fast. The fourth of their crew was at curbside in what was obviously the getaway car, and he was madly gesturing for them to hurry the hell up. But traffic was bottlenecking all around them—this was midtown Manhattan, after all—and they might not make it far enough away before the cops drew within distance. Plus there were witnesses who could identify the license plates and put the police on their tracks all too quickly.

All this went through Jack's mind in a heartbeat, and suddenly one of the robbers pointed a gun at Jack and snarled, "You! Come with us!"

"M-me?" said Jack, his voice going up an octave.

"In the car, now!"

Oh, my God, I'm a hostage, thought Jack.

Suddenly there was a collective shout, gasps, people pointing upward. Despite the fact that there were armed robbers standing on the sidewalk, they had abruptly become of secondary interest compared to the sight that presented itself now.

A lithe figure in tight-fitting red and dark blue descended from on high like an avenging angel. He wore red boots, a red belt, and a pattern that ran the length of his torso and down his arms, and his mask was frightening with its wide, silver-white eyepieces that obscured his face completely. An intricate, slightly raised web pattern ran along the red material, and there was an image of a spider on his chest. The rest of the costume was dark blue, although it was shimmering as he descended and appeared to have black highlights. He was swinging on gossamer strands of webbing . . . a gigantic spider crossed with Tarzan of the Apes.

He'd been heard about, rumored about, speculated about. But no one had ever seen him clearly in broad daylight. No one . . . until now.

It was Jack who spoke first, crying out in a startled voice, *"Spider-Man!"*

Immediately the bank robbers, as one, started firing right at him. Except he was no longer there. Releasing the web line so that the arc of his swing couldn't be tracked, Spider-

Man somersaulted through the air. Even as he did so, he crisscrossed his arms and unleashed sprays of webbing. With pinpoint accuracy it nailed the guns of the three robbers, gumming up the works and causing the weapons to adhere, useless, to their hands.

Spider-Man landed on the sidewalk right in front of them. They came in fast, the three of them converging as one. All they managed to do was slam into each other, because Spider-Man—having barely touched the ground—immediately bounced up as if he were on strings. Before they realized it, he was behind them. He grabbed the respective heads of two of them and slammed them together with a resounding crack. The duo went down as if they'd just been slammed with a two-by-four.

The third, the burliest one, swung his webbed-up gun hand, trying to use it like a club. Spider-Man ducked under each sweep, and as he did so, he said jovially, "Shall we dance? Cha-cha-cha . . ." It was as if he weren't in a life-and-death struggle and all. As if the whole thing were just a game to him.

On the fifth swing, he caught the arm effortlessly. The robber was stunned, unable to believe that he was being immobilized with so little effort, and then Spider-Man literally turned him upside down. "You know," Spider-Man said to him conversationally, dangling him by his feet, "when you open a new account here, they give you a free toaster. Should have settled for that. Let that be a lesson to you: Get a toaster . . . or be toast."

And with that, he tossed the robber on top of the heap of his already fallen associates. He started to get up, but a quick, casual spin kick from Spider-Man knocked him out.

The getaway car driver hit the gas, tried to pull out, but he was already too late. Spider-Man bounded over to him and called, "Nice car! I might buy it! Mind if I kick the tires?!"

He delivered a powerful kick to the right front tire that blew it out as quickly as if it had slammed into a concrete median strip.

Immediately the driver tried to leap out of the front seat in hopes of getting away . . . except he found himself webbed to the seat. Spider-Man cheerfully waggled his fingers at him. "When Spider-Man's putting on a show," he called, "there's never a dry seat in the house!"

And then, with the flashing lights of the police cars approaching, barely a block away, Spider-Man took a running start, bounced off the roof of the car and fired a web line all in the same motion. An instant later he had swung up and out of view, leaving behind four criminals and a wave of spontaneous applause from the onlookers.

Moments later Jack was at the nearest pay phone, dialing frantically. It rang on the other end and then picked up. "Hello?"

"Matt!" Jack burst out. "Son, wait'll I tell you about the genuine daredevil who saved your old man . . . !"

"Spider-Man."

The man who'd been introduced to Peter as Joe "Robbie" Robertson was looking him right in the face, and for a moment Peter thought that he'd been seen through just that easily. That this newsman had figured out that Spider-Man was, in fact, a nervous college kid who was trying to pull a fast one on the largest tabloid newspaper in New York.

But then Robertson looked back at the picture and said, "Spider-Man . . . he really exists," and he shook his head in amazement. "I was starting to think he was an urban legend. If you hadn't had us develop the negatives ourselves, I would have thought you doctored these with a computer or something."

Relaxing a bit, Peter said, "I thought you might think that. That's why I did it this way."

"Bright lad."

They were standing in the middle of the newsroom. Reporters made it a point of passing by, glancing over Robertson's shoulder with interest as he flipped through the stills. Word had spread quickly; unsurprising, since these were reporters, after all. Robertson pretended to be unaware of the fact that everyone was stopping by to sneak a look, first at the photos, and then at the unassuming young man who had snapped them. Peter forced a smile but then started looking down self-consciously and kept his attention focused on the floor.

Spider-Man swinging, flying, web shooting . . . they were all there, everything any newsman could ask for. "They're good. Very good. How'd you get 'em?" asked Robertson.

"If I tell you, you'll send your own photographer. Am I hired?" he asked.

"It's not up to me," said Robertson. "Mr. Jameson hires all staff personally."

That was when they heard shouting from an office down the hall. The person doing the shouting sounded as if he could out-holler a cement mixer. *"Is that what I said?! Is that what I asked? I said a picture, Eddie, not an ink blot! Why the hell can't anybody bring me decent art on that freak?! Get the hell out of here!"*

Peter didn't know which was more shocking: the volume and vehemence of the person shouting, or the fact that no one else in the newsroom really seemed to be reacting. "He fires 'em that way, too," Robertson said mildly. When he saw Peter's incredulous reaction, he seemed to intuit what was going through the lad's mind. "It's like living beneath an elevated train, son. After a while, the shock just wears off, and you barely hear it anymore."

A young man with dirty blonde hair, a camera slung around his neck, and a generally shabby appearance, emerged from the hall and stalked across the newsroom. He stopped when he saw Peter staring at him, saw the camera bag slung over Peter's shoulder. "What're you lookin' at, greenhorn?" he asked in a voice filled with pure venom.

"And Brock! Would it kill you to get a decent suit!?"

The bellowing voice's owner had appeared at his office door. How anyone could reach that volume while still keeping a cigar in his mouth was beyond Peter's ability to understand. His mustache was bristling as furiously as his flattop haircut. He looked like an angry porcupine.

"What?" he shouted at Peter for no discernible reason.

Without a word, Robertson held up the photos so Jameson could see them. Jameson blinked, squinted, then looked questioningly at Robertson. Robertson slowly nodded, silently affirming that these were the real deal. Jameson looked at Peter in disbelief, then shrugged and waved them into his office.

The moment Peter was in, Jonah practically pushed him into a battleship-gray chair in front of the desk, which creaked in protest. Peter looked around. The office didn't look as if a new stick of furniture had been put in there since before the Nixon administration.

Robertson spread them out on Jonah's desk as Peter tried not to pass out from the cigar smoke that clung to everything in the office. He glanced up and saw a smoke detector, hanging disassembled from the ceiling. That pretty much said it all.

"They're crap," said Jameson briskly, flipping through each one. "Crap. Crap. Megacrap."

Peter couldn't believe it, particularly after Robertson had been effusive in his praise. "But . . ." he managed to get out.

"Completely static," said Jameson. "You didn't follow the action at all. It looks like you shot them all from a third floor office window and were too paralyzed with fear to move your point of view around."

Peter gulped loudly. That was way too close to the truth

for comfort. "There was a lot going on," he said, sounding lame even to himself.

"A real news photographer doesn't keep a safe distance," Jameson growled. "You and your camera should have been right in the middle of this action."

Well, I was, Peter thought grimly. Then he noticed that Robertson was winking at him, sending him a silent but distinct message: Hang in there. And Peter tumbled to the fact that Jameson was being a hardcase, probably to lowball him.

"I'll give you three hundred for all of 'em," snapped Jameson.

Subtly, Peter's glance went over to Robertson. Robertson nonchalantly had his hand near his face, as if scratching his chin. And then, very slowly, he extended all five fingers as a mute signal to Peter.

Feeling buoyed, Peter said with confidence, "That seems a little low."

"Then take them somewhere else," Jonah said brusquely.

Peter shrugged, stood up and started to gather up the photos. But before he could, Jonah Jameson slammed his hands down on them and scowled furiously. "*Sit down!* All right, all right." He sighed as if he was offering to open up his chest and scoop his own heart out with a spoon. "I'll give you five hundred. That's the standard freelance fee."

Robertson nodded ever so slightly and Peter automatically imitated. Not realizing where the cues were coming from, Jameson scooped up the shots, making sure to keep one in particular on top. He tapped it. Peter noticed there appeared to be ink under Jameson's fingernails and wondered if it was there permanently. "Tear up page one," Jameson was saying to Robertson, "run that shot instead."

Peter couldn't believe it. Page one? He was going to be on the front page of the *Daily Bugle*!

No. Not him, he reminded himself. Spider-Man. He had to remember that. Spider-Man was exciting, mysterious, interesting. Peter Parker was none of those things, and if he valued his sanity, it was going to stay that way.

"Headline?" asked Robertson.

Jameson held his hands up as if envisioning the words on a movie theater marquee. " 'Spider-Man, Hero or Menace? Exclusive Daily Bugle Photos!' "

Immediately Peter was on his feet. "Menace?" he said incredulously. "Sir, he was protecting that bank from those—!"

Jameson rounded on him, scowling. "Tell you what, Atticus, you take the pictures, I make up the headlines. Okay? That all right with you?"

It was everything Peter could do to control himself. He wanted to shout that no, it was *not* all right with him, and that Spider-Man had been putting his butt on the line while Jameson was sitting on his, up in this ivory tower, making pronouncements that might frighten people, turn them against him. . . .

But he controlled himself. That wasn't going to accomplish anything. And besides, people didn't believe everything they read in newspapers, right? They'd know that Spider-Man was one of the good guys. Why, Peter would fight that perception himself, bringing in photos of Spider-Man helping people. Who cared about the words in a headline? Weren't pictures louder than words?

"Yes, sir," Peter said, although his fist was clenched and shaking slightly. "I . . . would like a job, sir."

"No jobs!" snapped Jameson, much to Peter's dismay. "Freelance. Best thing in the world for a kid your age. Bring me shots of that newspaper-selling clown and I might take 'em off your hands." He made shooing motions toward the door. Come on, get out of here! I got deadlines!"

Dear Mom and Dad:
I feel like I'm totally screwing myself.

For weeks now, I've been bringing pictures into the <u>Bugle.</u> Pictures I've been snapping of myself in action as Spider-Man. And with each new set of shots I figure, maybe this'll be the one that turns Jameson's opinion around.

Instead there are always new headlines about what a creep I am. Not me... the other me. And it's all Jameson. Robbie — that's Joe Robertson's nickname. I feel weird calling a man old enough to be my dad by a nickname, but he insisted after a while. Anyway, Robbie told me on the QT that Jonah Jameson personally skews the slant of all the coverage. There was one headline that was originally "NY Cheers Costumed Hero." And Jameson changed it to "NY Fears Costumed Coward." Robbie got so tired of having his headlines changed that he stopped making suggestions. So Jameson rose to the occasion and came up with things like "Spider-Man: Super-Hero or Super-Zero," "Big Apple Fears Spider Bite!," and, my personal favorite, "Spider-Man: Threat or Menace?"

Robbie started getting curious about my "luck." He took me aside one day and said, "Care to tell me how you're doing it, son? Do you monitor police band frequencies? Do you have people who alert you when they see the wallcrawler? Do you have some sort of deal worked out with Spider-Man himself, so he tells you where he's patrolling and you split the money from the photos?"

I just shrugged and smiled and said, "A magician never reveals his secrets, Robbie."

Robbie just kind of shrugged, and didn't push it. As for Jonah Jameson, it doesn't matter to him. As long as the pictures keep rolling in, he couldn't care less.

One day I couldn't take it anymore. I admit, when I first met Jameson, I was totally intimidated. But I got so fed up that I buttonholed him in his office and asked him why he was so hard on someone like Spider-Man who was clearly on the side of the law?

And he said, "He thinks he <u>is</u> the law. There's no place in this society for vigilante justice. Once one person takes the law into his own hands, it's anarchy."

I didn't know what to say to that. I mean, I don't think I'm taking the law into my own hands. It's not like I'm going around executing people or stuff. I'm just stopping bad guys. But how am I supposed to change Jameson's mind? It's not like I can tell him what's going through Spider-Man's head. I asked him if I could do something other than Spider-Man pictures, but he said no, I should stick with what I'm doing.

To my relief, Robbie stepped in. I think he realized how uncomfortable I was getting with the situation. "J. J., we need someone to cover the World Unity Festival. Let's send Peter."

Jonah kind of snarled and said, "World Unity Festival! Another epic display of OsCorp self-aggrandizement!"

"I thought you and Osborn were friends," said Robbie.

"We are! You should hear how I talk about my enemies."

I didn't need to. I knew already. It was in the headlines . . . and Spider-Man had never even done anything to him.

Finally Jonah said, "Fine, send him," and then turned to me and snapped, "but I never said you have a job! Meat! I'll give you a box of Christmas meat! Best I can do! _Now get me more pictures!_"

Christmas meat. There's something to live for. Knowing him he'll wait until it's on sale for half price, like during Easter. It'll be delivered in a hazardous waste container. Christmas meat. Sheesh.

I suppose the one joy I'm getting out of all this—aside from making money off the very thing that cost me my internship—is the knowledge that J. Jonah Jameson is paying me to take pictures of myself. He'd probably have a coronary if he knew.

XVII.

THE
FESTIVAL

Norman Osborn looked out across the New York skyline, of which he had a splendid view from his office at the top of OsCorp corporate headquarters. He stood there, taking in the fresh morning sun, feeling as if he could literally reach out and scoop up the entire city in the palm of his hand and say, "Mine. All mine."

There was some pronounced throat clearing behind him. He turned to them, his board of directors, all lined up like little ducks in a row, with their leather-bound folders open in front of them as they followed his description of the current state of affairs. Smiling over having made them wait, he slipped back into his chair at the head of the table and continued as if he'd never stopped talking. "In addition," he said, "we've secured three major new government contracts, and I'm proud to announce that—as of today—OsCorp Industries has surpassed Quest Aerospace as principal supplier to the United States Military. In short, ladies and gentlemen of the board, costs are down, revenue is up, and our stock has never been higher."

As one, the board members closed their folders, and Osborn sat back in his chair, arms folded, smiling. He remembered the legendary story of the host of a radio kid's show who—at the conclusion of one day's broadcast—ostensibly didn't know that he was still on the air when he muttered into a live microphone, "There. That should hold the little creeps for another day." That was exactly how Osborn felt at that moment.

Balkan leaned forward, a smile etched on his face. "That's wonderful news, Norman." He cleared his throat and added, almost as an afterthought, "In fact, it's the reason we're selling the company."

It took a moment for the words to fully register on Osborn. When they did, he was on his feet instantly. *"What?!"* He looked as if he didn't know whether to laugh in their faces or scream in them.

"It took us all by surprise," Balkan said, having the nerve to sound as if he were commiserating. "But Quest Aerospace is recapitalizing in the wake of the bombing."

Osborn's head snapped around to the nearest board member. "Fargas, what's going on here?"

Fargas didn't respond. Instead he simply glowered at Osborn, as if Osborn were some lower form of life. It was Balkan who replied. "Quest is expanding, and they've made a tender offer we can't ignore."

"Why wasn't I told about this?!" thundered Osborn.

"The last thing they want is a power struggle with an entrenched management," Balkan said, still trying to sound reasonable.

That was when Fargas stepped in, and if they were consciously doing good cop/bad cop, they couldn't have done a better job of it. "They want you out, Norman. The deal is off if you come with it. The board expects your resignation in thirty days."

"You . . . can't do this to me," stammered Osborn. "I built this company. . . ."

He couldn't understand how this could be happening. It was like some sort of surreal, demented joke, or a dream from which he would be awakening at any moment. Why, he and Fargas went back decades . . . he'd been the first to believe in him. "Max, please . . ." Osborn said, hating himself for feeling weak and sniveling.

As if tolling a death knell, Fargas said, "The board is unanimous. I'm sorry," he added, not sounding sorry at all. "We're announcing the sale right after the World Unity Festival."

Well, of course. Why have a cloud hanging over that? Why risk reporters turning out in droves, asking about Osborn's ouster, instead of focusing on the relentlessly cheerful and upbeat promotional spirit that was the festival's theme?

Norman Osborn felt as if a dark cloud was settling over his eyes, over his mind. He glanced outside, and although the sun was out, it no longer seemed bright. Instead it was overcast and threatening.

"You're out, Norman," Balkan said, driving the stake home.

And when Norman Osborn turned and looked back at the board of directors, there was something else in his eyes, that hadn't been there before. A quiet, deadly madness, that no one saw, and even if they had seen it, they would not have believed it.

"Am I," he said, and it was not a question. And in the fluorescent glow of the overhead lights, his eyes had taken on a distinctly green cast.

Peter hated crowds.

Not that he'd ever been wild about them, but the feeling had become more pronounced in recent months. The only thing he could figure was that it was because of his newfound freedom. Leaping among rooftops, hurtling among the spires of New York, it was as if he had the entire city to himself. When people surrounded him, all he could think about was leaping above them, clinging to a wall, webbing away with abandon, leaving gravity behind.

But he didn't have a lot of choice. His assignment was to take pictures of people enjoying themselves at the World Unity Festival in the heart of Times Square, not crowds of people pointing upward at the amazing webbed individual swinging over their heads. So he took a deep breath, counted to ten, and then snapped some pictures of the enormous multicolored globe that loomed over Times Square, trying not to get elbowed in the ribs in the process.

Behind him, on a stage, a singer was doing a soulful rendition of some pop tune. Getting a shot of that wouldn't be a bad idea, so Peter started wending his way through the crowd, putting his spider sense to good use by deftly moving his feet so he didn't get stepped on. As he did so, he continued to take pictures of the crowd, although he lowered his camera when he inadvertently focused on a young man reading a typically anti–Spider-Man headline in the *Bugle*.

Well, there were certainly plenty of other things he could shoot. There were booths set up with displays from various countries, and colorfully costumed people of all different nationalities were moving among the crowd, serving samples of their native cuisine. There were oversized balloons, there were floats celebrating global togetherness. Children were holding small balloon versions of the globe, or wearing T-shirts with the symbol on it . . . and with the OsCorp logo on the back. Yup, old Stormin' Norman never missed a trick.

Peter had no clue how many people were in attendance. It had to be thousands, and amazingly, no one else seemed annoyed or claustrophobic. The atmosphere was one of sweetness and light. That made a certain degree of sense to Peter. In the world itself there existed strife, war, poverty, genocide . . . but in a representation of the world, one got to pretend that everything was great. Then again, he figured, perhaps he was just getting cynical in his old age.

He spotted the reviewing stand, a converted balcony five

stories up, which had a huge banner that read OSBORN IN-
DUSTRIES WELCOMES YOU TO THE THIRD ANNUAL WORLD UNITY
FESTIVAL. Huge twin statues of Hercules—according to the
press packet that Peter had received—stood on either side of
the reviewing stand, appearing to support it. That seemed a
little odd to Peter, considering it was Atlas who—according
to legend—bore the weight of the world on his shoulders.
Then he remembered that Hercules had once been tricked
for a short time into shouldering the burden himself, and decided he could forgive the apparent misuse.

Peter got as close to the reviewing stand as he could, figuring that a shot of the people in the stand would be a good
one to have. He scanned across the balloons, past the floating streamers, up the torso of the Hercules statue, and discovered an assortment of men in dark suits engaged in
intense conversation with one another. He looked for a
familiar face. Maybe having Norman Osborn's mug in the
Daily Bugle might put a smile on his typically surly
demeanor. No . . . there was no Norman in sight, although
he did see Harry and . . .

"Mary Jane," breathed Peter.

Mary Jane couldn't recall the last time she'd felt so nervous.

She wasn't the world's greatest seamstress, but she wasn't
terrible at it, and she had put a ton of man-hours into sewing
the dress she was wearing. In terms of design it hadn't been
that difficult: It was a simple Chinese cheongsam, made of
red silk with a floral print. The neck was high, the collar
closed, with short sleeves, a loose chest, a fitted waist, and
slits up the sides to a modest height. All in all, it set off her
shape rather nicely, she thought.

She desperately wanted Harry to like it. She looked for
some hint of approval as he carefully attached a unity pin to

her bosom. He was visibly nervous, his hands shaking. She had a feeling that it had nothing to do with proximity to her, and his next words bore out her suspicions.

"Perfect," he said, once the unity pin was attached. "Except . . . how come you didn't wear the black dress? I wanted to impress my father. He loves black."

Mary Jane was instantly crestfallen. She knew the black dress he meant; it was slinky and sexy but not at all the thing she wanted to be wearing when trying to make a good first impression. The cheongsam had seemed the perfect idea; it was attractive and shapely, but didn't make her come across as . . . as low class. That's what she was the most concerned about. Norman Osborn, Harry . . . they were high society. And she . . . wasn't.

Rallying, she said, "Maybe he'll be impressed, no matter what? I mean, you think I'm pretty."

Perhaps realizing he had said the absolute wrong thing, Harry took her by the shoulders and smiled warmly. "Of course I do. You're beautiful."

He leaned forward to kiss her . . .

. . . and reflexively, for no reason she could readily understand herself, she averted her lips at the last moment, so that he kissed her on the cheek. Harry seemed slightly surprised, even a bit startled.

And then Harry looked even more startled. He seemed to be staring at something in the crowd, but when Mary Jane endeavored to follow his sight line, he quickly put an arm around her shoulder, turning her away, making forced conversation which only served to underscore how awkward the moment had been. She was still so flustered over her gut reaction that she didn't even bother to think about what it was in the crowd that had so thrown Harry for a loop.

Maybe it was his father, actually smiling, M. J. thought dourly. *That would be enough to confuse the hell out of anybody.*

• • •

Peter watched through his viewfinder, feeling sick to his stomach as Harry leaned forward to kiss Mary Jane, who in turn looked more ravishing than Peter had ever seen.

And then, to his astonishment, Mary Jane averted her face so that Harry kissed her on the cheek rather than the lips.

He couldn't believe it.

There was hope!

There was hope!

Jubilantly, Peter pumped the air, and something about the gesture caught Harry Osborn's attention. He looked down just as Peter had his arm raised, and they locked eyes.

Don't tell Harry, Mary Jane's warning sounded in his head, and he hadn't, except Harry had obviously gone and found out anyway. Because Harry saw Peter looking right up at them, and he was probably thinking, *Crap, Peter knows!* Except Peter had already known, so it wasn't as bad as it might have been, except maybe that made it worse.

It was making Peter's head whirl. How could there be this much confusion over love when Peter didn't even have a girlfriend and, by the looks of things, Harry didn't either?

Then Peter realized that his head wasn't just whirling. It was his spider sense, kicking into high gear, practically screaming at him that something was wrong, something was very very wrong.

Mary Jane felt as if she was being pulled along like a rolling suitcase as Harry made his way through the crowd on the balcony.

"Ah," Harry said, clearly having recognized a familiar face, and he brought Mary Jane over to two elderly men, one of them in a wheelchair. Quickly he introduced them as Messrs. Fargas and Balkan, although it happened so quickly that she wasn't entirely sure which one was which. "Have you seen my father?" Harry asked.

Balkan and Fargas exchanged uncomfortable looks. Immediately M. J. was cued to the fact that something was wrong. She knew that look all too well, because she'd seen it on her mother's face countless times: There was something to be said which no one wanted to say.

"I'm . . . not sure he'll be joining us," Fargas said in a slightly withering voice. And he gave Harry another look that Mary Jane again recognized, this time from her father. The look that said, *You are of no consequence. You don't matter.* It wasn't the way someone regarded the son of a valued company head.

She had no idea whether the same things were running through Harry's head, but at that moment their collective attention was diverted by a high-pitched whining sound. Looking for the source of the sound, Harry and M. J. made their way to the edge of the balcony.

It seemed to be coming from overhead. There was only a handful of clouds in the sky, but whatever it was, the sound originated from there. M. J. craned her neck, shielding her eyes against the glare of the midday sun. There seemed to be something . . .

"It's a bird," said Harry.

"No. I don't think so . . . kind of big," Mary Jane said.

Fargas and Balkan, along with the other members of the board, were also gazing heavenward. "A plane?" suggested Balkan.

"Too small," M. J. said.

The whining of the object was getting louder, as if . . . as if it was powering up somehow. "What *is* that?" Fargas demanded impatiently.

"Must be new this year," said Balkan. There had been some binoculars lying around the reviewing stand, for getting a better view of the crowd, and Balkan peered through one of them. Then he let out a gasp of amazement. "What the devil—? Is that our wing?"

Mary Jane had absolutely no idea what he was talking about. A wing? A wing of what? Like a building wing?

And then a demented cackle floated above the whining sound. With a rush of air and what sounded like a jet turbine, the object that was so high up suddenly got much closer, much faster. It dropped like a rock, but it wasn't in freefall. Instead it was moving with confidence and assurance. Quickly it was almost at street level, zigzagging through the floats and oversized balloons so deftly that the crowd automatically assumed it was part of the show. They started applauding.

But M. J. knew from the looks of the others in the reviewing box that this wasn't remotely intended to be part of anything.

The flying thing curled back up into the sky, banked and hovered, pausing to make a dramatic entrance, apparently. Then it moved right toward the reviewing stand, and Mary Jane couldn't believe what she was seeing.

It was some sort of large flying platform, crescent shaped, almost like a bat. Red lights were glowing on the front of it, with an array of cabling and armature underneath, running between the two wings and connecting to what appeared to be some sort of control sphere. Turbines were powering it from behind. But even the outlandishness of the device floating in front of them was as nothing compared to the rider.

He wore some sort of scaled green armor, glistening in the sun. It had a ribbed flexible look; in some ways it reminded her of the skin of an alligator. But it was layered with all manner of complicated circuitry that M. J. couldn't even begin to figure out. When he turned, even ever so slightly, at the arms or waist, there were little whispers of sound from servos or devices that seemed to be powering it.

But the armor itself was nothing compared to the face. It was more than a face: It was some sort of mask or helmet. With its glowing yellow eyes, the pointed ears that swept back, and the mouth that was permanently frozen into a demented grin with pointed teeth running along the top and bottom, it was the single most horrifying sight Mary Jane had ever seen.

Down on the stage below, the singer had stopped singing. The crowd, meantime, was still cheering. They had no idea that this—person, this creature—wasn't part of the show.

The creature was pulling something from a buckle on his belt. It was round, small, orange . . . a . . . pumpkin? Mary Jane wanted to laugh. Maybe this whole thing was some sort of gag, some sort of lively stunt, after all. Maybe he was some sort of juggler, planning to keep a bunch of pumpkins aloft at once. . . .

Suddenly the creature angled down and hurled the pumpkin toward one of the statues of Hercules. And Mary Jane's momentary laughter disappeared, along with the lower half of the Hercules statue. One minute it was there, but when the pumpkin struck it, the legs blew up.

The crowd's cheering and applause abruptly ceased, and an eerie silence filled the air. It was as if people were trying to figure out whether they'd actually seen what they thought they saw. For a moment frozen in time, the statue remained as it was, and then with a crack of stone the damaged monument gave way.

The reviewing stand, five stories up, began to collapse. The members of the OsCorp board of directors were shrieking and screaming in confusion, tumbling over one another. Mary Jane was thrown forward, grasping at air, trying to find something to hold on to. She called Harry's name, but he was pitched in the opposite direction.

The crowd's uncertainty was replaced with screams of panic as debris showered down upon them, nearly crushing several terrorized citizens.

The reviewing stand lurched another few feet, and Mary Jane slammed into the dangling balcony balustrade, barely holding on. She saw Harry trying to get to his feet, to get over to her and pull her back from the brink. Suddenly realizing the danger, she tried to shout for him to get back, but it was too late; his additional weight caused the balcony to shift. The shift caused the remaining sections of the Hercules statue to crumble into themselves even more, and the reviewing stand tilted further, flipping M. J. over the balustrade. Harry let out a terrified wail, and a five-story drop yawned beneath Mary Jane's feet. But she hadn't fallen, not yet; instead she was clinging, batlike, to the edge, dangling, her legs pumping the air as she tried to find purchase to haul herself back up.

The armored monster swung back around, his demented laughter ringing in Mary Jane's ears with such force that she felt as if the entire world consisted of nothing but his crazed cackling. She bit back her fear, didn't succeed, cried out in panic, and then saw him coming in fast as he hurled another pumpkin bomb.

This is it, I'm going to die, she thought, because another explosion would finish them off for sure.

Except it didn't explode.

Instead the bomb landed with a thunk right in front of the members of the OsCorp board. She heard it whirring, making a metallic sound, and she pulled herself up enough to see it rising into the air as they stared at it in confusion. None of them made a move to help her. Taking a deep breath, M. J. gave it everything she had and started to haul herself up.

Suddenly the bomb exploded, but not like the other one had. This one erupted in a flash of brilliant orange, so bright and searing that it irradiated half a dozen members of the board. Just as it went off, Mary Jane looked away. Being mostly blocked by the balcony itself, she was preserved from harm, but she was nearly flash blinded. And she caught a quick impression of those board members closest to it being literally turned into X-ray images of themselves.

The concussion of the blast caused the balcony to separate even further, and Mary Jane slid back, almost skidding off the edge completely. Harry was blinking furiously, apparently trying to get his eyes cleared from whatever damage the bomb had done to him. He was crawling across the balcony, trying not to cause it to tilt even further, and he was reaching out to Mary Jane to try and snag her hand. M. J. stretched her arm as far as she could, her fingers almost touching his.

Then she heard the roar of an engine, and a blast of heat from it enveloped her, the air rippling around her. She twisted and looked over her shoulder, and let out a scream as she saw the madman rising up on the glider behind her. His wide grin was solidly in place, his fingers twitching with anticipation of doing God-knew-what to her.

The creature mimicked her scream, then let out a bloodcurdling cackle that sounded as if it was emerging from the bowels of hell. . . .

XVIII.

THE

CONFRONTATION

. . . and then he was gone.

Just like that.

But not without help.

For what seemed the umpteenth time that day, Mary Jane couldn't believe what she was seeing.

At first she didn't understand. All she saw was a red and blue blur slamming into the green armored creature. It was moving so quickly, she couldn't even tell if it was a human or some sort of missile or what. What she did know for certain was that her attacker was no longer there. Instead he was falling down, down, knocked clean off the glider by the impact of the . . . the whatever it was. The creature plummeted, landed on one of the passing floats, bounced off it, somehow managed to twist himself in midair, and crashed feetfirst into a large tent serving Greek food. The armor he was wearing seemed to protect him from any serious harm.

And then she saw that glider of his coming after him, seeking him out. It let nothing stand in its way. It sailed through the replica of the globe, crashing in one side and out the other, knocking the globe off its stand.

At that moment, Mary Jane saw something land on a wall of a building across the way. She realized belatedly that it was the thing that had knocked the monster, however briefly, off its perch. And then she recognized him. How could she not? His pictures were all over the papers in recent days.

"Spider-Man," she breathed. And if she had ever been

inclined to believe any of those headlines about what a criminal mastermind he was, all of those went right out the window.

"A little help!" she tried to scream to him over the chaos below, because she still didn't have a firm grip and the balcony seemed on the verge of breaking off anyway. But Spider-Man wasn't looking in her direction. Instead his focus was elsewhere.

And then she saw it, too.

The globe that the glider had knocked over was rolling. Like a gigantic boulder, it was crushing everything in sight, and people were pushing and shoving and screaming to get the hell out of its way. Directly in its path was a small boy, staring in frozen shock as it barreled right toward him. His mother was screaming, waving her arms, trying to get to him and being carried in the opposite direction by the wave of panicked humanity.

Instantly Spider-Man raised his arm and something came hurtling out of his wrist . . . a web? *My God . . . how weird is that?* Mary Jane thought.

The web line snagged a billboard high atop a nearby building and, with no trace of fear, Spider-Man swung off the building in a huge arc, heading for the little boy, his right arm outstretched. . . .

I'm not gonna make it, I'm not gonna make it, thought Peter, as the little boy trembled in front of the rolling globe. And then he was right on top of the kid, and the globe was rumbling so fiercely that it hurt his teeth. He snagged the boy and whipped his body upward, arching his back as the globe rolled just under him, snapping a row of parking meters as if they were matchsticks.

"You made it!" the boy gasped.

"Never a doubt."

He hurtled past the tent where the green armored nutball who'd started all this was struggling to get out from under the fallen canvas. He was surrounded by police, and Peter heard him shout from underneath, "I surrender! I surrender! Media violence made me do it!"

What a loon, Peter thought as he angled himself toward a woman who was waving her arms and screaming "Billy! Billy!" over and over again.

"That your ma?" The boy nodded, and Peter dropped down next to the woman.

He saw the look on her face, the fear of his own masked features, plus who-knew-what-else thanks to the *Daily Bugle*. But he couldn't give it any further thought. Instead he handed the boy over to her without comment and turned toward the balcony where Mary Jane was holding on. She had managed to get some traction and had braced herself so she was no longer dangling over the street, held by the strength of her arms alone. Peter was about to swing up to get her. . . .

When suddenly he heard a roar, a cackling, and he spun just in time to see a half dozen of New York's finest flying off in all directions. Standing in the middle of the melee was the armored monstrosity that had come tearing into the middle of all this and terrorized so many.

Under his mask, Peter felt his fury growing even as he charged forward, his booted feet moving with precision and certainty across the debris-strewn street. He leapt through the air, did a series of handsprings and somersaults for no other reason than to show this monster just with whom he was dealing, and landed directly in front of his opponent.

"How dare you interfere with me!" snarled the green goon from beneath his mask. "What do you want?"

"World peace. But I'll settle for your chin."

His arm moved so fast that the armored man never even

saw it coming. Peter's punch lifted him clear off his feet and sent him tumbling heels over head into a brick wall. His heart pumping, Peter charged straight at him, cocking his fist to deliver another fierce blow . . .

. . . and the creature caught it in one metal hand, stopping the punch in midthrust.

"See what I did there?" he said almost conversationally, and then he drove a punch straight at Peter, and Peter had never, but never, been hit that hard in his life. Not even as a kid being smacked around by bullies. It was like being punched by a wrecking ball, and Peter crashed through an ice cream cart and into a lamppost.

The world was spinning around him, and Peter fought off a wave of nausea as he staggered to his feet. A heartbeat later, his spider sense screamed a warning and, operating purely on reflex, he backflipped high in the air. An instant later he saw why he'd felt compelled to do so: The bizarre glider the guy had been riding had come swooping in behind him and would have broken his spine if it had struck home.

With a gleeful cackle, his armored opponent leapt high in the air, landing smoothly on the flying wing. His boots snapped into place with an audible click and up he went into the sky.

For a moment, Peter allowed himself a breath of relief. He hadn't caught the guy, but at least he'd managed to chase him away.

The sound of machine-gun fire alerted him to his error.

Mary Jane, having managed to pull herself away from the edge of the balcony, bringing herself closer and closer to relative safety and Harry's outstretched hand, was starting to think that the worst was over. Then she heard the machine-gun rounds pumping away and twisted her head around to get a better view of what was happening.

The nut on the glider was diving down toward Spider-Man, and machine-gun muzzles had popped out of either wing. Bullets were chewing up the ground, and Spider-Man was moving faster than Mary Jane would have thought possible.

Spider-Man leapt, firing a web line at the same time. It drew taut and he ricocheted upward, staying just ahead of the gunfire's path. He swung up and over a huge float of a Rasta man, as the maniac on the glider disappeared into the sky.

Suddenly the reviewing stand moaned. With a creaking of metal, the struts began to give out, rivets popping like so many champagne corks. Harry was still trying to reach down to M. J., but she was out of range and slipping fast. She let out a scream that she hoped would attract Spider-Man's attention.

She succeeded in doing so. She saw Spider-Man look up at her, and an instant later he was moving. A procession of floats stood between her and Spider-Man, but not only did that prove to be no obstacle to him, they were in fact his means of getting to her. He bounded from one float to the next, drawing closer and closer to her. *He'll save me, he'll save me,* she kept saying to herself, trying to let that new mantra drown out the continued creaking of the overstressed metal supports.

Spider-Man was in midair when the monster reappeared.

He came ripping down from nowhere on his glider. Spider-Man obviously saw him coming, twisted around in midleap but was momentarily helpless. And the creature took full advantage of it. The grinning gargoyle smashed into Spider-Man, wrapping him in a bear hug and driving him into the building above the balcony. Glass and debris rained down, and Mary Jane frantically shielded her head as small bits of rubble and glass bounced off her.

Harry wasn't quite so fortunate. He tried to dodge, but

there was no room to maneuver, and a chunk of rubble bounced off his head. He wavered where he stood, trying to maintain his footing, but then Mary Jane watched in despair as his eyes glazed and he slumped over.

Spider-Man shoved away from the building with his legs and twisted around so that he had his toes on the edge of the glider. There he slugged it out with the armored monster. She could hear the sounds of the metal ringing under the pounding of Spider-Man's fists, but the creature didn't seem the least bit perturbed, as if—now that he'd readied himself—he could take whatever punishment Spider-Man was dishing out. Then the creature swung an elbow around, catching Spider-Man in the jaw. The impact sent Spider-Man toppling off the glider, and he smashed into the balcony.

The impact of his landing caused Mary Jane to lose not only her grip, but also the small measure of safety she had managed to obtain with her struggles. She rolled toward the edge, and she could have sworn she heard Spider-Man cry out. It was the balustrade that stopped her once again, bringing her to a halt but leaving her dangling perilously high above the street.

Spider-Man rose, started to move toward her, and suddenly the glider was right there, rising out of nowhere. The turbojet had gone utterly silent; perhaps he'd had it on only for effect before, or perhaps there was some other power source for simple lifting, like magnetism. She had no idea; she wasn't a scientist. Peter was the scientist. Deliriously, she wished he were there.

With a deft maneuver, the creature swung his glider around so that he was facing Spider-Man. There was a humming sound coming from the vehicle, the noise of a weapon powering up. The front section began to glow. Instantly Spider-Man shot out a web strand. It splattered over the monster's face with such force that, had he not been armored, it likely would have taken his head off. As the creature pitched back, clawing at his face, his change in posture sent the glider's aim off just as the weapon discharged. It appeared to be some sort of laser beam, although she couldn't be sure. But it was a pencil-thin beam of red light, and when it struck the wall next to Spider-Man, the wall blew apart. If it wasn't a laser, it was still a damned nasty piece of work.

The glider angled up within range of Spider-Man, and he leapt upward, grabbing at the underside of the glider. He came away with a handful of wiring from underneath. Immediately the glider began to smoke and sputter, sparks crackling from underneath. And its rider was still blinded by the webbing, howling his indignation as he angled the glider away from Spider-Man as quickly as he could.

Thank God . . . I'm safe, Mary Jane thought with relief.

That was when the ledge gave way.

Mary Jane clutched at the air, frantically tried to walk on it, and then she fell. Her arms flailed about, and insanely all she could think of was that the dress she had worked so hard on was going to wind up being totally ruined. The street sped toward her, and she hoped it wouldn't hurt too much.

Then, suddenly, she was in Spider-Man's arms. He was snapping back upward, and she had absolutely no clue what was happening. Then she saw that he was clutching a web line and realized that he had used his webbing to effectively bungee jump after her.

Spider-Man rebounded past the balcony, giving her a glimpse of the section that had collapsed. She saw Harry further in, away from the crumbling section, not in danger and just starting to come around. His eyes focused on her, and he seemed not to realize what it was he was looking at. Then he was gone as the arc of his web line took them up, up further, and then over.

They whipped through the canyon of skyscrapers, Mary Jane looking around in amazement. He moved with a speed, a certainty that she wouldn't have thought possible. She should have been terrified. She was being held aloft by a total stranger, swinging through the asphalt jungle as if it were a regular jungle and he was making his way on vines. When he would reach the end of his web line, he'd simply release it and there would be the brief start of a descent, whereupon another web line would take its place and off they went again. They swept low over the street, just brushing past the top of a cab, the driver of which stopped, exited, pointed, and bellowed to whoever would listen, *"What the hell's that?!"*

She started to wonder where he was taking her. To the spider cave under his mansion? Back to his place in the frozen north? No matter what, this moment was breathtaking. Particularly when she came to the realization that she wasn't afraid. That somehow she knew, beyond question, that he wasn't going to do anything to hurt her.

M. J. was mildly disappointed when she discovered that their destination was neither subterranean nor iced over, but instead a garden rooftop near Rockefeller Plaza. It was at that point that his intention became clear to her; he just wanted to make sure she was far away from the danger, just in case the nutball on the glider came back. They alighted on the rooftop, to the astonishment of several young folks who were relaxing with their lunches on benches, chairs, and a spread-out blanket.

"Don't mind us," Spider-Man said. "She needs to use the elevator."

It was the first time that he had spoken near her. There was something much more youthful about his voice than she would have expected. It was muffled, the exact tone hard to make out, but he sounded vaguely familiar. Someone she'd heard on the radio, perhaps.

Satisfied that she was attended to, he started to turn away, but she stopped him with a quick, "Wait!"

He looked back at her, waiting for her to speak. She

wished she could see through the eyepieces, at least. The lack of eye contact was the spookiest thing about him. "Who *are* you?"

"You know," he said.

Taken aback, she said, "I do?"

He paused for a long moment then, as if seriously considering saying something else. But instead he said simply, "Your friendly neighborhood Spider-Man."

Then he sprinted for the edge of the building. Despite everything that she'd just seen, she still felt a moment of panic as he vaulted off the edge of the roof, doing a double somersault as he went. But as he plunged she heard a *thwippp* noise, webbing shot out, and he swung gracefully away.

"Spider-Man . . ." she whispered, waiting for the excited beating of her heart to slow, but at the same time kind of wishing that it never did.

XIX.

THE
AFTERMATH

Harry burst into the apartment, the picture of a young man in turmoil. He had his cell phone in his hand, and he was frantically dialing a number. Peter, at the window, was a portrait of calm, serenely drinking a glass of milk. He could afford to be calm, of course, since he knew precisely where Mary Jane had been dropped off, and that she was out of danger.

But there was no way to convey this to Harry without tipping off to him things he was better off not knowing.

Besides, a small, sadistic aspect of Peter, one that he'd really rather have not admitted to himself, was pleased to see Harry in such a tizzy. After all, Harry had enjoyed the inside track to Mary Jane for a while now, and in secret. In the back of Peter's mind, it seemed justifiable payback to have his own secret about M. J. and to let Harry stew for a while.

"Pick up, pick up!" Harry yelled into the phone, as Peter took a deep breath and enjoyed the night air. "If somehow you get this, call me right away!" He snapped the phone shut, shoved it in his pocket, and walked quickly over to Peter. "Pete!" he said, his voice almost manic. "I'm glad you're here. Any word? Has she called?"

Any word? As it so happens, buddy, yes. The word is that M. J. didn't want to kiss you. Further word is that she looked at Spider-Man as if he was a god descended from Olympus. I'm on the fast track, friend, and you can eat my dust.

"Not yet," Peter said. "She will."

"She will?" Harry clutched at Peter's shirt. "How do you know! You don't know that!"

Peter delicately pried the hand loose. He certainly didn't need to have his shirt ripped open to reveal the costume underneath. "A feeling I have," he assured his roommate. "You okay? How's your head?"

Harry shrugged, as if his condition— and even the question itself—were of no consequence. "They patched it up. It's nothing." At that, he started pacing and talking rapidly, although to no one in particular. "What would he do to her? Thank God my father wasn't there. That whole scene, where'd that thing come from? What was it? What's that?" he asked, eyeing Peter's glass. "Milk?"

"Uh-huh. Got milk?" Peter asked lightly. He pictured what it would be like to appear in a milk advertisement, a little white mustache perched just under the masked bridge of his nose.

Harry stared at him incredulously. "Why aren't you worried?" he demanded.

"Oh. Right," Peter said, as if remembering to cue an emotion. "I am worried."

Beginning to pace again, like an expectant father, Harry announced, "I've put it together. Spider-Man knows she's my girlfriend. He'll want a ransom from my father."

Peter cocked his head and said, "Really? What could he get?"

Harry's cell phone rang. Harry quickly flipped it open and said, "Hello?" then he relaxed with visible relief. "Oh, thank God." He turned to Peter and said somewhat unnecessarily, "It's her." Then, back to the phone, he said, "Where are you? Are you all right? Did he hurt you?" He paused, listening. "He was what?" His brow furrowed. "What do you mean, he was incredible?"

Peter raised a hand to cover the smile.

Harry shook his head as if he were a dreamer trying to

shake himself back to wakefulness. "Are you sure you're all right? Are you . . . drugged? Where did he take you?" Another pause. "To a roof garden?" He looked to Peter as if to ask whether he was losing his mind or not. Peter just shrugged.

"No, I've never been there," Harry said, carefully measuring his words with forced calm. "Listen, I'm coming over." Yet again a pause. "Because you need to tell me everything, that's why. And what did you mean by incredible . . . ? What? You're going to sleep now?!" He looked as if he was going to argue the point, then remembered that Peter was standing there, and so he said, "Well . . . then call me in the morning. Are you sure you're feeling all right?" He scowled.

"Stop saying 'incredible!' " It was all Peter could do not to laugh out loud at Harry's frustration. "Call me when you wake up. We'll go for breakfast and . . . I'll buy you something beautiful . . . Why? Because I want to. It'll make you . . . feel better," Harry told her, sounding a bit uncertain. It was understandable. If Mary Jane felt as good as she seemed to, she'd float off the planet. "All right, g'night, get some sleep, uh . . ." Plainly he didn't want to disconnect and was searching for things to say. "Uh . . . sleep tight . . . don't let the—"

Mary Jane hung up.

Harry snapped shut the cell phone. Then he cleared his throat.

"She's . . . still a little rattled."

Peter nodded as he tipped back the glass, finished the last gulp, and lowered it. He glanced in a nearby mirror in approval. Milk mustache.

"At least she's all right."

"Yeah . . . look . . . about M. J. . . ." Harry said after a long moment. "I know that was a picture you didn't want to take."

Ahhhh . . . so Harry was going to admit that he'd spotted

Peter during the festival. "I didn't take it," Peter said indifferently.

"I know. I should've told you about us," Harry said, exhaling deeply as if trying to get the weight of the world off his shoulders. "But you have to understand, I'm crazy about her."

"We're friends. You didn't have to lie," Peter reminded him, sounding sharper than he would have liked.

"I always knew you wanted her for yourself, but you never made a move."

That was a bit more candor than Peter had expected from the moment. He lowered his gaze, his momentary anger replaced with self-reproach. "I guess I didn't."

Harry shook his head uncomprehendingly. "What was that thing that killed them? It happened so fast."

"I don't know. But somebody has to stop it."

"Right. Well . . . I'll pray in the bedroom."

He hesitated, as if there was something else he wanted to say, but apparently thought better of it and walked into the bedroom. Peter was left alone at the window, looking out at the night sky. Tomorrow the entire city was going to know that there was a genuine masked menace in town, because Peter had been smart enough to anchor his camera, set the automatic shutter, and get some extremely good shots of himself in battle with that goblin . . .

The Green Goblin. Peter winced. What a name. It sounded so juvenile, as if he should be sporting a little purple hat and booties. But it's what Jameson had dubbed him, upon taking one look at the photo. "Goblin" because Jameson thought he looked like a Halloween creature come to life, and "Green" because Peter's shots had been in black and white, and Jameson wanted to let the reader know what color he was in order to make even more of an impression—and sell more newspapers, no doubt.

"Ever since Spider-Man, they all gotta have a name. *Hoffman!*" Jameson shouted. "Call the copyright office! Trademark the name! I want a quarter for every time somebody says it!"

"But . . . 'Green Goblin,' " Peter said in weak protest. "It sounds so . . ."

"We have to make the name more memorable! And nothing makes people remember a name like alliteration!" J. Jonah Jameson said.

"Do you really think so?" Peter Parker asked the nearest bystander.

"I wouldn't know," Robbie Robertson commented. Then J. J.'s secretary, Betty Brant, informed him that he had a conference call with the noted scientists Bruce Banner and Reed Richards.

Left alone, Peter wondered where that armored lunatic was hiding out. He tried to picture what someone like that was like when they weren't wearing armor, a grotesque mask, and terrorizing people.

Did he have a wife? Did she know who, what he was? Did he have a daughter who adored him? A son who looked up to him? If he did, Peter had a feeling they had no idea what he'd been up to. He probably led some sort of double life. He felt sorry for that madman's friends and family.

Then again, who was he to talk?

The headline stared up at Norman Osborn, who was standing at the threshold of his apartment, the newspaper lying flat in front of him. He blinked against the brightness of the morning sun and couldn't help but feel that the paper was mocking him, somehow, as the banner shouted up at him, TIMES SCARE! SPIDER-MAN, GREEN GOBLIN TERRORIZE CITY!

Osborn licked his lips, ran his tongue along his teeth. He felt as if something had crawled into his mouth and died. He leaned against the doorframe, looked down at his disheveled clothes, and came to the realization that he couldn't remember having gone to bed. The last thing he could clearly recall was the board meeting. It . . . hadn't gone well. He didn't know what the details were . . . he just knew it hadn't gone well.

He picked up the newspaper, scanning it as if it could provide him with answers to questions that he didn't even know to ask. Then his gaze came to a halt on a smaller, less prominent headline . . . reading almost like an afterthought: OSCORP BOARD MEMBERS KILLED.

He blinked furiously, an owl in the daylight, trying to make sense of it. He was starting to sweat profusely. He felt disgusting. He felt as if he wanted to climb into a shower and just stay there for days.

Shoving the newspaper under his arm, he staggered away across the entry hall, kicking the door shut behind him.

And then, somewhere, far in the distance, he heard a faint cackling.

He stopped and looked around in confusion. Where the hell had that come from? Feeling vaguely uneasy, he lurched across the foyer and up the stairs.

The cackling continued as Osborn drew closer to what seemed to be the source: his den. But as he approached it, got within just a couple of feet, the laughter abruptly stopped. It was as if there were an intruder who suspected he'd been discovered and was trying to avoid detection.

"Somebody there?"

He should just be calling the police, but something stopped him. It wasn't just that the laughter had ceased. There was a palpable sense of emptiness.

He peered around the corner cautiously, aware that there could be some lunatic standing to the side wielding an axe, ready to behead him. Then again, considering how much his skull was pounding, that might be doing him a favor.

But there was no one. The room was empty. The only thing staring back at him was his collection of masks, and they obviously weren't posing any threat.

"Of course not," he said to himself. He took a deep breath, walked into the study, and moved to a small table that had a whiskey decanter sitting on it. He poured himself a shot, alarmed by how much his hands were shaking.

"Stop pretending, Norman . . ."

He whirled, the sudden realization that he wasn't alone a cold dash of water in his face. Sweat was rolling off him in buckets. The glass was wobbling in his hand, the whiskey slopping over the edges.

The voice was mirthful and otherworldly, and so damned familiar that it chilled him to the bone, especially in the informal tone it was taking, as if the intruder and Osborn were old friends. He stumbled to the middle of the room, spinning in place, trying to see everywhere in the room at once.

"Who said that?!" he demanded.

"Don't play the innocent with me. You've known all along." The voice spoke in a demonic monotone.

"Who are you?"

"Follow the cold shiver that's running down your spine. Look . . . I'm right here."

Osborn turned and faced a long mirror that was hanging nearby. He stared into it. His reflection was ghastly and pale, like a man on his deathbed. "I . . . don't understand," he said, his throat closing up on him. He wondered if he was going to keel over right there, before this intruder even showed himself.

"Did you think it was coincidence? So many good things . . . all happening for you . . . all for you, Norman . . ."

"What do you want?" Osborn shouted, his terror mounting, and he felt horribly weak for reacting that way. Sweat was dripping into his eyes. He rubbed them furiously to clear his vision, and when he lowered his hands. . . .

Something else was staring out at him from the mirror. Not his own reflection, no. No, it was that . . . that creature that had been on the front page of the newspaper. That Green Goblin, leering at him . . .

"What do I want? To say what you won't . . . to do what you can't . . . to remove those in your way," and with a slight inclination of his head, the Green Goblin indicated the newspaper.

The horrifying reality slammed home to Osborn all at once. "The board members? You . . . killed them?!"

"We killed them."

Osborn backed away, shaking his head, positive now that either he was dreaming or going mad, or both. "Oh God. Oh God . . ."

"Stop mewling," the Goblin snarled. *"You sicken me. You ooze weakness."*

Now . . . now he understood, more than ever, why the Goblin sounded so familiar. It was the way his voice sounded to himself . . . when he was talking to, or about, Harry. "I'm not a murderer . . . I'm a scientist, a respectable businessman. The police . . ."

The word hung there, the salvation. Osborn hurried for the phone, reached for it . . .

. . . and the Goblin was already there, no longer confined to the mirror, growing stronger in Osborn's psyche with each passing moment. His armored hand sat atop the phone, and he snarled into Osborn's face with putrid breath, *"Hypocrite! Liar!"*

The Goblin reared back, heaved the phone toward the balcony, and Osborn was inside and outside his own head at the same time, unsure whether the Goblin had truly sprung to life, whether the phone being thrown was an hallucination, or whether he himself had thrown it in the throes of a delusion.

And there was the Goblin, up on the den's balcony, ducking as the phone zipped past his head. The Green Goblin stood there, looking down at Osborn. *"Now shut up and listen! Try to understand the beauty of all this!"* he snapped at him. *"You are now in full control of OsCorp Industries. Your greatest wish, granted by me. Say thank you,"* he told him silkily.

Osborn didn't say thank you. But he stopped trembling, shaking in weakness. The truth was that he'd been more appalled at the prospect of getting caught than by the act itself. There was no love lost between himself and the board members, certainly.

"Hmmm . . . And . . . then what?" he asked cautiously.

Clearly pleased that Osborn was warming up to the situation, the Goblin continued. *"We'll eliminate your rivals. OsCorp will become the most powerful military supplier in history. You'll have limitless wealth."* He spoke in an increasingly seductive tone. *"Presidents and kings will court your favor. So don't be shy. Take what you've always wanted. Power. The weak will serve you. The world will be yours and mine. Yes. You and I, we can have a hell of a time."*

Osborn lurched toward his favorite chair, leaned on its back. "I . . . suppose the damage has been done, right?"

"Yeah."

"Can we . . . do it alone?"

"There's only one who could stop us."

Osborn drew himself up, struck by a better thought. "Or . . . be our greatest ally."

"Exactly! We need to have a little chat with you-know-who."

"But . . . how do we find him?"

The Goblin didn't have to answer out loud. The answer was already in his head, and without any further prompting

Osborn picked up the newspaper from where he'd dropped it. He stared at the front page with the picture of Spider-Man and the Green Goblin.

He gave a low, pleased laugh that sounded vaguely like a cackle.

XX.

THE REAL
TRUTH

J. Jonah Jameson was having a very good day so far, and all the nattering from Peter Parker wasn't going to ruin it.

Parker was stomping around Jameson's office as if the little twerp owned the place. Jameson made a mental note to slap Parker down; he'd been getting entirely too big for his britches lately. "Spider-Man wasn't terrorizing the city!" he told Jameson. "He was trying to save it! It's slander!"

"I resent that!" Jameson snapped at him, not even bothering to look in his direction. He was too busy admiring the front page of the *Bugle*. He wondered if perhaps he shouldn't have made the type even bigger. "Slander is spoken. In print it's libel." His cigar had burned down to the nub, so he flicked it out the window.

"You don't trust anybody," Parker said, stabbing an accusatory finger at him. "That's your problem, Mr. Jameson."

Whereupon he turned and strode angrily out of Jameson's office, which was just fine by Jonah. "I trust my barber!" Jameson called after him. Then, pointing at the picture of Spider-Man, he shouted, "What are you, his lawyer? Let him sue me and get rich like a normal person! That's what makes this country—"

The cigar that he had just thrown out the window flew back in. Jameson looked down at it, puzzled, and then turned to see if somehow there might have been a passing pigeon with a highly overdeveloped retrieval instinct.

That was when the Green Goblin, as if leaping off the

front page of the paper, smashed through the window frame. Jameson let out a yell of terror as the Goblin grabbed him by the throat with one hand and scooped him off his feet, his glider hovering over the floor of the office.

Outside Jameson's office, pandemonium erupted. People dashed about like so many headless chickens, shouting for security. Photographers were madly grabbing up their cameras. *How wonderful,* Jameson thought. *Front page coverage of his death.* Bleakly, Jameson hoped they'd snap his good side.

"Who's the photographer who takes the pictures of Spider-Man? I need to talk to him about his favorite subject. Where is he?"

Parker! He wants Parker . . . !

Jameson's first instinct was to shout the name, shout it as loudly as he could. But then something else kicked in: the oldest commandment in the world. Protect your source. Jameson had, on two separate occasions, gone to jail rather than violate that fundamental principle.

He looked hard into his soul at that moment, as the Goblin's face leered at him, and recognized himself for the money-seeking, headline-manufacturing, truth-bending leech that he was, but by God, he was just trying to keep his newspaper afloat, and at least his newsman's soul was still unblemished. That wasn't going to change.

Not even in the face of death.

Besides, if he blurted out the name, the Goblin might just kill him anyway. The longer he stalled, the more chance he had that security would get their slow, wrinkled butts in gear and take care of this nut.

"He's a freelancer," Jameson said. "I . . . I don't know who he is! His stuff comes in the mail!"

That sounded horrendously lame, and the Goblin obviously saw through it.

"You're lying . . . !"

"I swear!" Jameson choked out.

"This is your last chance—!" His voice was high-pitched, he was practically giggling the entire time, a green-armored demoniac.

"Please . . . air . . ." The world was starting to haze out. ". . . Stop . . ."

"Hey!"

It was another voice, from somewhere outside Jameson's fading field of vision. And then he saw the source.

Spider-Man was hanging, upside down, just outside the window.

"I wear the tights in this town," he said mockingly.

"Speak of the devil," the Goblin growled. He let go of Jameson, and the newspaper owner slumped to the floor, gasping.

But even as his lungs fought for air, he managed to get out, "I knew it! You and Spider-Man are in this together! I knew that creep was—"

There was a *thwipp* noise and suddenly Jameson couldn't move his mouth. A glob of Spider-Man's webbing was covering it.

"Hey, kiddo, let Mom and Dad talk for a minute, will you?"

The Green Goblin pointed at Spider-Man, as if about to challenge him . . . and suddenly gas billowed from his fingertip, spurting directly into the wallcrawler's face.

Caught completely unawares, Spider-Man gasped, tried to choke out the gas, failed . . . and toppled backward out the window. Instantly the Goblin was gone, as well.

My God . . . he killed him . . . Jameson thought wildly as he staggered to his feet, using the edge of his desk to haul himself up. He heard the sound of running feet coming up behind him, the useless security guards. He made a mental note to fire them as he stumbled over to the window and looked out, expecting to see Spider-Man's dead body splattered all over the sidewalk below.

Instead he saw the Green Goblin, arcing up and away into the sky . . . with Spider-Man's body slung over his shoulder.

I knew it! The Goblin saved him! He wouldn't have saved him if they were enemies! Damn! I need photos. Where's Parker when you need him! Jameson thought furiously as he pulled in futility at the webbing on his mouth.

He'd seemed . . . bigger, somehow.

That was the Goblin's thought as he hovered above the unconscious Spider-Man, who was lying on a rooftop just below him. When he'd been battling the wallcrawler the previous day, the bug man had seemed bigger. More powerful. Everywhere at once. But lying there as he was, moaning softly, rubbing his head . . . well, he looked pretty pathetic, actually. Maybe he wasn't really worthy of being an ally.

Still . . . when his fist had connected, especially that first time, the Goblin had felt it right through his armor. And hell . . . even Hitler had probably looked harmless— maybe even adorable—when he'd been sleeping.

Spider-Man was beginning to move, but he looked as if he couldn't coordinate his limbs. The Goblin knew why, of course. "Relax," he said.

The webslinger struggled to drag himself to a sitting position. He couldn't have moved any slower if he'd weighed a thousand pounds, and it probably felt as if he did. "My hallucinogen gas has slowed your central nervous system to a crawl," the Goblin said conversationally. "Just for a few minutes. Long enough for us to have a talk." He saw Spider-Man instinctively reach for his face, and he chortled. "Don't worry, I didn't remove your mask. I'll respect your privacy . . . for the moment, anyway. Because I respect *you*."

Spider-Man didn't seem to take it as a compliment. That annoyed the Goblin slightly, but he let it pass.

"Who are you?" Spider-Man demanded, sounding as if he had marbles in his mouth.

"A kindred spirit," the Goblin answered blithely. "A fellow traveler. You've changed, and now you want someone to tell you what to do, what to be. And there's no one who could possibly understand . . ." He leaned in toward Spider-Man. ". . . except me."

How cute. Spider-Man was trying to make a fist. All he managed was to move a couple of fingers. Perhaps he was trying for an obscene gesture. "They call us freaks," the Goblin continued. "But we're not less than human . . . we're *more* than human."

"I'm not like you. You're . . . a murderer. . . ."

"Well . . . to each his own," the Goblin said with a shrug. "I chose my path. You choose the way of the hero. And they'll find you amusing for a while, the people of this city. . . ." His glider rose and he hovered, making a sweeping gesture, taking in the entirety of the city with it. "But the one thing they love more than a hero is to see the hero fail . . . fall . . . die trying.

"The truth is, people don't *like* heroes. Who wants an example you can never live up to? Take my word for it, in spite of all you've done for them, eventually *they will hate you. Read the headlines!*"

He was listening. Spider-Man was listening to him, he could tell. And why not? Spider-Man read the headlines; he knew what the media was trying to do. He had to be aware of it. So why not milk that for all it was worth?

"We are who we choose to be," the Goblin continued. "But a day will come when you must ask yourself, did I choose wisely? Why am I risking my life for these ungrateful fools?"

"Because . . . it's right . . ."

The Goblin circled him, mockingly, out of reach. Spider-Man was glancing around, as if unable to focus on where he was.

"Right? Wrong? Capital R, capital W? You're young, aren't you." It wasn't a question. He was becoming more and more convinced that he was dealing with someone who was, at most, college age. "You believe in myth, beauty, professional athletes as role models. Well, here's the real truth. There are fourteen million people in this city," and he pointed all around them. "Those teeming masses exist for the sole purpose of lifting a few exceptional people onto their shoulders. You, me, we are exceptional. I had problems, but I used my God-given powers and poof . . . those problems vanished."

Spider-Man was focused on him now. The gas might be starting to wear off . . . and if that triggered a fight, then Spider-Man might not have time to dwell on everything the Goblin had said. So it was probably time to bring this to a close, to leave the "hero" with something to chew upon.

"Imagine what we could accomplish together. What we could create . . . or . . . We could destroy, cause the deaths of countless innocents in selfish battle again and again. And again . . . until we are both dead."

The glider, under his guidance, angled upward. "Think about it, hero," he called mockingly over his shoulder. Then he flew off into the glare of the morning sun.

Dear Mom and Dad:

I've got good news and bad news.

The bad news is, the early edition of the Daily Bugle carried a headline that read, "Spider-Man, Green Goblin Terrorize City." The good news is, the next day's edition didn't say that.

More bad news and good news. The bad news is that the next day's edition said, "Spider-Man, It's Time for a Bug-Free City," and featured an editorial from J. Jonah Jameson about how the Green Goblin and I don't care about who gets hurt, or about anything except whomping on each other. The good news is . . . well . . . there's not really any good news, I guess.

God help me, the stuff the Goblin was saying made sense. I find myself clinging on to one notion and one notion only, and that is that I'm "the good guy." Because I'm the good guy, I don't get pulled into the mindset that creates that sort of creature.

Except . . . well, it's almost Darwinian, isn't it. Natural selection. The strong survive. And the fact was that the Goblin had me cold. I got cocky and overconfident, he hit me with one whiff of gas, and _boom_, I was gone. If he hadn't caught me before I hit the ground, I'd be a pancake. He saved me for a reason. A twisted, demented reason, but a reason. And what he said . . . for a moment there . . . I was listening. Really listening. And worse, I think he knew I was listening.

The last thing I want to do is give a monster like him any reason to think that I could be swayed over to his side.

Still . . . the strong survive.

He may be stronger than I am. I mean, I'm still sorting out why I do what I do. Still trying to cope with the notion that I'm busting my ass for a citizenry that tosses aside common sense in exchange for believing tabloid headlines written by a man like Jameson.

But the Goblin, he was so sure of himself. He had so much conviction in his voice, in his attitude. He was like a living incarnation of chaos, and proud of it.

Me . . .

I'm starting to think I don't know what I am.

XXI

THE
STALKER

Mary Jane Watson stood in front of the casting director, holding the pages of the script in her hand, and she was practically trembling with indignation. She felt her eyes stinging and willed herself not to cry. It wasn't easy.

The audition room had been hot and cramped, and the casting director, a woman named April Reese, watched her with cold contempt, which was in startling contrast to the near-movie-star looks she displayed. M. J. had just read for a small part in the popular soap opera *Guiding Life* and was convinced she'd nailed it . . until she looked into Ms. Reese's eyes and saw otherwise.

Reese studied her meticulously manicured red fingernails a moment, as if pondering exactly what to say. "Normally, Ms. Watson, I'd say 'Very nice, thank you, next,' and move on with the audition. But I think I'd be doing you a disservice."

"You would?" Mary Jane said uneasily.

"Yes. But I'm going to make an exception in this case."

"You are?" For a heartbeat M. J. felt hopeful.

"I am. Ms. Watson, when I asked your agent if he had any fresh young ingenue types with red hair, your agent gave me the impression he was sending a professional over. Someone with promise. The reading you gave was hopelessly amateurish. Hopelessly, as in, no hope of improvement."

Mary Jane trembled, giving the acting performance of her life as she forced a smile and said, "Really."

"Really. At the very least, I'd recommend acting lessons. A lot. For a long time.

"At the very most," she said, shrugging, "I'd recommend finding some nice guy to settle down with to take care of you. In the meantime, don't quit your day job."

All the blood drained from M. J.'s face. She felt a sharp stinging like a thousand needles in her pores. "I appreciate your candor," she said in a very clipped voice.

"Good." When M. J. didn't move, Reese cleared her throat and said, "Okay, we've now come to the part where I say, 'Thank you, next.' You'll forgive me if I skip the part where I say 'very nice.' Doesn't seem appropriate."

"Well, good," said Mary Jane, fighting to keep her voice even. "And if it's all the same to you, we'll skip the part where I deck you. That wouldn't be appropriate, either."

She turned and stormed out the door, leaving April Reese sitting there, smiling. Then Reese pulled out a cell phone from her purse, briskly dialed a number, and waited.

"Flash," she said. "It's your Auntie April, the casting director. How are you doing, honey? Listen. That little girl who dumped you on graduation day? Picture this: She comes in here for an audition, absolutely nails the reading—probably knows she nailed it—and guess what I said to her . . . ? Yup. That's right, Flash. Payback, bigtime . . ."

Mary Jane stomped down the narrow stairs, almost tripping once, and then burst out the side door of the television studio. She spun, slammed the door behind her, then laughed bitterly at the sign that read, ARTISTS ONLY.

The temperature had dropped, and there were clouds rolling in, hinting at rain. She drew her coat around her, trying not to give in to the misery she felt. Never had she more wanted to see a sympathetic face than she did at that moment, but there was no one to . . .

"Hey!"

She turned and saw Peter Parker walking toward her. He was dressed in jeans and a brown coat, and had an umbrella tucked under his arm. She couldn't believe it. There were celebrity stalkers out there who had less of a track record than Peter did for showing up unexpectedly. Not that she was unhappy to see him; far from it. But he seemed to be turning into the king of the unexpected. "Hey!" was all she could think to say.

He stood in front of her, his hands shoved into his pockets. "How was the audition?" he asked.

M. J. was utterly taken aback. "How'd you know?"

"The hotline." Peter shrugged, as if it was the most obvious thing in the world. "Your mom told my aunt, who told me. We have no secrets from each other."

"So you just came by." She didn't know whether to be annoyed or flattered.

"I was in the neighborhood. I needed to see a friendly face." When he saw her skeptical expression, he admitted, "Took two buses and a cab to *get* in the neighborhood, but . . ."

And Mary Jane blurted out, "They told me I need acting lessons." When she saw his surprised expression, she just shook her head in disbelief. "A *soap opera* told me I need acting lessons."

The rain had indeed started to fall. Peter, prepared as always, snapped open the umbrella and held it over her head. "I'll buy you a cheeseburger. Sky's the limit, up to," and he reached into his pocket to check, "seven dollars and eighty-four cents."

She laughed at that. It felt good. Up in the audition room, she'd felt as if she'd never laugh again.

"I'd like a cheeseburger, but . . ." She paused, and then added apologetically, "I'm going to dinner with Harry." M. J. saw the disappointment in his eyes and thought of all the effort he'd gone to just to be outside when she came down from the audition. Just to be there . . . for her. "Come with us," she suggested.

"No, thanks," he said easily, and then, less easily, as if the relationship were a scab he couldn't help but pick at, he said, "I mean with you and . . . never mind, none of my business."

"It's not?" She cocked her head. "Why so interested?"

"I'm not . . . am I interested?"

"You're not?"

"Well . . . why *would* I be?"

And Mary Jane began to feel something stirring within her. Old embers being slowly stoked to life. The slow realization of the difference between being happy *for* someone . . . and being *with* someone who *made* you happy.

"I don't know. Why would you be?" she asked softly.

"Y'know . . . just . . ." He seemed totally at a loss for words. Was it because he was feeling emotions that he couldn't express . . . or that he just didn't have a clue what she was going on about, because he wasn't interested?

"I don't know," he said finally.

She smiled, waited.

Nothing.

She thought about saying more, of asking . . . asking questions she wasn't even sure how to frame. But she didn't know the answers she would get, didn't know if she'd make a fool of herself for a second time in the day. What she did know was that she simply couldn't cope with rejection again. "Sorry you won't come with us."

Mary Jane started to turn away, and Peter handed her the umbrella. She was about to hand it back, but he pulled up the hood of his coat, and walked quickly in the other direction.

Realizing she was running late, M. J. walked quickly to the corner of the darkened street and tried to hail a cab. She should have known better. In the rain in Manhattan, finding a cab was practically impossible.

"You need a ride?" a brusque voice said from behind her.

She turned and there were four punks approaching her. But they were quickly splitting into two groups, two of them coming around and at her from the street side, the others remorselessly approaching from the sidewalk.

"I'm fine. I'm waiting for my boyfriend, thanks," she lied.

"Well, we'll wait with you," said the closest of the punks, a guy with a shaved head and a ring in his left nostril.

"No, thanks. My boyfriend's the jealous type. He won't be happy to find you guys here." She tried to back up, but the other two had, as she expected, maneuvered in behind her. They were grouped around her so she wasn't even visible from the street, and they were starting to move, starting to guide her by their sheer presence, away from the curbside.

Then the big guy grabbed her purse, and M. J.—who had been looking for someone on whom to take out her frustration—found him. She kicked him in the shin, elbow-jabbed the guy next to him, turned quickly to punch the third one in the group, and before the fourth could make a move, she yanked free the mace canister that dangled from a keychain on her purse and sprayed it in his face. He let out an alarmed yelp, throwing his arms up over his face to ward off another attack.

She tried to squeeze past them, hoping to break loose and run for it, but then her luck ran out. They converged on her, snarling, and shoved her into a wall. There was an instantly identifiable *snikt* noise, and she saw that the leader had yanked out a switchblade and was bringing it toward her chin, while the others held her immobile. She knew at that moment two things beyond any question: First, that there was no way she was going to give these punks the satisfaction of hearing her scream, and second, that it was unlikely she would be able to maintain that resolution.

Suddenly there was another noise, more unusual, but she recognized it all the same. A loud *thwip* and abruptly all four punks were yanked together as if they'd been lassoed. They had just enough time to let out a cry of alarm, then they were pulled away and over into a nearby alley.

An instant later she heard the sound of bone hitting bone, and the bald punk came flying backward out of the alleyway, smashing into a window. Another emerged, also out of control, until he hit a brick wall and sagged to the ground. The third came flying out in a different direction, crashed into another window, and the fourth came rolling out as if someone had bowled him. He barreled into a garbage can and lay sprawled on the ground with the rest of the trash.

Slowly, barely daring to believe it, she turned and gazed into the inky shadows. She saw a figure standing there, but he wasn't coming any closer, and in the darkness she couldn't make out much beyond his general outline. But there was no question in her mind who she was facing.

"You have a knack for getting in trouble," he said.

She frowned. His voice sounded different. It was still deep, but it sounded more affected, somehow, as if it wasn't his natural voice. . . .

It wasn't muffled. That was it. It wasn't muffled as it was before. *My God . . . he's not wearing his mask. . . .*

She took a step toward him, and he retreated further into the shadows. She wanted to laugh. This guy had just manhandled four thugs, each of them the size of a small mountain range, but he was backing away from a one hundred three-pound redhead.

"You have a knack for saving my ass," she said slowly. "I think I have a superhero stalker."

"I was in the neighborhood."

She blinked, stopped, squinted at him in the darkness. There was . . . there was no way, but . . .

"You *are* amazing," she said.

Slowly but surely, she was drawing closer and closer, until abruptly he made a quick motion with his hands, and when he spoke his voice was muffled once more. "Some people don't think so," he said, stepping slightly out of the shadows, staring at her through the white and opaque eyes of his mask.

Mary Jane felt a small flicker of disappointment. "But you *are*," she insisted.

"Thank you." He didn't sound particularly convinced.

And she recognized that tone of voice. It was like hers: Sad, unutterably sad. She could sympathize.

He leapt up onto the wall above her, clinging there upside down. She stepped up underneath him. "Do I get to thank you this time?" she asked.

And before he could move, she put her hands to the underside of his mask and lifted it.

"Wait," Spider-Man managed to get out, but he made no motion to stop her.

Mary Jane pulled the mask up just far enough to reveal his mouth. And there, with the rain pouring down in buckets, she kissed him more passionately than she had ever kissed anyone. It would have caused Flash's toes to curl; it would have scalded the hair off Harry Osborn. Rain streamed down over both their faces, and over their lips when she finally parted.

She touched his lips with her fingertips and said gently, "That's so you'll remember where your mouth is."

She tenderly replaced the mask. He hung there for a moment, frozen, and then he turned and scampered up the wall, out of sight. She watched him go, eyes shining.

"Yowza," she said.

Dear Mom and Dad:
Please disregard previous letter. Am having wonderful time. Wish you were here.

XXII.

THE MOTH
TO A
FLAME

Peter Parker was sailing . . . literally.

He was sailing across the rooftops, feeling more alive, more invigorated, more filled with a sense of right than he ever had before. The city spread beneath him, and he regarded it through his mask and thought, *I am the protector of the city. I am one of the good guys, and that means something.*

All that from one kiss.

Even though several days had passed, he could still feel the press of her lips against his, like a fine wine. To some degree, he was still appalled at the chance he'd taken. He'd spotted the punks heading toward M. J., hurried to change into his costume, and run out of time, having to go into action before he could pull his mask on. . . .

Or was he kidding himself? Had he been playing a game of chicken with himself? Daring himself, seeing how far he would push it? Had he wanted M. J. to know who he was, wanted to drop the game? If so, then he had sure chickened out at the last minute.

Well, maybe next time. There was all the time in the world.

High over the skyscrapers, a blur of blue and red, and he knew people were looking out office windows and pointing and shouting. Maybe some of them were crying out in fear, while others were bellowing praise. Ultimately he would win them over. It was possible. With the taste of Mary Jane's kiss on his lips, anything was possible. And he was going to be seeing her tonight. Granted, it was part of a whole big Thanksgiving get-together, and Aunt May was going to be there, as well as Harry's dad—who was finally going to meet Mary Jane, and that alone was enough to make Harry a nervous wreck—but hey . . . it would all work out somehow . . .

Then he saw the black smoke rising in the near distance and angled straight for it. He swung down Fifth Avenue, then made his way over to the East Side with such confidence, such alacrity, that he might as well have been doing this his entire life. "Help is on the way!" he called out, adding "Yowza! Yowza!" for no particular reason.

Sure enough, a building was burning, fast and furious. It was an apartment house, surrounded by fire trucks, police cars, and ambulances. A crowd had assembled, and he could see that there were some people in the gathering who had been rescued from the inferno itself, swathed in blankets or getting help from paramedics.

He saw a young woman, two small boys clutching onto her skirt, literally being dragged away from the building by two firemen. She was struggling in their grip, screaming over and over that her baby was still inside. She was pointing toward the top floor of the building. Naturally it would be the top floor. Peter's heart lurched.

The waves of heat were already damned near suffocating, but when he heard the fireman cry out, "It's too late, lady, the roof's ready to collapse!" he knew he would spend every day of the rest of his life imagining that child's life being snuffed out.

Quickly he darted toward a window on the upper floor that didn't appear to have any flames coming out of it. He hoped it stayed that way; if it suddenly erupted just as he got there, he was going to be pretty damned toasted.

They'd spotted him. He heard shouts of "Hey! Up there! Look! It's him! It's Spider-Man!"

He'd never been more thankful that he'd chosen a mask that covered his entire face. It would provide him some minimal protection from the smoke . . . hopefully at least long enough to find the child.

He swung in through the window to cries of "What's he doing?!" and "He's crazy! He hasn't got a chance!" They were instantly drowned out by the roar of flames all around him. His spider sense was screaming at him to just get the hell out of there, and it was an unusual experience to have to fight to override it. When he'd dealt with a burning building some weeks ago, the fire had been nowhere this intense, and it had just been a matter of hauling people off the roof. Even then he'd gotten good and scalded, and a repeat performance wasn't his top preference.

But he had no choice.

He leapt to one side as a chunk of the ceiling, blazing furiously, fell right where he'd been standing. His leap carried him near another apartment with the door still closed. Suddenly he heard crying from within.

He kicked the door open with one booted foot and it splintered like a rifle shot. He ran in and noted with alarm that smoke was starting to fill the apartment. Dashing past the kitchen, he yanked his mask off, ran water over it from the sink, and pulled it back on. The cool wetness gave him a bit more protection against the smoke, and then—low to the ground—he darted through the apartment until he located the child in its nursery. It was sobbing piteously, terrified.

Peter scooped it up and said, "Hi. My name's Spider-Man. Maybe you've read about me?"

The baby looked at him with confused, wet, blue eyes.

Suddenly his spider sense urged him into motion. Peter leapt for the nearest window and, clutching the child to his chest, spun and smashed through the window backward in order to protect the infant from the impact. He heard a horrendous roar, a crashing of wood, and a fireball the size of a Buick frying the air behind him. His leap carried him a short distance away from the building, but there was smoke all around and he was falling blind.

Desperately, praying, unsure of which was up and down, he fired a web line in the direction he thought a building lay. *Please let this work,* he thought, and then he felt the familiar pull of the line as it anchored to something. It snapped taut and he dropped down, down, holding the child tightly to him.

Then he was clear of the smoke, and the ground yawned up at him, closer than he'd expected. But he had more than enough time to react, and he adroitly somersaulted for a perfect two-point landing on the street below.

From all around people were shouting, "He's alive!" and "I don't believe it!" and "He's got the kid!"

Then the applause started. Loud, genuine, and not a single person seemed to give a damn at that moment about the *Daily Bugle* or Jameson and his headlines or anything except for the fact that Spider-Man had put his neck on the line to save an innocent child.

Overwhelmed by emotion, he still managed to keep his voice steady as the mother ran up to him and he handed the child over. "Here's your baby," he said.

"Oh, God bless you, Spider-Man," she wailed, clutching the child to her bosom. "Bless you . . . bless you . . ."

Feeling that something herolike should be said, he turned to the boys, crouched, and said, lowering his voice to sound even more authoritative, "You children be good. Stop playing with matches. Don't start something you can't put out."

The boys were shaking their heads, apparently about to deny culpability, when the moment was ruined by a cop shouting, "Don't let him get away!"

The notion was actually amusing to Peter. As if a woman with a baby in her arms, or a grateful crowd that had just witnessed—as far as they were concerned—a miracle, would try to intervene should he choose to leave.

The cop burst through the crowd, his gun drawn, and he leveled it at Spider-Man. "Hold it right there! You're wanted in connection—"

"Heeellllppp! Heeelllllpppp!"

"Look! There's somebody else!" someone in the crowd shouted. Sure enough, several floors up, an elderly woman with a shawl and loose-fitting dress was standing in a window that already was dancing with flames. Her arms were outstretched and she was truly a pathetic sight, the smoke billowing around her.

Peter and the cop exchanged looks, and then Peter put out his gloved hands, presenting his wrists, as if inviting the cop to put cuffs on him.

"I'll be here when you get back," the cop growled, lowering his revolver. He had barely finished the sentence when Peter leapt away.

He skittered up the wall, hoping this was the last person in the building, because soon there wasn't going to be much of a building left. The old woman backed away, maybe in fear or maybe to give him room to gain access. He flipped in through the window, scanned the smoky room, and immediately spotted the woman, huddled in the corner.

"Everything's going to be okay, ma'am!"

She called out to him, in a wretched, wavering voice, "Oh, thank you, sonny. You're my hero." And then the voice dissolved into cackling, high-pitched demented laughter. And as the old woman stood fully erect, allowing the shawl to drop to the ground, "she" asked, "What's wrong with lighting up now and then?"

"Goblin!" shouted Peter. "You started this fire?!"

"You're pathetically predictable," the Goblin snarled, his

masked face etched in a permanent leer. "Like a moth to a flame. Perhaps you should change your name from Spider-Man to Moth Man." He giggled, chortled at his own cleverness, and then suddenly grew serious. "What about my generous proposal? Are you in or are you out?"

"It's you who's out, Gobby," and despite the flames licking the room around them eagerly, he assumed a fighting stance. "Out for good!"

The Green Goblin didn't seem the least bit impressed. Without hesitation he reached into his belt and hurled what appeared to be a small plastic bat. Peter swatted it aside with his left arm and then let out a yell of pain. Stunned, he looked down at the red and blue sleeve of his costume and saw a deep gash, oozing blood. The damned bat had been razor sharp.

The Goblin advanced on him, and Peter didn't hesitate. He fired a web line, snagging a beam above the Goblin's head, and pulling as hard as he could. Debris rained down and the Goblin vanished under the debris.

Immediately Peter turned and made for the window. He glanced behind, saw a trail of blood he was leaving as he scampered out the window and down the side of the wall. Behind him he could hear the Goblin howling, "I don't forgive and I don't forget! It breaks my heart! We could have been so good together!"

Okay. We've officially gotten into a weird area, he thought, but at that moment he didn't care about much beyond two things: Attending to the throbbing wound in his arm, and not dying before Thanksgiving supper, just so he could see how things turned out with Mary Jane.

XXIII.

THE LAST
SUPPER

She was wearing the black dress. It didn't seem to help. Harry still was as nervous as a cat at a vacuum cleaner convention, and Mary Jane had come to realize there was nothing that she, or May Parker, or anyone could do that would calm him down. The only thing that would help would be if Norman Osborn walked in, took one look at her, threw his arms around her, and claimed her as the daughter he'd never had. Somehow she didn't think that was going to happen.

Aunt May, with long-practiced expertise, removed the browning turkey from the oven and placed it on the stovetop, motioning Mary Jane to keep her distance lest she get burned. M. J. nodded and put the finishing touches on setting the table while May used a fork to satisfy herself that the bird was sufficiently cooked. Harry busied himself checking the living room, plumping pillows, and straightening chairs. M. J.'s heart went out to him. There were men on death row who weren't this edgy.

The doorbell rang and Harry let out a yelp. Trying to compose himself, he said, "Okay . . . he's here." Mary Jane emerged from the kitchen, removing her apron, and Harry looked her up and down with the scrutiny of a drill instructor. "You look great," he said, an efficient if perfunctory assessment that sounded as if he were complimenting her for having her M16 properly slung.

Harry walked over to the door, swung it open. *He doesn't have horns,* Mary Jane thought with amusement as Norman

Osborn stood in the doorway, attired in a very nice suit. She wondered if he was feeling well, though, because he was dabbing sweat off his forehead with a handkerchief. Mary Jane had thought the place was, in fact, kind of chilly. Osborn was carrying a small pastry box tied with a ribbon.

"Sorry I'm late," Osborn said. "Work was murder." Then he smiled, as if this was funny to him for some reason. Well, it was nice to see a workaholic with a sense of humor. "Here's a fruitcake." He passed the box to Harry, then glanced at Mary Jane and asked a question to which he very likely already knew the answer: "Who's this young lady?"

"M. J.," Harry said, trying his best to sound calm, "I'd like you to meet my father, Norman Osborn. Dad, I'd like you to meet Mary Jane Watson . . . M. J."

This was it. Set phasers on Charm.

Mary Jane flashed her most radiant smile, one that could have melted the hearts of the entire offensive line at Midtown High. Osborn stepped closer, holding out a hand to shake hers but also, unmistakably, narrowing his eyes. She felt as if he was mentally dissecting her. She tried to tell herself that there were worse things men could do with her mentally, but she still felt uneasy.

"How do you do?" said Osborn with the air of someone trying to force informality. "I've been looking forward to meeting you."

"Happy Thanksgiving, sir," she said evenly.

At that moment May Parker stepped forward, and if there was any reason to think that something was off with Harry's dad, she certainly didn't give a hint of it. "Hello, Norman. We're so pleased you're here." She turned to Harry. "Where's Peter? He'd better have remembered the cranberry sauce."

Suddenly a loud thud came from the direction of Peter's bedroom. The four of them looked at each other in confusion. "That's weird," said Harry. "I didn't know he was here."

"Peter?" Aunt May called. The only response they got was a thud so loud that they all jumped slightly. "My goodness," said May, looking at Harry. "Harry, dear, by any chance . . . did Peter take up anvil collecting . . . ?"

Every motion was agony for him.

Peter had become so accustomed to moving with agility and grace, but now—wounded and aching—he wondered that he could move at all. He had managed to swing past the living room window without being seen, had even managed to gain access to his room through a window with the most minimal of noise. But then, as he had crawled across the ceiling, the stab of pain that shot through his left arm was so fearsome, it caused him to lose his grip, and he thudded to the floor with the grace of an anchor.

He pulled off his mask and examined his injured arm. It was still bleeding, and swelling slightly. He wondered if that damned Goblin had treated the razor bat with some sort of toxin to give it some added bite. He wouldn't put it past him, because it was becoming clear that the Goblin was extremely creative in his penchant for sadism.

Suddenly he heard a noise, right at his door. It wasn't locked. Of course it wasn't locked; who locks their room behind them on the way out? Maskless, injured, panicked, Peter still possessed just enough presence of mind to leap upward. He flattened himself against the ceiling just as the door opened. Aunt May stepped in, with M. J., Harry, and Harry's dad standing just behind her. Great. Only everyone in his life who was important. All any of them had to do was look up, and he was a squashed spider.

"Pete?" called Harry into what appeared to be an empty room.

"But . . . there's nobody here," said a puzzled Aunt May.

Peter was sure they could hear the hammering of his

heart. How could they not? It was pounding in his ears, louder than cannon fire.

Osborn entered, and Peter felt that same vague thrill of warning from his spider sense that he always did when Harry's dad was around. Well, hey, no kidding on this one: danger was just an upward glance away. Norman scowled at the disarray he found around him.

Then Peter saw, to his horror, a drop of blood oozing from the cut on his arm, dangling right over the senior Osborn's head.

"Bit of a slob, isn't he," Norman observed.

Aunt May responded defensively, "All brilliant men are," which was kind of sweet of her to say considering the number of times in his life she'd said, "Peter, clean up this pigsty!"

Osborn smiled at that and turned to leave as the others filed out. He was the last one out of the room . . .

. . . and the drop of blood fell. It hit the light-colored carpet, right where he'd been standing.

But it was just a drop of blood. It's wasn't as if he could hear it. He'd have to have ears that would make a bat deaf by comparison.

Norman Osborn whirled and stared right where the blood had dripped.

Peter couldn't believe it. It simply wasn't possible. His eyes widened as Osborn stalked back to the spot where the drop had fallen. He stared down at the carpet, knelt, and as the wind blew briskly through the open window, he touched it and brought his fingers up to his face, rubbing them together. His eyes grew wide and he looked directly over his head.

Nothing.

Quickly Osborn crossed to the open window and leaned out, looking right and left, up and down. He could not, of course, look through the ledge that jutted out beneath the window . . . which was exceedingly fortunate for Peter, because that's where he was clinging.

He had never moved as quickly in his life as he had to get out of that room, and part of him still couldn't believe he had managed it. His arm was practically screaming at him in protest, and he bit down tightly on his lip to contain the moan of pain that desperately wanted to escape.

Apparently satisfied—although with what, Peter had no idea—Osborn pulled back in from the window. Moments later the door to Peter's room closed with a soft click. It crossed Peter's mind that it might be some sort of trick, but he didn't think so; his spider sense wasn't warning him of any immediate danger.

Minutes later, he had managed to make a perfectly silent reentry into his room, snag some clothes and some towels to wipe down the wound, get to the roof, change, and make it back down to the front hallway of the apartment. He had no idea whether he looked as exhausted as he felt, but he had to do whatever he could to put on a brave front. Only at the last moment did he remember that he was supposed to bring cranberry sauce.

Fortunately, there was a convenience store downstairs that was just in the process of closing up: Five minutes of begging and a five-dollar bribe had convinced the man to stay open long enough for Peter to fetch what he needed. He could brave fires, floods, famine, and the Green Goblin, but he had no intention of facing down Aunt May without cranberry sauce.

When Harry opened the front door, Peter had his broadest smile fixed firmly in place. "Hey, everyone," he said cheerily. He kissed Aunt May on the cheek. "Sorry I took so long. It's a jungle out there. I had to hit an old lady with a stick to get these cranberries."

"Oh, Peter!" Aunt Mary scolded him, slapping him

lightly on the shoulder as if he was an obnoxious five-year-old. Then, all business, she said, "Come on, everyone. Let's sit down and say a prayer."

They all moved for the table. Norman reached for the jellied cranberry log and, just to show she played no favorites, Aunt May slapped his hand. Osborn glanced at her, and a look flashed across his face, but then it was gone and he smiled gamely at the rebuke.

"And Norman," she said, indicating the turkey and the carving knife that sat near it, "will you do the honors?"

But as Norman Osborn moved to pick up the knife, Peter noticed that Aunt May was staring at him and had suddenly gone pale. He followed her gaze, and gasped.

His left shirtsleeve had a huge bloodstain on it, and it was growing. He cursed to himself. He'd thought he had the damned thing under control.

"Peter, you're bleeding!" Aunt May gasped.

Trying to sound as indifferent about it as possible, Peter said, "Yeah. I stepped off a curb and got clipped by one of those bike messengers." He wondered if that sounded as pathetic to her as it did to him.

She didn't seem to be paying much attention to the excuse anyway. "Let me see that," she said, rolling his sleeve up, revealing the distinctive X-shaped slashes that the whirring razor bat had left upon him. *"What in the name of heavenly glory!"* she cried out.

His spider sense . . .

"Everyone sit down, I'll go and get the first-aid kit."

. . . tingling . . . growing more intense . . . practically howling in alarm . . .

". . . and then we'll say grace . . . this is the boys' first Thanksgiving in this apartment . . ."

. . . drowning out everything that Aunt May was saying, pushing it far into the background, there was danger, danger in such thick waves that he was suffocating in it . . .

". . . and we're going to do things properly . . ."

And when Norman Osborn spoke, it was with a voice that bore only a passing resemblance to his normal tone. "How did you say that happened?" he asked. His eyes were focusing like laser beams on Peter's arm, as if he recognized the cuts, as if he expected Peter's answer to be a lie, because he already knew the truth . . .

". . . Bike messenger . . ." Peter said tonelessly.

. . . and his spider sense was at Defcon 5, as the world around him slowed to a crawl, each face he looked at frozen, each face the face of a friend, not an enemy, there couldn't be an enemy right here, at his apartment, at his table . . .

He snapped out of it, or snapped himself out of it, and now his forehead was beaded with perspiration. ". . . knocked me down," he managed to finish.

Danger, right in front of you, somewhere here, right here, not just to you, to everyone, find it you idiot, find it . . .

Mary Jane looked from Norman to Peter and back again. She couldn't understand what was transpiring. It was as if the two of them were eating a different meal entirely. That there was some sort of weird dynamic going on between them, at which the others could only guess.

And then, just like that, as Peter sat there and sweated as if he were in a sauna, Norman Osborn rose to his feet. "You'll have to excuse me. I'm afraid I've got to go."

Clearly Harry was dumbfounded. "What? Why?"

"Something . . . has come to my attention," he said, looking pointedly at Peter again. *What the hell was going on between those two?*

"Are you all right?" Harry asked. He was standing, tugging nervously at the neatly knotted necktie he was wearing.

"Fine, I'm fine. Thank you. Mrs. Parker. Everyone."

Even Aunt May was flummoxed. "What happened?" she asked. But she had no more luck deciphering Osborn's odd behavior than anyone else, for without responding to her question, Norman Osborn headed for the door. He stopped only to take a last look back at Peter, and then he was in the hallway. He didn't get far, though, because Harry was right behind him, and their voices carried.

"What are you doing?" Harry demanded. At least he was standing up to his father. M. J. had to give him credit for that. "I planned this whole thing so you could meet M. J., and you barely even looked at her!"

"I've got to go," Norman said curtly.

But Harry clearly wasn't going to let it end there. "Hey! I *like* this girl! This is important to me!"

And when Norman Osborn replied, it was with urgent desperation, as if he were trying to convince a stubborn drowning man to take the damned life preserver already. "Harry, please . . . look at her! You think a woman like that's sniffing around because she likes your personality?"

M. J.'s jaw dropped in astonishment. Peter and May were both looking at her, embarrassed on her behalf, astounded that Osborn would say such things.

"What are you saying, Dad?"

"Your mother was beautiful, too. They're all beautiful, until they're snarling after your trust fund like ravening wolves. . . ."

She wanted to crawl under the table, under the carpet. She wanted to die.

Harry spoke in a stunned, almost hushed voice. "Dad . . ." he said, and he didn't sound as if he was speaking with a great deal of conviction. "This girl's no . . ."

Osborn interrupted his son. "A word to the not-so-wise about your little girlfriend. Do what you need to with her and broom her fast." Then she heard his footsteps retreating down the hallway and, just like that, he was gone, leaving his son stammering behind him.

Slowly, like a woman in a trance, Mary Jane rose from

the table. Peter could barely even look at her, and May's expression was one of pity.

That's what she was. An object of pity. She wanted to die, just crawl away and die.

She headed for the closet just as Harry walked back into the apartment. He stood there, transfixed, as she grabbed her coat and headed for the door. "Where are you going?" he asked, dumbfounded.

The one she really wanted to lash out at was Norman. But the father was gone, and only the son remained.

"Thanks for sticking up for me, Harry," she said tightly.

"You heard?"

She whirled on him, pointing to the hallway that Norman had vacated. "Everyone could hear that creep!"

And suddenly Harry's own anger boiled over. Perhaps he, too, was misplacing it, since his father was gone, but he was no less vehement in his defense.

"That 'creep' is my *father! All right?* If I'm lucky, I've got the brains and the guts to become half of what he is, so you keep your goddamn mouth shut about things you don't understand!"

"Harry Osborn!" said Aunt May, shocked.

"You're acting like somebody's father—mine!" Mary Jane said. She was so furious, she started to shove the wrong arm into the sleeve of her coat. She wrestled with it, chagrined, twisted her torso around, got it to fit properly.

"I'm sorry, Aunt May," she said, and then she stormed out of the apartment, slamming the door behind her.

Well, the danger's gone . . .

That was the one bright spot that Peter was able to draw from the entire debacle. He stood there in stupefied silence as Mary Jane walked out the door.

"Harry, go after her!" he said finally.

To his astonishment, Harry replied with quiet certainty, "I don't think so."

He stepped toward his friend, shaking him as if trying to rouse a dreamer from his sleep. "Harry, come on!"

"No. I can't," he said again, with greater conviction than before, as if he knew that doing nothing was the right course. With bitter sarcasm, he turned to Aunt May and said, "Welcome to an Osborn Thanksgiving."

Then he stormed into his own bedroom, slamming the door behind him with as much force as M. J. had used on the front door.

A pall fell over the apartment, and Peter knew he couldn't just stand by. That he had to do something. The thing was, Harry wasn't going anywhere. Maybe something could still be salvaged of all this.

He had to face facts. He wanted Mary Jane, wanted his chance at her . . . but not like this. If M. J. and Harry had a relationship that ran its course and they parted, that was one thing. But this . . . this was an abortion. A total disaster. He wasn't out to play Cupid, God knew, but he had to do something to try and stitch some fabric of the relationship back together, for all their sakes.

"Sorry, Aunt May. It looked great," he assured her, as he grabbed his jacket from the closet and bolted for the door.

Behind him, Aunt May surveyed the wreckage of good sentiments gone bad and called, just before he was out the door, "We didn't even get to say grace!"

Peter sped down the stairs, vaulting them four, five at a time, since no one was around to watch. He made it down to street level, ran out into the cold night air and looked around frantically to see if he could spot where M. J. had gotten off to. It turned out not to be one of his greater challenges. M. J. was seated on the stoop of the next building over, sobbing piteously. Then the chauffeur-driven Bentley rolled past, and

Peter nearly laughed when M. J. showed enough spunk and presence of mind to flip the luxury car an obscene gesture.

He walked over to her and just stood there, hands folded in front of him. Mary Jane snuffled a bit more, then looked up at him. Her mascara was all over the place. Peter pulled out a handkerchief and held it out to her. When she hesitated, just staring at it as if it might be a hand grenade, he waved it slightly and said, "Take it."

She nodded and took it from him, blowing her nose loudly into it. Then she looked at him apologetically for having messed it up. He shrugged. "Keep it," he said with a ready smile. "It's yours. Got a million of 'em from Aunt May, a dozen every Christmas."

She laughed through her tears, blew her nose again, and this time made a very loud and pronounced "honk" that only provided louder laughter. Then, to Peter's surprise, her laughter swung back over to crying. Her shoulders trembled, then sagged, and it was as if every miserable moment in her existence had boiled down to this instant, and she was in the process of crying out a lifetime of tears.

He sat next to her, put an arm around her, literally giving her a shoulder to cry on. "That's okay. Good cry."

Between sniffles, she managed to get out, "I'm sorry I acted like that . . . but . . . but I couldn't stay there. Being treated that way . . . brings back bad stuff. I hate being thought of as if I'm not worth anything."

"I understand," Peter said with conviction. And that was no exaggeration. Not with newspapers coming out every day that questioned his actions, no matter how heroic.

"I know you do," she told him, and there was something in the way she said it that made him wonder. But then her mind was elsewhere. "Your poor Aunt May," she moaned, and it was reasonable to feel sorry for her, considering the amount of work she must have put into making the turkey. "But I can't go back in there," she said apologetically, frustrated over what she no doubt perceived as her own weakness.

Peter shrugged. "She'll be okay. She's tough." The stairs weren't the cushiest place to be, so he shifted to try and make himself more comfortable. It brought him closer to Mary Jane. She didn't seem to mind, so he didn't pull away. "I've never seen Mr. Osborn act like that," he said in bewilderment. "I've never seen either of them act like that before." He paused and then said the toughest words he knew he was going to have to say that evening. "But I know Harry really loves you."

"Sometimes I wonder why I ever went out with him in the first place. I guess because he liked me." She looked down at her ensemble. "Dumb black dress," she snapped bitterly.

"However, you do look extremely beautiful in it," he assured her.

She smiled at him then. "Thank you. You look very handsome yourself tonight."

She had sounded so tentative when she said it, but it seemed sincere, and now he was extremely aware of just how close he was to her. He realized that it wouldn't take much for him to lean over and kiss her. He was more in love with her than ever. He gazed into her eyes.

And did nothing.

Because he didn't want to pressure her. Because he didn't want to kick Harry when he was down. Because of a lot of reasons, really, but ultimately, because he didn't think it would be right.

She put an arm around his shoulder, and they sat there, holding each other close, and that was all they did . . .

. . . which was more than enough for Harry Osborn, looking down at them from the window of the apartment and glowering in the night . . .

"This changes everything . . ."

Norman Osborn felt as if his head was splitting in two.

He lay on the floor of his study, curled up, trembling, cowering in a pool of light from the end of the hallway. In his quivering hands he held the mask he wore as the Green Goblin, except he was doing everything within his power at that moment to convince himself that the Goblin was someone else entirely . . . not Norman himself . . .

. . . not Norman, who was no murderer . . .

. . . who wouldn't even consider what the Goblin was contemplating . . .

"Spider-Man is all but invincible," hissed the mask, *"but Parker . . . Parker is flesh and blood . . . we can destroy him . . ."*

"I can't!" Osborn was gibbering now, saying anything that came to mind. "I've been like a father to that boy. He's a good son . . ."

"Which is exactly what he wanted!" the mask snarled at him, clearly holding Osborn in contempt. Osborn's entire body was shaking now, his shirt soaked through with sweat, his lower jaw twitching spasmodically. *"He came to you, the greedy, open-mouthed scheming little orphan . . ."*

"He did," Osborn admitted slowly, as if puzzle pieces were being assembled in his mind.

"Plucked your heartstrings like a master. Connived his way into your heart, leaving no room for Harry, your true son and heir . . ."

Of course. Of course! How could he have been so foolish as to not be able to see it?

"It's true . . . oh, God . . ."

"And now," said the Goblin, moving in for the emotional kill, *"after everything you've done for Peter Parker, after everything you've taught him,* this *is how he repays you?"*

Years and years of guilt piled upon Osborn as he cried out, "What have I done to Harry?! What have I done to my own son!"

"Betrayal must not be countenanced . . . Parker must be . . . educated . . ."

Osborn sat partway up, propping himself on his elbow. In his dementia, he didn't think it remotely odd that he should be carrying on a chat with a mask. "What do I do?" he asked firmly.

"Instruct him in the matters of loss and pain. Watch him suffer, make him wish he were dead. . . ."

"Yes!"

"And then grant his wish!"

"But how?" demanded Osborn.

"The cunning warrior attacks neither body nor mind."

Instantly Osborn was furious. He didn't need cryptic hints at this point. He needed solid guidance. "Tell me how!" he fairly bellowed.

The mask was silent for a moment, and when it spoke again, it said, *"The heart, Osborn . . . first . . . we attack his heart."*

Ben Parker's mother had hated her.

That's what I should have said to her, Aunt May realized as she readied herself for bed. She did so in the same meticulous manner, with the exact same routine, that she had followed for more than a half century. It was so drilled into her that she gave it no conscious consideration, because her mind was elsewhere, dwelling on the poor, mortified Mary Jane Watson.

As she fluffed her pillow—three times, not two—and moved back the sheet the precise length—eighteen inches—that would allow her to easily climb into bed, she shivered slightly in her flannel pajamas. It was Thursday; Thursday, not Friday, was flannel pajamas. And she recalled a day—many years gone—when the debonair Benjamin Parker had brought a scared young woman named May Reilly home to meet his folks. Ben's father had been indifferent, and his mother had been positively scathing, critiquing everything from May's clothing to her hairstyle to her interest in Ben. May had tried to take it all, but eventually she had succumbed to her misery and bolted from the house, convinced she would never seen Ben Parker again.

Well, obviously it hadn't worked out that way, but she wished that she'd thought to say that to Mary Jane. Granted, tonight had been a disaster, and Osborn's behavior had been just abominable. But many relationships had hit similar rocks and managed to keep on sailing, just the same.

Thoughts of Ben affected her in that melancholy way they always did. She touched a framed photo of him that sat on the bedside table. The telephone answering machine was next to it. His voice was still on the answering machine. All these months he'd been gone, and she still couldn't find it within herself to change it. Every so often, she would play the message while staring wistfully at the photograph. "Hi, we're not around to take your call," his photo would "say," and she'd sigh heavily and wish that either he was still around . . . or that she was with him.

But there was no point dwelling on such things.

The good Lord had decided that she was to remain around for a while longer, that was all, and if He was inclined to reveal His purpose in these apparently capricious matters, then He would do so. In the meantime, she would simply deal with the hand she'd been dealt.

May knelt next to the bed, moaning softly as her knees creaked beneath her. Blasted arthritis was getting worse. Oh, for the youthful suppleness of the muscles she had once possessed. She had a young mind, she felt. What sort of perversity captured such a young mind in such an old and limited shell?

Well, the kind of perverse mind that would take Ben violently from her in a most untimely manner. Then May decided that further musings along those lines would most surely be blasphemy, and she didn't pursue them. Instead she rested her elbow on the bed, folded her hands and closed her eyes.

"Our Father, who art in heaven," she said with ease brought by long practice. "Hallowed be thy name. Thy kingdom come, thy will be done, on earth as it is in heaven. Give us this day our daily bread, and forgive us our trespasses as we forgive those who trespass against us. Lead us not into temptation, but . . ."

At that moment the wall behind her exploded. For a split second May thought she was back in World War II, back as a field nurse in that foolhardy, mad endeavor she'd never told Peter about, lest he consider it carte blanche to do something stupid himself. She thought that she was being shelled by the Germans or something. She hit the floor, plaster and glass flying over her head, and then she managed to gather together her scattered wits.

She turned toward the source of the crazed entrance, and was stunned. Floating a short distance away, the sound of his turbine engines roaring, was that ghastly creature the newspapers had dubbed the Green Goblin. She pulled bits of broken glass out of her hair as she gaped in confusion, watching as the costumed madman peered in through the hole he'd just created.

Green vapor was spewing out of his glider, filling the room. Then his face suddenly seemed to widen and widen, until it became impossibly distorted and filled the room, reaching from one side to the other. Those yellow eyes of his were glowing in the relative dimness of the bedroom. He let out one loud, demented laugh, and Aunt May tried to flee. Instead she fell to the ground, putting up her hands, trying to ward him off as she stammered, "But . . . but . . . but . . ." over and over again.

"Finish it! Finish it!" howled the Green Goblin.

She clutched at her chest, unsure of what "it" the Goblin meant, unless the monster was referring to her time on earth. But then she understood, and she cried out in terror, *". . . deliver us from evil!"* and suddenly there was a feeling like a massive vise across her chest, knocking the breath, the very life from her. Her back arched, tensed, and then she went limp as a sack of rice. Her eyes closed, her head slumping to one side, and the last thing she heard as the darkness claimed her was, *"Amen, sister!"* accompanied by a lunatic and very self-satisfied chortling.

XXIV.

<u>T H E</u>
<u>Y E L L O W</u>
<u>E Y E S</u>

Peter sprinted down the hospital corridor, out of his mind with worry. Nurses and orderlies scrambled to get out of his way. He almost collided with an old man just emerging from his room, pulling an IV on a rolling stand. But Peter darted around him with ease, so quickly that the elderly patient wasn't quite sure whether someone had just gone past him or not.

He reached the last room on the right, ducked inside, and stopped in his tracks. Despite the fact that he was in a hospital room, despite the fact that trained medical personnel were working with the frenzy of worker bees hauling ass to please the queen, still all he could do was flash back to that horrible moment that was Uncle Ben's last.

God, don't let her die . . . it would be like being orphaned twice . . .

If God was operating through the hands of the doctors, then He was working overtime. May Parker lay in a hospital bed, hooked up to so many machines that she looked as if she was ready to be fired into orbit. Her face was ashen, and although her eyes were wide open, it was unclear to Peter whether she was even capable of communicating. *A major shock . . . triggered an episode,* he'd been told. But the circumstances of May's collapse were maddeningly vague, and it was that lack of information that was threatening to drive him over the edge.

"Aunt May!" Peter called.

At first he didn't think she was going to respond. But then her eyes focused on him, and he was so overjoyed that his heart skipped a beat, figuratively speaking. Unfortunately Aunt May's heart also skipped a beat, but it was rather more literal, and she started to twitch in great agitation.

"What happened?! Is she going to be okay?!" Peter cried out.

"Sir, please!" said one of the nurses with a commanding voice. "Let the doctors work!"

Peter started to head toward his aunt, but the nurse—a stout woman who was to bedside warmth what wind shear was to airplane safety records—hooked an arm around his elbow and propelled him toward the door. Naturally, Peter could have lifted her over his head, slam-dunked her, used her as beach ball if he was so inclined. Instead, his attention fixed upon Aunt May's face, Peter allowed himself to be led out of the room, frantically looking over his shoulder repeatedly for a last glimpse of her. And that was when he heard her cry out, "Those eyes . . . those *horrible yellow eyes!*"

Those words meant nothing to the doctors and nurses who were attending her, trying to calm her. They undoubtedly figured she was experiencing some sort of delusion, a fevered and terrifying nightmare.

But for Peter . . .

At first his mind just locked up, hearing those words without fully grasping them.

And then he saw the face of the Green Goblin.

In his imagining, the Goblin's face—with those blazing yellow orbs filled with hatred—was on an upright domino. The domino was wavering slightly, and then it fell over . . . and struck another domino with Aunt May's face on it, which struck a final domino that had Peter's face on it. But it had Spider-Man's face as well. It was split right down the mid-

*dle, vertically, and it wavered and toppled, falling, falling as
the Goblin's hysterical laughter floated through the air . . .*

"The Goblin . . ." whispered Peter, standing in the hospital corridor.

All around him people lay in rooms with tubes attached to every possible part of their body, fighting for their lives, and here Peter's life was in mortal jeopardy, yet he was just standing there.

"He knows . . . oh God . . . he knows who I am . . ."

He bolted down the hall and dashed up the stairway, springing up each staircase as if he were on strings. He burst out onto the hospital roof and, as rain poured down upon him, let out a scream of mortal terror such as never had exploded from his chest before.

Dear Mom and Dad:

All my efforts to make up for letting Uncle Ben down have come to this: Not only is my own life in danger . . . which was mine to risk . . . but so is the life of the woman who committed the cardinal sin of loving me.

I haven't made things better. I've made them worse than they ever were.

I feel like I'm watching from a distance, like I'm outside my body, and my whole life is about to be flushed away.

What am I going to do? God in heaven, what am I going to do?

He'd brought a picture to set at her bedside: a lovely shot of a young Peter with a smiling Uncle Ben and Aunt May standing on either side of him.

And Peter Parker sat there, like a statue. He could have been there for hours or days. He'd often read the phrase "time had lost all meaning," in books and such, but the concept had never really meant anything to him until now. He knew it was night, since a glance out the window told him so. But for all he knew, he'd been sitting there for days on end. He really hadn't been paying attention.

The rain had soaked him up on the roof, but he'd dried off.

He stared at the picture that he himself had brought. Uncle Ben, dead . . . because of him. Aunt May, hospitalized, in mortal danger, because of him. This bizarre "gift" he had received came with too high a price tag, as far as he was concerned.

He leaned forward, kissed Aunt May on the forehead as he blinked back tears. "I'm sorry," he whispered.

He brought textbooks to keep current with his studies, but they sat in the backpack near his feet. He knew he'd get around to them, eventually, but at this point he was afraid to take his eyes off Aunt May, lest she somehow slip away into oblivion while he turned away even for a moment. At the end of visiting hours, the nurse who ran the ward tried to get him to leave. He ignored her. He simply sat in the chair, not moving. She could have been addressing a department store mannequin for all the luck she was having.

The nurse, annoyed, called the doctor, who came and told Peter much the same thing. He had to leave, visiting hours were over, his aunt's condition had stabilized, and he wasn't going to accomplish anything by taking up room. Besides, it was hospital policy, that was all, and such policy was well known, carved in granite and not to be trifled with under pain of . . . well . . . Very Bad Things.

Peter didn't acknowledge him, didn't even glance at him. He.

Just.

Sat.

Annoyed, the doctor summoned a burly orderly, who endeavored to pick Peter up bodily. Peter ignored him, too. He didn't fight back; didn't have to. He simply didn't budge when the orderly, who outweighed him by a good hundred pounds, tried to move him. Annoyed, the orderly tried to lift Peter's chair clean up, and was stunned when he had no more success at this than he'd had at his earlier attempts. He did not, of course, see the small globs of webbing Peter had taken the precaution of using on the bottoms of the chair legs.

So the orderly and the nurse and the doctor put their heads together and thought about calling the police. The orderly observed that the little guy was stronger than he looked, and if the cops started getting physical, things could get real ugly, real fast. The doctor asked if Peter was hurting anyone, the nurse admitted that he wasn't. That he wasn't a burden at all, and indeed, if not for the fact that they were making all this fuss, his presence would go completely unnoticed and unremarked upon.

The doctor shrugged, said "Keep an eye on things," and walked away. And that was pretty much that.

Peter hadn't realized that he'd drifted off to sleep, but before he knew it he was blinking away sunlight in his eyes. His shirt was soaked completely through with sweat. He didn't care.

He went downstairs, grabbed some snacks from a machine, went back to May's room and started reading the textbooks. He did this for a time, nodding to the nurses who came in every so often to check on his aunt. They'd stopped worrying about him, apparently choosing to think of him as one of the fixtures, no different than a chair or a bedpan. Perhaps they even thought it was kind of sweet.

Just after 9:30 A.M. Peter realized that May's eyes were open and fixed on him, the edges crinkling gently in that way she had when she was happy to see him. She murmured his name, and he didn't want to hug her for fear he'd break her. Quickly, Peter summoned the doctor, who checked May over, and a look of relief settled on his face. He asked her some questions while he jotted down readings from the machines that were monitoring her and seemed satisfied with the answers. When he asked if she knew what had happened, she just stared at him blankly.

Peter stayed with her as she drifted back to sleep. He was still tense and nervous, but the doctor seemed cautiously optimistic. Yes, that's what they always called it: Cautiously Optimistic. He informed Peter that he could go home now, and Peter just stared at him as if he'd sprouted a third arm, so the doctor rolled his eyes and walked away.

Since Peter's sleep during the night had been minimal, to say nothing of uncomfortable, he eventually fell back to sleep. He was awakened by a rapping, a gentle tapping, upon the chamber door. For a moment he was confused as to where he was. He looked up, licking his lips, his mouth feeling as if it was filled with cotton.

Mary Jane was standing there, a tentative smile on her face. She was holding a bouquet of flowers under her arm. "Can I come in?" she asked.

Immediately Peter felt rejuvenated. *How can one person have that much of an effect on another?* he wondered as he got to his feet. He popped a breath mint into his mouth as M. J. entered the room tentatively, casting a sad look upon Aunt May's unconscious form. Then, still holding the flowers, M. J. went to Peter and delicately put her arms around his shoulders. She drew him close in a comforting hug, and Peter let out a low breath that he felt like he'd been holding forever.

"I'm so sorry. I just heard about it," she whispered. He nodded, drinking in the closeness of her, and it was all he could do to hold himself together, rather than break down on her shoulder.

They stayed that way for a long moment, and then she turned toward the bed. Moving closer to Aunt May, she lay the flowers on the bedside table, gently touching the wizened woman's forehead. "Will she be okay?"

"We think so," Peter told her, shoving his hands in his pockets. "She finally woke up this morning. For a while. Thanks for coming."

"Who would do this to her?" asked a puzzled Mary Jane.

Peter's head snapped around. "How did you know that somebody 'did' something?"

She looked at him, surprised. "Peter . . . who do you think found your aunt? Called the ambulance? It was my mom. She heard your aunt screaming and howling, the noise. It was so unusual for your house that she went over to check on her. She found your aunt's bedroom wrecked, and there were burn marks, like someone had been trying to set the place on fire. . . ."

The glider, Peter thought grimly. *The turbos and thrusters would certainly leave burns on the carpet, on the wall. The monster . . .*

Mary Jane was shaking her head. "Your Aunt May . . . she's so loving, so giving. Why would anyone want to hurt her? Do you know who did it?" She said it skeptically, clearly not thinking that Peter would have an answer.

He wasn't going to tell her, but he blurted it out just the same. "It was the Green Goblin."

M. J. paled. "But . . . why?" she said when she found her voice. "Why would he need to attack her?" He didn't answer. What could he say? The truth? Oh, like that was going to happen. "I'm sorry, Peter. I know you've asked yourself these questions . . ."

"It's okay," he shrugged, trying to look bewildered when he, in fact, knew more than he wanted to think about. Turning it around, he said, "How about you? Are you all right about the other night?"

She looked down, obviously chagrined. "I'm sorry about that. Makes things worse for everybody."

"You were fine. Have you talked to Harry?"

M. J. shook her head, still not looking up at him. "He

called me. I haven't called him back." Then she turned her back to him completely, focusing on the sleeping Aunt May. She tucked in the bed sheet. "The fact is," she continued, still presenting her back, "I'm in love with somebody else."

Peter thought his head was going to explode. He cleared his throat. "You are?"

"At least . . . I think I am." Then she did turn back and look at him. "This isn't the time to talk about this."

"No, go on," he said urgently. Fighting to remain nonchalant, he took a step closer to her, closing the distance between them. "Would I know his name? This guy?"

"You'll think I'm a stupid little girl with a crush."

With as much fervency as he could muster, he said, "Trust me."

She looked into his eyes, long and hard, and suddenly she laughed as if tremendously embarrassed over having been caught at something. "I'm, like, head over heels!" she exclaimed. "It's whacked!"

"Who is he?"

"It's funny. He saved my life twice, and I've never seen his face."

It was all Peter could do to suppress a smile. Granted, he'd been hoping that M. J. would say that it was himself . . . except under the mask, it was. In a way, he was competing with himself. The absurdity of the situation struck him as amusing.

"Oh. Him."

She swiped at his shoulder in mock annoyance. "You're laughing at me!"

"No, I understand. He is extremely cool." *If I do say so myself . . .*

"But do you think it's true, the terrible things they say about him?"

"No way," he said immediately. "That isn't Spider-Man, not a chance in the world." Then he realized he'd said it with a bit too much intensity to sound natural, and she was looking at him oddly, as if waiting for an explanation. "I . . . know him a little bit. I'm sort of his," and he lowered his voice to sound very *entre nous,* "unofficial photographer."

"How do you always manage to find him?"

He shrugged. "Wrong place, right time, I guess."

M. J. looked him up and down, and suddenly he felt uncomfortable. As if he had opened a door he really didn't want to walk through. But it was too late to retreat as Mary Jane asked, "You ever . . . talk to him?"

"Sometimes," he said uneasily.

"Does he ever talk about me?"

"Uh . . . yeah. Once. Once he asked what I thought of you."

She drew a sharp intake of breath. She rested a hand on his arm as if wanting to touch someone who had once shaken hands with Elvis. "What did he say?"

He didn't have the faintest idea what to say. And then he reached deep, deep into his imagination, and he looked across the room into a mirror on the wall. There was Spider-Man, reflected at him, looking at him with his masked face, and maybe he was laughing under it, or frowning . . . it was impossible to tell.

He saw his own image reflected in the mirrors of Spider-Man's eyes, and he said, "I said . . . I said, Spider-Man, I said the great thing about M. J. is when . . . when you look in her eyes, and she's looking back in yours and smiling, well . . . everything feels . . . not quite normal because you feel . . . stronger. And weaker at the same time, and you feel excited and at the same time, terrified." He pulled his gaze away from the mirror to look at Mary Jane, and her eyes were moist. Peter was suddenly brimming with confidence; she was hanging on his every word.

"Spidey—I call him Spidey sometimes—the truth is," and he looked back to his reflection, saw the webslinger in the mirror, waiting to hear the "truth," "you don't know what you feel, except you know the kind of man you want to be and what it is, is . . ."

His confidence started to waver. He was getting tangled up in his mouth, in his thoughts. Now it was Peter who wasn't able to look into Mary Jane's eyes as he completed telling her the conversation that he had, indeed, had a hundred times with Spider-Man . . . in his head.

"It's as if, when you're with her, it's as if you've reached . . . the unreachable . . . and you weren't ready for it."

Oh my God, that sounded horrible . . . like some half-baked Don Quixote thing . . .

He looked back up at her and was dumbfounded to see that tears were welling in her eyes.

"You said that . . . ?" she said with a choking sound in her throat.

And suddenly Peter felt guilty and small. What he had done was voice his innermost thoughts, true, but he knew that he'd misrepresented himself. However he didn't have the faintest idea how to go about fixing it. "Uh . . . um . . . sssomething like that." Then guilt spilled over into embarrassment, for he knew he had said too much. In pretending to speak to Spider-Man, he had really, truly told M. J. how he felt, and she had to know it.

To his surprise, Mary Jane reached out and took his hand. Hers was warm and delicate in his, and suddenly he felt as if anything were possible. He couldn't take his eyes off her, and he was suddenly completely convinced that she was in the same predicament, unable to look away from him. He started to speak, with absolutely no idea what he was going to say.

"Hello."

That wasn't even remotely what he'd intended to say. On the other hand, it wasn't his voice. It was the voice of Harry

Osborn, who was standing in the doorway of the hospital room, staring at them with a smile that did not in any way touch his eyes.

Immediately, acting like two people caught at something, they withdrew their hands. But the damage was done, and Peter knew it . . . knew it all too well.

Harry, who had come in response to a phone message from Peter, remembered almost nothing of his visit to the hospital.

He made small talk, he tried to be polite. But the image of Peter and Mary Jane holding hands seared itself into his mind, obliterating everything else.

Had Peter set him up? Informed him of May Parker's condition just so he could show up and find the two of them looking at each other, like they were ready to get a room of their own . . . and he didn't mean a hospital room . . . ?

He felt as if he was incapable of containing the fury that welled up within him. He stayed for a few minutes, but quickly made his excuses, and the moment he departed, he expunged everything from his recollection except for that mental snapshot of those hands, those damnable hands.

Harry spent the rest of the day walking, just walking endlessly. And slowly, as the time passed, the anger burned less brightly, for it was impossible to sustain that level of white-hot rage.

But he didn't want to go back to his apartment and see Peter waiting there, fumbling with excuses, trying to determine what to say and what not to say. So instead he went to the place he'd come to think of simply as his father's home, even though he himself had lived in the townhouse for as long as he could remember.

It was night when he used the key to let himself in through the front door. A full moon cast its shadow on the doorway. Harry felt he could sympathize with the moon.

After all, did it not bask in reflected glory? Same with Harry Osborn, someone who could only trade on the surname built up by his father, or pass classes with the help of a friend who had stolen his girlfriend.

"Dad?" he called out as he stepped into the front hall.

There was no answer, but light was spilling from the staircase that led to the upstairs hall. Harry stood at the bottom of the stairs, and he could faintly hear voices. They were so soft from where he was standing that they were little more than murmurs, but the vehemence and anger in the tones was unmistakeable. There were two men, and he was reasonably sure that one of them was his father. "Dad? Is that you?"

The voices abruptly stopped. A moment later, his father appeared at the top of the stairs. He didn't move from the spot, though, appearing to his son like a great, dark shadow. "What is it?" he called down.

Harry took a deep breath. He was about to say the most difficult words he had ever uttered, and he wondered if his father would ever have any appreciation over how hard it was for him to say it. "You were right about M. J. You were . . . you were right about everything. She's in love with Peter."

He had no idea how his father was going to react. He expected laughter, perhaps, or sneers, or all manner of unbridled contempt. But instead there was simply a thoughtful pause, and then: "Parker?"

That was all, with no more emotion than a computer being fed a new bit of data.

No, Peter Piper. She's really into pickled peppers. But he held back the flip response that would be formed more by bitterness than wisdom. "Yeah," Harry said.

Osborn started to move down the stairs toward him, one leisurely step at a time. As he would walk, one foot would hang off the step a moment, as if even his feet were involved in deep thought, before he would descend to the next step down. "And . . . how does he feel about her?"

"Are you kidding?" Harry snorted. "He's loved her since the fourth grade. He just acts like he doesn't. But there's nobody Peter cares about more."

Surprisingly, he heard—of all things—a soft chuckle coming from his father. How in the world could any of this be remotely funny? But then, sounding extremely sincere, Norman Osborn said, "I'm sorry. I . . . haven't always been there for you, have I?"

Harry couldn't believe it. He'd never heard his father sound this sympathetic about . . . about anything. "Well . . . you're busy," he said. "You're an important man. I understand that."

"It's no excuse," said Osborn firmly, drawing closer. "I'm proud of you. And I lost sight of that somewhere. But I'm going to make it up to you. I'm going to rectify certain . . . inequities."

I'm dreaming . . . oh, lord, I'm dreaming. Maybe it's not my dad, maybe it's an impostor . . .

The shadowed individual drew into the light, and it was indeed Norman Osborn as he threw his arms around his son and—hugging him so tightly that one would have thought he'd almost lost him—Norman said, "I love you."

And from that angle, steeped in the joy and wonder of a scene that Harry imagined so many times, he was almost certain he'd lost his mind altogether. Hidden in all of that were eyes that burned with inner dementia, and lips that were pulled back in a wolflike sneer. It was the look of someone who understood love only in the context of the power it gave him over others. Power that he was more than willing to exploit . . . through whatever means necessary.

It was a pleasant dream Peter was having . . . he was webswinging through the concrete jungles of New York, but he was unmasked. Let the world know who Spider-Man is, because the world is a good and safe place where good people remain good and bad people don't exist.

Then he heard a voice, calling him from a very great distance, saying, "Peter? Peter . . ."

Peter woke up instantly, looking around in momentary confusion even as he sat up and knocked over the textbooks that had been lying in his lap. They lay on the floor, forgotten. Instead what he was gaping at was Aunt May, this time fully awake and looking far more lucid than she had earlier.

"You're awake!" he said, cunningly going straight for the obvious. "That's good! Good. You okay?"

"I'm okay," she said with certainty, and immediately switched over into overly concerned mother figure. "But I think you should go home and get some sleep."

He shook his head vehemently. "I don't like to leave you." He didn't want to add, *because then I can't protect you*.

"I'm safe here," she said dismissively.

"I should have been there."

Aunt May stared at him blankly, unable to determine what he might possibly be talking about. Then, of course, she realized: "there" meaning "with her." She shook her head. "You didn't know." When she saw that he looked no more mollified than before, she took his hand and held it tightly, with surprising strength. "Peter, the struggles we face in life are not ours to question. They're God's will."

"I know, but I could've done something. . . ."

Naturally she had no idea that the conversation was happening on two levels. No idea that her nephew meant that—as Spider-Man—he could have squared off against the Green Goblin, and possibly brought this madness to an end. Instead she chuckled at what she perceived as the pure absurdity of the notion. "Done something? You do too much! College, a job, all this time with me . . . you're not Superman, you know."

That comment, of course, prompted an involuntary smile.

How could it not? Not realizing the source of the humor, she was encouraged. "A smile! Finally. Haven't seen one of those on your face since Mary Jane was here."

He raised an eyebrow. "Hey! You were supposed to be asleep. What did you hear?"

Smiling enigmatically, she said, "You know . . . you were about six years old when her family moved next door. And when she got out of the car and you saw her for the first time, you grabbed my hand and said, 'Aunt May! Aunt May! Is that an angel?' "

Peter had only heard that story a hundred times. Nevertheless he put on an affected gosh-wow attitude and said, "Gee, Aunt May, did I really say that?"

"You sure did," she said, missing—deliberately or otherwise—the sarcasm. Then she lowered her voice and told him gently, "She'd like to know that, don't you think?"

Peter had been sitting on the edge of the bed. Now he stood and turned away, his hands draped behind his back. "Harry's in love with her. She's still his girl."

"Isn't that up to her?" she asked, blinking owlishly.

"She doesn't . . . really know me. She never will."

Aunt May had been lying back in bed, but now she pulled herself fully to sitting, and she spoke with such vehemence that it surprised him. "Because you won't let her! You're so mysterious all the time. More than ever lately." She blew air out through her lips in irritation as she rearranged the blanket around her legs, apparently quite frustrated with her nephew but not exactly sure where to start in letting him know just exactly how annoyed she was.

"Don't be so complicated," she said finally. "And don't let any more time go by. The one thing Mary Jane needs to know, the only thing she needs to know," and she waggled a bony finger, "is how you feel. Tell me, Peter . . . would it be so dangerous to let Mary Jane know how much you care? It's not as if everyone doesn't already know you love her."

He found himself nodding in mute agreement . . . and that was when the other dime dropped noisily in his head. He'd been so focused on Aunt May and her being targeted by the Goblin, that the full scope, the full horror of the situation hadn't been evident to him . . .

. . . until now.

He forced a smile, trying not to panic. "You know . . . I think you're right, Aunt May. I think I'll . . . I'll give her a call right now . . . tell her . . . try to, uh . . . make things right."

"How nice!" She pointed at the phone near her bed. "You can use that one right th—"

"No, I, uh . . ." He was stammering, backing toward the door. "There's a pay phone in the hall . . . I'll just, uh . . . privacy, you know . . ." and without another word he turned and ran out of the room.

Aunt May smiled, her heart soaring. "Ah, young love," she said.

Peter, meantime, was in the corridor, near the solarium where nervous family members were waiting to hear about their respective loved ones. He dialed the number, and as he listened to the phone ring, repeatedly, he felt as if he were one of them . . . except there was no doctor involved. The health of one of his loved ones depended entirely upon the whims of a lunatic.

"Answer the phone, answer it!" he muttered.

There was a click and his heart jumped, but then her answering machine kicked in. "Hi, it's me! Sing your song at the beep."

He waited impatiently. She had one of those phones that took ages to get around to the tone, and when it did he spoke so fast and with such urgency that he had to force himself to slow down part way through.

"M. J., it's Peter. Are you there? Just checking on you. I mean, making sure you're safe and sound. Give me a call when you get in. I'll give you an update on Aunt May. Hey, where are you? Okay, then, take care. Don't go up any dark alleys." He tried to make it sound light, but he knew there was no way he could leave "You're in terrible danger from a flying maniac" on a phone message.

Then, just as he was about to hang up, he heard another click on the other end. She'd picked up. "Oh, great, you're there!"

No answer.

"Hello?" he said tentatively.

And then a demented cackle sounded, and Peter almost crushed the receiver in his hand. All the blood drained from his face as a singsong voice inquired, "Can Spider-Man come out to play?"

"Where is she?" he demanded tersely. Some passing orderlies glanced at him. He half turned and squared his shoulders, so his agitated state would be less conspicuous.

"Be of love a little more careful, Spider-Man," recited the Goblin.

"I have better things to do than listen to you mangle e. e. cummings," Peter said, choking back his fury.

"An educated man," the Goblin laughed again. "Then again, a little knowledge . . . can be a dangerous thing. But there are so many dangerous things in the world, aren't there."

"Where . . . is . . . she?"

"She's having a little bridge work." And then he laughed again, and his cackling carried and carried, and Peter felt those yellow eyes burning into his soul. . . .

XXV.

THE CHOICE

It was the cold that caused Mary Jane to waken.

The cold seeped into her bones, needling her awake, and she felt incredibly heavy and clumsy as a result. She didn't know where the chill was coming from, at first, and then her mind processed the information—thanks to the steady howling—that it was the wind causing her to feel this way. The wind was blowing constantly, and that in and of itself was bad enough, but she also felt some degree of exposure that she couldn't quite understand. Exposure, vulnerability . . . perhaps she was dreaming. That could make sense.

She was wrapped in darkness, and then she realized that it was because her eyes were closed. But when she opened them, things didn't improve. She still couldn't make out much of anything. It was night, that much was certain.

Slowly she hauled herself to standing, disoriented, holding her head in pain. She remembered walking into her apartment, smelling something sickly sweet, wondering if she'd left the gas on . . . and then nothing. A haze of confusion had settled over her mind like a cloud.

She took a step backward, and suddenly, for no reason she could understand, she felt as if she were overbalanced. Instinctively she windmilled her arms, yanked herself forward with considerable upper body effort, and looked down.

She gasped as, hundreds of feet below her, headlights from cars became visible as unknowing drivers crossed the span of the Queensboro Bridge.

Years ago, the songwriting team of Simon and Garfunkel had been stuck in traffic on the selfsame bridge, and had used the opportunity to pen a song called "Feelin' Groovy." Mary Jane had always liked that song.

At that moment it plummeted to the bottom of her list, and only by falling to her knees did she avoid plummeting, as well, off what she now realized was the western tower of the bridge.

I'm losing my mind, I'm losing my mind, it's some sort of dream, everything's going to be okay, she kept telling herself, right up until the point that a familiar whine of an engine informed her that she was a damned sight far away from being "okay."

The Green Goblin arced past her, turbos roaring, and he tossed off a delirious little wave before angling away. But this wasn't just a flyby; he was heading somewhere, with a purpose. She watched him as he angled toward the Roosevelt Island tram station, leaving a trail of smoke behind him across the night sky as he headed down, down, toward a red tram that was halfway to the station. It was the cable car that carried passengers from Manhattan to the many apartment complexes on Roosevelt Island, there in the middle of the East River. Even from where she was, on her hands and knees, she could see that it was crammed with kids. The kids and their fathers were pointing at the armored green creature that was zipping toward them, an amber angel of death. She was too far away to hear what they were saying. Were they screaming? Laughing? Yelling at him to stay away?

And that was when a rocket launcher exploded to life from beneath the glider, hurling a missile toward the station. An instant later, the rocket barreled into the tram station, obliterating it in a massive ball of flame and smoke. Huge chunks of debris rained down onto the roadway below her. Cars screeched to a halt, many crashing into one another as the flaming chunks of the station plummeted from the night sky like death-laden stars.

Even from where she was, Mary Jane could feel the heat rolling over her, and she knew that all the prayers in the world weren't going to transform this experience into a simple nightmare. She wouldn't be waking up. This was real, this was happening, and those kids and their dads in the gondola were going to die, and she was going to die, and there was nothing, nothing that anyone could possibly do about it.

And then, in the glow of the fireball that lit up the night like a newly risen sun, she saw the familiar outline of a blue-and-red masked figure, crouched on a rooftop in the distance.

Her heart raced, and she was astounded that the first thing to go through her mind was a mental plea to the costumed hero: *Get away from here . . . save yourself . . .*

Funny . . . she'd never thought of herself as selfless before . . .

Too late. You're too late again . . .

Watching the carnage from behind the reflective eyes of his mask, Peter pushed that thinking far, far away. He didn't need to be bogged down by tons of guilt. Instead he fired a web line that hit one of the cables on the bridge, and arced toward the span as fast as he could.

It wasn't fast enough.

The sound of the first cables snapping was truly horrifying. A whip crack, the cries of terrified children, and suddenly the gondola was dropping like a stone, plummeting toward the water below. There was no way that Spider-Man could possibly get to it in time.

His entire focus was on the tram, even as he reached midswing, so he was startled and confused when he saw the car jerk to a halt. He thought it was a miracle.

He thought wrong.

* * *

Mary Jane couldn't believe it.

Just as the cable car had begun its plummet, the crazed monster that had condemned the tram and its passengers to death swooped down and snagged the trailing wire. The car stopped in midair, dangling from the cables, as the Green Goblin—displaying strength she could only imagine—soared upward effortlessly while holding on to the cable.

She could hear the children crying in terror, hear the fathers shouting to them that everything was going to be all right, in that way parents had when they were lying through their teeth as loudly as possible.

And suddenly the Goblin was there, right up on the bridge with her, and he wrapped one of his cold, armored hands around her. She tried to push him away, but a hand that was capable of supporting a cable car wasn't going to have a great deal of difficulty restraining a struggling eighteen-year-old. In the other hand, he still gripped the cable that was the only thing supporting the tram.

"Spider-Man!" he bellowed from behind his distorted mask, and that was when Mary Jane spotted the wallcrawler again. He had just landed on one of the suspender cables and was now in the process of clambering up toward the main cable that led to the tower. He backflipped upward as if gravity were a concept that didn't apply him, and landed on the main cable. But froze when the Goblin spoke.

"This is why only fools are heroes!" called the Goblin. "Because you never know when some lunatic will come along with a sadistic choice."

Mary Jane's frozen mind couldn't even grasp what he meant, but then she understood as the Goblin shoved her forward. Her toes went over the edge, and she almost lost her balance. Hundreds of feet below, cars were still trying to cope with the fallen debris. Within moments they might well be driving around the small bits of whatever was left of her, as well.

And all the fear she'd ever felt at her father's hands, all the abuse she had endured, that had made her feel small and worthless and unworthy to live, abruptly fell into proper perspective. The Green Goblin set a new gold standard for angst.

Perched atop the main cable of the bridge, Peter had never been happier that he was wearing a mask, because he never would have wanted the Goblin to see the expression of pure horror on his face as the lunatic crowed, ". . . you never know when some lunatic will come along with a sadistic choice! Let die the woman you love . . ."

Don't say that, you idiot! She'll figure it out, if she hasn't already . . . !

And then the Goblin's right hand, the one holding the cable, abruptly relaxed. The cable snaked through his gloved hand, the tram dropped with sickening speed, the children screamed, and then in an instant, the tram halted again in its plummet, as the Goblin's hand tightened once more.

". . . or suffer the little children," the Goblin continued, sounding almost conversational. It was as if they were sitting on a couple of bar stools, knocking back brews and discussing the latest scores. And it was at that point that Spider-Man realized how little it mattered whether or not M. J. knew his identity. Lord, first the Goblin had quoted cummings . . . and now he was quoting Jesus.

Peter had no intention of allowing a tram full of innocents to enter the Kingdom of Heaven before their time . . . but Mary Jane, the girl he'd loved for years . . . And they were strangers, he'd hear their screams in his head at night, yes, but at least M. J. would be curled up next to him . . . But there were, what, eleven, a dozen of them, one of her, one life against a dozen . . .

"Make your choice, Spider-Man!" howled the Goblin,

"and see how a hero is rewarded! This is your doing! You have caused this! *This is the life you have chosen! Choose!*"

Peter looked left, right, left, and right again . . .

. . . and the Goblin released them both.

Insanely, the only thought that managed to penetrate M. J.'s frozen brain at that moment was that she never got to tell off her father.

She plummeted, arms and legs pinwheeling, and suddenly Spider-Man was right there, tucking her under his right arm.

"Hold on!" he shouted, even as he fired a web line that snagged the underside of the bridge's center span, and Mary Jane thought giddily, *He chose me!* right before she was overwhelmed with guilt over the fate of the plunging cable car.

But Spider-Man wasn't done, not remotely.

Suddenly he released his web line, and there was the cable of the car whipping past them. She could barely see it, but Spider-Man homed in on it as if he had radar. He shifted Mary Jane onto his back even as he grabbed the trailing cable. She let out a scream as the two of them were yanked down, hard, hopelessly at the mercy of the tram's weight.

Then Spider-Man fired another web line at the underside of the bridge, and the white substance snared it, sticking with unbreakable adhesion. There below the span, the gondola slammed to a halt, bouncing up and down, kids and dads tumbling everywhere.

Mary Jane heard faint cheers floating down toward them. People were gathering along the Queensboro Bridge, all traffic having come to a halt due to the debris. Applause, shouts of encouragement, it was all very sweet, really, to witness such a gratifying show of public support.

But none of it meant a damn, really, because Spider-Man was hanging suspended in midair, his right hand clutching the cable line, his left hand clutching the web line. Mary Jane was hanging on his back, and every muscle in his body had to be screaming from the strain.

Peter thought he was going to die.

It might have been preferable.

He gritted his teeth beneath his mask to avoid the shriek that wanted to rip itself from his agonized body. His arms were on fire, his muscles trembling. When he did speak, his voice was a strained, harsh whisper, as he said to M. J., "Climb down. The cable to the tram . . . climb down . . ."

Her voice quivering, she said, "I can't."

"M. J., just do it."

"I'm scared."

"Trust me," he said, in the exact same tone of voice he'd used back at the hospital.

Mary Jane stared into his eyepiece, and it was as if she could see right through the mask, into his heart . . . as if she were seeing him in so many ways for the first time, and he said again, *"Trust me,"* keeping his voice level despite the incredible strain.

Without another word, M. J. eased herself down his body and wrapped her hands around the cable. She started to descend, and Peter couldn't help but think that if the Goblin wanted to pick the worst possible moment to show up, this was pretty much it.

Then his spider sense kicked in.

He barely had time to twist his head around before the Goblin zoomed in and slammed him in the jaw, and then rocketed away with only laughter floating behind him. Obviously he was in no hurry to finish things, and equally obviously there was no reason for him to be. He had Peter cold, and they both knew it.

• • •

Mary Jane was almost thrown from the cable. She barely managed to hang on, when the Goblin slugged Spider-Man with incredible force. The fact that the webslinger was still conscious, much less maintaining his grip, was nothing short of miraculous.

Nevertheless the tram dipped precipitously, again throwing around the kids and their fathers. *Hold on, God, please, hold on,* she mentally begged.

The Goblin swung around for another assault. He cackled as he extended his arm, exposing razor-sharp blades that adorned it. The webslinger watched, helpless, as the Goblin delivered a crushing blow to his stomach. Pieces of flesh and costume went flying, and that was it: He lost his grip on the cable.

Mary Jane couldn't help it: She screamed as she and the tram plummeted toward the icy waters below.

Spider-Man dangled from the web, grasping for the cable that was racing past him. As the last of it whizzed by, he lunged for it, catching it. And now it was Spider-Man's turn to scream, in agony rather than terror, as blood gushed from his hand. But the cable went taut again.

Mary Jane lost her own grip and fell, landing on the tram below. She raised her head and saw Spider-Man, his head lolling to the side, finished, looking for all the world as if he'd been crucified with his arms outstretched. And yet he was still holding on, impossibly, miraculously, to the cable in one bleeding hand and the web line in the other.

Then she heard the glider's engine as the Green Goblin circled in for the final blow.

But he stopped. He hovered in front of Spider-Man, looking at the hero whose body was stretched to the limit and beyond, looking like a pitiful rag doll that had been thrown on a scrap heap after a lifetime of service. For an instant, Mary Jane thought the Goblin was going to break off the assault.

Spider-Man raised his head, looked at his oppenent.

And then the Goblin threw back his head, laughed, and roared toward Spider-Man, his glider on full throttle.

It ripped at Mary Jane's heart. Her last thoughts—or at least what she believed her last thoughts were going to be—weren't of her own death, or the deaths of the children and their fathers, but rather of how ghastly and unfair it was that Spider-Man had suffered to such a degree, gone to such Herculean efforts, all for nothing.

A huge chunk of asphalt slammed across the side of the Goblin's head.

It sent him spiraling out of control, and he missed Spider-Man clean. He pulled himself out of the spiral, looked around in confusion, and more asphalt hit him. And then bottles, rocks, shoes, a virtual rainstorm of garbage and debris.

He craned his neck and looked upward, as did Mary Jane, and she was astounded to see dozens—maybe hundreds—of bystanders, lined up on the bridge, no longer satisfied with being sidelined like simple cheerleaders. Instead, they were pelting the Goblin with anything and everything they could get their hands on.

The creature howled with frustration, shielding his face with his arms, and angled down and away, vanishing into the darkness under the bridge, skimming near the surface of the water.

Peter was stunned, shocked beyond his ability to comprehend. His body was no less tired, his muscles no less spent. But as he saw the support and adoration being voiced by those most jaded of people—New Yorkers—strength began to flow through him, born of newfound confidence. He didn't know how long this second wind—second . . . more like fifth by that point—was going to last. But then he saw, at the bottom of the tower leg, a massive amount of rock that spread from the support piling. If the tram had simply fallen onto it, everyone aboard would have been crushed. That, however, was not going to happen.

Gently angling the gondola in a pendulumlike swing, he lowered it further and further until it touched down onto the rocks below. The moment it did, a new roar of approval erupted from the crowd. He almost passed out from relief as he swung his torn and bleeding right hand around to clutch onto the web line with both hands. He felt absolutely light-headed; in fact, he felt as if he were floating in zero-G, having gone from supporting the weight of the tram to simply his own body weight.

He saw Mary Jane, perched atop the cable car, looking up at him with concern, and more. Then suddenly her expression shifted to fear at about the same time his spider sense warned him of danger.

A cable snaked around Peter's waist, and for a split second he thought it was from the tram car somehow. Then the Goblin, holding the other end of the rope, swept past him. The cable went taut, and Peter was yanked off his web, high into the air, hauled behind the Goblin glider completely out of control. He thrashed about, to no effect, and the glider angled down and around, back toward Roosevelt Island.

The Goblin turned and cackled, clearly delighted at the costumed teen's struggles. Then, apparently having seen enough, he held out his arm, once again exposing the blades on it, and the blades sliced through the rope. Peter crashed into the abandoned, hulking ruin of a condemned smallpox hospital at the southern end of the island.

He staggered to his feet, and suddenly from everywhere they were coming at him: The bats. Razor sharp, sweeping in from all around. He had no idea where the Goblin got them, no clue how they functioned, no concept of anything except that they were ripping into him, shredding his costume, leaving glistening lines of blood on his chest, his legs.

Every time one struck him, pain exploded behind his eyes, to the point where there was so much that he just wasn't feeling it anymore.

"Enough!" bellowed the Goblin. But the bats, failing to heed their master's call, continued slicing at Peter as he staggered across the dusty floor of the hospital. *"I said enough!"* the Goblin bellowed, and this time some cybernetic circuit must have kicked in. The razor bats stopped their destruction, flying meekly away.

Peter didn't even realize he was on the ground, lying on his back, until the bats departed. He rolled over, leaving an outline of blood marking his resting spot. He looked up at the Goblin, who was hovering over him, and tried to stand. His legs turned to jelly and he crashed to the ground.

The Goblin, laughing, reached down onto his glider and pulled out a rod. At the top of the rod was a button, which he pressed, and three blades popped out of the front, giving the weapon the appearance of a pitchfork.

"Ahhh, misery, misery, misery," the Goblin said sadly, as if commiserating. "Again and again I've tried to make my case, but you won't oblige. Had you not been so determined, your sweetheart's death would have been quick and painless. But now, now that you've really pissed me off, I'll see to it that it's slow and . . . painful. Just . . . like . . . yours . . ."

The Goblin reared back with the spear, bringing it down toward Peter's chest. At the last moment, Peter caught it, and as he looked at the Goblin, stared into the face of hate, his strength returned. He yanked the spear out of his grip and smashed it against the monster's armored head so hard that it nearly decapitated him. As it was, it knocked the Goblin clear off the glider, sending him flying back ten feet and crashing to the ground.

Peter staggered back from the exertion for a moment, went down to one knee, taking deep breaths. There was

blood everywhere, all his, and the Goblin, who had terrorized so many, who seemed to exist purely to bedevil him,
was lying on the floor moaning. The fact that such a monstrosity could exist filled him with a nameless rage, and he
felt as if everything he'd gone through had happened purely
to bring him to this moment. To look into the face of evil and
say, *Your day is done.*

It was Peter Parker who had been knocked to the floor,
torn and bleeding, but it was the amazing Spider-Man who
got to his feet and snapped the pitchfork across his knee,
tossing the parts to the side. It was Spider-Man who grabbed
the Goblin by the chest, pulled him up from the ground, and
threw a haymaker that would have dislocated the Goblin's
jaw had he not been protected by his armor, and came
damned close to doing so anyway.

The Goblin went flying through a nearby wall. He rose,
managed to advance a few steps, and then Spider-Man
struck another devastating blow. The Goblin crumpled
against a nearby stone wall, and his voice was pathetic and
pleading when he said, "Please . . ."

Spider-Man didn't want to hear it, *would* not hear it. He
picked the Goblin up yet again, and he wanted to crush his
opponent's face beneath his fist. Wanted to see the Goblin's
blood, for once.

He ripped off the Goblin's mask, and the battered face of
Norman Osborn looked up at him and whispered, from between swelling lips, "Peter . . ."

Spider-Man's fist remained cocked, but this wasn't the
Goblin. This was Norman Osborn. It was . . . it was some
sort of trick, that had to be it. The Goblin had hypnotized
him or . . . or Spider-Man was hallucinating, that was it. Or
it was a trick of light, or an android, or a clone . . . something . . . it couldn't be . . .

The fury within him ebbed as disbelief pushed it aside.

Spider-Man pulled away his own tattered mask to make sure he was seeing what he thought he was seeing. He released Osborn, who slumped to the floor, looking up pathetically.

"Peter . . . thank God for you," Osborn said, as if waking from a dream.

Still trembling with rage, shaken by the overwhelming desire to inflict violence upon the man he saw before him, Peter said, "Can't be . . . you're a monster . . ."

"Please . . . Peter . . . don't let it take me back," Osborn begged him. "I need your help. I'm not a monster."

"You killed those people on the balcony," Peter reminded him sharply. "You could have killed your son. . . ."

Osborn was shaking his head furiously. "It killed. The Goblin killed. I had nothing to do with it. . . . Please . . . don't let it have me again. Protect me, I beg you. Talk to me about this. . . ."

Peter could barely comprehend. Protect Osborn . . . from himself? *Madness!* But . . . wasn't the Goblin mad? That certainly wasn't news. Maybe he really was the victim here. Maybe . . .

Then Peter's heart hardened. "You tried to kill Aunt May. You wanted to kill Mary Jane."

"But not you." Osborn was shaking his head desperately. "I would never hurt you. I knew from the beginning, if anything happened to me, you were the one I could count on. You, Peter Parker, would save me, and so you have. Thank God for you."

He had pulled himself to his feet. With his back against the wall, he held out a hand in pathetic supplication.

"Give me your hand. Believe in me, as I believed in you. I was like a father to you. Be a son to me now."

"I had a father," Peter said tightly. "His name was Ben Parker."

And then . . . Osborn began to laugh. It was the most bizarre thing Peter had ever seen, as the tortured face of Norman Osborn seemed to transform itself, and even though the tattered mask was on the floor, his face twisted into a semblance of the madness that the mask reflected.

"Godspeed, Spider-Man," he said.

That was when Peter realized that Osborn was manipulating, ever so subtly, an electronic pad on his wrist. He knew in a flash that Osborn had been doing it the entire time, and then his spider sense kicked in, seeing all around him simultaneously. And behind him was the Goblin glider, making absolutely no noise at all. It had risen up and was coming straight toward his back. As it did so, a spear snapped into place.

Peter hurled himself to one side, twisting and bending, and the glider's turbines kicked in for extra speed just as he leapt completely clear. It screamed through the air and terror suddenly creased Osborn's face.

He tried to get out of the way, tried to shut down the turbines, but it was too late. Momentum had taken hold, and the glider slammed into Osborn, the spear punching through him with a hideous *splutch*ing sound, like a sword through a watermelon.

Osborn was lifted off his feet and slammed against the far wall, pinned there literally by the shaft that went through his chest and out his back. His arms flailed about and he pounded on the glider, blood running down the spear, down onto the glider, which only at that point sputtered to a halt.

Osborn looked up at Peter with, at first, vague accusation . . . and then almost a sense of relief . . . before slumping over, the glider crashing onto the floor with him.

Peter stood there, trembling, not knowing whether to laugh or cry, and settled for both. In the distance, he heard sirens, heading for the hulking ruin of a hospital, and his first inclination was to just get the hell out of there.

But in his head, he heard the words of Norman Osborn, heard him saying how Peter Parker was the only one he could count on. It was the subterfuge of a madman, a clever dodge, a means of confusing him. He couldn't help but wonder, though, if that had been some aspect of the real Norman Osborn, making his presence known in his final moments.

Maybe there had been a germ of truth in what he'd said.

And he thought of what it would be like for Harry, whose life would be ruined by the revelation of what his father had become.

Before he had time to think better of it, Peter removed the spear from Osborn's chest and lifted him up as if he weighed nothing. By the time the police arrived, he was gone . . . and so was the Green Goblin.

Harry Osborn wandered aimlessly around the brownstone with a feeling of unease he couldn't shake. But this time, as he passed the door to his father's study, he felt a sharp breeze wafting from underneath the door. Perhaps his dad had left unlocked the French doors that opened out onto the balcony on the other side, and they had blown open. That was no good. He knew his dad kept important papers around, which could be scattered all over the place.

For the first time in ages, things had been going well between him and his father. He didn't want to risk any backsliding, and he could almost hear his dad's voice saying, "You knew the French doors were open and you did nothing about it. What, were you afraid to go into my den? What kind of son are you?"

He threw open the door, walked in, and froze.

Harry Osborn had never before seen a dead body. But he knew immediately he was looking at one now, and insanely, it took him a few more moments to realize it was his father, because his father was simply bigger than death, and Harry had never attached such a possibility to him.

Norman Osborn lay on a bed. He was naked, but covered by a blanket that was soaked through with blood. His head was slumped to one side, and one eye was open, as if he was winking.

Standing two feet away, about to step back out through the French doors, was Spider-Man. His costume was torn, his mask a bit ripped, but it was clearly him.

"You . . ." Harry managed to get out.

Spider-Man raised his hands, taking a step forward, and Harry retreated in fear. "No . . ." Spider-Man started to say.

But Harry wasn't listening. *"Murderer!"* he screamed, and he lunged for a table nearby where he knew his father kept a gun. He yanked it out of a drawer, swung it around as fast as he could, only to find that Spider-Man was gone, leaving behind curtains blowing in the wind, the corpse of his victim, and the sobbing figure of a son.

XXVI.

GOOD-BYES

Phil Watson opened the door of his home, blinking against the morning sun, to see his daughter, Mary Jane, clad in a simple black dress. She was standing there, just standing there, staring at him. She looked a little sad.

She didn't say hello. She just continued to stare. There was a taxi at curbside, which was obviously waiting for her.

"What, you need money? I hope you're not here asking for money," he said.

"No," she said, very calmly, as if she were addressing him from a very great height. "No, no money. It's just that, I'm going to a funeral today, and I thought since I was dressed for the occasion, I'd let you know that your daughter is dead."

He blinked at her. "What?"

"The daughter you knew, yes." She drew herself up. "The one who could be intimidated by your threats, by your bullying . . ."

"Oh, for the love of—"

Without hesitation, she continued, "The one who you made feel like dirt, so that you could walk all over her. She's gone. She's dead. She's never coming back. Now me . . . I've seen bullies and a face of evil that would chew you up and spit you out before breakfast. I'm the new Mary Jane. I'm a damned interesting person. And if you're inclined to get to know me at some point, that's your choice. And if you're not . . . that's your loss. Do we understand each other?"

He stared at her blankly. "I haven't understood you in eighteen years; why should I start now? You're being an idiot."

"And you're pathetic."

His temper flared, and he instinctively drew back a hand to slap her.

Mary Jane's eyes hardened, and a fiery warning flared in them. Slowly, he lowered his hand without being entirely sure why.

"Good-bye, Dad," she said, and without another word she turned and walked away.

A line of expensive cars was parked along the narrow, winding road. Peter walked a very quiet Harry Osborn over toward the Bentley, trying to ignore his imagination that had cackling laughter floating out of the grave, even after Norman had been lowered into it and dirt had been thrown upon the coffin.

Aunt May and Mary Jane were standing a distance away, talking quietly to each other.

"I'm so sorry, Harry," Peter said. "I know what it's like to lose a father."

"I didn't lose him," Harry corrected him firmly. "He was stolen from me. And one day, Spider-Man will pay." He stopped, turned, and faced Peter. "I swear, on my father's grave, Spider-Man will pay."

Peter had no idea what to say . . . and so said nothing.

They reached the Bentley, and the chauffeur opened the door for Harry to step in. Harry paused before doing so and said, "Look . . . about M. J. . . . . I was just trying to please my dad." He spoke as if admitting to a major felony. "I thought he'd be impressed . . . me with such a beautiful woman. I know she was never right for me. I wanted to make him proud, that's all. Now I'll never be able to." He clutched Peter's hand, shook it firmly. "Thank God for you, my friend.

You're all the family I have left." He pulled Peter toward him, embraced him once, then climbed into the car.

The chauffeur closed the door behind him, gave Peter a vaguely disdainful glance, then climbed into the front and drove off.

Peter turned and looked toward M. J. and Aunt May on the hill by Norman's gravesite. She turned toward him and smiled.

No matter what I do, no matter how hard I try, the ones I love are always the ones who pay.

He turned away and walked toward another tombstone, the gravesite of his Uncle Ben. BEN PARKER, BELOVED HUSBAND AND UNCLE, it read. As if half a dozen words could come close to summing him up.

He stood there, hands folded, head lowered, and drew his coat closer around him as a chill breeze cut through him. "Hey." Mary Jane's voice came from behind him. He didn't turn to look at her, and in a lowered voice she said, "Your aunt thought I'd find you here."

"M. J.'s here, Uncle Ben," he said to the tombstone.

She moved closer to him, putting her arm around his elbow. "You must miss him so much."

"He was a beautiful guy."

They stood there for a short time, and then she tugged gently on his arm, indicating with a nod of her head that it was time to leave. He wanted to protest but instead allowed himself to be pulled along.

Abruptly, she stopped.

"There's something I've been wanting to tell you," she said. "I heard the message you left on my answering machine."

He tried to remember exactly what he'd said. He'd been so caught up in the panic of the moment—trying to warn her without tipping his identity—that the words were a blur to him. "Uh, yeah . . . I uh . . ."

"You didn't finish, but I know what you were going to say, and I want to say it first. When I was up there, and I was sure I was going to die, there was only one person I was thinking of, and it wasn't who I thought it would be.

"It was you." Peter started to tremble inwardly as she continued. "I kept thinking, I hope I make it through this, so I can see Peter Parker's *face* one more time."

"My face . . . ?" *Meaning . . . with no mask . . . ? Did she know . . . ? She had to. That had to be what she was dancing around . . . wasn't it?*

"Sometimes," she said softly, "what you want . . . you have to go to the edge of your life to find out it was right next door. I've been so stupid for so long. There's only one man who was ever there for me, who has always been there for me. Who makes me believe that I'm . . . more than I ever thought I was. That I'm just me . . . and it's okay. The truth is . . . I love you. I really love you, Peter."

And he could hear Spider-Man's voice in his head, shouting at him, *tell her you love her tell her who you are*

She knew . . .

She had to know . . .

But maybe she didn't . . . and if she didn't, it might send her running in fright at the risks he had taken, and would continue to take . . . maybe . . . maybe . . . so many maybes . . .

When he was in the middle of a fight, he knew what to do, immediately, instinctively. Faced with one young woman, he was stymied.

"I . . . can't . . ." he said.

"You can't what?" she asked, puzzled.

"Tell you everything," and quickly he added, "I mean . . . there's so much to tell."

"Yes. So much to tell . . ."

"To tell the girl next door . . ."

"But isn't that all I am?" she asked.

"Oh, no, no," and he started to laugh, "you're the amazing girl next door. Mary Jane, the amazing, amazing girl, and I want you to know that I will always be there for you, I will always be there to take care of you. I promise you that. I wish I could give you more than that, but you must know . . . that you will always be safe."

She moved toward him, embraced him, and then kissed him gently on the lips. Something seemed to build within him, and he murmured ". . . can't . . ." even as she drew him close once more. And this time when she kissed him, it was like that other time, when he'd been upside down and only the lower half of his face was visible. A kiss filled with passion and intensity and heat that he felt through every nerve ending in his body. When their lips parted he could still feel hers on his, like a man who's lost an arm can feel the limb as if it were still attached.

She pressed her body against his, wanted more . . .

. . . more than he was willing to give. More than he dared, for fear of what happened, could happen, to his loved ones.

He pulled away from her. Her eyes went wide. Slowly he shook his head. The wind was kicking up, and he shoved his hands deep into the pockets of his coat, drawing it closely around him, and walked away as quickly as he could, leaving M. J. standing by the gravesite.

Because he knew it was the right thing to do.

And he couldn't afford to stop doing the right thing . . . ever again.

Several days later, J. Jonah Jameson sat in his office, chomping on his ever-present cigar, looking out the window at the people moving through the streets far below. Robbie was leaning against the doorway.

"Spider-Man. I don't get it," Jameson said in frustration. "First the town thinks he's trash, and now he's a glamour boy."

"He's a hero, J. J.," said Robbie, as if it should have been self-evident.

"Don't give me that line again," Jameson said, stabbing a finger at him. "I don't trust heroes. They're nothing but criminals in disguise. Hoffman!" he shouted as Hoffman went past the door, and the nervous little man stopped in his tracks. "Where's Parker? I want some pictures."

"He just left," said Hoffman.

"Left? He's always leaving."

"He went to cover the hostage story."

Jameson stalked his office, waving his arms in the air as if the world existed just to be a gross inconvenience to him. "Sure! Another hostage story! But where is he when the Green Goblin busted through my window? The Goblin and Spider-Man in front of our noses! A golden opportunity, and the photographer went to lunch!" He squinted at an office boy heading in the other direction, holding an odd bundle. "And what's that?"

The office boy turned, held up a pair of trousers. "Peter Parker's pants."

"What?"

"They were in the closet."

"Parker's pants?" Jameson said slowly, trying to make sure he'd heard this right.

"With his shirt and tie and shoes and socks," the office boy said cheerfully.

"What's going on here?!" demanded an increasingly be-fuddled Jameson. "Who's he think he is: Tarzan? Where is he, running around the town naked? Or does he think our storage closet is his own personal armoire? And who put flowers on my desk?!"

Betty Brant stuck her head in. "I did, sir. It *is* your birth-day."

"What're you looking for, a raise? I don't want flowers, I want Peter Parker. *Not* his pants!" He grabbed the bouquet and threw it in the trash. "I want pictures! I want to sell papers! I want Spider-Man!" He thumped repeatedly on his desktop, sending everyone scattering until he was alone in his office.

Alone.

And he knew that somewhere out there, Spider-Man was likely speeding to help hostages. To help people.

Helping people. That's what he did.

Jameson glanced at the motto of the *Bugle,* situated in block lettering beneath the masthead, just as it had been for decades: THE TRUTH OF THE MATTER, was what it said.

He stared out at the skyline and, as if Spider-Man could hear him, said softly, "That is what you do . . . isn't it. Help them. Unselfishly. With no thought of compensation. You're everything I can never be. And if someone like you is considered a hero . . . what does that make me?

"You're everything I aspired to be . . . and never can be . . . because I'm too damned weak. And my greatest weakness . . . is that I'm going to continue to try and drag you down, because . . . God help me . . . I'm jealous of you."

At least he, Jameson, knew the truth.

Even if it never saw print . . . ethics were satisfied.

Dear Mom and Dad:

Had a busy few hours.

I swung by the cemetery late this evening to visit with Uncle Ben, and found some punks trying to trash the place. I scared the hell out of them, then I just hung out and talked with Uncle Ben until the sun came up.

Oh . . . I saw Mary Jane the other day. I know she was hurt a little by what happened after Norman Osborn's funeral. She thinks I rejected her. Or maybe she knows the truth about me, and is willing to wait until I'm ready to tell her . . . if ever. Man, I'd trade all these powers for the ability to read minds.

You know . . . last night . . . when I was at the cemetery . . . I told Uncle

Ben everything that was going on with me. The whole story. I mean, I've been writing to you guys, so you've stayed in the loop, but Uncle Ben... well, I figured he deserved to know. So I brought him up to speed.

Wasn't an easy thing to do. And no one can say I didn't warn him. The story of my life isn't for the faint of heart. Like the man said, it's hard to be a saint in the city. And whatever life holds in store for me, I now accept: I will never forget these words again...

"With great power comes great responsibility."

This is my gift. It's my curse.

Who am I?

I'm Spider-Man.

ULTIMATE SPIDER-MAN ADVENTURES DESIGNED FOR NEW READERS!

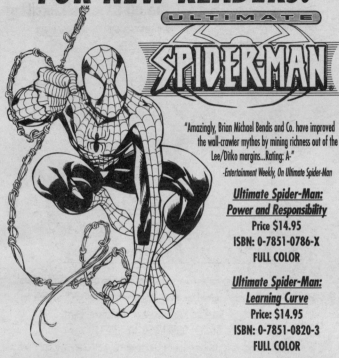

"Amazingly, Brian Michael Bendis and Co. have improved the wall-crawler mythos by mining richness out of the Lee/Ditko margins...Rating: A-"
-Entertainment Weekly, On Ultimate Spider-Man

**Ultimate Spider-Man:
Power and Responsibility**
Price $14.95
ISBN: 0-7851-0786-X
FULL COLOR

**Ultimate Spider-Man:
Learning Curve**
Price $14.95
ISBN: 0-7851-0820-3
FULL COLOR

Ultimate Spider-Man, the comic book publishing event has hit the bookstore arena! Starting over at the beginning, the story of how a tortued teen is embued with startling powers has been completely reimagined to appeal to a new generation of readers!

Available at a bookstore near you or check with www.bn.com and amazon.com!

marvel.com